To Lane ~~~
Hope you enjoy this
little excursion into the
West

The End of
the Old Ways

a novel by

Harold M. Brannan

Harold Brannan

• HAROLD BRANNAN •

Publishing Comany

PO Box 90030
San Antonio, Texas 78209

Though many of the names, places, battles and dates are authentic, the book is purely a work of fiction and any words ascribed to historic figures used in the story are simply part of the imagined happenings.

Cover painting by
Madeline Low

Book design by
Mark Mayfield

Brannan, Harold
The End of the Old Ways
ISBN 978-0-615-41810-0
Printed in the United States of America, Litho Press Inc.
First Printing January 2011

Acknowledgements

I am particularly grateful to Marie Laine and Nancy Price for the many hours they spent editing this book and whose thoughtful suggestions made it a better story.

I want to express my indebtedness to some of the works which especially served to whet my interest and helped to furnish a basis for locating the time and places of this story.

Robert G. Carter, On the Border with Makenzie, Reprint by Texas State Historical Association, 2007, Austin, Original printing, Eynon Printing Co. Washington, D. C.

Charles L. Kenner, The Comanchero Frontier, University of Oklahoma Press 1969, Norman

Deborah Lamont Newlin, The Tonkawa People, West Texas Museum Association Journal, XXI, 1982, Lubbock

Dan Flores, Caprock Canyonlands, The University of Texas Press, 1990, Austin

T. R. Fehrenbach, Comanches The Destruction of a People, Alfred A. Knopf, 1974, New York

Robertson, Pauline D. and Robertson, R. L., Panhandle Pilgrimage, Paramount Publishing Company, 1978, Amarillo

Morehead, Max L., New Mexico's Royal Road, University of Oklahoma Press, 1958, Norman

Timanus, Rod, An Illustrated History of Texas Forts, Republic of Texas Press, 2001, Plano

To Margaret, Madeline and Marie,
my three muses who urged this work to completion

CHAPTER 1

The autumn moon had moved far into the west, though it was still luminous enough to cast the shadows of the trees as an eerie grid work upon the ground. The hunters had an extra advantage when stalking in these shadows, the trees swaying minimally from the soft breeze so that the competing patterns of darkness and light danced everywhere, and even the furtive movement of the stalkers simply blended with the movement of the shadows leaving the browsing fawn unable to detect subtle motion, and thus, vulnerable. The sun was already probing just beneath the eastern horizon, and would soon appear above the rim of the earth and erase the last vestige of the moon's pale illumination, replacing it with the defining clearness of day.

The pair emerged from the tree line and strode across the treeless flat at the edge of the mesa. From as far back as when he first began to walk, Thomas had loved this rise at the edge of the bluff, a vantage point for viewing the whole valley below, the little valley where the farmstead nestled just above the flood plain of the Guadalupe River. His father had often held him in his arms and pointed out the features which could be seen from this distance: the farm house with its dogtrot porch, the bend of the river with its towering western cypress trees, the horse corral made of sturdy rail fencing, and the barn with its tall hay loft, a hoist protruding from the wall above the upper story door. The sight always evoked a feeling of assurance, a knowing that just ahead was the trail down to his home, his refuge, his security, not just the place where he was given life and nurtured, but the place where he was cherished. The path from the mesa to the valley led through a break in the rim rock, then twined down the steep scarp, switching directions just at the right places, as though nature had placed it there, which indeed, it had, for the earliest settlers, and the natives before them, had only followed a deer trail, long ago sculpted by tiny hooves.

Both of the early morning hunters topped the rise, and began their descent down the south trail toward the farmstead. Their steps were in rhythm, not because they were affecting such a pace, but because they had stalked and hunted so much together that repetition had formed a bond of similarity between the two. Each of them carried a rifle in his hands, and the leader had the young deer strapped across his back. The large Tonkawa was in the lead. The younger Thomas, his Texan compatriot, followed about five yards behind.

Across the valley, a Great Blue Heron arose from the river shallows and flew off toward the east, squawking in angry protest at whatever intruder had disturbed its early morning repast. The bird caused the older hunter to pause and drop his load to the ground, it being far too early for anyone from the farm to be down by the river. He put his hand back and to the side as a signal to the boy, then, slid behind a wild persimmon bush. There was something disturbing about the quietness below.

"I hear no sound," he said as he listened intently, but in vain, for the usual noises of the farm, the cluck or crow of the chickens, the bleat and low of the live stock. There was a lack of nature's songs as well, even the usual chortle of the Mockingbird and the staccato squall of the Flicker were missing. There was only stillness and silence as though a rent had been torn in the fabric of the earth, allowing leakage of the sounds of living creatures to clear the valley, and flow into another realm.

He took in a deep breath, holding it so he could hush the sound of his own respiration as he listened even more intently. He squinted his eyes and scanned the still shadowy scenery, then, breathed in slowly, but deeply, trying to get the scent of something that might be new. The normal resinous smell of the cypress wafted upward from the river, but nothing unusual.

"Listen!" whispered Thomas as a faint shuffling sound broke the silence, the noise arising from the direction of the thicket by the little creek near the point where it joined the river. A frown played across the older man's forehead for he felt certain that something was amiss. Both hunters were now absolutely motionless except for the slow turning of their heads as they repeatedly scanned the valley.

The imposed stillness below was suddenly ended, as two riders emerged from behind the underbrush. The first had the two farm mules in tow, and the second, the two ranch horses. The riders were bare skinned except for breach clouts and moccasins, but their faces were smeared with the black and red paint of the warpath. "Comanches" whispered the Tonkawa. He pointed to his rifle, then held up one finger and pointed to himself, then, two fingers and pointed to the boy. The hunters waited until the raiders cleared from behind the brush, and until enough of the early sunlight hit them to unmask their profiles. Sequential shots pierced the quietness. The lead Comanche's head jerked and he fell from his horse abruptly to the ground. The second shot, followed in only an instant, but the other rider was already in motion, rapidly sliding behind the silhouette of his mount, running between the cedars full speed for the timber in the far end of the valley. "He's gone," said the Indian. "There is no use in shooting more."

The two riflemen approached warily, always under the cover of brush, easing through the copse with soft feet, without audible sound or sudden motion, carefully surveying the whole of the valley in an effort to sense whether or not other intruders were about. The lead Comanche was obviously dead, lying face down, both arms out away from his body. His lance point stood impaled into the earth from the force of his fall, its free end, even yet, quivering in the air. A fresh scalp was tied and draped over the forward part of its shaft. A sickening smell of fresh blood arose from the scalp and mixed with that of the dead Indian.

"He was arrogant," said the Tonkawa. "Instead of being careful, as he knew to be, he acted as though he were already riding back into the camp of the war party, strutting on his horse, and showing off his trophy," the Tonkawa, always the scout, explaining the scenario to himself, seemingly oblivious to the likely tragedy that awaited them.

The boy had no such leisure. He turned and started for the house in a dead run, his body tingling with dread. If they had arisen and dressed earlier than usual, if they had already gone over to the neighbor's house, if they hadn't been caught out on the open trail, maybe they were safe. His mentor followed swiftly, but stayed in the shadows, lest he become a victim of arrogance himself.

Thomas Sutton found his mother face down about ten yards from the house. A large depressed gash opened the back of her skull and the hair and scalp had been removed from the front of her head. Thomas let out a whimper, then, began searching for his little sister.

She was not in the house. "Trudy!" he called, already knowing there would be no answer. He could see her tracks coming from the house straight toward her mother, then a chaos of prints around the body, both those of the child and also moccasin clad feet. Two sets of tracks led on down the trail away from his dead mother, the strides elongated, those of runners. Thomas searched the edges of the path leading away from the front of the home. His practiced eye caught sight of a trampled branch in the edge of the brush. Immediately, he saw the trail and followed it to his sister who also laid face down about thirty yards from her parent. Thomas studied the larger tracks that had followed her, prints of feet, broad, but short and stumpy, attesting to them likely being Comanche. There were four large wounds across the girl's back and a final one in the back of the head. Her favorite dress of royal purple, which she was wearing to visit the neighbors today, had been ripped away, though in the violence of tearing off the garment, one of the ribbons parted and caught on the limb of an adjacent agarita bush, dangling as though it had been purposely placed there by the child. He saw her bloody head, but he could look no more.

The import of the scene came down on Thomas like the sundering blow of the blade of an axe, an irreparable separation of his "before" from the hereafter, the remnants of his beloved family now only a history. The decimation pressed him down to his knees as he sobbed in agony. He was still kneeling as the older man walked up. The Tonkawa placed his hand on the boy's shoulder, for a long time remaining both silent and still. "How could it be?" murmured the boy.

The violence of such deeds, though not uncommon in raids on the Texas frontier, was beyond civilized reckoning, acts of some alien, ghoulish world not encountered in rational life. "The nature of the Comanche is a mystery to us all," interjected Oswego, "perhaps, to the Great Spirit as well. It simply cannot be fathomed by anyone of my people, much less yours. We have no power to change what has been done," he finally said. "There are now tasks that you and I must do."

Oswego wrapped the bodies in blankets. He carefully folded the remnant of the purple dress and handed it to the boy; then carried the girl out beneath the big oak and laid her beside the gravestone of Amos. Before he picked up the body of the mother, he stood for a long time examining the tracks, then, seeming to understand what he had examined, carried her out to place beside the child. Thomas put the folded ribbon in his pocket, wiped his tear-stained face on his sleeve, and numbly followed Oswego back to the area of the encounter with the two Comanches.

The young hunter stood gazing at the dead Indian, his stilled limbs flayed upon the ground. To the boy, the raider's fingers, even in death, seemed curled and claw-like, in a raptorial posture. Oswego took out a knife and deftly took the scalp of the dead man, placing his foot on the neck of the Comanche as he stripped the thick skin and hair away from the skull. Thomas had never seen this act before. He cringed at the wanton disregard of dignity that one human could have for another, even for this creature he loathed, though he suddenly caught his breath and recoiled in rage as he realized that the alien hands that had caught his attention had just perpetrated the same atrocity upon his mother. He glanced at the Comanche's right foot, then kicked it hard. At that moment, Thomas swore to be an everlasting and unrelenting enemy of the Comanche people.

The riderless Indian pony now stood with the four farm animals, oblivious to the role it had so recently played in the depredation, now only swishing its tail and occasionally stamping a foot, a prime example of nature's unconcern with human tragedy.

CHAPTER 2

Oswego began to study the scene of the fallen Indian. "The second rider was hit too," he said, pointing to a tiny spot of blood on a tree branch, five horse lengths behind the dead man. "If he has taken a bad wound, we will catch him before nightfall; if not, we will not see him again." They quickly led the horses and mules back to the barn, saddled their own two sorrels, strapped on their gear, and rode by the neighbors to tell them what had happened, and warn them of other Indians that might still be about. Oswego asked them if they would tend to the graves. The two riders started for the trail, there being no time to mourn. The only acceptable thing among the people of this frontier culture was vengeance.

Tracking an injured enemy, who was moving rapidly, was little problem for Oswego. He had been a military scout for both the Texas Rangers and the U.S. Army, leading hundreds of troops across the western part of Texas and northern Mexico. His ward was already better at the same task than nearly any professional. For four years now, Oswego had taught him how to track and read the signs, even the smallest, pointing out every bend in the grass, every tiny imprint in the dirt, every scuff on a rock, displaced leaf, or newly broken stem, that were the hallmarks of a new trail. Oswego liked to say, "Even one's shadow leaves a trail." The eyes of the trackers followed a line of progress of which the uninitiated had no hint.

The Tonkawa had taken over the training of the boy when his only close friend, and Thomas's father, Captain Amos Sutton, lay dying of what had been termed the colic. The dying ranger had recognized and accepted his fate, and turned to his brother in arms, asking that the

Indian mentor his son in order to prepare him for his future in this harsh and unforgiving western world.

Oswego's life was a unique mixture of two very different cultures. Thirty-five years prior to the death of Amos, a Methodist Circuit rider on his rounds, just southwest of Austin, heard a small cry as he was crossing Barton Creek. He rode over toward the sound and to his amazement saw a baby, held in a cradleboard, simply lying on the bank of the stream. Recognizing the cradle board as Tonkawan, he was not overly alarmed about danger to himself. The preacher knew, however, he had come upon an unlikely scene. He started to ride on, thinking the careless mother must have set the child there, and gone off into the adjacent woods.

As he crossed to the opposite bank, his horse snorted and shied away from the bushes that grew low beside the water. "What's the matter?" the pastor asked aloud. He regained control of his mount, and with his spurs, roweled his skittish animal back in the direction from which it had shied. The horse repeatedly snorted, was loath to go forward, and drew deep breaths, but the rider spurred on. Slowly venturing through the brush, he came upon the bodies of three adult Tonkawas, arrow riddled, scalped, and brutally disfigured. The victims included an Indian woman, whom he thought was likely the baby's mother.

Reluctant to become involved, he sat on his horse and pondered, "What in the world will I do?" Though he had never before admitted it to himself, he abhorred the idea of personally being involved with an Indian, but he knew that his professed faith held that this creature, too, was a child of God, and bid him to either abandon his life's calling or act the Good Samaritan. He waded back across the creek and looked down at the infant. The child was wide awake, but now it made no sound. The penetrating look of the small dark eyes convinced him he simply could not leave a baby there to die. He picked up the infant, strapped the cradleboard across his shoulder and carried it home to his wife.

All her life she had wanted a child to love, but she had given up the thought more than thirty years ago. Her reaction to this gift was immediate. She adored the little papoose, quickly bonded with him, and lovingly cared for him for the first eight years of his life.

The elderly woman was born and raised in northern New York on the banks of Lake Ontario so she named the child for her home town, Oswego, because the name sounded proper for an Indian, and there were many pleasant childhood memories in that place.

While the child was an infant, and then a toddler, the parishioners and neighbors accepted the baby with benevolence, though more as an orphaned pet than as a human being. As he grew older, and began to interact with the other children, however, a rather harsh animosity began to appear from the neighboring Texans toward the child. The circuit rider and his wife knew they had a major problem. The neighbors were beginning to see Oswego only as an Indian, and regardless of his upbringing, as alien to their way of thinking. Many Texans held that the only way to deal with their Indian problem was to eradicate all red men, friendly or not, and there was no inclination to make an exception for this orphan. In no manner could most of the rural people accept a child of Indian blood, living and acting as an equal among their own children.

The smoldering attitude became more and more confrontational, beginning to have a severe and debasing effect on the young lad, as he experienced the trauma of being disliked for a tribal affiliation he didn't even know he had, so his foster parents, by this time, well into their sixties, began to dread the possibility of having their son left alone in a white society. The heart-wrenching decision was made to try to return him to his own people.

The pastor and his wife were referred to Major Robert S. Neighbors, the well-known, able, and kindly Indian agent who enjoyed an excellent relationship with the Tonkawas, and was their most ardent advocate to the government of Texas.

"Let's go talk with Placido, the major chief of the Tonkawa people," the agent suggested. The Indian leader was well-known among the rangers and soldiers of Texas as a staunch ally, his braves scouting and fighting alongside the Texans in both Indian battles and skirmishes with Mexico. In fact, shortly after Texas became independent from Mexico, and before U.S. forces became more plentiful in the Southwest, the Ranger force might not have been able to hold off the Comanches without the help of the small band of Tonkawa warriors.

"I will adopt him and take him as my own son," offered the Tonkawa, and Oswego, thereafter, grew up with the Indians. The Tonkawa leader's wife was a Comanche woman, previously a captive serving the Tonkawas as a slave until she was claimed by Placido as his spouse; therefore, Oswego learned, not only the society of the Tonkawas, but many Comanche traditions, and many Comanche expressions as well.

Being abruptly plucked from one culture and plopped down in another, many precepts of which were diametrically opposed, was a daunting experience for an eight-year-old, and for many weeks it was obvious that Oswego desperately longed for his home. Within six months of his departure from the Texans, however, both of his foster parents had died, and he had no home to return to.

Placido recognized the culture shock the eight-year-old was going through and endeavored to ease his pain and make him feel welcome. "The Great Spirit has sent you to us," Placido assured him. "You are destined for wise leadership among your people and the Tonkawas will always consider you a great blessing."

The benevolent attention gave the boy confidence and soon thereafter Oswego determined he would thoroughly learn the ways of the wild. The effect of his first years in the home of the minister and his wife never faded, however, and he could never completely accept the value system of the natives. Forever, he was adrift between the two cultures.

"You must always retain your ability to converse, and read and write English for the white society will increasingly dominate the West, and good relations with them will be essential," the chief told the boy.

Placido's endeavors were aided by the Indian agent, Major Robert Neighbors, who took a great interest in the rearing of the orphaned lad. The agent not only dropped by to check on him in the Indian village, but with Placido's approval, occasionally brought him into his own home for visits, instruction, and practice in reading and writing among the members of the Neighbors family. He also promoted a childhood friendship between Oswego and another orphaned lad called Amos, the son of an admired acquaintance of pioneer stock, named Sutton. Amos's father and mother had died during an epidemic of typhoid fever, leaving the young boy with no nearby kin.

The bond between Amos and the Neighbors family had begun one day when the agent, hearing about the catastrophe in the Sutton household, rode up to the dogtrot house to see about the boy. He found him sitting on the breezeway porch, his father's pistol in his hand, looking grimly out over the country side.

"Howdy," said the agent, "I just rode over to see how you were getting along."

Amos had seen Neighbors once before when the agent had ridden by to talk to his dad about Indians straying through the area. "I'm fine, I can take care of myself," said the boy.

"I guess you can, sitting there with your dad's pistol all cocked and ready," replied Neighbors. "You look about as entrenched as a mad javelina, but that's not what I came over here to talk to you about. I was wondering if you might be able to take care of me."

The question took Amos completely by surprise, causing him to drop his feigned mask of self-sufficiency. "What do you mean?" asked the boy.

"In my work as Indian agent I have to ride out over a large territory, some of it a bit dangerous. I was wondering about hiring you to ride along with me as a bit of protection."

"I never thought about such a thing." said Amos, "but I'd probably be pretty good at it."

"Well, since this should be a business deal, why don't we ride over to my house and we can talk over our business during supper. I don't know whether you can remember it or not, but my wife was a good friend of your Ma, and they both liked to cook and share recipes. I'll bet my wife's cooking might taste a lot like your Ma's."

Amos's victuals had consisted of nothing but poke salad, parched corn and clabber for the last two weeks so he was quite susceptible to such an invitation. That night Amos ate like a starved wolf pup, and the older people smiled and watched him with much satisfaction. "Maam!" said the boy, "I know you've got to be the best cook in Texas."

The next morning he was riding beside agent Neighbors, though the older man persuaded him to put his pistol in his saddle bag because he said it might scare the Indians of the friendly villages they needed to visit.

When Major Neighbors brought Oswego home with him for a few

days, the two lads met, immediately recognized their similar status, and a bond formed between them quickly, both boys desperately in need of such security. Amos displayed none of the prejudice that Oswego had encountered elsewhere, and their friendship soon developed into a highlight for both boys, both always looking forward to the next visit.

Neighbors did not stop with just an introduction and an occasional visit. He gave the two boys the thrill of a lifetime, taking them, together, to accompany him on a government trip to Galveston. The mighty city, the largest and most prominent in Texas, with its ocean, broad streets, mansions, ships, and commerce, so astounded Oswego, that he almost decided he no longer wished to be an Indian.

The three travelers rode up in front of the government building. Neighbors got off his horse and handed the reins to Amos. "You boys ride around a bit and look over the town. This business of mine will take me about two hours. Just stay on your horses and mind your manners and you'll have no trouble. You might like to ride down to the docks and watch the ships unload."

Neighbors walked up the steps and disappeared behind the large door, and the two boys chucked their horses and rode down to the wharfs. Both lads were spellbound and sat watching the stevedores hook ropes to bales and with pulleys and cranes, swing them on board the ships.

There was so much activity, with people coming and going around the wharfs, that, as the boys sat looking at the spectacle, neither noticed two shabbily dressed seamen walk up. One took hold of the reins of Oswego's horse. "Well look here," he said. We got us a genuine Injun right here in the middle of Galveston. Maybe we should pull him off this horse and see if he can do a buffalo dance. Get down, redskin, and let's see you dance."

Amos reached in his saddle bag and pulled out his dad's pistol. "Get your hands off his reins," said the boy.

"Well, listen to this shavetail a telling us what to do," laughed the other sailor, "aint he a mean looking hombre. I believe I'll walk over and see how mean he really is."

The gun clicked as Amos pulled back the hammer and cocked the pistol.

The sound made both derelicts freeze. "That ain't no play gun he's got pointed at you," said the one next to Oswego. He turned loose of the reins and backed away. "Now don't get nervous, boy, we was just joshin' ya."

"Joshin' makes us nervous," answered Amos. Both seamen backed quickly out of sight, melding into the crowd.

The Galveston visit was an epiphany in the young Indian's life, after which he knew that there was another world out there, a vast geography, technology, culture and history, of which he had no previous comprehension, but which he now resolved to learn about, and to make part of his understanding of the world. It was at this time that Oswego first knew he would never live solely in the Indian sphere. He would catalogue it, would strive to master its insights, techniques, and its physical discipline, and would claim many of its mores and much of its value system as his heritage, but his intellectual awareness, the being which he considered to be "himself," would also include the wide world of the whites.

When he became eighteen, Oswego hired on as a scout with the Texas Rangers and at later times, with the U. S. Army as well. By those years, he was completely adept in the ways of the Tonkawa, and the ways of frontier war. He had an uncanny gift for tracking, and for detecting a nearby enemy, and a thorough knowledge of Comanche habits and tactics. He detested the feared Comanches. Not only was he aware that his blood parents had been murdered by members of the tribe, but he had witnessed raids where the howling horde had stormed through Tonkawa villages, leaving random death, mutilation, and devastation in their wake. He grew up eager to join with the Texans to meet the Indian raiders in a planned campaign, or to lead a tracking party in quest of revenge. With the extra advantage of knowing the Texans' language, he was much sought after by both armed forces. Of no small importance to the military, he could read and write English well enough to fill out army reports.

This same year Sutton was twenty and had already served in the Texas Rangers and twice as a scout for the U.S. Army. Through his years of association with Agent Neighbors, he had acquired a thorough understanding of the country west of the Brazos River and of the aborigines it harbored. Oswego and Amos reunited a few years later when they were both assigned to the same Ranger Company, Amos, as one of the youngest Texas Ranger Captains, and Oswego, as an accomplished scout. During their ensuing hard years in the saddle, the Ranger and the scout extended their childhood friendship into adult years. Such a relationship between an Indian and a White was a rarity in the frontier culture, seeming quite mysterious to all those who were not of the inner circle of the Ranger company. Amos and Oswego however, considered it completely normal, each recognizing in the other a gateway to a wider understanding of the world around them, both working hard to fathom the skills, the mores, and the collected wisdom of the other man's society.

"This Indian is too aloof," said one of the Rangers, "he seems to think he's better than the other soldiers."

"He probably is," laughed Sutton. Though aloof he might be around most of the company Rangers, he was both happy and intrigued to be around the captain. Sutton always made sure his scout was armed and equipped as well as the other Rangers, and in times of privation on their forays, he saw to it that the scout was included in sharing equally, the last of the food or water. Often, the food they ate, Oswego scavenged from the countryside rather than it being what the quartermaster had allotted to each man, but he seemed never to mind turning it over to the captain for distribution to the rest of the company.

CHAPTER 3

In the late summer of 1862 raids by the Comanches became more frequent and more severe than ever. With the withdrawal of the American Army, because of the Civil War, the Indians realized they were again free to prowl, almost unmolested, over the frontier. Clashes between the two peoples, called raids by the Comanches, and depredations by the Texans, were occurring more and more often, until the roster of ravaged ranches and rural homesteads became catastrophic. The undermanned Ranger force, markedly depleted by the Civil War, was deployed in an effort to stem the tide, but most of their efforts were ineffectual because of the lack of men, weapons, and supplies, in the face of the vastness of the exposed territory.

Sutton's small group of Rangers patrolled an area between the headwaters of the Guadalupe and San Saba Rivers, sparsely settled and uncharted country. Clashes occurred any time one race thought they had an advantage over the other, with vicious and brutal actions taken by each side, skirmishes and running battles so numerous that most were not even recorded. The enmity was so fierce that just the sighting of one by the other was sufficient reason to kill.

A small patrol of six riders, including the scout, Oswego, was sent out to investigate the country where some livestock had recently been taken. After reaching the north bank of the Llano River, the troop had been surprised by a large group of Comanches which almost encircled them. As the Rangers maneuvered to get out of the trap, Oswego volunteered to act as the rear guard, while the others began to retreat back across the river and up the hill. They, in turn, were to produce covering fire while Oswego made a dash for the river to join them. As soon as the Rangers had broken out of the near encirclement, however, they realized how little ammunition they still had, and simply bolted for the pass above, leaving their scout to his own circumstances. The Comanches realized that the Tonkawa scout was alone, and quickly encircled his position leaving him with no hope of escape. Oswego knew better than to be captured by Comanches and was determined to die at his post, but an arrow pierced his forearm and the enemy braves swarmed over him instantly.

The five Rangers, having retreated all the way to the next rise, looked back to see their scout with a noose around his neck and his arms bound behind his back, being led out of the valley, the lead of the rope tied to an Indian pony.

Upon returning to base camp the Rangers had to report to Captain Sutton. "Where is Oswego?" he asked. He began to find discrepancies in their stories and quickly arrived at the truth. The five surrogate rangers acted relatively blasé about their loss. Though they certainly valued Oswego's ability as a scout and as a fighter, to these unseasoned recruits, he was not one of their own. "He's just another Indian," said one of the troopers, "They've probably already made him one of their chiefs."

The look the young Ranger got from Sutton was more than contempt. There was no mistaking that there was malice in his expression, and the glare caused the novice to shrink back.

"You have just deserted someone who would die before he deserted you, and now he faces an ordeal the horror of which you would never be able to imagine, and you're being flippant about it," said the Captain. "My advice to you is to be gone from here before I get back." To Sutton, their action constituted desertion in the face of the enemy, unacceptable no matter what the circumstances. Amos knew that the force had many inferior men because of the depletion of their ranks by the war, but he could not imagine them abandoning their basic precept of never leaving one of their own behind.

Without pondering the advisability of the mission, he immediately saddled two horses, put an extra rifle on the mount he was leading, a shotgun and a rifle on his own, and headed toward the battle site. Reaching the spot of the encounter in late afternoon, he rode on north toward the San Saba River. Examining the trail, Sutton thought to himself, "There must be at least twenty Comanches in the party." He had no trouble finding the bloody foot print of the now barefooted prisoner. A mile beyond the river, the war party split into two groups and rode in different directions, but the barefoot tracks were still easy for him to find. The smaller party of Indians, leading Oswego, had now reduced their number to ten.

The Indians were making no attempt to cover their tracks so Sutton was able to follow the party past dusk. At first, he could not fathom why the Comanches were so uncharacteristically careless with their trail, but finally decided that the raiders would not imagine the Texans being concerned enough about a Tonkawa to follow them into dangerous Indian Territory. The one chink in the armor of the Comanche warriors was that sometimes, the young and inexperienced were separated from the main force and relegated to a lesser responsibility, such as trailing captives, and hazing livestock toward the Indian camps, while the more experienced warriors extended their raids. Sutton hoped this was the circumstance of the party he was now following.

When darkness fell, and he could no longer see the trail, he decided to take a calculated risk, and simply ride for the split in the next ridge of hills where he knew the frontier path passed over the rise. If the war party had continued their careless ways they might have stopped over night for rest. If so, he could close the distance between them. It seemed never to occur to Sutton that even if he caught up, the odds would still be ten to one.

• *HAROLD BRANNAN* •

CHAPTER 4

As the first glimmer of light began to creep over the hills, Sutton had already established himself over the brim of the pass. He scanned the scene for any sign of danger or sentry, but he could find none. Having been over this same route many times in the past, it was more his home territory than that of his adversaries. He knew there was a small spring at the mouth of a side canyon below, often frequented by travelers, including Indians, so he hoped they had stopped there to camp. Studying the ground, he saw the tracks go right through the pass, continuing on the well-established trail. Oswego's barefoot prints were still among them. He saw where the captive had fallen and had been dragged for several yards, but then, the footprints resumed. Sutton knew that he was fortunate, because the group had still made no effort to conceal their tracks. "Yes," he thought, "they must all be initiates on one of their first raiding parties, and too young and inexperienced to be sufficiently careful." The thought gave him some solace. If his reckoning was correct, the lack of mature Comanche skill might reduce the Indians' vigilance, and thus, their advantage.

He had already found a hiding place for his extra pony, fifty feet behind the top of the ridge. This horse was tethered in place, one of the extra firearms was transferred to his own mount, and he carefully worked his way into a group of junipers growing on the crest close to the pass, taking his horse across the top without exposing its silhouette to anyone in the valley. He led the horse through the brush, farther down the slope, and then tied him behind an outcropping of rock so that neither the horse, nor any creature below, could see one another. The last four hundred yards, Sutton made on foot and on all fours, carrying the shot gun in his hands, a rifle strapped across his back, and his own pistol in its scabbard. He began to hear the faint hum of voiced Comanche interaction.

As he crawled and scooted through the underbrush he saw off to his left, a shadowy mound, which at first, in the early morning hours, he couldn't make out. Crawling completely behind a large tree trunk and slowly raising his head he realized it was Oswego, staked to the ground in a spread eagle position. Sutton guessed he was likely over an ant bed. If the young Comanches had intended to trail their captive all the way to the Llano Estacado to serve as the victim in a torture fest, they had been much too harsh on him – the vitality of his body already rapidly ebbing. Sutton guessed the young Indians had given up on the long trek for the prisoner and meant to kill him here, probably with as much pain as they could inflict.

The bushes back down toward the spring rustled slightly and Sutton saw three young braves approaching up the trail, each with a long flint knife in hand. They walked up and stood over Oswego. One kicked him in the ribs and the victim let out a low moan. Another of the young braves grabbed a large shock of Oswego's hair. He called out toward other companions coming up the trail and bent down with the scalping knife.

Amos stood up, swinging his shotgun at the young Indians. All three whirled toward him, startled, but instantly exuding a countenance of malice. They were too late, as both barrels flashed, and all three braves were knocked backward to the ground. He rapidly put a rifle bullet through the head of two, and took his pistol to the last. Sutton reasoned the enemy would have heard three different guns, and would have to wonder if there were several rangers. In a flash he took his knife, severing the thongs holding Oswego to the stakes. He took one arm and dragged him away from the ant bed, then grabbed his guns and sprang for cover behind a large downed tree with several small junipers growing up in front of it. Oswego stirred slightly but could not rise.

The ranger saw distant bushes move and knew that other Indians were spreading out and coming his way. Out of the corner of his eye he saw the legging of one limb protrude from behind a large oak trunk. Slowly the ranger moved his rifle barrel toward the partially concealed Indian who had not yet seen Sutton. The gun of the Comanche eased around the oak and pointed toward the prostrate Oswego, perhaps, to make sure this enemy could not be salvaged. As the young Comanche took aim his hand came forward to steady the barrel of the gun. Since Amos had no head or body silhouette to aim at, he fired at the hand. The young Indian howled in pain and several shots answered with splinters flying off the downed log from where Sutton had fired as the Comanches immediately located the site of concealment of their enemy, but the experienced ranger had already scooted behind the log toward the far end of the tree near the bared roots. The captain reached for the barrel of his shot gun, breached the weapon, and reloaded just before two more young fighters rose up with a whoop, took courage from the sound of their own voices, and ran straight for the barrier of the downed tree. As they leaped over the log he caught both in mid air by sequential blasts from the double barrels. Their riddled bodies fell in a heap into the junipers, twitched and turned for a moment, then were still.

For several minutes all was quiet, then, he heard the "uh oh oh ooh" call of a mourning dove coming from the direction of the camp. Sutton knew no dove would still be in the vicinity after the noise of such a battle, so he waited, listening to learn what the signal might mean. Soon, he heard the stirring of unshod horses' hooves and desperately hoped the Comanches had had enough. He knew the young braves would be severely scorned by the members of their tribe for losing half of their number, just for one Tonkawa prisoner. He hoped they would not risk losing others.

The captain did not move for almost an hour, and would have remained concealed much longer, in fear that the Comanches might have circled around rather than heading home, but he knew Oswego was in dire straits even though he could see that he was still alive. Oswego had his eyes open and focused on the Ranger but he did not stir. The Ranger reloaded his shotgun and crept over to a large, partially fractured hollow tree. He poked the stock upward in the hollow until it was tightly wedged and then walked over and knelt by his friend. His body was covered by ant stings and numerous cuts, bruises, and abrasions. Both feet were badly macerated, a rope burn printed deeply around his neck, and there was a wound completely through his right forearm with a piece of broken arrow shaft still in place. Amos glanced back at the ant bed. The bloody bodies of the three young warriors lay across one another with ants already swarming over the corpses. Amos looked at the three faces and was struck by how young they were, more like children than men. He realized that if this fight had been with the kind of accomplished warriors he was used to seeing, the confrontation would have turned out quite differently.

He walked over, picked up one of the long flint scalping knifes and stuck it beneath his belt, later transferring it to his saddle bag. He brought up his horse, and with all the effort he could muster, pushed Oswego up into the saddle and bound him in place.

They were four days getting back to the Ranger station, much of the time used in allowing Oswego to rest. Only short stretches of travel were possible, during which he had to be tied in the saddle as he alternately went in and out of delirium.

Riding back slowly over the long stretch with no one to talk to gave Amos much time to reflect over what had just happened. He had been in many Indian battles, some at close quarters, where death was a common occurrence, and he was certainly hardened to war. Usually he shook off the gory memories of a vicious encounter like a dog emerging from water, shaking the wetness out of its coat, but the events of this last day would not let his mind be at ease. It was not just the wastage of Comanches, for whom he held no benevolence, but the youth of those involved, the vestiges of child-like expressions on their faces, the incongruity of death enveloping the young.

When the two returned to base, all of the force gathered round in bewilderment with wild hurrahs, though neither Oswego nor Sutton would speak to any of them. After one week, Sutton thought his scout could ride, so they saddled the horses and made their way back to the Sutton homestead on the headwaters of the Guadalupe where the Ranger's wife, Maria, and the two Sutton children were living. He now deemed the straggly group of troops in his unit unfit to serve, believing they were doing more harm than good. He sent a message to headquarters in San Antonio, advising them to disband the force.

CHAPTER 5

Maria's parents had been in Texas before the revolution, her father, one of the Tejanos who had fought on the side of the Texans against Mexico. He was also one of the few Tejanos who had ever served in the Texas Rangers. Eduardo Velasquez, originally a son from a wealthy family in Mexico, had met Maria's mother, Monique, a young French girl, in New Orleans, where he had been sent for schooling in America. Marrying outside his social circle of the Mexican elite, and especially to a French girl with no illustrious family background was unacceptable to his family and Edwardo was disowned. Nonetheless, Monique was the prettiest, perkiest and most loving person he had ever seen, and being a maverick himself he chose his true love over his heritage, and the two moved to San Antonio to start a life of their own. After the Texas Revolution, Edwardo had gained considerable social status, and the husband and wife established a rancho south of town on the San Antonio River. Part of the land was made available to him from the government of Texas, as a reward for fighting against Mexico.

As the daughter of such a family, Maria had grown up being self-reliant, knowing the heartache of the lonely, sparsely settled country, but also the exhilaration of the wide open spaces. She had first seen young Amos Sutton at the Rangers' Christmas Ball, where she was introduced to San Antonio society. Her comely appearance and vivacious deportment quickly attracted the attention of everyone there. Amos thought she stood out like a canary among sparrows. Though the girl was carefully chaperoned, all of the eligible young men sought to make her acquaintance.

Amos walked up to her father and introduced himself. "Senor

Velasquez, I know you were one of the early rangers after the formation of the Republic of Texas. If you ever have the inclination, I would love to hear your account of the battle with the Comanches at Plum Creek."

Sutton, himself, was well enough known among the present group of law men, that Senor Velasquez had heard of him, and, knowing what the young Ranger really desired, postponed any tales about the early days, and introduced him to his wife and daughter.

Both Amos and Maria realized, almost from first sight, that they were meant for one another. After a courtship, somewhat abbreviated for a Mexican family, Maria, left the security and comforts of her home, to move with her young husband to a large tract of land they were able to acquire on the upper Guadalupe, where they dreamed of creating a grand estancia. A small farm headquarters was initially established beside the river with adjacent pasturelands extending into the hills. A boy and a girl had been born to the young couple by the fifth year of their marriage.

The Sutton neighbors who helped populate the frontier were a unique mixture of people. Most of them were repeat failures from the location of their origin, being unable to succeed where they had lived before, but willing to face danger and deprivation to wipe away the past and make a new start; some were immigrants from the old countries of Europe, some were fugitives from the law. Nearly all of these accumulated settlers were subsistence farmers, living essentially on the crops they could raise and the game they could shoot, only minimally setting themselves apart from the wild natural creatures of the surrounding frontier. There were a few who were visionaries, trying to establish themselves in a position to build their own empire as the population grew and the frontier was pacified. Maria and Amos thought they were such people.

When the Civil War erupted and Indian raids once more became severe, they might have moved back to San Antonio close to her parents, but when Amos was pressed into service with the Rangers to protect the frontier, Maria refused to go home. She wanted to be close enough to see her husband from time to time, and she felt safe with the several neighbors close by.

CHAPTER 6

Maria and Amos nursed Oswego constantly for the first tenuous two weeks; then he slowly began to improve. The Indian hated the inactivity of recuperation, and longed to be off to himself, but the constraints of his injuries were beyond his abilities to cope so he compromised with Maria who made him his own living space away from the house, converting the nearby tool shed into the Tonkawa's living quarters.

It was a full year before Oswego was back to his original strength. During the whole time Maria and Amos's small boy, Thomas, came to see him daily. At first, he brought only food, water, and firewood. He would quickly place the wood in the fire box, the food and water on the stark table and then stand straight and face the Indian until the patient dismissed him with a nod. There were no words exchanged between them.

One day as he began to lose some of the fear he had of the austere Tonkawa, Thomas ventured an offering. Following the nod he reached in his pocket and held forth a scarlet red tail feather of a rooster cardinal. "I brought you a present," he said. The Indian first looked at the feather, then deeply into the boy's eyes. He took the feather and slowly his other arm reached out and he placed his hand on the boy's shoulder. A broad smile spread across the Tonkawa's face. "A red feather is a symbol of bravery to the Tonkawas," he said. "I can see that you will one day become a very brave warrior." The boy smiled too and a soft chuckle came from both the lad and the scout. Thereafter, Thomas would often bring things that a young boy would fancy; pet rabbits and squirrels he had caught, bird eggs, strange rocks, insects, and animal bones. Oswego knew much about all these things, and he intrigued the boy by telling him what they meant in the Tonkawa way of understanding nature.

Oswego, who had no son of his own, became more and more interested in Thomas, and began to share with him many insights into his surroundings that only one raised in the wild can acquire. He taught him skills of hunting and tracking, and how to use a knife, and a bow and arrow. He practiced with him on how to use the most primitive weapon of all and certainly the most available. For long periods of the day they threw rocks together, the boy becoming ever more accurate and effective. There began to develop a bond between the teacher and the pupil, that time worn and honored duty of one generation handing down to the next the accumulated lore of generations past, each participant inherently attracted to the other, each adapted and called to the task.

Oswego worked to instill in Thomas a heightened awareness of the five senses, and the realization of the great potential they have to widen one's world.

"The ears of most people hear only a fraction of what is available to them, and their eyes see only what is most obvious. You must learn to look through the pall of what is readily evident to learn the extent of what is really out there." He taught how the breeze will carry one's scent to the animals they stalk, and when the air is relatively still, how to detect the direction of its motion by taking a single thread from a spider web, attaching a tiny leaf to the end, and dangling it from an exposed tree limb to watch the subtle direction in which it drifts. Thomas delighted in these new insights and resolved to be a master of such sensitivity.

Oswego taught him to sharpen his sense of smell, to detect the aromas of the wild, the leaves and blossoms of different plants, the repugnance, but uniqueness of the spoor of the different creatures. "Note how wolves and dogs recognize their competitors by the spoor they leave behind." He talked about how the mothers of the animal kingdom differentiated and recognized their young by smell. He even taught him to shut his eyes and differentiate the various horses of the farm by his own sense of smell alone, to delve deep enough to detect the uniqueness of the one, from the generic of the many, taught him to detect a rattlesnake den, then to develop his sensitivity enough to smell a single close rattlesnake. Oswego impressed on the boy that smell is one of the things that will endure longest and most acutely in one's memory, but it is the most neglected sense among men. If one thoroughly honed such sensitivity when he was young, these abilities would remain with him for life.

Oswego spent endless hours teaching Thomas to listen, to become familiar with normal background noise, and to distinguish it from the abnormal.

"No matter how skilled you become, you must still understand that the animals are much more skilled in hearing and odor detection than you are, and it is necessary to recognize one's own limitations, especially in comparison to the creatures of the wild," said the Tonkawa.

"Watch the animals and see how they react to the noises you make or hear, and if you again see those same reactions when the world is silent to you, they are probably hearing something beyond the limits of your own ability, perhaps the noise of your approach, if you are stalking." He told Thomas that he would only rarely have the chance to intently watch predators, but when the occasion came, to carefully study coyotes, wolves, cats and bears noting how they used their keen senses to explore the landscape, to detect and stalk their prey, and to protect themselves from dangerous encounters. He taught him to spend much time observing horses, seeing how they reacted to what they heard, saw, and smelled, and how one's horse would most often detect game, danger, or other horses before the rider.

The Tonkawa made the boy his own bow and several arrows, and taught him to fashion arrows of his own, then to shoot with steady arms, and to practice daily. "There should never be a day that you do not practice," he said.

He taught him to taste all things, except those that he knew were dangerous and to feel all things he could by day and by night, to refine his senses of touch and taste. He taught him what was edible in the wild, and where such food could be found. He impressed upon him that the senses do not go completely dormant when one sleeps, especially those of smell and hearing.

He worked with him on how to imprint a scene upon his memory, and to recognize what was changed when he again saw it, practicing with him to markedly reduce his recognition time, so that if he saw something only for an instant, he could visualize it, stamp the vision in

31

his memory, and hold it there until he had time to reflect upon what it was he had seen.

The core lesson that Oswego wished to convey to Thomas was that the only external information that went into the mind was brought there by the senses. "If you hone the acuity of your senses and glean twice the information as the ordinary person, your own world will be twice as large, and you will be twice as able to deal with the environment as the other person," he said. Oswego was very patient with the boy, as if time were of no importance, for he knew from his own upbringing that there was no "royal road to learning," only long and difficult hours of application and study.

The culmination of this extended effort, the thrill it afforded, the activity in which it all coalesced, was the hunt. It was the hunt in which Thomas could pit his skills against nature, against the inherent skills of the animals he sought, in which he could join the cult of his ancient ancestors and become a predator himself, a mighty hunter. His first grown rabbit, his first fox, his first deer were all gained under the tutelage of the Tonkawa, and he could hardly wait to get to the house to see the reaction and obtain the praise of his parents when he was successful.

Oswego reminded him there were predators besides man in the wild, ones which might consider him prey, the bear, the wolf, the cougar, and if ever confronted, not to run, but not to provoke, simply stand up as tall and wide as possible in order to make himself a more imposing image and slowly back away.

His lesson came one early morning, after he had just turned nine. The family needed meat and he and Oswego contrived to get a deer by working together. Thomas was to descend into a shallow canyon and drive the game by Oswego who stood concealed aside the mouth of the gully.

Thomas silently crept down the steep wall to the bottom where there was a tiny stream, but just as it was time to make noise to start the drive, he sensed a danger. What was the sensation, a sound, a sight, a smell? Whatever it was it caused the hair on the back of his neck to stand up. His eyes became accommodated to the shadows around the tiny stream, and he drew back as he caught sight of the carcass of a deer lying outstretched by the creek. There was blood around the neck and along the underbelly. He looked beyond the kill and searched the underbrush. At first he saw only plant life, but what he saw did not explain the slain deer. His eyes swept back and forth, then, began to peer intensely into the shadows. Suddenly his eyes met two others. They were deep in the shadows but reflected a pale yellow stare. They moved slightly toward him and the movement let him see other features. A tingling fear swept trough his body as he began to recognize the form of a mighty cat, the tawny coat which blended with the underbrush barely discernable in the early morning light, but the animal was almost close enough to see the whiskers on its face. The deep cold eyes stared directly into his as the cat stood motionless. Thomas raised his bow high in the air in one hand and his arrows in the other trying to increase the size of his silhouette. Nature urged him to flee as fast as he could, but Oswego had told him no. He slowly began backing away but the cat slowly came forward. A nine year old boy probably did not look very imposing to a cougar, but the animal hesitated, innately sensing danger from the human scent. Thomas saw the slight cock of the animal's head, then the slow back and forth undulation of the tail, and he thought he saw the curl of the lip, and the tensing of muscle as a muffled snarl seemed to define the cat's intent.

A rapid sschup sound split the air from above as an arrow hit the cat in the lateral chest and protruded out the opposite side. A chilling scream echoed down the canyon and the cat reached back to bite the arrow which impaled him, but two more arrows almost instantaneously hit the cat and it began to flay itself upon the ground.

Oswego waved for the boy to back up the canyon wall to where he was, and the two stood watching the cat which now lay on its side, a complete stillness now pervading the canyon and the cat. Oswego told Thomas to put another arrow into the animal and as Thomas held his bow his arm began to quiver. The Indian reached out and closed his hand around the boys arm, steadied it, then loosed his grip and nodded. The arrow went straight into the belly of the cat. There was no flinch, no stir of life, but still the two sat watching for a long time. "I think you and I have done it," said Oswego, then he slowly approached the animal, bow and arrow at the ready, leaving Thomas in place at the top of the ledge.

"How did you know to come back for me?" asked Thomas. "I heard no noise when I knew you had already reached the bottom of the canyon," answered the Tonkawa.

When the two hunters knocked on the farmstead door Thomas stood holding the huge pelt.

In an attempt to contribute something of his own to their relationship, Thomas practiced reading and writing with Oswego and discussed with him what he had learned about geography and science. The Indian had maintained his knowledge of reading and most words which had been a part of his education when he was still with his foster mother and father and later when he was in the home of Major and Mrs. Neighbors, though he was amazed to realize how much more there was than he had ever learned. With the help of Thomas and Maria he increased these skills rapidly, and was soon reading some of Maria's complicated texts. Maria tried to include Oswego in parts of Thomas's home schooling without embarrassing him, though such a relationship between an Indian and a white woman was so foreign to Oswego that his inhibitions blocked him from many of the mathematical and language skills he could have acquired.

CHAPTER 7

After his year of recovery Oswego temporarily went back to his people, where his wife and two daughters lived with his extended family. The scout was one of the wealthiest of the Tonkawas because of his desirability to the army, and his wealth was shared with the large family. The actual remuneration for a scout on the Texas frontier was only a pittance, though any money at all among the Tonkawa people stood out as extraordinary. Though he and his family were used to being separated for long periods of time because of the scouting assignments, they had almost given up hope that Oswego was still alive until his whereabouts had been relayed to them by a Texas Indian agent.

Captain Sutton continued to work as a ranger, when called upon, but as the war ended, more and more he stayed close to Maria and the children on the homestead, building up the land and the home, and directing protection from the Indians only for the surrounding community of farms. For the first few years after the war, the settlers had to protect themselves, the U. S. Army only giving lip service to the task. Sutton often said "The army was willing to fight the Comanches to the last Texan before they engaged themselves."

Maria diligently taught her children to read and write, to work mathematics and to have more than a basic understanding of geography and science. In the early years she taught a daily community school, with the neighboring Beasley children attending as well. Virginia Beasley was only a little younger than Thomas, but she was definitely the scholar of the group. Eager to learn and intelligent, she served as an impetus to force Thomas and his sister, Trudy, to work harder. The two Sutton children grew up speaking both English and Spanish, but as they grew older, both Maria and Amos realized that the education available in their home was not enough of what they desired their children to have, so each autumn, they sent them to San Antonio to go to school.

Thomas was sent to the only institution, of which his parents were aware, that was available for such boys, a Catholic Marianist school named Saint Mary's Institute. His grandfather was a close friend of Father Bernard, a learned monk, and a teacher at Saint Mary's University, who agreed to look after his grandson in the evenings and at night. The lad went to school during the day, but many of the nights, after he had finished with his studies, were spent in talking with the priest and his friends, discussing science, philosophy, geography, art and literature, topics usually reserved for a more advanced age. Thomas deeply respected the monk for his knowledge and for his fairness, even toward other religions.

Trudy was sent to the Ursuline Academy, and on many occasions the two were allowed to visit with one another, where they loved to sit and talk by the river. The two siblings adored each other and their bond became much stronger because of being away from home.

One visiting day was on Thomas's birthday. When they first met, he could see that Trudy was exceptionally excited. She held her hands behind her back, and when they sat down on the river bank she brought her hands forward and handed Thomas a wrapped present. He gingerly opened the paper, and there was a plaited belt, eight strands of yellow leather, woven into a strap with the two ends of the strap frayed into single strands, a heavy bead tied to each of the eight free thongs, the pattern repeated on the opposite length of the strap. "Sister Angeline helped me make it for you" she said. "It's very strong."

"Like you are Trudy," he responded. "This is the best present I've ever had. I intend to wear it when I am grown and am the father a young daughter. I hope she will be just like you." He sat on the river bank with his arm tightly around the young girl for a long time. When the children returned home Thomas asked his mother if he could keep the belt on the mantel, and the family agreed that its intricate beauty was such that the mantel was where it should be.

In the early spring Thomas could hardly wait to get back to the frontier and the wilds. His homecoming and the reunion with his parents was paramount, but Oswego had usually returned in the spring, and year after year, the two of them would continue their affair with the great outdoors, exploring the countryside, learning to live off the land, and melding with what grew in the wild. Thomas would try to tell Oswego about all the things he had studied in school. The boy could see that Oswego was quick to grasp even the most difficult concepts of the Anglo and Spanish worlds, ones that were usually far outside the realm of Indian lore and society, his mind ever probing, ever claiming as his own, features of the white society and bits of the storehouse of their knowledge of the world.

The Tonkawa scout would work for the Ranger force in protecting the settlements, and would help the captain do those jobs that needed more than one adult, but like many other semi-nomads, he was never a happy farmer, so he made forays into the hills and brought home game for the table. Thomas usually wanted to go with him and often, the two hunted and gathered together.

Oswego was always considerate and friendly to Maria, but for the most part kept his distance, as though it were not his place to be an intimate part of the family life. The one exception was a time when the ranch was visited by a pair of riders from San Antonio. They said they were tax assessors for the state, and were here to inspect the land, wondering if the property might be undervalued. Amos was away, but Maria recognized immediately that they were carpet baggers, and the tone of her voice attracted Oswego who strolled up to the edge of the porch. He was holding a sun-bleached remnant of a dead mule's rib in his hand, the artifact appearing more like a weapon than a relic. The huge Indian stood to one side and just listened, a slight frown playing across his face, alien, and with the hint of savagery. The chief inspector looked uneasily at Oswego, turned back to Maria, and asked her what the Indian was doing here. "He is the property manager," said Maria. "He will show you around as you inspect the farm."

In his bare hands, Oswego bent the bone, which made a loud cracking sound, and snapped into two pieces. He pitched the pieces to the ground, slightly toward the feet of the two strangers, and without a word, beckoned for them to follow him. The chief assessor stood in awe, swallowed twice, then said that he believed he could see the property well enough from the homestead, and thought there was no reason to change the numbers. The two visitors made a hasty retreat.

CHAPTER 8

As Oswego and Thomas rode out of the valley of the Sutton homestead, leaving the tragedy of the massacre behind, the trail was fresh and easy to follow. They pushed their horses hard. Sensing their quarry's desperate flight, they were not overly afraid of an ambush from the one they pursued, though Oswego reminded Thomas that it was very unusual for only two marauders to travel alone, more likely having branched off from a much larger force, with plans to meet again at some designated spot. Every three or four miles Oswego would dismount and study the tracks, intensely trying to discern how old they were. He told Thomas that they were gaining on the fugitive and twice they saw spots of blood along the trail. Before they rode over any rise, they would carefully survey the distant scenery for any sign of other Indians.

When the trackers reached the Llano River, clouds of grackles arose from the nearby trees and flew off into the sky. Oswego frowned because he knew this many birds could be seen for some distance by an enemy, and that such a sudden flight might well be interpreted as due to fast moving human intrusion, even trackers following one of their own. The two hunters followed the hoof prints into the water, but thereafter, they disappeared. "He either knew, or believed, he was being followed," Oswego said. "The new concern about his tracks probably means he has seen us, so he has to be close."

They began to ride in both directions on the north side of the stream. Though no emerging prints were seen arising from the banks, there were plenty of places where rock surfaces touched the water that could have been used as an exit. Thomas had dismounted and was minutely looking at the terrain when his eye rested on a low, broken branch of a cypress tree growing between two sheets of granite. He almost passed it by, the break of the branch not being fresh, but a tiny fleck of color arrested his attention, making him examine the protruding wood more closely. Caught on a sharp spike of the broken end of the limb was a single, tiny fragment of purple thread, not much more than a fiber. Thomas called for Oswego who soon joined him and began to intently inspect the surrounding area to the north of the far bank

"He must be wearing the cloth of the dress as a bandage, perhaps, scraping the branch against the cloth as he rode through", said Oswego. The two spread out from the riverbank and soon found the horse's trail, the hoof prints again becoming visible where the river rocks ended. The older scout thought they were not more than one hour behind. "His pony is tired," said Oswego, pointing out the scuffs in the soil where the forefoot had faltered by scraping the front of the hoof along the ground.

They rode steadily for the rest of the afternoon. Toward evening, they sighted a cloud bank in the west, the clouds beginning to drop sprinkles as they drifted near. Both riders sensed they were closing in, and they pushed their horses harder. Just as the two cleared the next ridge they saw their quarry below. Sure enough, there was a purple cloth tied around his left shoulder, the rider slumped forward on his pony, the pony itself stumbling from near exhaustion.

As Oswego and Thomas went over the top and started down into the valley Oswego caught sight of movement to his left, far up the canyon. A flock of wild turkeys rose in the air, and flew about two hundred yards down beside the creek into a large group of trees. The Tonkawa scout led his ward straight down the trail until they passed into a thicket of brush and timber where Oswego immediately detoured away from the path, motioned for Thomas to follow, and both riders made their way far to the right and back over the ridge where they could remain concealed from below. "Why are we going backward?" whispered Thomas.

"Didn't you see turkeys?" asked Oswego and Thomas nodded. "Turkeys always prefer to walk or run, even away from danger. They do not fly unless they are flushed by something big, at least as large as a coyote. They would hear and simply get out of the way of a lone rider. They were most likely flushed by a war party. I did not bring you here, just to have you scalped by Comanches. Your day will come, but it is not today."

"Oswego, I am not afraid of the danger. I'm not concerned about what happens to me. I just want to get my own hands around his neck, so he can, if only for a moment, know there are consequences for what he did."

"No," said Oswego, "life is much too precious to be traded away for vengeance."

Sheets of rain began to fall, thoroughly drenching the countryside. The two riders traveled far to the side of the most obvious and easy way home for Oswego knew that the two of them might have been seen by the war party, the thirst for revenge possibly residing as avidly in the hearts of the savage Comanches, as in their own. They slept in a cold camp under a ledge that would be easy to defend, and took turns standing guard, but they heard nothing, nor saw anything hinting of danger. The next day they rode into sight of the farmstead.

Thomas dreaded going back into the empty farm house. He was now fourteen, and, with some advice, could manage most things on the farm by himself, but he had little heart for his tasks ahead. He walked into the empty rooms, even his own footsteps faintly echoing with a vacant sound. He went over to the fireplace and reached to the mantel to bring down his plaited belt, just to hold it close as a reminder of Trudy. It was not in its place. He stood staring at the empty shelf.

"It is time for me to return to my people, "Oswego said," you are welcome to come with me but I do not think you would be happy there." Thomas nodded his head in agreement. "I belong here," he thought, "I need time to myself, and I need time with the neighbors."

Oswego could sense the boy's bitterness. "Do you think you would feel any better if we had caught him?" he asked. Thomas clenched his jaw, his eyes narrowing, "I have missed him this once, but destiny will let our paths cross again. The next time, I will be ready, and he will pay an awful price for what he has done."

"What you are talking about, Thomas, may require a lifetime, and also, it could well require of you, your own life," said Oswego, "When, and if, you finally meet him, you will probably have no way to recognize him, and the retribution will only be heaped upon others that were not directly responsible. In most conflicts, it is more often the innocent who are harmed rather than the belligerents."

"There are no innocents among the Comanches," said Thomas, "a nation of people who will openly admire a warrior for the wanton killing of women and children needs to be removed from the earth." He was quiet for some time and then continued, "This warrior thinks he can simply flee back to the plains and be safe, but I pledge to spend the rest of my life to show him it isn't so. There will be no sanctuary on the face of the earth for this person or his kind."

"Be careful to what you commit your life," said Oswego, "you must know that you and he, both, are simply a part of the handiwork of nature, and children of the Great Spirit. You are the way you are, because of where and to whom you were born, and the way you were nurtured, and he has the same connection to his heritage.

"Your heritage reaches through your grandfathers to Europe and back through thousands of years and two hundred generations of civilization, societies that learned to hand down their knowledge to the next age by writing it down. His heritage reaches back through his grandfathers to the harsh wilds of North America, where his people stoned, clubbed, and speared the living into the food they ate, where his ancestors had no transportation but their own feet, and where previous lore and history could only be handed down by the spoken word, very often, only to be forgotten. The past barely exists in his mind as some large, vague, 'before.' The past of your world nourishes you with education and wealth, religion, agriculture, technology, and written history.

"You need not forgive his deed, but you can be aware that it occurred as an act not solely of his own initiative.

"I prefer you the way you have always been, a humane being, with a moral view of life, a gift bequeathed to you by your ancestors, a gift which it should be your lot to add to. In the free ways of the wild, there is no such thing as hate or revenge, only the daily following of our own destinies, the same as would a wolf or a buffalo. Do not keep hate or the lust for revenge in your heart. Hate is a false concept, conjured only by the human mind. It has no basis in nature."

The boy realized Oswego was giving wise council. The Tonkawa had an inner calm that he knew he did not have, an objective pattern of thought, a maturity, more suggestive of restraint and common sense than of obstinacy. He tried to be logical and look at the subject dispassionately, but he could not forgive the unforgivable, and as soon as he started reflecting on the tragedy, the visceral urge to strike back gained mastery of his being, leaving him seething with rage, conjuring up in his mind pictures of the deadly blows of retribution that would be his to deliver with his own hands.

"Oswego, I have no confidence in humane feelings, or for that matter, even of God. Explain to me what you mean when you talk of The Great Spirit."

The Indian did not speak for some time. "I doubt that I can translate my own thoughts into your mind," answered Oswego, "because I believe the Great Spirit is only a process existing between nature and your own essence, and thus, is different for all creatures.

"Tell me, when you think of the little creek that runs down to the river just east of the homestead, what is its outstanding feature?"

"I suppose it is the waterfall," Thomas answered.

"Yes, and in dry season there is no waterfall, is there?"

Thomas shook his head, "no."

"You see! The waterfall is not an independent thing; the waterfall is not the water, and it is not the creek bed, it is a new reality that only occurs when the two interact. The same may be said about the shadow of a tree. The shadow is not part of the tree, nor is it part of the sunlight; it is a new thing, a new reality that occurs only when the tree and the sunlight interact.

"Most of nature is similarly the consequence of two or more, or possibly many things interacting or combining to produce new realities. That is true about us as human beings. We are the consequence of numerous things interacting, of blood, bone, hair, skin, sight, voice, and hundreds of other components too numerous to mention. The results of this interaction is our own essence, not only our bodies, but also the magnificent attributes of our minds, self-awareness, heightened memory, and ability to contemplate so that we are creatures who do not just react or follow the dictates of our instincts. The combination of our bodies and our brains and our ability to speak, all functioning together, creates a new reality; a reality greater than the sum of our individual parts, defining our beings and allowing us to operate and function as we do.

"If you and I are complicated, with many components combining to create our being, think how much more complicated and organized is the entire world with all its creatures and all its features in which you and I are only tiny contributing parts.

"I believe this entire world, constructed of millions of parts, is, like us, the result of interactions producing a living thing, although on a plane of reality immeasurably higher than ours, the world itself, having thought, and insight, and self awareness.

"I believe this living awareness emanating from the world is the Great Spirit.

"When you understand this design and feel a kinship to it, even though the feeling may be only an infinitesimal bit of the greater awareness, you feel that you have spoken to, and are a part of, the Great Mystery itself."

Oswego looked deeply into his young ward's eyes. "I will come back to see about you in the spring, Thomas. Your spirit will mend if you let nature heal you. Don't spend all your time thinking, scheming, or remembering the past; feel and enjoy the soft grass beneath your feet, the cool breeze blowing on your face, the warmth of the winter sun upon your back, and look up into the beauty of the blue sky. Allow yourself to be one with nature. You will be able to feel the peace and power of the Great Mystery, and you will learn much of how you became who you are. You still have plenty of time to become a man of great wisdom and friendship." Oswego then got on his horse and slowly rode away.

CHAPTER 9

Thomas was determined not to let the farm deteriorate, working tirelessly on the fields and crops, the fences, the livestock, and the buildings. The work helped him heal. He sought the help of his neighbors, the Beasleys, who were always kind, and forever helpful to him. He loved being invited to eat with them, to be a part of a family, especially, because young Virginia Beasley, who was only a little older than his sister had been, was always particularly interested in making him welcome, and at every opportunity, she manipulated to be near him. Thomas went to his grandparents every winter, and again enrolled in school, but through the months of study he dreamed of the day in May when he would be free to return to the frontier.

Oswego did come back in the spring, and the next and the next. They went on hunts and explored together, and rode up as far north as Fort Concho where he met many of the soldiers, some of whom remembered his father. They did a bit of tracking for the Army, and once patrolled with troops and three other Tonkawa scouts as far north as the Big Spring at the foot of the great escarpment, the most reliable source of water between the Llano Estacado and the Concho Territory. Scouts and a small contingent of troops left on an exploration, riding up the North Fork of the Concho River as long as it was a source of water. After resting the troops and the stock for a day they filled all canteens, watered the horses, and rode north. Two days later, they came upon a small dry arroyo with green plants in the bottom, running east from the base of a nondescript mesa.

Thomas rode down the bottom of the draw on a well-worn trail through a mass of increasingly thickened and tangled growth, and came upon an uncontrolled invasion of plant life surrounding a circular limestone depression, where several huge pieces of the sedentary surface stone had broken off the ledge, and were half submerged in a magnificent pool of fresh, cool, clear water, the "Big Spring," undoubtedly being fed by underground flow from the high plains to the north. The overflow of the pool ran east down the draw for several yards, then disappeared back into the shallow aquifer through several crevices in the floor, emerging again farther down stream, finally becoming the original source of the headwaters of the Colorado River which flowed through Texas all the way to the Gulf of Mexico.

Having scouted and fought in the area several times before, Oswego explained to Thomas that this was the principal watering place on the Comanche Trail after the Indians descended the escarpment of the Llano Estacado riding for Mexico.

At the Big Spring the trail broke into three separate routes, one going southeast into the Concho country, a second, straight south to Castle Gap and the Pecos River, and the final trail veering southwest toward the Willow Springs area, and from there to the Pecos, all three routes eventually arriving in Mexico.

Thomas rode up out of the depression to get a better look at the countryside, thinking to memorize the topography in case he led people here in some future time. He rode out of the draw, and started toward a hill, its base girded by a limestone ledge. To his astonishment, he came face to face with a band of about twenty Indians.

The Comanches sat resting on their horses, wearing little but breach clouts, moccasins and head dresses, the head coverings bedecked in an array of feathers, horns, and streamers, their eyes as black as their long hair, and their bodies and faces daubed with clay and war paint, attesting to their savage intent.

Both parties sat in their saddles staring at one another for almost a minute. Thomas's life-long eagerness to wreak vengeance on the Comanches was suddenly and completely staunched by the peril of his situation. He turned slowly around and started methodically and slowly riding back toward the spring as if nothing were amiss. One of the warriors suddenly gave a war hoop and the whole party came after him like a wolf pack after a fawn. Thomas instantly spurred his horse into a mad dash, and yelled at the top of his lungs, "Comanches!" Oswego, who was already in the saddle, yelled for his Tonkawa brothers to hold them away from the water, then headed toward Thomas in a hard run. The Comanches, realizing that there were enemies at the spring, split their force and circled around both sides to surround the defenders, though one determined brave continued his murderous pursuit of Thomas. The boy heard an arrow hiss right beside his neck, ducked as low as he could over the steed's back to make as small a target as possible, and spurred the horse on. The Comanche was so intent on slaying his victim that he didn't notice the bushes on his right until he looked up and saw the huge Oswego and his horse almost upon him.

The breast of Oswego's mount hit the astonished pursuer directly from the side and sent him and his smaller pony sprawling. Oswego realized that he and Thomas were both cut off from the spring, so he waved for his ward to follow and went straight up the side of the mesa, a place with which he had long been familiar. He came to the outcropping of limestone, which formed a ridge around the base of the rise, then up a defect in the ridge that, first, his horse, and then Thomas's, had to struggle to ascend. They rode into a clump of juniper dismounting with their rifles while the horses were still on the run.

Oswego knew what the Indians would do even before the braves themselves had decided. The pursuing Comanches had to go through the single ridge defect to follow up the side of the hill, necessitating that all the Comanche ponies had to go through the same small opening one at a time, completely losing their speed and maneuverability as they climbed the steep escarpment. Both Oswego and Thomas were sitting in the juniper, both rifles aimed exactly at that spot. "Shoot the horses," said Oswego, "you won't see enough of any Indian to have a target." The pursuers rode into the gap with their bodies draped around the far side of the ponies with nothing visible to the two scouts but a foot. The rifle fire was accurate, however, the missiles going straight into the lower necks of the animals. The first three horses fell and tumbled back down the slope, the other pursuers pulling back to consider another plan.

This was the first time Thomas had experienced the role of prey, with someone intent on killing him, and he didn't like the feeling. He could imagine what it would be like to be a species that lived its entire life being hunted and attacked by some predator.

The Indians gathered in council to plan the route of their next attack, but a bugle sounded from behind the hill as the troops who were following the trail of their scouts, heard the shots, and came riding into view. Seeing the soldiers, the war party broke off their attack, beating a hasty retreat, appearing to head back toward the plains, though Oswego said this was only a ruse.

On the way home from Fort Concho, with much time spent idly in the saddle, Thomas turned to his friend and said, "Oswego, I have always wanted to ask you about the tracks at our house the day that my mother and Trudy were killed. Explain to me what you think the tracks meant."

Oswego knew that Thomas had long wanted to talk about the episode, but until now it had been too painful for him to confront. "I believe Trudy's tracks coming from the house to your mother means she was in the house when your Maria was surprised and caught outside, and that she ran out to defend her mother, to confront, and, even though a child, to attack the Indians, with what weapon, I have no idea. She must have inflicted some kind of injury or insult, however, because the brave who killed her was obviously enraged, wounding her in several places. Ordinarily the Comanches would have taken such a child captive, so I believe she must have been somewhat successful in her attack."

CHAPTER 10

When the two returned to the Texas frontier, Thomas accompanied Oswego to his home in the Tonkawa village rather than proceeding to school in San Antonio, the boy hoping to become adept in his understanding of the wilds and Indian fighting. Although most of the Tonkawa were residing in the vicinity of Fort Griffin, where they had been moved to a reservation by the Texans and then the U.S. government, Oswego's clan, a band of mavericks, ranged farther south in Central Texas near the settlement of Waco on the Brazos. Thomas remained with the Tonkawas about six months before returning to his own home. In the village he was highly regarded because everyone knew he was the son of the legendary Amos Sutton, who as a lone Ranger had rescued Oswego from a band of Comanches. Thomas was able to hone his frontier skills while living and interacting with the young Indians of the tribe. For the first time the boy began to recognize the bonds that civilization had placed upon his life, and, conversely, the exalting feeling of freedom accrued from living in the wild – these feelings, of course, enhanced by the exuberance of his youth.

Oswego justified his domination of Thomas's time, even supplanting his formal schooling, in order to prepare him for the war clash that he recognized was yet to come, and in which he felt sure Thomas craved to be a participant.

The village youth tracked one another and learned to move without leaving an obvious trail. They learned how to stalk, and to walk and crawl with almost no sound, how to remain concealed, how to shift their own weight silently, and to be aware of the wind which they knew carried both scent and sound. It became second nature to always know in which direction the air was moving, almost as instinctive as knowing to open one's eye lids in order to see.

They were warned not to assume that, even though they could not hear themselves, other things could not hear them.

"One is never protected by his own curtain of silence because the hearing of others can be superior to yours. Besides, the animals or the enemy may detect you by using other senses, for this superiority will reside in most animals and in some special humans."

Most of all, they became as one with their bows and arrows. These weapons were even by their side at night and were taken along on any venture, whether great or small. Oswego's skilled cousin made the bow and many arrows for Thomas; the bow stronger, and the arrows truer, than those of most of the other boys.

The young men learned to mimic all of the bird and animal calls of the region. Oswego's foster brother taught them to make reed whistles which, by changing the reed tones, they were able to emulate the sound of an injured rabbit, the bleat of a lost fawn, the shrill call of the Red Tailed Hawk, or the less sibilant cry of the eagle. With this call they could lure predators within range of their bows, or even draw in a doe as she hunted for her fawn. The boys were never without their call. Oswego was particularly proud of the hawk cry that Thomas performed. "The chirp of small birds and the coo of the doves is most often incidental," said the Indian, "but the cry of the hawk always has a purpose." The boys ran and hunted and wrestled, testing their skill and strength against one another in the manner that only adolescents can do. Oswego knew this activity was good for Thomas and tried to help him understand the Tonkawa ways and the Tonkawa language as best he could.

In preparation for the dire circumstance of possibly being pursued on the trail, the boys were taught how to make booby traps and snares. They were made by bending green elastic limbs which were held in place with twine, easily triggered to release with major force by stepping on or pushing against some minor obstacle in the trail. Finally the teenagers were instructed on how to come onto a vista, where one could see across great distance, and discern from the topography of what they viewed, how to ride across it with the least likelihood of being seen by strangers or enemies.

Although Thomas did not recognize it at the time, many of the skills being taught, besides those of the hunt and escape, were the ominous skills of war.

The Indian boys began to range over more and more territory, going north up the Brazos River, staying the night, then making their way back on a hunting spree along the river banks. Thomas and Two Bears, his closest friend, decided to go it alone and try their luck in making a raft to float the twelve miles home. It was early spring and the soft and washed green covering of the trees harbored a wealth of new life and excitement. "Let's take only our bows, arrows, knives and fire tools," said Two Bears, "that way we can be free and swift as nature made us."

"We must take an axe, to help with the raft, said Thomas, "and also hooks, to fish on our trip back down the river."

The trek up river was the happiest occasion of Thomas's young life. "I feel like this is the first time I have really found where I belong," he said. They probed the dense growth along the river bank, tramped through the long pecan bottoms, and used their bows to acquire food, procuring squirrels, rabbits, and armadillos abounding in this habitat. The two boys sat by their campfire late into the night discussing what they would do when they became grown men, their planned exploits, epic and heroic, as is the way the mind fantasizes in the younger years.

Next morning they diligently went to work, finding a slope to the river bank where they could push a raft into the water, then gathering and chopping old dried timber, binding it together with grape and briar vines. The work went slower than they expected so they decided to spend another night in camp. Firewood had been gathered and placed between stones when Thomas heard the simulated mating call of a rooster cardinal, (Cheep – chir, chir, chir – wurp, wurp, wurp, wurp). He touched Two Bears' arm, frowned and shook his head. It was nearing dusk, and mating calls of the red bird most often permeate the morning hours. A similar call came from below camp, but Two Bears whispered it was not distinct like a Cardinal. As both boys reached for their bows six riders came charging out of the brush, firing rifles as they came.

"Into the river!" yelled Two Bears, and both boys sprinted toward the bank. One of the shots found its mark and Thomas saw blood and flesh explode out of the front of his friend's chest. As the young Tonkawa fell to the ground he cried out a muffled and gurgling, "run Thomas run!" Thomas streaked to river's edge, diving into the muddy water, and stayed for a long time beneath the surface though quickly reversing the direction of his plunge and turning back toward the bank, coming up in the midst of a large tree, which had tumbled into the stream, the dirt having eroded from its roots until it was claimed by the flowing water. The tree and much debris were caught in the shallows and partially clogged the flow through two adjacent sand bars. As Thomas's head emerged from the water and he gasped for air, he heard a rustle to his side as three disturbed water moccasins plopped from their resting spots on the limbs, into the muddy river and swam away. Thomas breathed as slowly and quietly as he could, and did not move a muscle.

"I believe I hit the red bastard, he's probably drowning, but let's take a good look." "The other uns still tryin' to breathe," came a twangy voice. "Scalp the damned heathen," added another. Thomas heard the scream of his friend, then the tramping of the men as they searched the bank looking for him.

Thomas was seized with a fear he had never known could exist. He lay quivering in the water and fought to keep from crying out. After the sounds on the bank dissipated, and no other human activity was heard for a full hour, Thomas swam down under the tree and back to the river bank. He reached for a low limb and pulled his way to shore, crawled back to the path of their flight and found the spot where Two Bears had fallen. The site was redolent with the smell of blood but no body remained.

Thomas ran the twelve miles through the dark to the Tonkawa camp, and lay gasping for air as he related the tale to the men of the village. They quickly mounted their horses, and Thomas, aching with exhaustion, led them back to the scene.

Early morning sunlight penetrated the forest and it was easy for the Tonkawas to find the site. They could see the blood-stained trail where the body was dragged to the river's edge and apparently tossed in. Oswego quickly found the trail of departure, and a war party was immediately on their path, tracking the group fifteen miles up river to the landing of a ferry. No one was there on the west side, but a corral was filled with hard ridden horses. The ferry route ended across the river onto a path that led to a small Anglo settlement.

The warriors cut the ferry ropes that spanned the river, then killed the entire horse herd and rode away. Thomas was aware that he was now riding with Indians against his kindred, Indians who many white settlers considered the enemy rather than the allies they had always been. He could not, however, mentally ally himself with the rogue band of killers, be they white folks or not, and he rationalized that he was choosing the side of justice. As soon as they got back to the Tonkawa village, everything was quickly gathered and packed and the villagers fled north. Thomas slept on the back of his horse, staying with the Tonkawas as they moved out of the shadow of retaliatory danger.

Grief and guilt overwhelmed young Sutton, almost overshadowing his experience after the death of his mother and sister. The guilt factor arose from his thought that he had failed his friend, leaving him alone to die while he himself cowered in fear. Oswego recognized what was troubling the boy, and told him he was having feelings that anyone would have, but that he must keep to his quest because his friend knew he was mortally wounded, was dying, and could not be helped, thus bidding Thomas to run. "There are times when one must choose the expedient, when the selfless sacrifice of oneself serves no purpose."

Thomas had trouble accepting the fact that his own race would perpetrate acts as violent and despicable as were those of the Comanches, but indeed he had to recognize that the Whites who murdered Two Bears had much of these same such qualities themselves.

"Cruelty and depravity are not traits that abide only among a few tribes," said Oswego. "They lie hidden in the heart of all men, all clans, all nations, and it is left to the people to either suppress them or extol them." Thomas decided that among the members of the tribe into which he was born, the morals they claimed to support, were no morals at all, only conventions, rules that kept them from trampling on one another during their own interactions. He clung to the hope that the killing of Two Bears by the white men was an aberration, and not a rule.

Thomas was endowed with great natural ability and physical dexterity, but more importantly he incessantly labored at learning, becoming extremely adept with Indian methods of tracking and stalking and with the use of the bow and arrow. He loved sitting around the campfire with the other boys, sharing the camaraderie that was afforded them by being raised together in the wild. He loved to watch the images shown in the distance by the flicker of the firelight, attempting to recognize their origin, even with such a momentary illumination cast from the ever-changing, dancing, flames.

Once again he practiced the most basic hunting and defensive skill of all – the throw of the rock. Day after day, the boys of the village would have long throwing contests.

Thomas realized that his emerging understanding and oneness with his surroundings gave him a new power, not over other people or other things, but over himself. He felt as though he had broken through a barrier, and was, thus, freed from the constraints of the domestic and ordered life, affording him entrance into the wild, now understanding nature in a way he had never before recognized, and with which he was, now, himself a part.

"I don't understand what it is about living in the wilderness that so separates it from the domestic life I have always lived", Thomas said to Oswego. His mentor thought for some minutes and then answered. "It is a matter of fetters. Wild things and free men are restricted only by the natural habitat in which they live, and by their own inborn ability and instincts, so that they are only very minimally inhibited. Domesticated things have to live under unnatural laws." "Animals don't have laws," replied Thomas. "A fence is a law, the same as is a cage; it tells you where you can and cannot go. A bridle or a collar, or even a house is a law."

"I wonder why men would ever forfeit their freedom to give allegiance to laws?" questioned Thomas. "Food," said Oswego, "the quest for food is the most driving force that animals experience, aside from breathing itself. If I control the food, I can tame anything on this earth. I remember one time when I came upon a water snake in a shallow stream that had a live fish in its mouth which it was trying to swallow. It was repulsive to me to see the snake swallowing a living creature so I impaled the snake with a sharp stick, and it started writhing, trying to escape my spear, and in doing so, slung the fish out of its mouth. The fish started flopping in the shallow water in an effort to get away, and the snake, even though still impaled with a life ending injury, desperately tried to reach and regrasp the fish. It is the law of the forest; 'first you eat, and anything else you do comes after.' Men who have become domestic, or as they prefer to say, civilized, did it to better insure a stable supply of food."

Oswego gathered all of the boys of the village, and spent much time in instructing them in the techniques of fighting at close quarters, of clubbing with the butt of a rifle, and parrying with a spear or bayonet, or even with the barrel of a gun – all of these methods made available from the training received by the veterans who were now returning from the civil war, which Oswego had eagerly learned in order to pass them on to the young Tonkawas.

CHAPTER 11

When he returned home, in addition to tending to the farm, Thomas continued to practice his hunting skills. He used his bow and arrows as much as his rifle, steadily improving his ability with both, shooting an arrow at least a hundred times a day. He threw a rock a hundred times a day as well.

He tracked his own horses, learning the difference between the tracks of a walk, with its repetitive symmetry, a trot with its choppy scuff of the ground, and the lope with its longer stride, its double print of the forefeet and the deeper imprint of the hooves of the driving hind legs. He learned to pick out the distinct tracks made by a single animal from those of another, and to recognize hoof tracks made in the night by the depressions the animals had stepped into, and the rocks hit because of their poorly lighted marches. He tracked deer, even bear, trying diligently to keep most of his tracking abilities intact.

He rode daily and practiced the horsemanship he had learned from the Indians, even shooting arrows from beneath the neck of a running horse while clinging to its side, like the wild natives he had seen, always rehearsing for the battle he was yet to fight. He rode bareback for hours, perched only on the skin-covered raw spine of the horse. The many tasks of his expended efforts allowed him to live in two worlds, part bending more to the civilized, part counter-pointing toward the wild.

When Thomas returned to his mother's parents, they were always delighted to see him, begging him to remain with them, instead of going back to the frontier, but Thomas was intent on honoring his oath – to wreak his justice upon the Comanches. He stayed with his grandparents on his weekend leaves from school, and the holidays that occurred during the school year. While there, the family spoke totally in Spanish. He certainly noticed and appreciated the comforts of such a home, and was deeply pleased and grateful for the love of his grandparents.

"Thomas," said his grandmother one evening, "you must realize even as a young man, that there is a family history of which you are a part, but which you have never been close enough to totally understand and enjoy, nonetheless, a past which has endowed you with much of your being, and the continuation of which it will be your responsibility to pass on to the next generation."

"I accept that duty, *Abuela*," he said, though he didn't exactly know what he was accepting.

Back in San Antonio he sought out and became acquainted with some of his father's old ranger friends, being taken along on some of their lesser missions. They flattered him, calling him an honorary Ranger. He once asked them to help him get a job, so he could ride with a trading caravan into Mexico, and found a short one that took him to Laredo and on down to Monterrey south of the border. This country he was vicariously familiar with because of family stories, but, now, found much more exciting to experience in person.

Post Civil War San Antonio was becoming a boom town, serving as the gateway to the Southwest. It had, at last, become safe from Indian raids or Mexican forays but was replete with every sort of drifter, confidence man, escapee from a criminal past, failure, misfit, incompetent, and gangster – a veritable stew of the undesirable. They circulated mainly among themselves, hoping to chance upon some unwary rube or innocent citizen with some token of value upon his person. Thomas wandered through this den as an observer, eyeing the displaced rabble, but he stood clear of any close encounter. He knew well enough that any business he could ever have with this crowd would be only as a victim.

When Oswego returned the fourth spring, he told Thomas that he, and several of the Tonkawas, had enlisted to scout for Colonel Ranald S. Mackenzie and the U.S. Army on an expedition into Indian Territory against the Comanche and Kiowa tribes who had refused to settle on the reservation, and were continuing to plunder the Texas frontier. He had asked for, and obtained, permission to include Thomas as one of the scouts. Thomas would also be assigned to serve as an interpreter and liaison between the officers and the twenty-five Tonkawas attached to the Fourth Cavalry. The old feeling of retribution came back to Thomas, and he decided this was his one good chance, an opportunity to satisfy the deep need in his heart to seek atonement for the massacre of his mother and sister. He rode over to talk to his neighbors to see if they would tend to the farm in exchange for the crops that it would produce. They readily agreed, but they all considered the venture rash and foolish for a lad of his age, and tried to talk him out of going, especially Virginia.

As he turned away from the Beasley house, Virginia walked with him. "Thomas," she said, "you have good prospects for a wonderful life here, and you have your grandparents in San Antonio for support. You will be throwing away your years as a normal young man, for a life of danger, crude surroundings, and uncertainty, perhaps for the rest of your days. I want you here, so I can see you, while we grow up together."

Thomas was jolted by what she said, having never considered someone caring for him in that manner, suddenly feeling an obligation in response to what she thought, admitting to himself, he did care how she felt.

"Virginia, I have to go. If I don't, I will always be haunted by the image of my mother and Trudy, lying on the ground amidst their own blood, and me not caring enough about their memory to make the sacrifice to do something about it. I have an unusual ability as a scout, that only a very few people are able to acquire. I've worked four years to become skilled enough to be a part of this campaign, and I owe it to the settlers of the frontier, and to the memory of my family to help put the scourge of the Comanches behind us, once and for all. I would never want to raise a family of my own which would be in danger of the same thing that happened to my people. Please try to understand the way I feel." He knew this was an intimate experience for both of them and he didn't know how to proceed, how to share his own feelings with hers, and his face blushed red, but he drew her to him and kissed her on the lips and she responded in an embrace that both would remember forever.

Virginia lowered her eyes because she knew she would cry if she looked directly at him. "I will be here waiting for you to return, Thomas; I will miss you so, and every night that I live I will pray for God to watch over you."

CHAPTER 12

The unlikely pair of scouts saddled their ponies, packed minimal gear and headed north, both men with a feeling of exhilaration as they rode forward across open country, first to the South Llano and through its valley, on across the river's main branch and then north across the San Saba.

It seemed to Thomas that an uneasy feeling still lurked in the mind of Oswego as he approached the location of his previous Comanche ordeal. They continued north out of the river valley until they climbed up to a high ridge where Oswego stepped off his horse and looked through the oaks, persimmons, and juniper bushes far down to a winding canyon below. "There is a spring up that canyon and a good place to spend the night," said Oswego. He stood there gazing for some minutes before both travelers led the horses over the top and into the trees, slowly picking their way to the canyon floor. Thomas could tell that there was a preoccupation to Oswego's actions, but he said nothing.

The two scouts crossed an old trail, leading toward the spring. "This is the place where your father came to take me back from my captors," said the Tonkawa. He got off his horse and stood gazing at the ant bed which was still alive with the scurrying insects. "Would you like to build a fire over the bed?" Thomas queried. Oswego slowly shook his head. "The ants only followed their natural instincts, just as the Comanches probably did. I try not to make this a personal enmity between any specific thing, or anyone, and me, though in the heat of conflict I forget my musings and become wolf-like as do most warriors." A small horned toad scurried in front of his foot and Oswego reached down and picked it up. He laughed, and said, "Horned toads will be nature's way of dispensing retribution on the ants. These little lizards make a diet of them."

"You don't seem to have a lasting enmity toward those people, who so abused you. You have forgiven. I never could."

"May be that will come later for you, Thomas. Perhaps you will come to believe that this war is motivated by things much larger than our own individual grievances. We like to say that our purpose is to wreak vengeance for some ill deed perpetrated against us personally, or our loved ones, or our property, but these raids, which are inflicted on both sides, and often with unspeakable horrors, are only the tools of war. This war, like most wars, probably is only a struggle to see who will dominate and thus control the land which both the Texans and the Comanches think should rightly belong to them.

"You and I are joining the side of the Whites in an effort to rid the plains, and thus, the frontier, of the Comanches so that the Texans can take over their land. I believe this may not be a just thing to do, and that perhaps I am not taking the right side of the conflict even though my people have been bitter enemies of the Comanches from as far back as my forefathers can remember. I often worry that the white man's avarice may be much more dangerous to my tribe than is that of the Comanches."

"They don't deserve consideration," said Thomas. "Everything about the Comanche race is an affront to the world, everything they do, a clash against decency."

"In your eyes, yes," returned Oswego, "but in their eyes everything about the Texans is an affront to nature and to the ways of Great Mystery. I think that each of our worlds is only a tiny sample of all that exists. The Great Spirit has room for many worlds. We are not able to see into the world of our foes, nor they, into ours, so since there is no understanding among us we both choose to fight."

Oswego stepped off his horse, and walked up to the huge hollow oak tree. He took a stick and probed upward, then reached in with his hand and pulled down a shotgun. There were spider webs at the end of the barrels and some rust around barrels and hammers, but the weapon was in surprisingly good condition. "How did you know that was there?" said Thomas. "I dimly recollect your father putting it there, because he could not carry me and all the weapons at once." Oswego opened the breach and pulled out the two shells and examined them. They too, were in good condition. He returned to the tree and wedged the gun back up into the hollow, then walked over to a long-downed log, and began probing with his knife into the partially rotten wood. He pried out a rifle slug and walked over to Thomas, handing it to him.

"This bullet was aimed at your father," he said. "Keep it always; it will remind you of the price your father was willing to pay for his loyalty to a friend." He pulled his flint knife from the scabbard on his belt. "This knife, your father asked me to wear, for it was directed at me in a like manner as this rifle slug was meant for your father."

The two travelers took water from the spring, but rode far away to make camp. They found no hint of danger, no hint of other people, but caution was never far from their minds. Thomas could hear Oswego turning and tossing far into the night. Before dawn they were again in the saddle and heading north. Three days later they rode into Fort Concho.

The fort was one of several such bastions strung across the Texas frontier, extending all the way from the Cross Timbers area to the Mexican border. Forts Concho, Griffin and Richardson were relatively new, built in an effort in which the army was trying to shore up the frontier defense. All the posts were undermanned, however, and though the menacing nomads were no longer swarming into the settlements, they still raided with impunity, in spite of the tokens of federal troops spread across the border area.

Things were busy when they arrived at Fort Concho, troops training, stores accumulating, and supply wagons being packed. Most of the Tonkawa scouts were already there and were at work for the army, making short probing forays into the countryside, hunting for trails, watering holes, and Indian signs. As the scouts returned to the vicinity of the fort that night, Oswego and Thomas went out to meet them. Oswego knew all of them and Thomas actually knew several from the short time he had lived among the Tonkawa.

Thomas treated all of the scouts with the utmost respect, praising both their tribe and their many abilities. For their part, the Tonkawas were very receptive to Thomas, many having known his father, all very familiar with the details of the rescue from the Comanches that Amos Sutton had carried out for Oswego. The scouts readily taught the son anything they knew about the Comanches, especially Comanche tactics in war and raids, or about tracking, or the natural habitat in which they worked. Thomas listened and watched attentively as though he had a deep thirst to learn it all. He began to be comfortable in speaking the Tonkawa language and actually, became rather adept in using the Indian sign language commonly employed among the tribesmen who lived or traveled across the plains. He also began to accumulate many Comanche phrases and words which were known by the Tonkawas.

CHAPTER 13

Colonel Mackenzie decided to send a group of his own emissaries on a trip to the Indian Reservation at Fort Sill, to determine in detail which of the Comanche and Kiowa groups were still on the reservation, and which might now be out on the Plains, and to learn the relative strength of the warrior groups from each tribe. Thomas heard about the trip and immediately applied to be one of those on the mission. Oswego thought it would be good training for the young scout, and, since he personally knew the Colonel, he asked that Thomas be allowed to accompany the party without Oswego, himself, being present. As a special favor to Oswego, and since the trip was not thought to be a dangerous one, Colonel Mackenzie granted the request.

Two days later the detail, consisting of one officer, a Lt. Deighton, four troopers, one experienced sergeant, and Thomas left for Fort Sill, taking the road first to Fort Richardson, and then northward to the headquarters of the Indian reservation located beside the Oklahoma fort. The trail was well-worn and the group traveled in a relaxed manner, though all of the men were acquainted with frontier life, and, for the most part, prudently exercised caution.

Toward the end of the third day on the trail, Thomas heard a strange sound off to the north which he couldn't categorize. "What is that?" he asked the lieutenant. The officer shook his head, aware of nothing. To Thomas it sounded somewhat like an interrupted bray of a mule, a noise which abruptly stopped, and then was heard no more. He looked at the other members of his party, but no one else showed any sign of concern, nor was there any indication that they had heard anything unusual. Nonetheless, what he had heard made Thomas look more to the left of the trail as they traveled on. He noticed that his horse often looked in the same direction and once gave a faint nicker as his head was turned toward the north. As dusk approached, a small flock of birds arose in a flush from a far distant tree. It was a time they would usually be settling in to roost for the night. This time, Thomas told his compatriots that he thought someone might be following them. They all laughed, and assured him that every young soldier felt the same way when they first began to ride out on a mission bordering on Indian Territory.

"A man always hears what he fears. In this country we call it phantom warnings," the old sergeant explained.

The soldiers bivouacked and staked out their horses to graze in a small *sendero* very close to their camp. Just beyond the edge of the savannah there was a small spring where they were able to obtain water for themselves, and to replenish their stock. Thomas walked around the small open area, finding unshod horse tracks, though they were a few days old. He was hesitant to mention the tracks for fear they would call it another phantom alarm, but certainly, other riders had been there before. A guard was posted and the remaining travelers wrapped themselves in their blankets to rest for the night. When Thomas's turn for guard duty came around, he took some extra time to look over the adjacent scenery. He knew they were surrounded by a belt of rather thick cedar interlaced with post oak enclosing a small, open sward of grass where the animals were grazing. There was only one narrow, treeless passage into the savannah to the east and, also, only one to the west. Thomas double-staked the horses and then walked over to the narrow inlets and stretched lariat ropes, just higher than a horse's back, across from side to side. Finally, he climbed up a large tree, taking his two weapons, and sat with his back to the campers.

A full, yellow, moon arose over the tree tops, illuminating the grass and trees, the savannah glowing blond with a ghostly hue. At the line of timber, the taller canopy blocked most of the moonlight from the cedars below. They stood close together, druid-like, shrouding the ground in darkness where the tree line abutted the edge of the pasture.

In rapid succession, the croaking of the frogs down by the spring was stilled, and there were two plops into the water that sounded to Thomas as though they might be bull frogs, jumping back into the pond for safety. Once again, everything became quiet. Thomas's senses were acutely on edge. He could smell the leaves, the freshly cropped grass and the horses, but there was another faint suggestion, a different odor, one that he had experienced before. He struggled to remember the context of the smell. Slowly it came to him, a smell reminiscent of the day his mother and sister died. It was an odor which made the hair on the back of his neck tingle, giving him gooseflesh. Thomas strained to hear more, but there was only silence.

In unison, all of the grazing horses raised their heads, turning their necks toward the far side of the opening. Thomas still could hear no different noise. His senses and the emotion of the moment combined to create a stirring in the mind, a mental reality, telling him an enemy was there, even before he could formulate thoughts to confirm it. His eyes followed the direction of the stares of the animals, and slowly a shadowy figure emerged from the tree line and crawled for the nearest staked horse. The figure rose slightly and began to gently stroke the horse on his neck. He stopped stroking and bent down, and Thomas recognized the glint of the metal knife blade in the moon light as the intruder reached to cut the leather hobble from around the horse's front legs.

First, Thomas reached for his rifle, but a gunshot would undoubtedly startle, or, perhaps, even stampede the horses, so Thomas folded his left hand around his bow and clinched it tightly. He brought his arrow into place, and leaned forward, his heart accelerating its rhythmic beat, a faint nausea in the pit of his stomach. He pulled back the bowstring and let the missile fly. The twang of the bowstring sounded, followed by a startled cry from the intruder.

Suddenly, all was chaos, as a howling troop of mounted Comanches took the sound to be their signal, and came dashing out of the nearby east woods, heading for the narrow inlet into the savannah. The roused army troops, struggling to their feet and running to defend the horses fired a few wild rifle shots into the dark as they came, but the Comanches got there first. The initial four hard-riding Indians were abruptly jerked from their saddles by the lariat stretched in the shadow which they hit at full speed. A concert of guttural cries rang out, the intruders hitting the ground in complete disarray. Three of them arose and started running back to the east, from whence they had come.

After the first four riders had fallen from their mounts, the braves of the war party realized they had been caught in a trap and whirled their horses in the opposite direction. Their companions behind them were still coming into the gap at full speed and a mass of human and horse flesh collided in the shadows as a chorus of terror issued from the throats of both horses and men. Soldiers had reached the clearing and were randomly shooting toward the movement. The Comanches speedily gathered up all those who could still move, then dashed for open country.

Because of the double staking, only one of the troopers' horses had broken loose during the melee. There were two new Indian ponies now mixed with the army ones, and all were quickly secured. Two Comanche braves lay on the ground. The one shot with the arrow was dead, the arrow having gone through his chest and probably his heart. The only one still breathing was one who had hit the rope. He had a broken neck and could not move. He was quickly dispatched by the sergeant, who, in a grisly fashion, scalped them both.

"You are very much like your father," the veteran sergeant said to Thomas. "Where did a kid like you acquire battle skills?"

"It was much more luck than skill. What little I know I learned from Oswego and the Tonkawas," replied Thomas.

Lt. Deighton called Thomas to one side. "I was very foolish this night," he said. "This raid could well have been a catastrophe. I will never be trivial with a warning again, even from a new recruit." He asked Thomas to tell him how he knew to prepare the trap with the lariat ropes.

Thomas related to him the hearing of what he thought was the broken-off bray of a mule, which he thought probably had been squelched by the Indians right after the animal opened its mouth, then of the flushing of the flight of birds, and of his horse continually looking to the North. "I was pretty sure someone was out there, possibly Indians, and was afraid they would be after the horses, so when it became my time to guard, I tried to get ready. I thought Indians had probably been here before and knew of the inlet and exit from the savanna because of the hoof prints of the unshod horses. If they knew the savanna, they would probably try to stampede our herd by dashing through this area after one or two infiltrators had cut some of them loose. The inlet area was shaded by the tall trees, making it impossible to see the stretched rope."

Although Thomas's feeling was not that of smugness, nonetheless, he felt quite satisfied with himself, attaining, he thought, a higher status among the other men. At least, they would look at him as an equal and no longer as a mascot.

He was not sure what he thought of having killed a human being. He had tried to rationalize that these raiders should not be regarded as humans, especially since he could personally attest to how brutal they could be, killing with relish, wantonly and sadistically dispatching their victims. He wished he could have no more compunction about killing them than he would a rattlesnake, but when Thomas remembered the appearance of the very young Indian, lying mute and still, with a Tonkawa arrow through his chest, he kept having a gnawing feeling that all was not right with the world, and began to take less and less satisfaction in what he had accomplished.

The remainder of the trip into Fort Richardson was uneventful. A very sleepy Thomas had to fight to keep from dozing off in the saddle. The garrison and officers at the fort were surprised that there had been an attack so close to their facility but were very lavish in their praise of the party for fighting them off. The official report turned in by Lt. Deighton commended Thomas for bravery and extreme ability under attack, but said nothing about the laxity on the part of the rest of the company.

For two days the group stayed in Fort Richardson. It was a splendid place to camp. The troopers' barracks and several of the smaller buildings were made of picket poles arranged in an upright position, the gaps filled with mud. The hospital, guard house, and armory were made of more substantial stone, and the officer's quarters were a mixture of stone and sawed wood. All of the habitats except the guard house and armory had at least some glass windows, all of which had been transported over wagon road from Galveston. The buildings were symmetrically arranged around a broad parade ground, and the back of the fort abutted a small creek with constant water.

Thomas walked over to the guard house and asked the sentry if he could talk to some of the prisoners. Four tiny rock cells held three men each, and the facility was full, the cells fetid and dark, the facility and its population vividly displaying the harsh discipline of the army. "What are you in for?" Thomas asked the men from one cell. The charges were drunkenness, dereliction of duty, and attempted desertion.

"Why would you want to desert?" he asked.

"This is the most Godforsaken hole on earth," was the answer. "It's drill, drill, drill, and then what you get for relief is clean the stables, go on kitchen duty, or sweep the barracks. This place would bore a toad frog out of his water hole."

"Don't you fight Indians?" he asked.

"There ain't no Indians, just reports of raids, and stories of how bad it used to be in the old days."

"Oh, there are Indians, all right, you've just been in the wrong place," Thomas rejoined.

After the twenty-four hour rest, the party moved out on the route to the north. Four days later, they rode up to headquarters of Fort Sill.

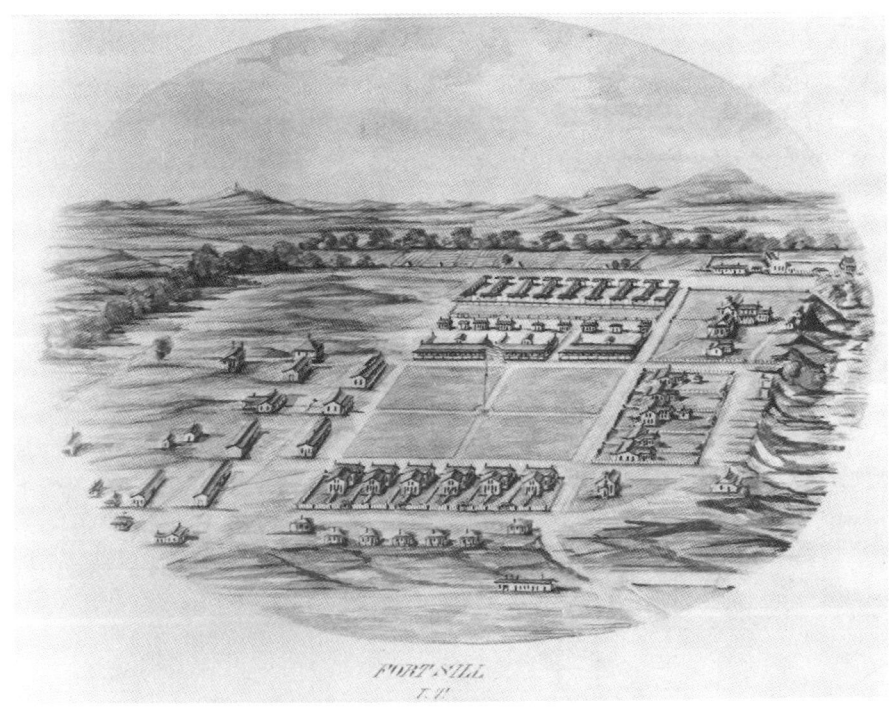

Early Map of Fort Sill

CHAPTER 14

At first, the young scout was quartered with the enlisted men but after the story of their Indian clash on the trail became known, Thomas, who was hired by, but not an official part of the army, so not an enlisted man, was brought into the company of the officers. The Fort commander, Colonel B. H. Grierson, had known of Thomas's father. Both Lt. Deighton and Thomas discussed Colonel Mackenzie's request with the Fort Sill staff, but only heard from the army personnel the numerous stories of conflict between the Indian Service and the army, the soldiers claiming the army was totally hamstrung to inactivity by the federal policies of the Indian Service, policies which army personnel considered absolutely insane.

In effect, the army knew very little about the actual make up and whereabouts of the Comanche tribes that were supposed to be on the reservation, because they were forbidden by the Indian Service to go out into that area.

In view of the utter failure of the previous reservation system, the desperate politicians in Washington had loosed the Quakers on the tribes, and now the religious brothers were the agents in charge of the system at the reservation beside Fort Sill. It was the Quaker theory that the wild Indians could be brought into compliance with the desires of the government, and persuaded to desist from their ways of war and violence, by simply treating them with kindness, respect, and Christian love. On the reservation, the Quaker and Comanche systems, common only in their demonstration of complete chaos, mixed like oil and water. The Comanches readily gave their amity in exchange for the annuities furnished by the United States, but giving life style compliance to the wishes of the government was quite another matter. They acknowledged no borders for themselves but claimed to be lords of the entire plains of the Southwest, maintaining that any other people that traveled across or lived within the area they considered Comancheria were either there by invitation or were trespassing. Many government agents (not Quakers) in turn exploited the Indians by stealing their supplies, and the Indians exploited the reservation system by using it as a safe haven for launching their raids into Texas and Mexico, returning to the reservation only when hotly pursued, or in the hard winter months.

Some of the Quaker brethren were assigned to travel over the reservation, trying to become friendly with the tribes, and to assure the natives of the government's good intentions. Though the agents seemed not to realize it, their only protection was the desire of the tribes to obtain more goods. These riders were all in the field at the time, so there were none available at the agency for Mackenzie's envoys to consult. Colonel Grierson thought they would be uncooperative even if they were available.

Discussions with the officers during the long evenings and nights were informative in other ways. For the first time, Thomas began to grasp the overall organization and assignment from a perspective much larger than just that of Texas. General Phil Sheridan was overall director of their region of Fort Sill and the Texas frontier, which constituted only a part of his entire command. His office was Commander of the Military Division of the Missouri, consisting of more than a million square miles of frontier country, ninety-nine separate Indian Tribes, and an estimated 192,000 Indians.

At that time, the entire U.S. Army consisted of just over twenty-five thousand officers and men, of which only ten regiments of approximately five hundred soldiers each were available to Sheridan for controlling the frontier. The mission of the army was generally referred to as "Settlement of the Indian Question," which in the mind of most of the military, and certainly the settlers, meant extermination of the natives.

Colonel Grierson introduced Thomas and Lt. Deighton to the official interpreter of the fort – a colorful, well known, and able Horace P. Jones. Jones had been raised and schooled in Missouri, moved west at an early age, and had been adopted by a Comanche tribe. He lived with them for several years, and was completely adept with the Comanche tongue and with the sign language which was so well understood by all the tribes of the plains region. He was one of only a very few Whites that the Indians trusted, for he had been meticulously honest in every dealing he ever had with them.

For the first time, Thomas began to hear stories about admirable attributes of the Comanche people, also hearing, again, about the unspeakable abuse heaped upon them by the incessant encroachment of the Whites, on what Comanches considered their territory. "Territory is a very important concept to these people even though they do not discretely define its borders," said Jones. To them, all of the Comancheria is their home; it has been their domain for almost two hundred years, and anyone coming onto it, without an invitation, is committing an act of war. The Indians defend their land in the only way they know how, violently." The complete ineptness and the lack of reliability of the United States governmental policy and that of the Indian Service somewhat embittered Jones, and certainly embittered the Indians. These programs were also discussed in detail with Thomas.

Jones took him to see the Quaker Indian agent, Lawrie Tatum, who, with his Quaker brethren, was the advocate of the policy of persuading the Indians to be docile by treating them with kindness and respect. Though Thomas had heard of Quakers before, he absolutely could not comprehend their pious outlook on life, to which he was now introduced by Mr. Tatum. The young scout was repulsed by the attitude of the Quakers toward their "Comanche brothers," though he was careful to keep his opinion to himself.

The Quakers had established a school for the children of the reservation, in the hope of preparing them for their future life to be patterned after the ways of the whites, using Mr. Tatum as one of the instructors. Although some of the reservation children, such as the Caddos, enrolled, the effort was wasted on the Kiowa and Comanche tribes which steadfastly refused to let their children attend.

Mr. Tatum invited Jones and Thomas into his office one day to witness the possible return of a male captive known to be living in one of the villages. The Indians were nearly always reluctant to give up captives, and many times the captives themselves had integrated into the native culture and did not want to leave. Agent Tatum had considerable coercive power over the tribes, because, as the agent in charge, he had the power to withhold their allotments. It was the policy of the U. S. government to seek the return of any captives, so when the agent would get word of such a person, living among the natives, he would persistently insist on seeing the person and usually he could compel the tribes to bring them in. Terms of this meeting were prearranged to the effect that the captive could decide for himself whether or not he wanted to return to his original home, or go back to the wilds and continue living with the Comanches. In the past, decisions had been made each way, with a surprising number of children relishing the Indian lifestyle and opting to continue their role as a Comanche, though most who had lived with the natives for only a short time longed for the chance to return to their own people.

The young captive brought into the agency was a Mexican boy, nearing fourteen years of age, elaborately bedecked in the finest Comanche regalia, with a feather headdress, bracelets and fringed buckskin. He was surrounded by a group of fifteen young Comanche warriors. Jones whispered to Thomas, "The braves were sent along to intimidate and scare the boy into choosing to return with the tribe." At first, while surrounded by all the natives, the lad said he preferred living among the Indians, but the patient Mr. Tatum told the group through his translator that he had to hear these words from the boy in a room apart from the Comanches, so he beckoned the boy to follow him through the adjoining door and into the kitchen. A Mexican lady was by the fire cooking food and the aroma permeated the room. Thomas followed as though he were an official of the process.

The two young people stared at one another, Thomas realizing that the boy was close to the same age as the Comanche he had killed in the horse raid, and wondering what might be racing through the captive child's mind. "*Buenas dias,*" he said, but the captive boy made no answer, just continued his searching stare. Neither Mr. Tatum nor Thomas knew what to do to break through the emotional tension.

The *senora* reached up and took two tin plates off the shelf and placed in each a tortilla on which she dished a ladle of *frijoles* and a piece of *cabrito*. She walked over to Thomas, motioned for him to sit down, handed him the plate and told him to eat. She then walked over to the young captive and did the same to him. *"La cocina de su mama,"* she said, (the kitchen of your mother). Both boys began to eat. *"Si, mi mama,"* said the youngster, "I want to go home, but today I die."

"No," said Mr. Tatum, "the army is here to protect you." When the boy was convinced, that as long as he was in the presence of the Indian Agent, he would not be killed by the group of young warriors, he walked back into the room and announced he was going home. The leader of the warrior group walked up and spat in Thomas's face. The Indians rapidly stripped the boy of his Comanche trapping, took the possessions, and left in a huff.

Lt. Deighton decided to leave Fort Sill with what information he had received and return to Fort Concho, but to leave Thomas, who had established considerable rapport with the interpreter, Jones, to see if he could work his way into more knowledge about the status of Comanche whereabouts.

Thomas asked Horace Jones to use his good offices to arrange for him to live inside a Comanche camp. "I don't have such influence over the Comanches, nor would I betray their trust with such an arrangement if the purpose is to spy on those people. In addition, the Indian Agency would not stand for it." Jones added that the Comanches were not fools and would immediately recognize him as a spy, and he would not be alive the next morning. Jones also let it be known very emphatically, that he would participate in nothing with the Comanches not based on absolute truth and openness, his steadfast honesty being the basis of the trust that he had achieved with the people. He had no desire to give up that trust for the sake of some young daredevil, especially for that of a spy.

He did work hard with Thomas to teach him the rudimentary aspects, pronunciation, and usage of the Comanche language, partly because the boy seemed so eager to learn, when nobody else did. "Don't think because you have translated a Comanche sound into an English word, that the particular expression means the same thing to you both; otherwise, you will let these sounds do your thinking for you, and you will commit grave errors." Thomas began to realize that language was a very different thing for the natives than it was for the Anglos. "As much meaning is conveyed by gesture, stress, and cadence as is imparted by the enunciated word."

Jones suggested to Thomas, "There is an area far back in our minds where concepts and insights can occur that are not arranged as words, these being the basic units of our mental pursuits. We try to package these ideas into words so that we can more easily communicate, but the concepts and connotations contained in a word are so different from one person to another that it is a wonder that we are able to talk to others at all. Do you think the word birth could ever mean the same thing to both you and your mother? Then, think how much more complicated it becomes when you add different racial heritages to the translation. The number of words in the American vocabulary must be from six to eight times as many as that of the Comanche, but it does not follow that we have more mental concepts. There are many ways to communicate besides the spoken language and the uncivilized natives rely on these methods much more than the Whites. I often think they actually have more mental concepts, and certainly more accurate ones, than we. One has to dwell intimately with these people to achieve an understanding of such things."

Jones also introduced Thomas to a half-breed woman who worked for the Indian Agency in helping to distribute rations, saying she would be a good source of information since she was always in direct contact with the Comanches.

A dark copper tone, squatty stature, and broad flat face gave the woman unforgettable features, but her eyes shone with an intensity asserting that she was both intelligent and sly. Her affect was affable, affording an easy approach. The woman loved to talk, second only to her love of eating. She turned out to be an excellent interface with the tribes. One day, Thomas took out a leather packet from inside his shirt, carefully opened the leather flap, and unfolded a small piece of bright purple ribbon. "Have you ever seen anybody wear a piece of cloth the color of this ribbon, or decorate anything with it?" She sat still and quiet as if she were mulling the answer over in her mind before she gave it vent. "I've seen it in the braids of one of the warriors," she said. "Do you know him?" pressed Thomas. She shook her head from side to side, and scooted uncomfortably on her seat.

"What does he look like?" he continued. "A Comanche," she

shrugged. The curt answer angered Thomas and he snapped at her before he thought. "He is no warrior," Thomas declared. "He took a dress attached to this purple ribbon from a young girl he had killed. He is a coward. He fights with women and children, and is a disgrace to the Comanche nation." She rose and turned to leave, but Thomas harshly called her back, cut off a tiny bit of the cloth, and handed it to her. He said no more, but left the room before she could. Recalling the events as he walked the path to the fort, he realized he had made a mistake, both his acts and remarks falling short of what he had hoped to gain. He knew he had burned a bridge, a pathway that might have led him to identify the one enemy he most sought.

Thomas visited the trading post and became acquainted with its manager, Jack Evans, who traded with all of the major chiefs and consequently had a fair idea of who was on the reservation and who was not. The Indians continually bartered with him, often using their allotments to trade for goods for which they had more desire, sometimes for only baubles. The position of major trader, however, made him a more accurate source of information than was either the army or the agency.

On the day that the allotments of food and supplies were issued, Thomas was invited by agent Tatum, to witness the event. Never had he seen anything like it. An entire village would come in to receive their allotment of goods, bringing a menagerie of braves, squaws, papooses, Indian ponies, pack mules, and dogs. The braves' apparel ranged all the way from nothing but a breechclout, to gaudy clothing, probably taken during raids against the Anglos, to full feathered head dresses. In Thomas's eyes, the militants had no notion of modern hygiene. They were smelly and both their clothing and persons were greasy and soiled with grime. Most of the squaws were wrinkled and leathery, looking older than the dirt that encased them.

The most forlorn, however, were the old people, most of whom were likewise mounted on the older horses, the animals thinner than those of their kindred, their-keel like backbones thinly fleshed, reaching upward to saw at the strides of their riders. Though their numbers were few, because the Comanche life style was almost impossible to survive once one became at all disabled, the few that remained were bent and feeble, shawled in timeworn raiment, looking out from their dark and swarthy faces through rheumy eyes.

The braves sat, or stood around watching, while the squaws sat on the inside of a circle, their pack animals directly behind them. The circle was the only organized part of the process. The Indians were allotted their respective annuity goods, mostly meat, flour, blankets, and clothing, and the thing the Comanches most prized, coffee and sugar. The tribal Chief first had to deliver his certificate to the agency clerk, then, he was given the allotment and he and his aides in turn doled the goods out to the squaws, supposedly in proportion to how many mouths each had to feed. The Indians were uniformly sullen, seemingly with the attitude that this ritual was a charade they simply had to endure.

As Evans walked up to watch, Thomas turned to him and said, "It seems to me these braves are not so much a group of courageous warriors as belligerent warriors."

"Oh no, what you are seeing here," returned Evans, "are not the real Comanches; their society is so distorted by the imposition of our white culture that one can no longer recognize them as the people they truly are. Get them back out on the plains, however, and they ride like the wind, endure like the desert sand, and fight like a pack of wolves. They sustain themselves in a lifestyle as only they, and their ancestors before them, knew how, and they wage war with guerrilla tactics that we do not yet know how to counter. We Whites could never have displaced a single village in a one on one confrontation, but we can control the entire West by the magnitude of our population and our gigantic arsenal."

"In what manner are their war tactics so different from ours?" asked Thomas.

"In battles waged by the U. S. Army, most actions are planned, so they are ideas long before they occur, and we tend to think of them in terms of specific localities, times, and borders; in battles waged by the Indians, most actions are generated by instinct or by reactions, and these reactions include moving swiftly away from clashes that are likely to carry a high death toll, then returning with a vengeance when we least expect it. That's why those who are not seasoned fighters sometimes think they are not valorous, but their culture is so different from ours that we usually cannot see them for what they are, often until it is too late. Since they recognize no borders, moving away from a plodding army column is not ceding land in their interpretation of war, but don't sell their instincts short. These traits have developed from generations of constant warfare, and are uniquely adapted to these hills and plains."

Evans pointed out to Thomas the dark, malicious stares of the braves, who seemed capable of infinite contempt. "You see," he said, "these people are, in effect, prisoners in their own land. The only thing the males live for is prestige, which they call honor, and there is no honor in being forced from their homes and haunts, restricted to a reservation, and receiving doles from the government. The squaws are not so severely embarrassed as they are used to being slaves, and being told what to do, the males having always relegated them to such a status."

"Indian honor may not be wholly honorable, but I'm not really sure what we ourselves speak of when we talk about our own honor," ventured Thomas, "it's probably not the same as Indian honor." A faint smile drifted across Evans' lips. "Honor is only what you think you have when you are satisfied with yourself," he said. "When you think on those things of which you are not satisfied, you find that you suppress them, and store them in a hidden trove that no one else can see. It takes a very special man to look honestly at both sides, and thus, see himself as he truly is, honorable at times, dishonorable many times.

"What you see here today," continued Evans, "is probably the least important reality regarding the Comanches. You mistake them because you have never lived among them in their native habitat. It's like judging the attributes of a wild duck by observing it in a chicken coop. These natives don't hesitate to submit themselves to long crusades where they absolutely know they will have to endure great physical suffering, but this endurance and determination created an empire upon these arid plains, established trade and commerce that dominated all their neighbors, subjugated whole Indian nations, stopped the Spanish empire in its tracks, and halted the Whites for decades."

The women packed the allotments on the horses and mules and sometimes on a travois pulled by a dog. The dogs were barking and snarling, mules were braying, braves complaining, and squaws yelling, so that the sum effect of the raucous event was overwhelming, confusion rampant. The only ones that were quiet, throughout the whole ordeal, were the papooses, strapped in their cradle boards, peering out from their dark, searching eyes, almost never crying. Thomas stood close by, watching the happening. Although he was, for the most part, ignored, he saw a few of the squaws cast a brief glance at the small purple ribbon he had left slightly protruding from his shirt pocket.

Thomas decided he had gleaned about as much information as possible from the headquarters, trading post, and the Indian agent. Since he had no chance of safely riding out onto the reservation, he decided to return home. He had already been warned by Jones that he must be extremely careful, but now, the translator called him in, and told him that word had leaked out, and the entire Comanche nation knew he was one of the Whites who had successfully ambushed the war party west of Fort Richardson. "They are seething for the chance to get revenge," he said. Jones also told him that all of the Indians knew about the purple cloth, and that, whatever was going on in that regard had uniformly angered the reservation tribes. "The only sensible thing for you to do is to get away from here as quickly as you can, and stay away."

CHAPTER 15

Thomas walked over to the trading post and asked to see Evans. "I'd like to trade for one of those decorated cradle boards. Would you tell any likely Comanche that I would pay a good price and will be here again tomorrow afternoon?" He quietly bought a set of steel wolf traps from Evans, put them in a sack to conceal them from sight, and went back to the Fort. At midnight he saddled his horse, tied on his gear and headed out for Fort Richardson, hoping that the ruse of wanting to trade the following afternoon, would lower the vigilance of the Indians for this night, and keep any Comanches from already being stationed on the trail to interrupt his journey. He wished to be twelve hours south before the Indians even conjectured that he might be gone. Through the first night he simply rode hard, keeping close to the trail, trying to put as much distance as possible between himself and the Comanches, but starting the second day, he remained extremely cautious. Every two to three miles he would stop his horse and listen to the noises of the countryside. The sounds seem normal to him. When he rode up to a vantage point he scanned the surrounding territory, being careful not to ride completely out in the open where his silhouette would stand out against the skyline.

Thomas loved to ride, but riding day after day exacted a toll from the rider as well as the horse. The inside of the legs chaffed, knees and hips and stride ached, and the spine longed to be stretched and extended. Nonetheless, Thomas kept a steady pace, pushing his mount into a foxtrot gate, which was usually easier for the rider and the animal.

In forty-eight hours he had crossed the Red River and both branches of the Wichita. Without incident, he rode into Fort Richardson, where he reported to the local commander and talked to him about his mission for Mackenzie. The officers thought if he was going on alone to Fort Concho he had better change horses, or let his mount rest for a few days, but Thomas was so intent on getting his message back to Colonel Mackenzie, that the local commander traded with the scout, giving him a fresh and sturdy steed, and put him in an Army uniform, so he would not be identified from a distance as the same rider who had been at Fort Sill.

Thomas started his trek to Fort Concho the next day, leaving just before noon, traveling about fifteen miles with one of the local ranchers who knew the country well and had been able to keep his scalp all these years. After arriving at the ranch, Thomas accepted an invitation to spend the night with the settler and his family. Following a good night's rest and obtaining food for himself and his horse, he set out well before sun-up on the trail to Fort Concho.

His course closely followed that of the well-established, but now discarded, Butterfield Stage route, going by the location of the old Fort Belknap ruins where he crossed the main trunk of the Brazos River and on westward to Fort Griffin, a fort located on a bend of the river's clear fork. Shortly after leaving the ruins of Fort Belknap, he came to a small stream where he was watering his horse when he noticed several hoof prints of unshod ponies, rather fresh, obviously being ridden together as a group. The findings certainly suggested the possibility of Indians on the prowl. All day, Thomas scanned the countryside, looking for any sign of trouble. He saw nothing, nor did he ever notice his horse reacting to anything unusual.

Once more, he picked out a camp site where he could sleep with his back to a bluff, and place his horse in a small area of dense trees, only thirty feet away. He set his three traps, easily covering them with the plentiful leaf debris. The horse was allowed to graze until well after dark, then was led into the enclosure, and tied from both front and back legs, restricting the animal so it could get right next to, but not on top of the traps. Thomas inadvertently dozed off for about an hour, abruptly wakening at the sound of an owl. His eyes searched the direction of the sound and spotted the form of the big bird sitting on a branch of a large tree, allowing him to realize the owl noise was no signal. In the dark, he climbed up into his predetermined roost in a big cedar-elm.

Except for a slight breeze rustling the leaves, there was silence. After about two hours, Thomas became aware of his heart beating faster. He couldn't say what had caused the reaction, but he was suddenly alert, as though the very vibrations of the air were prodding at his nerves. From the corner of his eye, he saw movement, the silhouette of a sapling slowly bending to one side as though being pushed from below. The intruder remained darkly invisible, no light penetrating to the ground. The horse snorted slightly and suddenly he heard one of his traps snap followed by a whelp-like cry.

Dropping down out of the tree and coming around the front of the horse, Thomas confronted the most feral thing he had ever seen in his life. Tethered to an oak tree, his wrist caught in a trap, and the trap chain locked around the tree trunk, was a young Comanche, a knife in his free hand slashing through the air at his tormentor. The Indian was a veritable tornado of fury and frenzy. He lunged at Thomas who easily stood out of his reach. He made terrible, guttural, growling noises, turned half around, and kicked with all his might, but the foot only plunged into thin air. Thomas swung hard with the butt of his rifle, catching his victim on the chin, and as the young warrior fell backward to the ground he sprung a second trap which clamped down on the shoulder of the free arm. Thomas turned his attention to the near-by trees and strained his senses trying to detect any hint of other Indians. He detected nothing.

He looked down at his stunned, half-conscious enemy, his features, at first, indistinct in the moonlight. His adversary slowly began to stir back into consciousness. Thomas wanted to make no more noise so he pulled out his hunting knife, but when he looked again into the face of the trapped intruder, what Thomas saw was no longer ferocity, but terror. The Indian was just a boy. He could not be more than twelve or thirteen years old. "He is here, to prove his courage, and to gain Comanche honor by taking a horse," thought Thomas. He loosened his grip from around the hilt of his own knife, and placed it back in its scabbard; put his foot on the free arm of the Indian, bent over and took the native's knife out of the young combatant's hand, then stepped on the spring of the trap which had clamped down on the shoulder and scooted it away, then stepped on the spring of the second trap and gently pulled out the wrist. Thomas gave a wave of his hand, and uttered the Comanche word, "go!" The puzzled Indian boy lay still for a moment, then rolled to his feet, and disappeared like a wounded deer, into the surrounding forest.

Thomas went back to the bluff, and sat down, his whole body aching with fatigue. He laid his pistol by his side and his rifle across both knees, and waited for morning.

The dawn came crisp and clear. Thomas stretched his sore limbs and carefully began to survey his surroundings, even out into the far terrain. Two male cardinals flitted from limb to limb in a chase for mastery of the territory. Nothing seemed amiss; he heard no unusual sound. The horse stood in a relaxed pose, certainly not alert to anything unusual.

He pulled a small strap of jerky out of his saddle bag and began to chew on one end. It felt and tasted like chewing dried mule hide. Thomas walked over to the horse, sprung the one remaining trap, and began saddling the animal and loading his gear. He took off the hobbles and went forward to untie the halter rope. Something was on the rope right next to the knot. Thinking it a bug, he flicked his fingers to brush it away, but it did not fall off. It was hard to see in the still dark shadows, but he looked carefully and realized it was a small rag tied around the rope. He untied it and held it up to the light. A chill surged through his body, his muscles tensed and there was an odd feeling in his stomach. The rag was a piece of bright purple cloth. Quickly he resurveyed his surroundings, again seeing and hearing nothing of alarm. "If the bearer of this cloth came here to kill me I would already be dead," he thought. Anyone tying a strip of cloth to the halter rope could, unquestionably, have put a bullet or an arrow through me."

He remounted and got back on the trail to Fort Griffin, taking no unusual precautions, for he was totally preoccupied. Again and again his mind raced back over the past events of the night, trying to imagine the scenario which allowed the placement of the cloth strip around the halter rope. Each time, he found himself back at the same conclusions. The person who had tied the cloth knew who he was; he had undoubtedly trailed him here from Fort Sill or else cut cross country to intercept him; he, Thomas, had not been sufficiently alert to protect himself, and finally, his life had been spared by this arch enemy, an enemy he had always thought of as neither proffering nor receiving quarter. He wondered if he was still alive because he had not killed the boy.

He rode on toward Fort Griffin, a very subdued and sober scout, and though he was warmly greeted by the troops who had already heard about the horse raid, and his part in the defeat of the Comanches when the emissaries were on their way to Fort Sill, he could not talk about it. He told no one what had happened during the previous night.

The layout of Fort Griffin was similar to that of Fort Richardson, comprised of all the standard buildings, widely separated around a large parade ground. The position of the fort, however, was magnificent, situated high on a plateau overlooking a bend in the Clear Fork of the Brazos River, offering a vast panoramic view of the valley below. Thomas walked out to be alone, and sat looking into the distance to review, in his own mind, the quest that he had assumed, and weighing his ability to attain it, a quest that had been his total preoccupation since his family had been killed.

The ride on into Fort Concho was an easy one. A group of replacement officers was on the way to Concho so Thomas went with them, joining a group of six troopers who were sent with the officers for support duties and protection.

Upon arrival at Fort Concho he went immediately to report to Colonel Mackenzie. The Colonel had already been apprised of Thomas's part in thwarting the night raid of the Comanches, so he was congratulated and warmly received by the commander. Thomas reported all he had ascertained about the Comanche, Kiowa and Arapaho Indians, who were both on and off the reservation. He was amazed at how much the Colonel knew about the Indians, and at how Mackenzie quizzed him concerning every detail he had learned about the native people, particularly the individual chiefs. Thomas returned to his position with the Tonkawa scouts, telling the colonel nothing about the Indian boy, or of the purple cloth.

CHAPTER 16

Both Thomas and Oswego were delighted to be reunited, but right away the Tonkawa sensed that something was deeply troubling his young friend. As soon as they were able to be alone, Oswego said, "there is something on your mind that is bothering you, since we were last together. Is there some way I can be of help?"

Thomas then began to relate to Oswego what had happened since they were last together. He told him of his trip to Fort Sill, of the Comanche raid on the road, and of his sojourn at the reservation, where he had done all he knew how, to learn more about the Comanches. He related the story of his provocative use of the purple cloth and of his telling the half-breed Comanche squaw that the Indian who possessed the material was no warrior at all, but a cowardly killer of children.

He told Oswego the story of the attempted theft of his horse on the trail back to Fort Griffin, of his trapping the Comanche boy, his inability to kill the young Indian, and the boy's subsequent release. He told of finding the purple cloth tied to the halter rope the next morning. "All of my life since my mother and sister died I have hated the very thought of the Comanche who helped kill them. I have spent my life trying to become superior to him, and was prepared to give him no quarter if we ever met. Now I find that this Comanche is not only a better soldier than I am, but that he spared my life. I see no reason to go on."

Oswego smiled at his young ward. "You are dismayed because events have not turned out the way you always imagined they would, but the imaginary world rarely turns out to be the real one. It's hard to admit to yourself that someone you hate bested you, but then treated you with leniency. He was, however, probably not being benevolent, but simply following the dictates of his common tribal mores.

"You are probably right about who it was that left the cloth. He undoubtedly was the same fleeing Indian whom you shot in the shoulder and whom we almost caught the day your women were killed. The boy you spared was most likely a close relative, perhaps a son, to whom his fellow Comanches gave the opportunity to steal your horse before you were attacked, so that he could gain his own prestige as a budding warrior. The father probably did not spare you for the same reason you spared the boy. You spared him because you have compassion for human beings and a sense of what is morally permissible, attitudes that reside in you because of your heritage. It is deeply embedded in the mores of some Indian tribes that the beneficent deed of an enemy must be returned in kind, before the enmity can be resumed. That is why you are still alive, but also, why you are still in danger."

"I'm not fit to compete with the enemy if I can be stalked so easily," said Thomas. "I'd convinced myself that I was an extraordinary scout, but I can see that I'm only a boy and have achieved practically nothing. I suppose I'd rather sleep than shoulder the demands of a frontiersman. Since I'm still alive only because of some tribal superstition, I should return home and be a farmer."

"Your time as a farmer will come," said Oswego, "right now, in spite of what you tell me, you are the best young scout, and I repeat young, that I have ever seen, and yes, you are lucky because you are alive and you have another chance. A boy does not get to be an able warrior or an able scout just because he works hard and desires that end; he achieves the goal only when he has experienced both many victories and many failures of his pursuit, when he has acquired the hard-earned skills, and when such an able scout is called for. You are being called for, Thomas! The Texas frontier is calling you now.

"The one who tied the purple string is older and probably much more seasoned than you, and there is no other thing, nothing at all, which can take the place of experience. You may regret your lack of experience, or your lack of knowledge in the art of scouting, or the art of war, but you have no reason to be ashamed of it. You are actually more trained and educated than 'battle wise.' Battle wisdom comes from only one thing – experience."

"I've always thought of some day being the best scout on the frontier, and I thought I had been going in that direction, but now I can see, that is not true," said Thomas

"No one guaranteed that any numbers of endeavor would make you the best, nor even if you were the best, that you would win out every time," returned Oswego. "There is, actually, no such thing as best. Best is never permanent; best this time, second best next time, last at times, always changing as one treads through life."

"I don't see what you're doing out here, serving the army of the Whites and risking your life, Oswego. You are never extolled, or honored, or especially rewarded by the army and you don't have the same deep enmity in your heart toward the Comanche that I do, yet you are more dedicated than I am to their downfall."

"I am sufficiently honored by my own people, and I do it for them. There needs to be a world of peace, where I and the members of my tribe, who have been sorely beset by these Comanches, don't have to fear a horrible death every time we ride out on the plains to hunt the buffalo, buffalo which should be ours as well as theirs and where we don't live in constant dread of returning to the village to see our horses stolen, our home and possessions pillaged, and our families ravaged and killed. If these Comanches are not deterred, they will wipe out the Tonkawa.

"If the Comanches did not have this fetish for violence, or if they were not so successful with it, there would be many things to admire about them. They exhibit physical endurance, stealth, and the will to persist beyond imagination, and are skilled in the knowledge of the natural world around them like no other humans. They are both brave and resolute, and will let neither physical nor emotional set backs, come between them and their goals. There is a reason why the Comanches rule the southern plains instead of some other tribe. I believe it is their persistence and resolve to excel, and their willingness to endure whatever is required to meet that end."

Very shortly after Thomas returned from Fort Sill, the Fourth Cavalry headquarters was removed to Fort Richardson, from where Mackenzie launched his first foray into the heart of Indian Territory. In the early fall of 1871, Oswego, Thomas, and other scouts were sent out to probe the western edges of the canyons which broke off from the escarpment of the Great Plains. It was their duty to look for signs of Indians, but also to become familiar with the terrain, find the watering places, and learn of any established trails which coursed through the area.

In September, 1871, Mackenzie led the troops of the Fourth Cavalry into the canyon land of the Comancheria, camping along the headwaters of the Fresh Water Fork of the Brazos River, where he established his supply base. The scouts were out daily through the edges of the canyons and even up near the rim of the Llano Estacado. Signs of the Indians were abundant and the scouts reported to the army that the Quahadi were very near.

Scouts for the U.S. Army were not the only scouts about. The Indians knew every inch of this canyon country, and carefully watched the army troops moving into what they considered their homeland, trespassing upon their sacred soil, an act of war, justifying any means of retaliation.

On October 4, 1871, Mackenzie and his Fourth Cavalry moved out toward the Clear Fork of the Brazos River on which they were to establish their base camp for their subsequent foray onto the plains. There were about six hundred men, with a large herd of horses and around one hundred pack mules. Thomas, with his friends, the Tonkawa scouts, were fanned out ahead of the column, widely scattered across the countryside, looking for signs that might guide them into a Comanche village.

The column traveled northwest and crossed the Double Mountain Fork of the Brazos River in easy sight of the Double Mountains for which the fork was named. The Double Mountains might well have been named the Triple Peaks, for one of the uplifts had two rises near its crest. The peaks were the highest landforms for almost two hundred fifty miles in any direction and for hundreds of years had served as reference points for human travelers. The army marched on, through miles upon miles of small hills, interlaced with broad flats close to minor streams or dry creek beds, almost always finding Indian signs, especially around the water, the location of which the natives seemed to know intimately. Mostly, the signs were trails which had been recently used, but often there were utensils and remnants of clothing or broken pieces of armament that had been lost or discarded by the nomads as they, forever, kept on the move.

As the troops continued to the Northwest the land changed, appearing more eroded the further they traveled, and the closer they came to the escarpment of the Great Plains, and the more solid rim rock which kept the boundary of the higher flat land intact.

The escarpment country was the very essence of badlands; born of erosion over thousands of years it was blanketed with a lifeless rust color, a kingdom of red clay and caliche, the desiccated clay crumbling to cascade downward, clogging the crevices below. Only occasional plants were able to take root and grow atop the eroded ridges. The gnarled tentacles of the few mesquite and juniper trees situated at the top were grappling with the chinks of soil in a race to penetrate deep enough to take hold and stabilize before the wind, water, and gravity prevailed, and tumbled even this bit of flora onto the floor of the gulches below. The never-resting wind strewed dancing eddies of dust over any denuded spot of ground. Wherever the land had been stirred, rolled over, or trampled on, there was dust; not just dust that powdered and lay upon the earth, but dust that pervaded the very lower layer of the atmosphere, and so laid its mantle over the travelers that when they ceased their march at day's end, they had assumed the very color of the red earth. When the wind blew hard, the stinging grit would eat into their faces, leaving bleary eyes and abraded lips.

Most nights, Thomas could hear the far away yapping howl of the coyotes. He sometimes got to see them in the early morning or at dusk. They trotted over the ridges and down the canyons, silently, ears forward, nose ever probing in different directions, trying to get a scent or a sound that would lead them to their prey. Rarely, he saw a successful one trot across the prairie carrying death in its jaws.

The flora of the dry country had a waxy shriveled appearance to the outer layers of the leaves and stems, helping them to survive the dehydration that the unshaded landscape impressed upon them. Beneath the few scrubby junipers that grew on level land lay a profusion of ciliate sprigs which had been shed through the previous dry season and the long winter. They did not decay and merge into the soil as they did back home beside the Guadalupe, but lay whole, withered, curled, and brown, lasting ghosts, in defiance of the wind and the sun. Thomas could not imagine how a nomadic people could subsist, much less develop a society in this forbidding land.

CHAPTER 17

A sense of expectation engulfed the scouts, as though some great revelation lurked before them, imbuing all with a subliminal sense of dread, a fear of the unknown. Thomas studied the Comanche signs minutely, and talked about them with the Tonkawas who were adept at telling how old they were, and how many might be traveling in a party. The scouts crossed one ridge after another in a seemingly endless landscape of erosion and small gullies which issued out of the plains. Small Indian trails converged, branch canyons converged, and both the topography and the trails seemed to beckon them onward and upward. Then, it happened. Thomas rode up a steep declination, found a small crumbling defect in the rim rock, chucked his horse to urge him upward, and suddenly his mount was standing on level ground; the Llano Estacado.

To the north and to the west, the land, as level as a calm sea, reached out into a boundless emptiness. There were no hills nor valleys, no rocks nor trees, just an immeasurable, unimpeded stretch of flatness that would not cease. The eyes of the invaders were not trained to evaluate such a landscape – there was nothing of comparative likeness in their minds. The Llano seemed impenetrable, not from any physical barrier, for there was none, but from its sameness and vastness – the sum of the scenario, more an emotional idea than a geographic entity.

The grass was not green and lush, but gray hued, matted, and thick, with rootlets filling the ground with organic tunnels that clung to and encased the earth, defying the sun and space to turn it into a wasteland.

The topography was so strange that Thomas felt he was standing on forbidden soil, exposed, vulnerable, making him want to flee back to some token of familiarity. He watched as the other Tonkawa scouts now rode up through the rift in the rim rock and topped out onto the plains. He sensed they all were suffering the same foreboding feeling, the men seeming very small and inconsequential, even to themselves, as though the very vastness was ready to swallow them up and transform them into a gust of the prairie wind. The one glory of the landscape was the vault of faultless blue that stretched overhead, unmarred by a single obstruction between them and any glimpse of the horizon – a house of sky.

Thomas minutely examined the grass, finding it relatively short but thick and his horse began to graze it with relish. He led the horse for thirty feet, then knelt down and looked back at the path, so as to introduce himself to what he would have to face when tracking across such a country. In the thick turf the tracks were more shadow than imprint. Thomas discerned that as the sun rose higher they would be harder to see because the minute shadow affected by the slanting sun hitting the rim of the print, would no longer be present. The Tonkawas stayed on the top for about an hour, letting their horses graze, and talking to one another about the new kind of ocean that lay before them and the diligence that would be required to follow the Comanches across it.

The scouts, used to the refuge of ridges, sinks, rocks, and trees, were loath to go farther across this prairie without more connection to the main body of the troops, so they descended off the Caprock and began looking for the army column. As the last token of sunlight began to ebb below the canyon rims, they spotted Mackenzie's encampment below. Several camp fires were aglow, causing Thomas to frown, wondering why the officers would allow such an explicit understanding of the position of their entire encampment to any Indian spies that might be hereabout. The camp was in a pocket valley with a stream of water issuing from the base of steep bluffs at the head of the canyon and the site located between the stream below and a set of rather steep hills and gullies to the north, which the unseasoned officers considered a barrier.

"I don't like the position of the horse herd," said Oswego. "They are bunched together with an easy outlet to the south and no protection from the north. If we lost one we could lose them all."

"The officer in charge probably picked the spot because the grass in this area is quite good," Thomas said.

"The officer has not fought the Comanche before," grunted Oswego. The two compatriots walked off into the dim light next to the wall of the canyon and selected a spot away from the main body of the army where they had a tiny *sendero* only twenty yards wide, and where they could actually tie the horses to a substantial mesquite rather than tether them to a stake driven into the ground. They were in direct line with an easy crossing of the stream. They made no fire and ate only some of their own reserve of pemmican that night. The two alternated between sleeping and sitting guard.

After midnight the moon arose high in the sky, its pallid light seeping through the mesquites and openly bathing the savannahs where the animals were grazing. Occasionally, glowing embers from the soldiers' campfires would blaze up, spew a few sparks into the night sky and die back down. Far to the north, along the edge of the escarpment, could be heard the wail of the prowling coyote.

An abrupt end to the rest came with a chorus of spine tingling yells from the hills and gullies to the north. Moving as suddenly as flushed quail, a howling pack of screeching Indians came pouring over the ridges above, riding at full speed toward the camp and the horse herd below. The barriers of steep hills which the officers had picked were no barriers at all to the Indians and their agile horses which had been long inured to such country. Cow bells were clanging, buffalo robes flapping, and gunshots were popping as the Comanches dashed through the camp in an effort to stampede the herd. The army horses and mules went berserk, neighing, snorting, braying, rearing, and lunging in a desperate attempt to get away. Ropes began to snap and stake pins were pulled from the ground, as the horses that were able to free themselves dashed for the unknown in a wild stampede of animals, popping leather, flying ropes, and stake pins. The sounds of crashing brush intermingled with the other noises of the din, the horses and mules blindly fleeing through the growth in the bottom of the canyon.

Officers were yelling for the troops to get to their mounts, and a desperate scramble to do so began as soldiers intermingled with the remaining, but crazed, horses that had not been able to free themselves from their tethers. Several carbine shots whined through the air as troopers tried to retaliate but all were ineffective and the Indians rampaged right through the edge of the herd and on down the valley which echoed with taunting shouts from the raiders who quickly faded and then disappeared.

Oswego had awakened Thomas just before the raid began. He could not say why, but had sensed something to the north, a danger, perhaps. The scouts had learned to heed their premonitions, so both scouts saddled and mounted their horses, then, slipped into the shadows of the grove. As the horde came rushing toward them, Oswego placed his hand on Thomas's arm and said, "We must stay where we are; we have no chance to affect this raid." They stayed completely concealed as the braves rode through, but then a lone trailing raider came riding hard, trying to catch up with his comrades. He headed directly to the tiny opening in the trees immediately beside where Oswego was hidden. There was a sudden crack of wood as Oswego swung a dead oak branch, and hit the rider squarely in the head. Oswego was on him like a wasp lighting on a worm. He pierced his chest with his knife and then scalped him as the raider was still struggling. He then cut the throat of the hapless victim took his gun, shield, and scalp, and rode with Thomas back to join the soldiers.

All was still confusion among the troops, officers trying to account for their men and to see how much stock they had lost, eventually amounting to almost one hundred head. A single soldier had been killed and only the one Indian, but the confidence of the troopers had been severely shaken. To make matters worse, one of the campfires, which had been run through during the confusion, spread to the adjacent dried vegetation and then swept up the canyon toward the escarpment ahead.

Several of the soldiers had to fight the fire to keep it from engulfing their equipment. After the chaos began to abate, a substantial number of able pickets were posted around the camp to warn of any further incursion by the Indians, but there was no rest for the remaining part of the night. Long before dawn, scouts were in the saddle with orders to fan out and see if they could determine where the Indians had come from, and more importantly, where they had gone. A second group of soldiers, officered by two captains, were then assembled to follow the trail of the missing horses to see if any were retrievable.

Thomas mounted his own horse, rode away from the other scouts, and looked back down on the camp. Though there was, yet, no cloak of daylight, silhouettes emerged through the beams the moon still cast down. Charred branches of the newly burned Mesquites appeared like relics of some bygone kingdom of devils, brandishing their forks into God's holy sky. He had never had such a sense of desolation. He turned his horse away from the other scouts and rode a couple of miles to the southwest, then, turned north, again angling toward the main body of explorers. He rode up a ravine running parallel to their former location but about a mile away, looked back to the east, and blinked into the sunlight as it first broke over the top of the canyons.

CHAPTER 18

Thomas began to hear gunshots off to his right, so he rode up to the top of the ridge where he could see a small troop of cavalry running their steeds toward the top of a broad plateau. Just as the riders disappeared over the top, a crescendo of piercing screams, whoops, and howls echoed down the gullies, followed by a din of rising noise that sounded like the moans of hell, with all of the armies of the earth screeching their defiance and hatred toward one another.

He kept riding upward until he was just below the rim of the plateau, then dismounted, and concealed his pony as best he could, in a small clump of juniper. He scrambled to the top, concealed himself in the scrubby cedars, and peered out onto the flat. A huge gathering of Indians was fanned out over the mesa, attacking a small group of soldiers who were caught out on the bare prairie, and were trying their best to stay in formation and hold them off as they slowly retreated back toward the ravine from which they had originally come. The Indians were on the move, running in an oblate circle, firing sporadically at the Blue Coats each time they dashed around the circular path nearest the troopers.

As the Comanches came in line with the soldiers they swung themselves down on their horses' opposite sides, holding on to a platted mat of hair woven into the steed's mane, with a single foot draped over its back. They shot at the troopers from beneath the horse's outstretched necks while galloping at full speed. The scene was horrifying, yet fascinating, the union of the Indian with the Indian pony becoming more than just a rider and his mount, but a new form, a new existence, a veritable centaur of the staked plains. Thomas's mind flashed back to the escape of the Indian at whom he had fired, after the death of his mother, and the way he rode with one foot draped over the pony's back.

The young scout recognized that the soldiers had pursued the Indians into an ambush. Suddenly, six of the men on the left flank, including their captain, abandoned their years of army discipline, forsook their defensive formation, mounted their horses, and made a desperate run back to the rim of the plateau, leaving the remaining six soldiers in a dire position with their left flank completely exposed. The warriors, outnumbering the troopers thirty to one, closed into the flank area of the trapped force. Though they could easily have overwhelmed the soldiers with one direct assault, the natives would not close in a direct charge. They kept feinting at, but never assailing, the final perilous space that was the dividing line between the two hostile groups, as though still cowed by the deadly fire of the carbines, even from only six remaining troopers, and preferring to let the army unit be disabled by running out of ammunition. It seemed they were loath to lose a single Indian, even to kill six of the hated Blue Coats.

Steady fire from the native cavalry kept the troopers pinned down and unable to retreat. If an Indian pony was wounded and fell, the catlike brave always seemed to land on his feet, a comrade sweeping by and picking the unsaddled Comanche off the ground, as he sprang up behind his rescuer's saddle and rode to the far side of the circle. A squaw in the rear immediately brought a fresh horse to the warrior, and he was remounted at once.

Meanwhile, the women of the tribe, behind the circle of warriors, let out a continuous howl, punctuated by piercing screeches, as though the might of the entire attack was derived from their eerie sound. The drama of the interaction would be unforgettable, the clash of arms, the sounds of the running horses, the howling Indians, and reports of the rifles with the pungent smell of the exploding gunpowder, the gaudy color of the whirling natives, and the grim but desperate steadiness of the Blue Coats, all melding into a new externality, greater than the sum of warriors and soldiers, tribes and landscape: the fearsome essence of war.

Out of the corner of his eye, Thomas saw a subtle movement to his left. He squinted in order to diminish the ambient light, and realized there were three unmounted warriors crawling down over the edge of the escarpment, working their way behind the soldiers in an effort to surprise them from the rear. Thomas became motionless as they passed behind him, not sixty feet away, thinking surely, they must hear the surge of his racing heart. A sudden clamp of fear enveloped him, stirring again the memory of his fright while hiding beneath the half submerged tree in the Brazos River. He fought to hold his breath steady and slow, so it would not signal the stalkers, as though unaware that the clamor above would have completely muffled any such sound.

As the three Indians climbed up the opposite steep and crumbly slope toward the next ridge, the trailing man slipped, saving his fall, by grabbing onto a tiny bush. His two companions formed a human chain to pull him up, but just as they were most extended, Thomas raised his rifle and squeezed the trigger; automatically the rifleman shucked his carbine and a second bullet was sent on its way. The two braves standing atop the ridge keeled forward and fell head long down the slope. Thomas winced at the sequence. It was almost as though he pulled the trigger, but never expected such a thing as this to happen. With no one left to hold on to, the third Indian slid hard to the bottom of the ravine where he was completely exposed, allowing Thomas to riddle him with shot.

The whole episode was over in ten seconds; it arose not as a plan calculated by the young scout, but as an automatic thing, a reflex, something devoid of intent, devoid of design, mindless, a thing over which he had no control, an impulsive act of war. Time suddenly seemed suspended, the world static, his being suddenly stripped of thought, stripped of any ideal or moral principle, then slowly regrouping to once again allow him to catch up and be aware of the events. The complete melee and den of the activity above was so loud that no others noticed the ancillary fray.

Thomas looked down upon the scene where the three lay, crumpled over one another, still and mute in their unlikely repose. The first thoughts that came to him were, "what have I done, then, why am I alive while they are dead?" but as the bidding of war entreats, those thoughts quickly passed from his mind and he went on.

Thomas worked his way closer to the battleground and back up to the rim of the escarpment, then into a small clump of juniper in order to see if he could outflank the Comanches while still keeping himself concealed. He immediately saw one of the troopers, caught out in the open and too far removed from the defensive formation of the other soldiers, mount his horse and try to gallop back in order to close ranks. The soldier turned backward in the saddle to fire at the Indians but his rifle jammed and then his horse began to reel from almost complete exhaustion. Four warriors, who sensed the desperate plight of the isolated fighter, were charging hard, directly toward him, their killer instinct at a raw edge. The leading attacker was arrayed as a war chief, feathered bonnet flowing behind and large rings in his ears. Black and red war paint marked each side of his face. Riding a splendid black horse, he flew at his enemy. To Thomas, the Indian looked like the devil incarnate.

The trapped soldier seemed to collapse into a trance of inaction, as the Indian warrior, zigzagging his horse to avoid giving other army men an easy target, only increased his speed as he rode at the struggling, fumbling trooper, never wavering in his forward motion until he was upon the lone soldier, putting a pistol to his head and executing him on the spot. The Indian's horse whirled, altering its course back to join the line of ponies circling ever closer to the remaining five Blue Coats.

As the warrior whirled, Thomas's carbine rang out and the Indian chief immediately slapped the side of his neck where blood smeared across his hand. The wound was, apparently, only a superficial crease, and not a disabling injury. The chief whirled once more and looked directly at the bushes from whence Thomas's bullet had come. The urge to flee was overpowering, but Thomas fought to maintain his self control, for he dared not move, knowing a lone scout on foot would be easy prey for the mounted Comanches. The visage of the war chief was startling, demanding submission, head held back with eyelids halfway closed as though he were looking down on mere mortals – the consummate master, the consummate warrior. The image so stamped itself in Thomas's mind that it would linger with him as long as he breathed.

The wily chief abruptly seemed to think better of the situation, and instead of engendering another confrontation in his exposed location, he again turned and quickly sped away, his retreat followed by at least thirty of his warriors whose running circle had pressed to within forty yards of the beleaguered soldiers.

The circling attackers, along with the rest of the horde, then sped off toward the butte at the head of the small area of level ground. To his left, Thomas saw the actual cause of the Comanche retreat. The Tonkawa scouts, under Lieutenant Boehm, were dashing and whooping straight into the fray. An entire cavalry unit was right at their heels. A running battle ensued, with the circling Indians slowly retreating toward the butte and finally over the top and onto the plains before the main column of Mackenzie's troops could become engaged. The officers decided that further pursuit at the time was dangerous and probably useless.

Members of the column retraced their steps back to the dead soldier who lay as he had fallen when shot out of the saddle. He was buried with a simple military funeral, far out in this alien land, in disregard of any connection to home, family or heritage, as was the stark necessity of military death when war was being waged. There was not so much as a cross or stone to mark the freshly dug dirt apart from nothing at all. The troops rode off the butte and went into a temporary bivouac to wait for the coming day.

As the men left the burial, Thomas walked up beside an old sergeant who was a known Indian fighter of many years. "I have never seen people ride like that," he said, "do they always fight that way?"

"Listen boy," answered the Sergeant, "never try to outride a Comanche. Them Indian ponies look scraggly but they're tougher'n dried cactus, and them Comanches, they even speak horse. It don't matter whether you shoot the Injun or the pony, the other'n 'll be right back fightin' ya. For myself, I just try to shoot the ponies, cause there ain't no way you're going t' get a clear shot at one of them Injuns."

Thomas walked back to the ravine where his own private war had taken place. All three dispatched fighters had tumbled to the bottom of the ravine. Though they certainly looked dead, he checked all three to make sure. Looking down at the carnage, he was torn between the urge to boast and the urge to flee. The impetus of war is to do to the foe what they would have done to you. Following that dictate, he shut his mind to who he was and who he had always been, and did not pause to let contemplation lead him to his own decision but allowed the compulsion to become as one with his compatriots urge him on. Stepping across the line of which his civility and his conscience would, heretofore, have not allowed, he took out his hunting knife and quickly scalped all three – his mind's eye immobile, unseeing, as though the repugnant act was being done by some automaton, not himself.

He put the scalps in his saddle bag and rode back to the troops, saying nothing to any of the soldiers or to the Tonkawa scouts until he was alone with Oswego. He told his only confidant the entire story, including the description of the war chief and the doomed soldier's almost trance-like willingness to yield to the warrior, as a small bird yields itself as prey to feed a snake.

"Quanah," said Oswego, "Chief of the Quahadi." Thomas shuddered slightly at what he said, gave him the scalps, and walked off to be by himself.

Oswego took the three scalps and found Lieutenant Boehm who was commander of the scouts. He related the entire report of Thomas's experience, showed him the three scalps and told him where the bodies of the Indians could be found. He also told him the story of the captain who had fled, leaving the six exposed soldiers to fend for themselves. "Nothing is more hypocritical than a professed warrior averse to battle," said Boehm. He probably reported the story to Colonel Mackenzie, but Oswego was never sure.

The chief scout then rode off into the midst of the Tonkawas, gave them the three scalps and told them the story. There was much excitement among the tribesmen who considered Thomas one of their own, but that night Oswego suggested to Thomas that he make his bed with the army instead of the scouts.

After dark had enveloped the canyons, Thomas heard weird sounds coming from the Tonkawa camp. He walked closer in the dark and saw the warriors around a large fire in a frenzied dance. In the center was a pole to which the three scalps were tied, the Indian scouts circling the pole making debasing gestures and taunts at the relics, then raising their hands into the air to give thanks to the Great Mystery. He could see Oswego in the circling clan, participating in the rite but seeming totally out of place to the young Texan. Over the fire he could see a sizzling haunch of meat and wondered where the fresh supply had been obtained.

Suddenly it dawned on Thomas what this represented. He had

heard stories that the Tonkawa were sometimes cannibalistic, but never believed that the stories were true. He had never seen a hint of such behavior, either in the Tonkawa village, or in his several months with the scouts. He could not believe that this relatively civilized tribe was responsible for such a scene. Why hadn't Oswego told him? Was this some atavistic, bestial trait, long sequestered in the far depths of their beings that had always lurked beneath the veneer of civility, ready to express itself when the occasion was right? Were all humans of such a nature? Was he of such nature? Would the compulsion to be part of the group have had him circling in the dance if Oswego had not warned him away? There was much in the heart, mind and history of these people which he decided he should not attempt to understand.

Just after midnight, the following day, the Tonkawa scouts were already out hunting for the trail of the fleeing Quahadi. Around three o'clock in the morning they came back to camp, claiming to have found a trail beyond the butte, and onto the plains, that must certainly be leading to the Comanche village. Even though the troops were already bone weary, part of the cavalry now on foot, and the horses grossly taxed, Mackenzie ordered the army to push onto the Llano and trail the Indians.

The soldiers found a vivid trail apparently of the movement of a whole encampment, and soon sensed they were gaining on the fleeing villagers as they began to find more and more discarded gear, but instead of daylight emerging with the dawn, an engulfing bank of black, roiling clouds came down upon the column. Snow flakes began to fall in an increasingly swirling tempest, buffeted by an unimpeded arctic wind. The unlikely autumn storm was on the side of the natives, who were accustomed to enduring bitter cold, while the soldiers were not. As the intensity of the storm increased and began to form an opaque whiteness in all directions, the Indians gradually disappeared through the curtain of swirling flakes into the vastness of the plains.

Since the army was not equipped to continue in such weather, they reluctantly set a course back toward base. The men, wearing only clothes for a fall campaign, shivering and numb, were only too glad to turn their backs to the north wind, and trudge back to the shelter of the canyons.

Glancing through the falling snow, Thomas was startled to see a phantom-like column of figures, seemingly trailing them, staying slightly behind, but along a parallel line to the northeast. At first, he thought they might be crouched Indians. He veered his horse toward them to get a better look but their easy movement always kept them the same distance away from his horse. He edged back into his column and pointed out the figures to Oswego. "A pack of wolves," he said, "the large lobos, hoping to find something we discard, or better yet, have some disabled animal stray too far from our midst. If a living thing gets far from its own circle in this part of the West, something'll eat it; this is a hungry country." Thomas stopped his horse and watched them intently; each ghostly figure showed a slight swaying motion as they glided forward, the pack moving in unison, coalescing into a single unit. He wondered aloud, do they dare to follow the Comanches in the same manner?"

"They frequently trail the nomads," said Oswego; "the moving villages always leave a trail of abandoned trash, including scraps of food."

Riding back off the escarpment and into the canyons, Thomas turned his horse and rode south back to the spot of his encounter from the day before. The three Comanche bodies were gone but blood, skin and bits of raw muscle were on the rocks. Stuck into the ground was a Comanche spear, and tied to the free end was a blond human scalp, the relic torn and shredded and smeared with the blood and entrails of a small animal. Thomas realized that there was yet another chapter in the enmity between these two tribes, the Comanches and the Blue Coats, waiting to be written, the Indians giving warning that no quarter would ever be given.

CHAPTER 19

Mackenzie knew many military men would consider this campaign a failure, but he and the men of the Fourth Cavalry had learned much about the Quahadi, and how to fight them on their home territory. He also had learned never again to expose a horse herd to the wily natives.

Thomas sought out the commander of the scouts, Lieutenant Boehm, who, like the old sergeant, was also a seasoned Indian fighter. "Sir, I don't understand the battle yesterday, when our six troopers were surrounded by more than a hundred Indians. The natives could easily have overridden us any time they wanted, but they only kept riding in circles."

"Yes, they could easily have overridden the six and killed them all," said Boehm, "but they would probably have lost one or more of their braves, and they never fight in a manner that would swap even one of their own for ten soldiers. If our troopers had not maintained their discipline and held their formation, and if their ammunition had not held out, they would all be dead, for Comanches instantly close on fleeing or disabled foes, but almost never charge a formation head on, even a small one, unless they are able to take it completely by surprise. The death of an enemy or anybody that is not Comanche, doesn't matter any more than a spit in the dust, but let them lose one of their own warriors, and they take it as a tribal catastrophe. That's why some of our soldiers don't think of them as brave fighters, but they are plenty brave; they just don't think a Comanche life should be traded for anything."

Back at Fort Richardson the Tonkawa scouts were released for the winter with plans to rejoin the army in the spring for renewed campaigns against the Plains Indians.

Colonel Mackenzie called Thomas to his office, singling him out for a one-on-one talk. He congratulated Thomas on his skill and commended him for his coolness under fire, but he also told Thomas that he was lucky. "These people we are fighting are formidable foes, and since we are in their territory they are usually more skilled than we are.

"You go off to yourself and engage as a lone warrior too often, and the Comanches are usually deadly when they catch a soldier alone or isolated. Don't think that the considerable skill you have acquired will always allow you to win out or that you can continually take chances and still stay alive." Thomas knew that he had taken rash chances, especially in taunting and then engaging the enemy without the close support of his compatriots, something that one with more experience would consider quite unwise.

He suggested to the colonel that his personal desire for revenge was so strong he had not been rational, but that he had been so devastated by his loss of a mother and sister that he had thought he would do anything to see that the Indians were punished.

"Neither a soldier nor a scout can let his own emotions take precedence over the mission of the entire army," said the colonel. "We are one force, with one mission, to subdue the Comanche Nation. We must always think accordingly. I have a war to win. This campaign is not a revenge fest and I cannot afford to lose a good scout just to gain a few scalps."

Colonel Mackenzie added that the Comanches were certainly a scourge to the Texans, but, in fairness, he noted, "you must also realize what a scourge we have been to them. We keep establishing settlements, encroaching more and more on their territory. Because they attack these encroachments, army headquarters has ordered that we either drive the Comanches back on the reservation, which means depriving them of their own culture, or else, that we annihilate them. Since we can never engage these guerillas in a frontal assault, we will do that by strategically attacking their camps, and destroying their homes, food stores, and families. I hope for the first of these alternatives, to drive them to the reservation, but if that does not come about, we will have a gruesome task; yet this is what President Grant and his cabinet say has to be done.

"I understand you speak Spanish," said the Colonel. "Yes Sir, my grandfather is a Tejano, and since my mother spoke it so well, she had us learn it and speak it as we grew up," Thomas answered. "I have also spent much time in my grandfather's home, where nothing but Spanish is spoken, and I have traveled in Mexico."

"Do you know what a Comanchero is?" asked the Colonel. "Yes Sir, it's a Mexican trader who traffics with the Plains Indians. They are generally from around Santa Fe or Taos, and I understand a few are Indians who come from the pueblos."

"Do you think you could go among them without their discovering who you really are?"

"Do you mean, become a spy?" asked Thomas.

"I guess that's what I mean," the Colonel responded.

"I could probably pass myself off as a half-breed Mexican along the Texas-Rio Grande border, because that is what I am," Thomas answered, "I don't know how I would do in New Mexico. I think I would stand out as different."

"We have good reason to know that there is a large and active network of Comancheros which operates in concert with the Comanche bands, and that barters with them for the livestock that they are taking from raids into Texas and Mexico. This trade is thought to be the basis for most of the trafficking in stolen goods and now is the major factor in keeping the Comanches an able, fighting force," said Mackenzie. "I believe that if we could ferret out more of their routes of trade, we could intercept them, and not only break the power of the Comanchero, but also stop most of the raiding into Texas. I intend to cross the Llano Estacado next year, first, to demonstrate to the Comanches that they no longer have free rein to wander and hunt across the plains as they please, and second, to learn to cope with the land and its conditions like the Indians do. Although I may chance upon some of the trading routes, I will by no means understand the entire system."

"It would take a very special person to be able to infiltrate this network, but I think with your background in Spanish, your skill as a scout and frontiersman, and after some intensive training, you might be the one to do it." Mackenzie pulled out the John Arrowsmith Map of Texas, dated 1843, and pointed out to Thomas the features of the Staked Plains, and the few known landmarks and trails in and around it. "I would want to teach you to become a map maker yourself, and I would also want to have you thoroughly indoctrinated into the New Mexico frontier culture."

"Would I be totally on my own, or would I have some authority?" queried Thomas.

"You would be an official agent of the United States Army, and after some training in San Antonio, you would be commissioned to your assignment," answered the Colonel. "You would then have the full backing of our country, but there is no doubt that you would be exposed to considerable danger, possibly finding yourself in circumstances where the authority of the U. S. Army was simply scorned. If you are successful and return in time from your trading trip across the plains, I want you to go into Northern New Mexico and see where all that livestock is being taken."

Thomas asked for time to think it over, and promised to say nothing to anyone but Oswego. He walked out of the office with a feeling of great exhilaration, because the colonel had made him feel important and extraordinary, though he did not totally recognize why an army colonel could give him such a sense of self-worth.

Thomas found Oswego, and they rode out away from the fort to talk. He told Oswego all that the colonel had said to him, and they discussed the mission from every angle, but in the end, Thomas had to decide whether or not he was willing to take such a risk for very little prospective personal reward. As Oswego knew he would choose to go, rationalizing that he still could not discard his personal vendetta, but in reality, because he was thrilled with the flattery and the new status the colonel was offering him.

"We are just like the Comanche braves," the Tonkawa said to himself, "above all else, we seek adulation from our own people." Thomas had been told he was special – an extraordinary person – and Oswego did not try to point this out to him. It was the right of the young to feel they were extraordinary and unique; they would be brought down to earth soon enough. Oswego knew that Thomas's attitude was, in a major part, his fault. He had taught the boy to be exceptional and to think of himself as out of the ordinary. He just hoped his young ward would not die as a result.

Thomas returned to the colonel with his answer. Mackenzie told him that after his military training in San Antonio, he was to study with a cartographer, who had been a useful consultant to the army. He was to learn the techniques of making and reading maps, and learn to calculate bearings, when traveling in a strange land. He also said he wanted Thomas to remain the rest of the year in San Antonio and in Paseo del Norte, then to travel up the Rio Bravo to perfect his Spanish and become very familiar with the New Mexican frontier society. "The mission could require as much as two years," the colonel stated. He gave Thomas a letter of introduction to any U. S. Army force he might encounter.

CHAPTER 20

The next morning, Thomas set out on the road to San Antonio. He was on a strong army horse and led another. This trail was now a very familiar one, and he was quite confident, though he always knew it was prudent to be very wary, especially when traveling alone. He left the Fort on the Concho River, with a feeling of exhilaration, a joy in the solitude – a time to take stock of himself, a time to mull over hopes and likely outcomes for the future, a time unfettered by the expectations of others.

On the third evening he approached the San Saba River, deciding that, one more time, he would visit the spot where his father had saved Oswego. He had the feeling that this was holy ground for him, now quite familiar and so ingrained into his being, that he could almost commune with his dead father at the site.

As he came to the top of the ridge that looked down on the valley containing the old Indian spring and camp, he saw four riders below with two pack mules. They certainly were not Indians, so he cautiously rode closer, leaving the main trail and swinging into the low trees, and far to the left, so that he could not be seen, either from above or below. Coming nearer he could tell that there were two men and two women, with the two pack mules heavily loaded. They appeared to be "Tejanos," as both men wore sombreros and both women had *sarapes* wrapped around their person. Thomas called out and then rode down to meet them.

"Como estan, senores?" Thomas ventured. His greeting was cautiously returned and they began to converse in Spanish, which seemed to make the four more comfortable. They were on a foraging

party for pecans along the river and creek bottoms of the hill country, and apparently had been quite successful. Thomas questioned them about the advisability of being in Indian Territory with such a small party. The Tejanos said that the pecan crop was so good this year that they had thought the risk worthwhile, especially because it was getting closer to winter and Indian raids were very infrequent this time of year. They did, however, tell Thomas that they were not alone in the region. They had seen several fresh horse tracks, mostly of shod animals, and were sure other riders were close by. They invited Thomas to join their camp for the night, both for the camaraderie and the extra protection. Thomas happily accepted the invitation.

The foragers were *campesinos* from just west of San Antonio. Thomas enjoyed the evening meal of tortillas, beans and venison, with a handful of pecans to shell. He enjoyed talking with the group in their own language. He did think they were naïve, being out here with no more protection or experience than they had. There were two muzzle loaders between them, weapons which couldn't be very accurate for any distance, usually sending bullets at random over the general direction in which they were pointed. However, one of the Tejanos had brought down the deer that they were eating.

Having already staked their animals, the foragers simply let the fire burn down and the two pairs made their bed close to the embers and went to sleep, apparently oblivious to any serious precautions. Thomas took his blanket and equipment off into the trees, and lay down in the middle of a brush thicket, staking his two horses away from those of the four campers.

Well after midnight Thomas sat up and listened intently. He had awakened to the sound of the snap of a twig and then he heard another, followed by the subtle noise of small chittering birds, as they were flushed from their perch and took wing. Thomas was well concealed so he knelt and waited. He could see all four of the slumbering company by the light glow of the dying fire. Thomas's eyes turned toward the tree line on the far side of the opening, the sense of danger outpacing the reality, though already sure that a menacing presence was on its way.

A huge figure emerged from the tree cover and walked out into the open circle. He was armed. Thomas guessed he was carrying a shotgun.

It was immediately evident that he was not Indian. His appearance was brutish, and Thomas imagined that his eyes were squinted as part of a cynical fat face, a feature that should accompany such a corpulent body. A rancid smell pervaded the air. The gun he carried in his right hand was pointed toward the ground.

The large figure stepped up to one of the sleeping men and gouged him with the toe of his boot. "Wake up, my sleepy friends," he said. "Don't you know that you're camping on my land, and you were not even polite enough to ask for my permission? I must tell you that you have angered me, and you must pay a price for such a disturbance." All four of the Tejanos were now sitting up, and were huddled together. "Ah ha," he said, as he raised his shotgun. "I see that you have brought us some women. We can make use of them, but *senors*, I am sorry, we have no use for you."

It was the last word he ever said. An arrow flew directly into the base of his neck, severing his trachea and lodging in the spine. He staggered as he tried to draw breath, but blood was already welling up into his mouth and throat, and as he fell, he triggered the shotgun which only sprayed into the fire, sending a myriad of tiny embers flying up into the darkness. The two couples were still cowering away from the body when Thomas said, "We need to move out as fast as possible! This bushwhacker is not out here alone even if he was careless enough to come into this camp without help, and also, someone unrelated to him may come upon this scene and misinterpret it." Thomas stood guard as the others gathered their things. They were packed and in their saddles in a matter of minutes. He had his group head back to the north for half a mile, then separate into pairs, veer first to the left, then circle back and intersect the trail, crossing it over a bed of gravel which would leave no prints. From there, they were to meet at the foot of a small peak which could be seen on the distant horizon, even in the fading moonlight. Thomas said he would be there first, and they would know where to assemble, by his call of the whip-poor-will.

Thomas and his party crossed the San Saba River before dawn, then, rode up the south side of the valley where they could look back over a mile of territory just as the morning sunlight gave it a clear illumination. Thomas stopped and began to scan the country over which they had traveled. He had a small Army sighting scope and he pulled it from his saddle bag and looked intently. "Six of them," he said, and pointed toward what the *campesinos* thought was nothing, but then the nothing began to move. With his scope Thomas could clearly see the leader. He was dressed as an Apache. "They have a tracker," he said. "This one has to be an expert to have followed us."

Thomas's mind was in a whirl. He knew he could outdistance the trailers, but he did not know how to do it without abandoning his companions. "We may have to leave the mules and their loads, He said, "but, not yet. We still need their tracks." Thomas was sure he knew the country better than those who were tracking him, so a plan began to evolve.

They rode down to the next creek which crossed their path, and Thomas led them single file four hundred yards down stream, carefully scanning the bank for a place to exit. He chose well. The bank was rocky, but not rocky enough to fool an expert tracker. The path was not only stony but was engulfed in a profusion of plants and tangled bushes and briars so that one had to bend right down to the back of his horse to get through. Branches had to be lifted for the mule packs.

As soon as his group had cleared the underbrush, Thomas pointed out the notch in the next rise for his companions to ride through, saying he was going to prepare a diversion, then catch up with them beyond the rise. He had his four friends lead his extra mount with the mules so he had only one horse to manage.

Quickly, he bent back a large elastic juniper branch protruding across the trail, tied it in place with his rope and stripped off the small limbs and greenery. He notched the back of an oak trunk against which the branch had been pulled, placed the bottom of a stick into the notch to use it as a lever, took some twine out of his saddle bag and tied it to the top of the fulcrum, then ran it down to the ground and across the trail to use as a trip wire. The strain on the twine was relieved by the length of the lever which held the limb in place close to the fulcrum. Thomas had practiced this technique numerous times with the Tonkawas, and he knew how to disguise the twine, and how to leave the tripping mechanism in a precarious state. He rode three hundred yards up the rise and picked a place where he could remain concealed but see the trail. He readied his rifle in case his ruse failed.

Within twenty minutes he could see the riders trailing the Apache down the stream. He heard the scout laugh as he found the place where they had exited the water, and Thomas watched him emerge from the stream, bending low to avoid the crossing branches. Suddenly the trap sprang, the limb breaking loose from its lock and hitting the tracker directly in the face, knocking him completely off his horse. Other riders quickly surrounded him, cursing in angry voices, but Thomas did not wait to hear more. He knew he could escape if they had no expert tracker.

Thomas and the four foragers traveled on but rode to the left of the beaten path. Three days later, the party crossed the Pinta Trail which led southeast to San Antonio, a trail long established, even prior to the frontier settlements, the path originated by the natives on their way to the welcoming headwaters of the San Antonio River. Thomas parted with his new friends at Sisterdale, a small German settlement on the Guadalupe River. While the Tejanos continued south, Thomas turned up river toward his family homestead on the headwaters of this same stream.

Thomas was surprised to see the home place looking completely tended. The fields were plowed, rows aptly contoured to the sloping land, even in width and depth, showing obvious careful husbandry. The fences were cleared of weeds and gates were all intact. He rode up to the house and called but no one was there. The house was as neat and clean as it had been in the past after his mother had finished her morning chores. He remounted his horse and turned up the trail beside the river that led to the Beasley home. About one hundred yards away, he began to hear loud voices and a barking dog. The noise came from outside the house, down toward the river. "This certainly doesn't sound like the Beasleys," he thought. He started to turn back, thinking he shouldn't appear during a family argument, when he made out the emphatic words, "get off our land." The voice sounded like that of Virginia. Thomas pulled his rifle from its scabbard and walked down toward the disturbance.

Mr. Beasley was confronting three men, Virginia standing at his side. Her jaw was clinched and her eyes narrowed. She had grown up on this land, their family wrenching it from the wilderness, and she stood there as though she would defend it like a tigress would defend her den.

The man talking to them was well-dressed but the other two appeared quite shabby. Mrs. Beasley was standing just off the porch and their two young sons were close to her. The dog was standing by Mr. Beasley growling at the three strangers. "Trouble is following me around like a lost puppy," Thomas thought to himself

"We have a valid claim to take the large cypress trees on both sides of the river and yer jist gonna hafta stay out of our way," said the stranger, "or else we're gonna hafta run ye off. I got this here paper sez it's my right, and that's the law."

"It may be your idea of a law, but there is no such law in Texas, and it holds no sway out here," interjected Thomas, as he stepped out into the clearing. Of the three men, only one appeared armed. He wore a holster, with a large pistol on his hip. Though Thomas spoke to all, he kept a fixed and steely stare on the one with the pistol, undoubtedly an Army issue Colt Forty-five.

"I don't know who you are, young sir, but we're from this shingle company…"

"Your company just went out of business," interrupted Thomas.

"Drop that rifle or I'll blow your head off," growled the one with the holster. Thomas turned slightly more toward the *pistolaro* and stood staring at him, rifle cocked and pointed in the direction of the man, the scout's jaw tensely clinched much like Virginia's.

"Jerome, I don't believe you'd better mess with this boy," advised the leader, "he's got a steely and confident look in his eye, and he seems to handle that rifle like an expert."

"You'd better heed what he says; it's the last warning you're going to get," said Thomas. The man froze, though his stare was brimming with malice. "If you want to keep breathing, don't look at me like that," said Thomas, "it makes me edgy." The man dropped his eyes to the ground.

Thomas glanced at the original speaker and asked him his name. "I'm Jesse Purvis, and these here, are jist my workers," he answered. The twang in his voice made Thomas remember the day his young Tonkawa friend, Two Bears, was slain on the Brazos. "May I ask who you are, young Sir."

"My name is Thomas Sutton and I'm a Texas Ranger and a scout for the U.S. Army."

"Be ye the son of the late Amos Sutton of the Texas Rangers?"

"That's right," returned Thomas.

"Boys," said Jesse, "We've made a bad mistake; let's get out of these people's way."

Thomas squinted at the gunman, "drop your belt and holster on the ground and step away." His voice was calm, but the inflection sounded stern and there was no hesitation in the message. Once more, the belligerent did as he was told. "You two others take out your weapons and put them in the same pile," Thomas ordered.

"We ain't got none," they both said. Thomas turned Jesse around and frisked him. He found nothing. He walked over to the other one, had him lie face down, and found a small pistol tied to his leg, just above his boot. Thomas took out the gun, had the man stand and cracked him on the back of the head. The intruder fell back to the ground, but Thomas kicked him in the ribs and told him to get up. Blood flowed from the back of his scalp, but he staggered to his feet.

Thomas turned to the holster wearer. "If you have any hidden weapon of any kind, put it on the ground now. If I find anything on you, you'll have no further warning, and we'll see who gets his head blown off." The man pulled a small knife from his boot and added it to the pile. "Now get out of here, and if anything bad ever happens to these people, I'll consider it your doing and I'll personally lead a company of Rangers, hunt you down, and hang all three of you from that cypress." The tree cutters lost no time in heading down the river, stumbling over cypress knees as they rushed away.

The reunion at the Beasleys was a joyous one, a reunion of hugs and tears, especially from Virginia, who held Thomas as though she would never let go. "At least, let him get his breath," said her mother. Thomas could feel the warmth of her body firmly pressed against his own as she clasped him around the waist, a clasp that unabashedly laid claim to his person and which gave him right to lay claim in return. He had felt nothing at all like this since he said good bye to Virginia when he left for the campaign. The feeling both startled and pleased him.

The evening was continued with a grand dinner, after which Thomas informed them that he was under orders from the Army to undertake a mission which might take as long as two years.

Virginia, certainly not pleased with the prospect of a two-year mission, saw her young life slipping by, her hopes of a future with Thomas, perhaps, in vain. She and Thomas sat on the porch and talked into the late hours, but it was obvious to her that he would not consider giving up his assignment nor his quest. She began to doubt if maturity would ever take hold and overpower the oath of vengeance he had held onto for so long.

Two days later, Thomas left for San Antonio and the hacienda of his grandparents.

After a three day trip to the city, he followed the general course of the San Antonio River southward. Ancient oaks spread their gnarled limbs over the sides of the streams, Spanish moss draping a curtain of nature's finery over the lower branches and engendering a feeling of tranquility over the scene. He rode up to the hacienda and tied his reins to the corral fence. Walking down the trail to the patio door, he peered in, where a small white-haired woman stood trimming a flower bush. She was stooped and wrinkles ran across her face and forehead. To Thomas, her features still evoked his memories of calm and kindness. "*Abuela*," he called softly. She turned and gasped in surprise, holding her arms out to him, tears already streaming down her face. "Oh Thomas, Thomas, we miss you so when you're away." She held one arm around his waist as she opened the door and called her husband; "Edwardo, God has sent us back our boy."

The three sat together, all feeling the deep emotional bond between them, each realizing that the blessing of this reunion might never occur again, each knowing that they constituted a dwindling family. They eagerly exchanged questions and answers with one another. Even in the short time he had been away, Thomas could see considerable difference in the old couple. Time was exacting its toll, a toll that had taken away much of the vigor and sparkle of former days. He told his grandparents stories of what he had seen and done, but omitted most of the violence. He told them nothing about the danger of his present mission, but did say that he was under binding Army orders and had no option but to finish his assignment. The grandfather told Thomas that this beautiful and prosperous hacienda was being saved for him, "You must come here to live and work and raise your own family," he almost pleaded. The grandson answered that he looked forward to the day he could return. "That day has not yet come, *Abuelo*. I owe it to the memory of my mother and sister to see this obligation through."

"Thomas," she said, "we would concede a lack of revenge for the death of our daughter and her child a thousand times, rather than not see you again." Thomas felt a sudden surge blush his neck and face, and his eyelids blinked rapidly to hold back tears, but they were too much, and he wiped his sleeve beneath his eyes. "When I first went out from the frontier, I admit my heart was set only on revenge, and I took dangerous chances, but I have grown past such thoughts and actions now. Within three or four years the frontier will be at peace forever, and the things that I can do will have helped make it so. I hope we all can take solace in that."

Colt .45 Revolver

CHAPTER 21

Thomas found the San Antonio Army Headquarters located in the Alamo, and reported to the commanding officer. He showed him his letter from Mackenzie and asked for his help in enrolling with the cartographer and then in traveling to El Paso. He also related the story of the bushwhackers at the springs north of the San Saba. The general told Thomas that there were many such gangs straying across the frontier, at times seeming worse than the Comanches, preying on anyone they think is weaker than they are, having no regard for any law, no remnant of human decency.

"Colonel Mackenzie has already written me, and has asked that I obtain some instruction for you," he said. "First I will send you to the Army for an abbreviated time of training, then, turn you over to the best teacher of Mexican culture in the United States. He is familiar with the land and life of the people along the Texas border and all the way from Mexico City to Santa Fe. He knows the Mexican frontier area intimately."

After an abbreviated stint of Army training and indoctrination, in which he solidified his sharp-shooting by practicing with hundreds of rounds of ammunition, he was returned to the general. The commander sent Thomas to one Carlos Huerta. Carlos took his assignment with the utmost seriousness. For weeks he conversed with his pupil totally in Spanish. Thomas ate every imaginable Spanish and Mexican dish, learning to, at least act like, he cared for jalapenos. Carlos told him what he might expect in Nueva Mexico that was different, even to things as minimal as blue corn tortillas. They wandered through the barrios of San Antonio, and went to the Mexican *cantinos*, and cockfights. They visited the small churches and the small farms. They went to see the *charros*, and Thomas mounted a borrowed horse and tried his own hand in their special kind of rodeo. Carlos even got Thomas in barroom fights, but intervened when the knives came out. He practiced with Thomas on how to fend off a knife-fighter, but advised him to always walk meekly in places of danger, and finally he taught him the actions and demeanor of a peon, telling him that he might be occasionally abused, but to just endure it, as part of his disguise. "Being meek and little noticed, will do more for your safety than any amount of bravado and fighting skill ever could. You will be going into a lonesome country, so prepare to keep most of your thoughts to yourself."

Next, Thomas went to his cartography school and studied, one on one, with his teacher. He became familiar with all the available maps of the area where he was going. Since he would not be able to take sophisticated instruments or survey equipment to establish his position on the plains, he was taught how to make crude judgments as to where he was, just by using his knowledge and memory of maps and landmarks, his reminiscence of distances he had traveled, and by orientation via sightings of the heavens at night. He did carry a pocket compass. He learned how to make close estimates as to the distance he had traveled, how to use triangulation to estimate altitude and distance, and how to record his findings so they would be legible to a cartographer. He memorized the few known elevations of the landmarks of the area where he might operate, and learned all of the Spanish names and any known Indian names of the different landmarks, arroyos, and streams.

Two months later, the Army dispatched a group of twenty raw troopers to Paseo del Norte, passing over the upper road so they could drop off supplies to the forts along the way and exchange some personnel. The caravan and the enlisted men were to be accompanied by one officer and three veteran sergeants. The soldiers welcomed Thomas, being very happy to have an experienced scout along. One other assignment of the soldiers was to escort two civilian business people wanting to get some goods to Paseo del Norte, and at the request of the Archbishop, a young, recently ordained Franciscan Friar, named Dominic Castaneda, on his way to the church in Ysleta, was allowed to join the caravan. Three army wagons pulled by four mules each and an extra set of four spare mules, in case of complications, were included in order to freight a load of supplies to both Fort Davis and Fort Bliss. The business men had only one small wagon with only a span of mules.

The party started out of town on the old Pinta Trail that went through the settlements of Boerne, Sisterdale, Caine City, and Fredericksburg; then on to Fort Mason, where they dropped off a few supplies, and picked up an additional six troopers who had already attained some frontier experience, and were no longer needed in the fort where they were serving. From Mason, they traveled by the ruins of the ancient San Saba Mission, where, in 1758, the Comanches attacked and burned the isolated compound, killing most of the mission workers. "The savages haven't evolved toward anything more civilized in more than a hundred and twenty years," said Thomas. The priest looked at him and smiled, "I have great sorrow for the Christians who perished here, but none of us ever recognized that we Spanish moved into this territory, not as invited guests, but as self-proclaimed superiors, with the intention of enforcing our ideas with the use of Spanish arms. It does not usually occur to us that the Indians' purpose might simply have been to defend their home territory from foreign invasion."

It was on to Fort McKavett for a one-day-and-night stopover, before winding northwest to intersect the middle fork of the Concho River, following it to its source, then proceeding across a barren, water-sparse stretch to Horse Head Crossing on the Pecos River. From the Pecos, the trail continued westward to Comanche Springs and the community of Saint Gaul, then further southwest to Mescalero Springs, and on to Fort Davis. The trek from Fort Davis to the Rio Grande was the last dangerous leg of the expedition. Once they reached the river there would be well-worn trails and available supplies on into Paseo del Norte and Fort Bliss.

The first part of the trip was routine, with considerable boredom in riding long stretches of open country accruing to those of only an urban orientation, but much the opposite to those who loved the open spaces and delighted in seeing nature's grand display. Fort McKavett was newly built, Colonel Randal Mackenzie having been placed in charge of revamping the fort after its dereliction during the Civil War. The buildings were recently erected and made of stone, the inside of the barracks and the utility buildings were whitewashed, and the fort sat on a grassy hill close to the springs giving rise to the head waters of the San Saba River. The company spent only one night at the fort and moved on.

Thomas took the young priest under his wing and endeavored to teach him some of the insights of the outdoorsman. The curate had been schooled in New Orleans, then sent to San Antonio, and now was to be head of his first parish. Thomas knew that he was very intelligent, but considered him somewhat naïve to the ways of the world. Dominic was an accomplished scholar and Thomas began to relish riding with him just to listen to the young curate discuss Spanish culture, history, and world politics, the like of which was very seldom available in such a traveling party, most enlisted men, mule skinners, and frontiersmen sharing in a total abstinence of anything learned.

The prelate was quite open to learning what Thomas knew, mostly about the local flora and fauna, and the interrelation of the two with climate and topography, the essence of the ecology of the great outdoors, which he was now minutely observing for his first time. He endeavored to fathom what it meant to be in wild country and to enjoy it like Thomas, but the starkness of the grey land, its unordered forms, and its vast distances offended his sense of aesthetics.

Thomas intuited what was transpiring in his friend's mind. "The reason you can't see the beauty of this land is that your eyes are not yet trained to see it. The appreciation of the beauty of the West only comes to those who want to see it and will work to develop a perception which is keen enough to recognize it. Here in the desert it lurks in unexpected places. The visual joy afforded to you in the green and lush world in which you grew up served you well in that region, but the subtle pastel colors of the earth you see in the west will take both time and training to appreciate and enjoy. Your eyes have not yet adjusted to such a country."

Thomas taught the priest how to cook his own meals, find the most comfortable available place to sleep, search for water and food and, most of all he began to indoctrinate him on how to be wary of the dangers of the open, unsettled territory. In turn, Dominic decided he must work to save the soul of this fellow traveler, so he started gently delving into religious subjects: salvation, faith, and love, even for one's enemies.

Respect for the enemy Thomas could fathom – but love, no! "You have to understand, priest!" said Thomas, "my relation with the enemy is not just theoretical. The enemy raided our home and wantonly murdered my mother and little sister, then disfigured and scalped them, for no reason except their savagery. The only way I will love this enemy is when he ceases to draw breath." Thomas told the priest about his pursuit of the Comanche killer immediately after the raid on the Guadalupe, and of the Indian's subsequent escape when he and Oswego thought they were about to confront a war party, and finally, of his life-long and determined quest for revenge. He related vivid stories about the cruelty of the Indian depredations, but Dominic thought he had no mature concept of the depredations of the Whites upon the Indians.

He told Dominic about the continuing yearly raids during the Comanche moons of the late summer and early fall in which the Indians not only captured livestock, but took women and children prisoners, and viciously dismembered and scalped any others who crossed their path. Thomas said the Comanche held in equal regard the animals they had stolen and the captives they had claimed, except they did not intentionally torture the livestock.

Dominic steadfastly held that the Indians, too, are God's children, and that Christ bids us to offer them the path to salvation as well as to our own. "If we let the Indians in on these concepts, they, too, may feel the power of a loving God, and turn away from violence."

Thomas, in turn related to the priest the Quaker experience as Indian agents on the reservation, and how they have attempted to pacify the Indians with kindness and love. "The army and rangers consider the policy nothing but ludicrous politics and it has done nothing but make the situation worse, as the Comanches use the reservation as a haven when they need it, draw their allotments of supplies from the government, then continue their raids on the Texas and Mexico frontiers whenever they desire."

"Perhaps the Quaker effort will some day bear fruit, even in ways we may not be able to see," said the cleric. His own thoughts were that much of the failure was because the missionaries were not Catholic, but he chose not to venture upon that argument with Thomas.

"One must first accept God and his divine son," said Dominic, "then, one uses faith to carry oneself through the doubts and the vicissitudes of life. Once you have faith, you no longer have use for arguments.

"This, I do know!" Dominic emphasized, "I only have the ability and steadfast courage to go out into this wilderness, and face its hardship and danger, and endure the extreme loneliness which I must endure, because of my faith in God, and His holy purpose."

"I don't understand this thing you call faith," said Thomas, "but in your choice of profession and your destination, your courage is likely to be severely tested."

Thomas knew he hadn't the ability to debate theology with Dominic so he decided that further discourse had no purpose. "You have indeed bitten off a difficult task," he said. "I wish you well." He then spurred his horse and caught up with some of the other members of the caravan, and rode on through the day. When night came, however, he again sought out the young priest and helped him make camp for the night.

Pecos River

CHAPTER 22

As the convoy reached the headwaters of the middle fork of the Concho, the water in the river began to be only a trickle and the soldiers knew they were in for a rather dry trek to the Pecos. The last ten miles up the Concho, the stream bed was only a bottom of flat limestone, crusted by the salts of evaporated water, easy to cross by simply stepping over the occasional small pools which joined one to another by small rivulets of tepid liquid, the limited flow inching forward to form another pool where the creek bed had used one of the limestone ledges to form another small dam, the balance between flow and evaporation almost equal. Every two to three hundred yards the ledge would be high enough to form a pond six to twelve inches in depth. For the last three miles upriver the water alternately came to the surface for a few feet, then, disappeared beneath the rocks, to appear once again farther down the stream bed. Farther west, they encountered only dry ravine.

Dominic had noted that for the last three days of their proceeding into the west, the landscape kept being progressively depleted of green pigment, the earth covered with ocher and other red tones, grey ledges, and white caliche. "I am a long way from New Orleans," he said to himself.

Thomas was approached by the military captain and asked if he would ride on ahead and scout out the watering places between the Concho and the Pecos to see if the area was passable with their wagons and teams. The plan was for the convoy to stay in place where adequate water was still available until he returned. The priest begged to go with the scout, and though it was against his better judgment, Thomas relented. He did, however, see that Dominic's horse and gear included an extra canteen and a rifle with considerable ammunition. When the priest protested, Thomas told him they might have to hunt for food for the convoy and, thus, both of them needed the rifles.

After leaving the vicinity of the creek bed, the two riders continued west, over miles of unturfed ground, the ocher powder cauterized by the bleaching sun, the sun unimpeded by a cloudless sky. The only interruption of the monotonous plain was the occasional appearance of greasewood, creosote bush, cholla, or, very rarely, a struggling mesquite, all plant life widely separated, as there was not sufficient moisture for a density of growth. The only animal life to be seen was a sporadic lizard, and even for these creatures, nature's predator, the chaparral which the Mexicans called *paisano*. Thomas pointed out that the creosote bush does not share any water with adjacent flora, because it exudes a toxin in the soil that keeps other plants from growing nearby.

From the river headwaters, they first sought out the Mustang Ponds, located in the sand dunes deposited against the southern escarpment of the Llano Estacado. The arid country reached out to form a vast and grisly cyclorama of wasteland for the two horsemen to behold. As far as the eye could see the desert rolled on, the sides of the trail strewn with the residue of previous cattle drives, decayed and decaying corpses of steers and horses. Occasionally a cross driven into the ground indicated that humans were susceptible to death by desiccation as well.

The Mustang Ponds were relatively easy for Thomas to find, but they contained only a trace of tepid water. About twelve miles farther west, they encountered the Flat Rock Ponds which consisted of several small basins, spring-fed by outcrops of the Edwards limestone. Myriads of Indian pictographs were graven on the rocks, and mortar holes were scattered on the surface of the flat limestone. Dominic studied them intently. Thomas walked up to him. "Do you feel like you are standing on holy ground?"

"One cannot help being humbled by the marks of centuries of human habitation, and the reflections these people harbored about their surroundings."

It was obvious that the graven images and the utilitarian mortar holes were quite ancient, existing long before any contact with the whites. "Does it bother you that none of these artists and artisans had the benefit of knowing about your God or His salvation?" scoffed Thomas. "How were these people to be saved?"

There was water for themselves, and their animals, but certainly no abundance. Thomas considered there was enough for the caravan to come this way, though because of the slow trickle of water to the surface, they might have to take half a day to water the stock. The two pathfinders quickly moved on, making a cold camp that night, close to, but slightly removed from the main trail. A tiny amount of bunch grass was found for the horses in and around the mouth of the draws, but when it came time to bed down, Thomas brought the animals in close to where they slept, cross hobbled them, and also staked them with their lariats. This seemed an extravagant precaution to Dominic who thought Thomas was putting on a bit, but he said nothing.

The next morning they were riding well before sun-up and before noon were at the Wild China Ponds where they located a group of small holes that had formerly been filled with water, though none was present now. The ephemeral watering holes were surrounded by a small stand of dwarfed soapberry trees. "It seems unfair," said Dominic, "that the trees have roots that can reach down to have a drink, and we can have none. Both had their last canteen less than half full, and Thomas felt very foolish that he had let himself use his reserves so rapidly. He carefully restricted the use of their remaining water and for the first time in his life Dominic began to feel the agony of thirst. "How long can we go on like this if we find no water at the next spring?" asked Dominic. "With the little water we have left, about two more days," answered Thomas. "You will know what suffering is if we have to travel waterless all the way to the river before we can have another drink."

A day's ride to the west brought them to a split running through the Castle Mountains, the historic landmark of Castle Gap. In the narrow pass, they, at last, found a small pool made by a seep from the side of the rift; water that had fallen from the sky months ago was swallowed by the land surface and had slowly percolated through the limestone to this place of freedom, only to be swallowed again. "*Weick Pah*," said Thomas, "the Comanche words for gap water. I have read about this spring on old maps. This narrowed gap has been the crossing place out of the Pecos region for as long as people have inhabited this land."

Since there was only a trickle of water available at the spring, the two took almost an hour to slake their own thirst and fill their canteens. It took another two hours for the horses to get water, but they rode on before the animals were completely satisfied. The narrow part of the gap had walls almost perpendicular, with immense cacti growing out of the crags between boulders. The two riders looked down from the pass onto the greasewood plains of the Pecos valley, the stream only twelve miles away, but there was no sign of a river from where they stood. "Come to the desert and let its vastness stretch your soul," quoted the priest.

Just before dusk, as the heat was abating, Thomas walked a short way into the brush with his bow and arrows to see if he might find a rabbit, his choice of weapon dictated by the fear that sound from a rifle might travel a long distance and thus arouse an enemy. Dominic thought this action would provide meat to cook, so, trying to be helpful, he had a small fire burning when Thomas returned with his game. "What in the world are you doing?" exclaimed Thomas as he stomped out the fire. "Do you want to let every Indian within fifty miles in any direction see the smoke and know that we are here?" Dominic was quite chagrined and quickly began to help scrape dirt over the fuel.

"We have to move," said Thomas. "We cannot chance the likelihood that that we have been detected by the Apaches. The Comanches used the word of their Ute cousins and called them *tontos* (fools), but they were masters, not fools, of this desert land. The two travelers ate raw rabbit and then topped off their canteens, drank all they could and brought the animals up for another try. They rode back east to the level of the plain, then, ascended about a mile up a dry gulley away from their original camp being careful to walk over bare rocks to conceal their tracks. They stopped where the walls of the gully widened out, but where the banks were high enough to conceal their horses. Once again they slept next to the horses but this time, Thomas insisted that the possibility of the Indians having seen smoke from their fire constituted a threat, so they alternated with one another at standing guard to watch for hostiles and avoid the possibility of a surprise attack.

Dawn saw them again on the move, and already far back down the gulch, this time leading their mounts in order to maintain a profile lower than the horizon. Thomas insisted that both of them carry their rifle in hand. Dominic said that was foolish because he would never shoot at another human being, but Thomas insisted that even the appearance of a rifle could serve as a deterrent against trouble. As the two came to the end of the gully where it breaks completely out of the watershed of the Castle Mountains and onto the flat below, it was now possible to see in all directions. Waiting for them, both to the left and to the right sides of the dry delta, were six mounted Apaches, sitting immobile, on their horses, watching them emerge from the arroyo. Threateningly, two of the warriors rode across their escape route toward the open country, a definite gesture of malice. Dominic could plainly see their faces which were hard and grim, their skins blackened by the desert winds, winds of a moving furnace fueled by the unremitting sun. Though his heart was pounding, he murmured to himself, "God's blessings upon you; brothers in Christ." Thomas had his rifle in his hands, but pointed it at no one.

As if led by a choirmaster, the Apaches began howling in unison and brandishing their weapons. Then, they charged. Thomas, who was not in the saddle, knelt upon one knee, aimed his carbine and shot, knocking the lead warrior from his horse.

Inexplicably, Dominic dropped both his horse's reins and his rifle and started fleeing back up the draw. "Come back!" shouted Thomas, "you're committing suicide!" but the priest ran on. He had not gone fifty feet farther, until he saw another mounted Apache slide down the embankment into the arroyo directly in front of him. "Oh Heavenly Father no," he screamed, and turned again to flee back toward Thomas. With a blood curdling whoop the Apache bore down on the novice, but Thomas's carbine sang out with a whine followed immediately by an audible thump, and the horseman fell abruptly to the ground, the riderless pony continuing down the draw past Dominic and toward the horses of the other Apaches. Thomas whirled in the opposite direction toward the oncoming foe, and the carbine exploded for the third time, the horse of the lead rider lurching to the side and then falling heavily against the bank. By the time the horse hit the ground, his rider was already clear of the saddle and running for cover.

A beating sound arose and then hovered above the din as a large owl took wing from the nearby grove of scrubby trees, and flew directly over Thomas and his friend. The Apaches pointed to the bird, and immediately whirled their horses and sped away back toward the gap. "What has happened?" cried the astounded Dominic. "I think we have just been saved by an owl, a bird some Apaches take as an evil omen," said Thomas.

Dominic walked back to the dead Apache who had charged him. Even in death, his hand was still clinched around his weapon. Dominic glared at the clinched fist of the infidel, bent down, and loosened the stilled fingers, took the rifle and dashed it against the ground. The priest dragged him into the shade and made the sign of the cross over the corpse.

The two men mounted their horses and warily started back down the trail toward the troops and wagons. Thomas told the young priest that it was a common belief among many Indians of the Southwest, that the owl was an evil omen, and that the Indians who had such a belief would not ever continue with an action which had been despoiled by the blight of an owl. He said nothing about Dominic's behavior during the fray.

For miles Dominic spoke not a word, morose and badly shaken, even his horse seeming to reflect the priest's feelings, plodding along with his neck pointed toward the ground, making his head appear bowed. Thomas was also searching his soul to know what to say. He had just demonstrated to Dominic that he was better at violence than the savages were.

Finally Dominic spoke. "I know you can see that my claim of a life dedicated to God and faced with vigilance and courage is absolutely fraudulent. I have no escape from the fact that I am an abject coward, and, in time of crisis, think only of myself. God has tested me and found me unacceptable. My duty is to return and bury the Apaches and accept my fate in the desert."

"Who are you to interpret the mind of God, and decide for Him what is and is not acceptable?" retorted Thomas. "What you need is to get out of your self-contrived world, and start trying to recognize life and this creation as they really are. In the first place, the dead Apaches are no longer there. Their bodies have long since been retrieved by their people. What you did back there was natural, and you must recognize yourself as limited by what nature has bestowed upon you. It is the nature of an animal or a human to flee from dire danger." Thomas told him the stories of the Rangers who abandoned Oswego, and of the army captain and his troops fleeing from the swirling Comanches on the Llano, leaving the remaining six troopers to their fate. "These were all brave men, but, in the face of mortal danger, they couldn't rise above their natural instincts for self-preservation. There was a saying among the old battle-worn cavalry sergeants that there is no such bravery in the heat of battle as on the road thereto. Were you coming out here, to this howling wilderness, thinking you were already prepared for whatever the West would present to you?"

"You think of yourself as part of nature, and you did not run," returned Dominic.

"There have been plenty of times in my life that I ran, and this time was one when I wanted to." He told Dominic about the time on the Brazos when he hid in the river while his friend was scalped alive. "I have spent the last twelve years being schooled not to run from Indians in a situation such as this one, because it only makes your circumstances worse. If you had trained those same twelve years, you probably would have done better than I."

Dominic could not let himself off that easily. "There is no escaping the meaning of what I have done, and the recognition of what I am," he said. "The happening causes me to feel like all my previous life has been wasted. If there is any way for me to continue in the service of the church I have to start over while realizing how worthless I am without the help of God."

Thomas related to him the incident of finding the strip of purple cloth tied to his horse's rope on the way back from the Fort Sill Reservation, and how the experience totally wiped out his arrogant supposition of self-sufficiency. "Only the slow ticking of time removes the desperate heartache you suffer from this awareness," said Thomas. "In my hour of this same circumstance, I was told that all I could do was to persist. If you are willing to endure, the endurance will make you whole again.

"Oswego says that we human beings are not entities but ever changing processes. I believe he is right."

The two horsemen wound their way back through the dust to the column without much else said between them, each man discrete unto himself, but the two conjoined in their youthful quest for greater understanding of the order of creation and of their own inadequacy. They rode across a forsaken land, the only flora of the region, withered and thorny, the only fauna seen this day, the buzzards, ever circling in search of death. Both young men rode on, deeply absorbed in their own thoughts.

CHAPTER 23

When they got back to the column, Dominic was surprised, but also relieved, that Thomas said nothing about their encounter with the Apaches. He only mentioned that there were abundant, fresh Indian signs in the area, and, probably, extreme danger. He told them that they would need all their reservoirs completely filled with water, and they must constantly conserve every drop, but that they could make it to the Pecos.

After a night in a safe camp, the two explorers guided the column on a three-day trip by the waterholes, on through Castle Gap, and then the twelve miles through the greasewood plains to the Horse Head Crossing of the Rio de Cicuye, or Pecos River. As advertised, the mostly barren soil on both sides of the river was littered with sun-bleached bones from the livestock which had perished there, usually from the rapid intake of too much salt-laden water. A few fresher corpses were littered about, but they were already shriveled and darker than adobe, curling into leathery decay even before the bloating had disappeared. "First the sun turns you to jerky, and then the blowing sand bares your bones," said one of the sergeants. Numerous horse skulls were impaled on the dead snags of the scrubby mesquite trees nearby. The travelers took in the scene, enduring it, even more than seeing it – the desperate and dread feeling of men plying through the land of insufficient water.

The stream looked more like a crooked canal than a river, the water alien to the land it traversed, the land to the west giving no respite to the eye, affording no point of focus upon the brushy plain from the river to the horizon. A flock of wild ducks arose from the narrow channel, circled out to the west and set their course up-river, never out of sight of the winding stream which coursed through the blistered land below. The ducks flew in formation, twisted and turned as one, as if offering their audience a sky dance.

One could walk within a few yards of the flowing water without even knowing it was there, as almost no bloom of nature defined its border from the surrounding country. There was no great corridor of green paralleling its course, only dust and a thin line of mesquite trees extending to the very edge of the precipitous bank which descended vertically into the turbid water. The two merchants who had accompanied the column walked over to stare down at their own images, but the swirling eddies and suspended gypsum blighted out even their noonday reflections, leaving only their ill-defined shadows.

Just to the south was the crossing; where the water seemed to free itself from the confines of the narrow channel, the river banks were hewn down to a gradual slope, the water spreading out into a shallow pan. Horses and mules were frantic to get to the water, and when freed to do so, ran to the edge and waded on out to midstream, plunging their noses into the bitter mixture, shaking their muzzles back and forth as if to oar away some film of contamination, but when the bitterness of the water would not go away, they drank huge gulps, the boluses visibly rippling along the bottom of their necks with each passing swallow. Intermittently, the animals would raise their heads, coming up for rest, drops of dark fluid falling from their thick lips. Even though the river flowed, it reeked with the odor of stagnation and the bitterness of the alkali it flowed through, but the column had no choice but to replenish, both men and animals, with the only thing nature had provided.

From the Pecos crossing, the column continued west, riding toward the Mexican border. They passed through a land-form of rock and dust, with meager flora, nearly all of which consisted of spined things. They rode by Comanche Springs and the adjacent settlement of Saint Gaul, a motley assembly of *jacals* and shacks, destitute, desolate, and dilapidated. They rode on, passing close to the foot of the mountains, through land of sparse, widely separated, and withered bunches of grass, the desert surface punctuated by *sotol, lechuguilla,* and limey rocks.

At night, they bivouacked on the open plain. To the west they could see the looming, violet cordillera silhouetted against the fading light of the heavens. Lightening assaulted the night sky, and scintillated across the tops of the ridges, the momentary and distant flashes giving testament to how vast the land was that they were passing through.

As darkness settled, Dominic often walked to the edge of the encampment and stared into the distance, as though weighing whether distance itself might be the enemy. He remembered having felt alone back in the South after he had made his life decision to go into the priesthood, but in that land he was alone with God. Here he seemed alone with himself. He would wake in the night unsure of where he was, having dreamed of this hinterland, this barren distance, this loneliness and isolation, questioning whether he had wandered too far, wandered even beyond the realm of what he held holy. He lay beneath his blanket, half conscious, restless, and fretting, wondering in his cloudy, sleep-deprived mind whether he had actually discovered hell. He would toss and turn trying to drive the fear from his soul until he was finally crushed back into sleep from the weariness of the long days on the trail.

The company paused at Barilla Springs, an oasis, a welcome place of quenching, then, continued south toward Fort Davis, entering the mountains, and climbing through the two mile Wild Rose Pass, coming to a canyon carved by Limpia Creek. The running water was clear, sweet, and cool. Giant, ancient cottonwood trees arose from the adjacent alluvial plain, many still endowed with pictographs from the days the site was known as Painted Comanche Camp.

As the wagons labored over the rough stony path, one of the older sergeants, their best mule skinner, dozed off, allowing a front wheel to hit a large sharp rock, the impact throwing the sergeant off his seat and under the rolling wheel of the wagon. Everyone scrambled to restore order, but the mule skinner's leg was broken and the train, with no extra seasoned driver, had considerable difficulty with the mule team as they trudged on into Fort Davis.

The fort was located on a flat, nestled between the creek and the steep edge of the mountains, tall basalt turrets rising from the valley floor to serve as sentinels – stark, impregnable – the guardians of the lonely citadel. The wagon train and its company halted for two days at Fort Davis, making their camp between the troop barracks and the creek, among the age-stained cottonwoods.

The young officer, Dominic, Thomas, and the two merchants were entertained with an elegant dinner at the home of the commanding colonel and his wife – a most welcome interlude from everyday camp life for the travelers. It was news from home and a brief respite from the monotony of the wilderness to those stationed in this forlorn outpost. After the meal, the officer of the train turned to the fort commander: "We have lost one of our wagoners from a broken leg and need to leave him here in your hospital. We're having considerable difficulty with our balky mules since we lost our driver, and I'm a bit desperate to get the rest of our load to Fort Bliss. Do you have a good mule skinner you could loan us?"

"We have one," returned the colonel, "a colored corporal, who used to haul cotton along the Mississippi in his slave days. As white folks like to say, he has a rapport with mules. He's too valuable for us to lose, but we'll loan him to you until you get to Bliss and you can send him back on the stage."

Following the party, Thomas and Dominic walked down by the creek, where they could hear the gurgling stream while gazing up at the moonlit mountains. By chance, they came upon a lone trooper, himself strolling beside the water. The two quickly engaged him in conversation. He was a Buffalo Soldier, one of a regiment of black troopers, now stationed at this isolated bastion of the West.

"Where are you from, soldier?" asked Thomas. "New Orleans, suh," he responded. Dominic told him of his student days in New Orleans, and they quickly became animated in discussing places they both knew.

"What do you miss most from back home, corporal?" continued Thomas.

"Ah misses the mud."

"The mud?"

"Yesah, when your feet was hot at home you could walk down by the river and the cool mud would work up between your toes and give you a feeling of heaven. If you bare your feet out here, you're lucky if you just get rocks between your toes; most likely you get cactus."

"Have you ever had to fight the Apaches?"

"Yes suh, we ran into a group of twelve, who was raid'n some settlers east of here. We charged straight into the buggers and they scattered like a bunch of quail. We never saw none of 'em again. Mostly we don't fight, we just drill, sweep, and tend to the stock. Sometimes we give escort to the stage when it comes through on its way to Paseo del Norte."

"Your officers must have been very proud of your charge," said Dominic.

"We was proud of ourselves. Most soldiers hope for praise from the officers, but Buffalo Soldiers jist hope to be spared censure."

"Are you lonely out here?" asked Dominic.

"Suh, jist talkin' to you tonight will probably be the highlight of my year. There ain't no decent women, and except for a few officers and their wives, there ain't no decent white folks neither. The only enjoyable thing, there are a few good horses and mules to work with."

"What are you going to do after your five-year stretch is up?"

"I'm goin' back to the Mississippi, where they's girls wants to get married, and where you get a little bit of meat in your greens and pot liquor, even if it's hog jowls or only an old possum."

Before the caravan continued on, Thomas had a chance to talk again with the fort Commander. He related what the soldier said about his fight with the Apaches.

"Many of the officers were quite dubious about the fighting ability of black troops in their first years, but they have proved themselves to be as good fighters as any troops we have. I hope to imbue my officers with a more appreciative attitude. It's interesting to note that the desertion rate for the colored troopers is about one tenth as much as it is for the white enlisted men. I think it's because they have more will to make something of their lives since they were only very recently freed from slavery. You'll get to know more about this corporal on your journey to Paseo del Rio," he added. "He's our resident mule skinner, the one I told you about last night."

Corporal Dobie Chance was his name. He was informed of his new assignment when he got back to the barracks from his stroll by the creek, and he was out handling the mules before daylight. He let the animals smell him, and he smelled them. He began to muzzle-feed them small tastes of corn by hand. When harness time came, he asked to do that all by himself. He brushed down the animals, putting grease on the galls along their withers, and checked the shoes on all sixteen feet. While he was putting on the collar pads, then the collars and hames, he actually crooned to the team. "You the best two spans of mules I seen around these parts in a long time."

The teams were in their traces and hitched to the singletrees just after sunup, and the officer in charge signaled for the train to move out. Reins flapped on animal rumps, and occasionally a whip cracked, but Dobie just chucked to his four. He leaned forward on the wagon seat, his knees extending out as a brace for his sinewy forearms, his large calloused hands forward and resting, their long black fingers interlaced with the reins, the leather lines only quivering when he gave the faint flip to go, the quivers barely perceptible as they oscillated down the lines to gently vibrate the bridle bits, but the mules surged forward, their powerful breasts pressing against the collars, and the wagon began to roll. "Hyah! Look sharp you Army Mules, you's on review!" Long ears flicked alertly forward, as if in salute, and the wagons wheeled out of Fort Davis.

Two miles farther up the canyon, as the progress became routine, Thomas tied his horse to the back of Dobie's wagon and crawled up on the seat beside him. "They tell me you're the best mule skinner in the territory," he repeated.

"A mule skinner is somebody who's s'posed to be smarter than a mule," said the trooper. "That's just man talk, ain't no mule agrees with that. I've worked with lots of mules but I ain't never worked with one that warn't smarter'n me."

"Then how do you get along with them so well?"

"I just try to act like a mule, like I was their mother looking after 'em, making sure they's fed and watered and their feet ain't sore and their hurt'n places is tended to. I just try to think how I'd want to be treated if I was a mule." At first Thomas thought Dobie's philosophy a bit primitive, but the longer he rode with him, day after day, the more he admired the trooper, his accommodation to his lot in life, and the clear mastery he had of the tools with which he labored.

"I want you to teach me how to drive a team like this," said Thomas.

"I'll try," Dobie answered, "but you got to be born with a rhythm in your hands and ain't everybody that's got it." By the end of the week, however, the pupil was driving like a veteran. Dobie told him he was a "natural." Thomas loved the ordeal; something mesmerizing resided in the action of these hybrids, their flopping ears in rhythm with their striding haunches, their lot in life, only to bear the burdens of the moment, to leave no progeny, no record of themselves except the work they had done, their only expectation for the future, a bucket of corn and a bit of hay, the only assignment nature required of them: "Be yourself, be a mule."

When the caravan reached the pass where the wagon train had to come out from the Limpia Valley, the incline looked formidable. The young officer came back and asked Dobie how they usually went about it. The mule skinner told him that it was so hard to get ordinary teams to pull over the pass that it was nicknamed Mule Flayers Trail. He persuaded the officer to hook eight mules at a time to take the wagons over the top, and even though this was slow, it was well worth the trouble. Dobie, himself, rode one mule and guided the eight mule teams to the crest. The remainder of the day was taken up by resting the animals and the hard labor of rearranging and stowing the supplies which had been bumped and bounced out of place as they had gone over the rocky pass, but when they topped out, they all could look down to the Marathon Plains spread below.

Thomas sat very still on the wagon seat. "I thought when I saw the Llano Estacado I had never seen so much space. Here, I've never seen so much land."

"It ain't what you sees, your eyes don't know what it is they sees, it's what you feels that's important," said Dobie. "To understand this land you got to be one of them people who reaches outside hisself. You knows you is kin to all this some way, but you hafta reach out with more than jist your eyes to understand why."

"It's times like these that make me wish I was a painter," said Thomas. "Some of the officer's wives tries to paint the desert," Dobie told him, "but that ain't possible. It'd be like paint'n God. People want to paint it, or pick up stones or other little pieces of it so they can decorate their yards and houses and make the desert belong to them. They's wrong, they jist need to let theirselves belong to it." Thomas tried to penetrate the meaning of what was being said to him, but it was more than he could sort out. Was it that Dobie was unable to express what he was feeling or was it that he, Thomas, hadn't the capacity to understand? At least he understood this much; Dobie was trying to ponder the Great Mystery himself, and to recognize his own kinship to it.

The train stopped for the night at the Pineries, a small sawmill and spring on the southern slope of the mountains garrisoned and worked by only four of the Buffalo Soldiers. As Dobie unharnessed each mule, fed it the daily supply of corn, and finally staked the animal so that it could graze on what little vegetation there was, he gently slapped each mule on the haunch. The gentle slap was almost a caress, but he wanted to be sure that each animal was touched, the time-honored "laying on of hands," a soothing feeling, an action bonding one being to the other.

He was glad to see some of his own friends, and he camped with them that evening. Thomas and Dominic could hear all five of them singing late into the night.

CHAPTER 24

The caravan headed southwest out of the mountains, traveling through a strange desert. Relics of ancient lava flows in the form of basalt outcroppings rose above the flat land and peered down from their towering outposts. Scattered herds of pronghorns dotted the distant flats, the small herds sparse and long miles apart, as were the limited crisped plots of grass upon which they fed.

In the act of riding forth upon the plain there was much more to sense than what the rider beheld with his eyes, an extension far beyond the alkali dust and the basalt outcroppings; it was a world one could feel, a world to be a part of, a world of obedience to a master plan, land and sky coagulated by thousands of years of arid climate, climate that not only sculpted the land, but directed the type of flora, allowing only for bunch grass other than turf, for tiny curled leaves other than broad green ones, creating short spindly and thorny brush and limbed cacti rather than trees tall enough for shade; likewise restricting the fauna, placing upon the dry earth animal species that were fleet of foot and could traverse over immense distances for the water and food that sustained them, or reptiles long adapted to quenching their thirst with only occasional bits of dew – an immense interplay between the dusty desert landform of the arid plains and the living things which cycled their lives within its restrictions.

The soldiers followed the ancient Querecho trail southwest toward the Rio Grande, a path first established by the Apaches, but now claimed by the Butterfield Stage Line as a portion of its route, the trek, the longest stage route in the world, extending all the way from St. Louis to California. Many of the watering stations kept mules for the stage as one team was dropped off for rest, and a fresh one hitched to the coach to take it either east or west depending on which carryall was passing through. They passed by Barrel Springs Station, named for the wooden barrels buried around the springs to collect the seeping water, then, on to Dead Man's Hole. Next, were Van Horn's Wells, where they went through a low mountain pass, then Eagle Spring, and on into Fort Quitman on the Rio Bravo. On the north side of the stream the land reached out into a long flat plain, but just across the river were the mountains of Mexico, unknown land, forbidding in its appearance to the caravan.

When the caravan camped to rest the animals and men at night, Dobie moved out alone for his bivouac, but both Dominic and Thomas, who were civilians, not Army officers who were directed not to mingle with the enlisted men, walked out to join him where they ate and shared together.

Riding up the Rio Grande was more pleasant travel, the caravan now in the region of small irrigated plots of land which occasionally hugged both sides of the river, the land, peopled with *campesinos* who tramped up and down the dusty roads as they walked by the green irrigated fields and the tiny villages, Thomas noted Dominic nodding to everyone he encountered along the way. "Why do you nod to people you don't even know?" asked Thomas.

"It tells them that you recognize that they are valuable, and worthy of your attention, even if it is only a nod," said Dominic. "There is no greater affront to a person than to pass him or her and not even give them a glimpse, as though they were of absolutely no concern or worth. It's much easier to think that you yourself are significant if you consider everybody significant."

When the caravan left Fort Quitman, Thomas turned his mount over to the army, and asked that his personal belongings be sent back to San Antonio. He donned a sombrero, loose Mexican shirt, pants, and sandals. He and Dominic said a fond farewell to one another and the military convoy moved out without him. Tomás walked the trail to San Elizario, and on to Socorro. He paid a pittance for a bed with one of the poor farm families where he stayed for a month. In that manner, he got to talk with villagers and *campesinos*, working in the soil, side by side with the farmers, discovering what kind of life they led, and listening intently to the nuances of the Spanish they spoke.

Finally, he bought a mule, saddled it with native tooled leather, and slowly made his way toward Paseo del Norte. He passed through Ysleta, a small village of Mexicans and Tigua natives, the intermixed descendents of Indians and Spaniards from the pueblo region of Isleta, a small village below Albuquerque. The Indian people, allies of Spain, had fled for their lives, marching south with the Spaniards after the Pueblo Revolt of 1680. Their new settlement, Ysleta, was said to have been established in 1680, and thus was the oldest town in Texas. He asked the locals about the church, and was enthusiastically told about the new, and already beloved, priest, Father Dominic, who had so recently arrived.

Thomas walked into the back of the church, *La Mision de Corpus Christi del Sur*, already an ancient relic of centuries past, the first of the Spanish missions of Texas. The fleeing Tigua Indians of 1680 had carried the icon of their patron saint from the Isleta church they were abandoning to the new church they were to build on the land where they reestablished their community.

Father Dominic was working near the altar. He glanced back, and due to the Mexican clothes of the visitor, did not recognize his former friend. "What can I do for you *mi amigo*?" asked the priest, as he continued with his chore. "I have come here on a long journey to receive your blessing," answered Thomas. The priest dropped his books and ran to meet his former companion and the two embraced warmly. They walked behind the chapel to Father Dominic's living quarters. The room was austere, with a simple cot, two chairs, and a small table, bare except for a single candle. A rod on which to hang clothes hung down from the ceiling, and a crucifix was tacked to the rear wall. Low on a side wall, almost hidden by the hanging clothes, was a crude picture, the drawing of an owl with the inscription, "God's miracle for me."

They talked all afternoon, and Dominic told Thomas that he must stay for Vespers, a supper, and rest, and also insisted that he remain the following night for the parish festival, a holiday which he was reviving after it had been dormant for many years. Thomas placed his mule in a small pen behind the church, gave the animal some corn and hay he had bought in the village, and bided his time.

At the Vespers hour he sat in the back of the chapel and watched the faithful come reverently into the church to partake of the ancient rite.

Following Vespers, Dominic prepared their supper, a meager dish of gruel and goat's milk. "I have not yet had time to make my garden, but the next time you come, it will be flourishing, and I will serve you better fare," the priest told him. The two talked late into the night, wandering again into the realms of life's meaning and of God, God who seemed to mean Holy Director to Dominic, a reverence for nature, to Thomas, both men wondering what it was that forged the connection between the two of them.

Father Dominic told his friend how he had already started working to become more courageous, and how he was planning a way to begin atoning for his guilt in the death of the Apaches. Thomas nodded and said, "I know these things are of great concern to you, and you will never let them rest, but I hope you don't make them your priority, because you have more important work to do than to try to justify yourself to some agnostic, like me, or even to your God, who, as you say, can see into your heart without your striving to convince him." Dominic promised Thomas he would spend time thinking on his views.

At bed time, the priest would have no other arrangement but for Thomas to sleep on the cot and he, himself, to sleep on the floor.

Both men were stirring well before sun-up. Thomas wandered through the tiny town, talked with the merchants, and then wandered outside the village to visit once more with the *campesinos*. Most of the farming plots were located on the silt-laden bed left over from the frequent change of the course of the river that the spring floods usually brought about. The pueblo and the church were both now located on the north side of the river, though the original settlement had been on the south side, the annual meanderings of the stream responsible for the change.

As the evening hours approached, the church came alive with activity, the festival at hand, memories emerging among the older parishioners of happy, exciting times in their own childhood, memories long repressed by the drudgery of frontier life. The congregants wore their brightest clothes and two members brought guitars and played music. The excited children ran back and forth between adults, squealing with delight as they were caught and tickled by the parents and the older youth. Foods were in abundance and there was one senora making taffy candy. She boiled the sugary syrup and then had the young people and many of the women pulling it into the white sticks it eventually became. Thomas asked her how to make it, and if there was any way to take butter into the wilderness. She gave Thomas the simple recipe, and told him that if he would boil the butter, scald the bottle he was to put it in, and then seal it with a wax top, that it would be good for many days.

Thomas stood apart, watching the scene. Dominic was already the father of his flock. He watched a small toddler hold out his hands and run to the priest and Dominic bent down and picked up the smiling child. Thomas felt a strange stirring. This priest had a family, he was no longer alone, no longer a stranger in a foreign land, as Thomas, himself, remained.

Early the next day the two friends again bade one another good bye. "I believe you have helped me rediscover my lost lane to heaven," said Dominic, I hope the same thing for you." Thomas gave him a faint smile. "If anyone could lead me to mine, it would be you, Dominic."

CHAPTER 25

The trip upriver was at first slow, but safe. Thomas stayed out of Paseo del Norte on the south side of the river and slowly plodded through Franklin, on the north. He was able to purchase some American goods which he packed on a burro. He did not tarry, but as quickly as possible began his way North on the ancient road, the *Camino Real*, which followed a route alongside the Rio Grande.

Most of the surrounding country was desert, interrupted by an occasional green oasis afforded by irrigation from the river, though imposing saw-toothed mountains lurked at a distance both to the right and the left. The *camino* was a worn and dusty road, appearing much more plebeian than royal. Though dusty and plebeian it might be, there was no mistaking its route; it had been stamped into the desert and rutted into place since 1598, when Juan de Oñate first came out of Mexico through the pass to the north, then over the low water ford of the Rio Del Norte, to follow the river up through the rift that split the territory all the way northward where its headwaters drained high elevations of the Rocky Mountains.

With Oñate came the first Europeans on their way to a new home, to colonize a new land that centuries later was to become part of America. The time well predated the appearance of the English pilgrims who landed on America's eastern shores. The road had been the sole lifeline to civilization for these western colonists for almost two hundred and fifty years until the Santa Fe Trail was opened in the 1840's. The *Camino Real* at first was traveled only once every three years, but it endured through centuries until it had become the path of thousands of trading vehicles, and the only route of commerce in this part of the Southwest.

As Thomas followed the trail, he saw little commercial enterprise except the occasional caravans of freighters, men with timeworn faces sitting on the creaking, mule-powered conveyances. These animals, some of the most ill-treated creatures on earth, their ribs showing through their skins, hides often bare of hair from the chafing harnesses and the lashes applied to their rumps, having nothing to look forward to the next day except more hours in the traces straining against their heavy loads. Thomas began to feel somewhat uneasy as he noticed that most of the caravans had armed escorts and he encountered no other lone travelers.

One day, one of the old teamsters stopped his wagon and beckoned Thomas to his side. "Where are you going, that you have to travel alone?" he asked. "To work with my uncle in Socorro," answered Thomas. "*Los bandidos* and *los Indios* eat *ninos* like you," said the *viejo*. He reached back in his wagon and threw him a dirty brown shirt. "Put your white shirt in your pack and wear this one. It cannot be seen from ten miles away, and when you get to the next village wait until you have company to travel on."

From time to time, Thomas came upon old abandoned towns and pueblos, reportedly vacated because of repeated Apache incursions, the ruins lying sad in their clutter of deserted abodes, the adobe houses collapsing, melting, and gravitating back into the valley floor from which they had been fashioned.

He availed himself of the conveniences of the few army forts established along the Rio Grande, Fort Seldon, Fort McRae, and Fort Craig where he was able to introduce himself with the letter from Colonel Mackenzie. At the forts he was always treated cordially and most often he obtained companions to accompany him for some distance along the way. There were twenty-five recognized communities along the river from Paseo del Norte to Santa Fe, though several were not much more than camping grounds with access to water where the stock could drink.

Aside from his respite at the forts, as often as he was able, he paid a pittance to stay in the homes of farmers which were clustered in the small adobe villages, the natives always being very hospitable, though they had the vexing habit, when asked for the price of the lodging, of saying, "*lo que guste*," (whatever you like), reckoning that the traveler would pay more than the service could rightfully command. He learned to live within their austere circumstances, and strived hard to learn their mores and to speak with their particular Spanish dialect.

Because most of the irrigated plots of land were so inefficiently operated, the United States Government was striving to introduce the steel plow to the farmers which made the tilling of soil tremendously more efficient. Most of the peasant farmers, however, could not be coerced into using them, feeling that the metal violated the sacred soil which had forever been tilled with wood. Some priests agreed, and absolutely banned the use of the God-forbidden metal instrument within the boundaries of the parishes where they lived and worked.

The rare farmer who could generate enough produce from his plot of land to pay his yearly debt to the general store, his tithe to the priest, and still have enough to feed himself and his family was indeed a successful man.

Though Thomas was too early in the summer to witness the custom, most of the farmers raised many watermelons, and from July to October, lived almost entirely off the fruit, preferring to eat them green, consuming them right to the outer rind.

At Fort Seldon, he again ran into contingents of Buffalo Soldiers stationed far from what any of them had known in slave days, but many had adapted quite well, and were proud of their army life. Traveling north from Fort Seldon toward Fort McRae he could see the residual of an ancient lava flow, which formed the dominant land-mark of the region, the Black Mesa, looming to the east of his pathway, guiding him to Rincon and to the beginning of the long arid path, *El Jornada del Muerto*, the Journey of Death.

The waterless journey was actually a shortcut, joining points on two limbs of a great bend in the course of the river. It was almost eighty miles across the *Jornada*, but it also saved many days from the journey by guiding the travelers over flat land, rather than over a route by the water where they had to laboriously climb over the steep canyons and *barrancas* that descended from the mountains right down to the eastern bank of this portion of the river.

At Fort McRae, which had been built to protect travelers going through the *Jornada*, the commanding officer persuaded Thomas to abandon his plans for going alone, and wait for a larger force thus gaining both increased protection from the Apaches, and the improved ability of a larger and more experienced group to cope with the lack of water. The fear of Apaches was no idle threat. Cochise and his band had just raided the village of Palomas, taking four hundred sheep and goats and killing two shepherds.

The party that Thomas was introduced to was a group of six soldiers from Fort Craig who were returning home after having ferried orders originally sent from Santa Fe to the small contingent at Fort McRae. The group was led by a rather diminutive noncommissioned officer, appropriately named Sergeant Ryder, probably in his early forties, who was a self-styled expert on the region they were traveling through. Thomas soon chose to ride beside an enlisted trooper, because he was somewhat offended by the sergeant's grating personality.

The initial part of the trek followed a flat mesquite terrace, totally arid, but hard and relatively smooth. The sergeant told them they would come to a waterhole, the Laguna del Muerto, that would refresh them with drink, since it was now the rainy season of the year. When they arrived at the landmark, the lake was nothing but a sink hole, several yards across, with large cracks in the earth across the bottom, but without a vestige of moisture. "Somebody forgot to bring the wet along with the water," said one of the troopers. The sergeant, irritated by the reaction of the rest of his party, told them there was abundant water only three weeks ago and it should not be gone by now.

The group had not gone forward over another mile, when a covey of quail suddenly flushed immediately next to the riders. The mule, bearing most of their water reserves, jerked back and broke his lead rope and ran across the flat, bucking and scattering his precious load across the dry ground, bursting open the water bags, leaving nothing but wet spots on the ground by the time the troopers could get to them. The sergeant excoriated the private who had been leading the mule, then told him that he and Thomas were appointed to take the pack mule and fill the remaining water bags at Dead Man's Spring, a small watering hole shown on the map as located five miles westward into the very heart of the mountains that lay between them and the river.

Thomas, having been warned that the spring was noted as a frequent haunt of the Apaches, suggested that the group ride on the forty remaining miles, simply enduring the thirst they certainly would be facing. He received a withering look from the sergeant who said, "I believe you have heard my orders."

Thomas reluctantly accompanied the trooper down the trail which was soon a narrow winding canyon with very steep cliffs to each side. They had gone down the canyon only a mile when a side trail came out of an adjacent *canyoncito* to join the main path. Thomas saw tracks coming into their route and dismounted to inspect them. They were tracks of several unshod ponies, very fresh, and obviously being ridden as a group. Thomas turned the trooper around and they rode back to the party reporting to them what they had found.

Sergeant Ryder was furious, and ranted that he would court marshal them both for deliberately disobeying orders. Thomas emphatically reminded him that he was only accompanying the group, was not in the army, and the sergeant had no actual authority over him. "If there is a job to do it seems I'll have to do it myself," said Ryder, where upon he took a different trooper with him and headed the mule once again toward the canyon. Thomas rode up beside the pair. "Sergeant Ryder," he said, "those were not just wild donkey tracts up that canyon. I have scouted many Indian trails, and those in this canyon are only a couple of hours old and very ominous." The sergeant simply sneered and rode on.

Though not asked to do so Thomas thought it was wise to follow the impetuous sergeant at a distance. Instead of riding down in the canyon, however, he and his cohort rode up on the rim, and though the high trail was most difficult, they could see a long distance into the gully below. They rode far enough to see the intersecting trail where they had previously stopped and turned back. Suddenly, a barrage of rifle shots was heard from farther down toward the river, and as they sat on their horses, the shots came closer and closer to them. Thomas correctly surmised that Sergeant Ryder and his aide were being pursued by a band of Apaches. Thomas took out his rifle, beckoned his partner to do the same, and began firing shots into the wall of the canyon. The Indians, hearing shots from above, and not knowing from whence they came, broke off their pursuit. Soon, Sergeant Ryder and his trooper dashed out of the canyon to safety. He told the party that they had been attacked by a host of Apaches, but had fought them off. The pack mule and all the empty water bags had been lost.

Thomas rode up beside the shaken sergeant and said quietly, "Sergeant Ryder, you need to apologize to this group of men and rescind your threat of court marshal for this trooper who rode the trail with me. The report of what actually happened here would not look good on your records. The sergeant glared at Thomas, his eyes full of hate, but the scout returned the stare without a blink. Most reluctantly, the Sergeant nodded his head but no apology was forth coming, and the party slowly straggled in to Fort Craig, a desiccated and weary group of men and animals.

North of the *Jornada,* mountain ranges narrowed close together around the river, allowing silt to raise the course of the bed enough to produce miles of marshland, marshes acting as a welcome succor to the sandhill cranes and other migrating water fowl, unlikely inhabitants of such an arid land.

At Fort Craig, located twenty miles south of Socorro, Thomas came across a caravan of pottery traders, on their way south. They had stopped at the fort because the commander was an avid collector of such wares, and this group from the pueblo of Acoma often stopped by on their treks to Paseo del Norte hoping to sell him some unique piece. Thomas was extremely impressed by the artistic quality of the work, learning that the roots of the art went back many centuries into the unrecorded past, most of the motifs decorating the pottery relating either to the belligerent or benign gods of their culture. In Acoma, pottery making had flourished and now offered a valuable trade source for the isolated people. Thomas tried to converse with the artisans, but they knew only a smattering of Spanish so most of the intercourse was done by pointing and gesture. He found them a very affable and intriguing people.

He visited throughout the region around Socorro, already known as one of the oldest communities in America. The region was reputed to have had a wealth of silver mines, all of which were abandoned, closed, and hidden by the natives, following the pueblo revolution, and live on, only in the imagination of treasure hunters.

By the time the young scout was halfway from Paseo del Norte to Santa Fe, he believed he could exhibit the demeanor of a peon without flaw.

His trip through the small settlement of Albuquerque gave him some respite from the desolate land of the trek farther south. The looming gigantic granite uplifts, the Sandia Peaks off to the east dominated the landscape, and the watermelon shape of the two large mountains gave the area a unique appearance, seeming to alleviate the somber drudgery of the austere life style of subsistence farming in which most of the inhabitants were engaged.

Thomas had been warned that, on some of the large haciendas, the owners were a law unto themselves, and that a traveler could easily be put upon by these people, even if he stayed to the road. He kept a low profile and never ran into any problem until he arrived beside a large estancia, about forty miles below Santa Fe. He was plying the road, the sole traveler, when a group of ten horsemen came galloping out of the hills and reined up beside him. The men were boisterous and laughing, obviously on a spree.

"You are trespassing upon the land of Don Jose Elizondo, *haciendero* of this estate," said one of the riders, "do you have a permit to do so?" Thomas answered in Spanish in a very subservient tone. "*No Senor*, I do not. I beg your forgiveness for not knowing that I needed to obtain such permission."

A large, well-dressed man on a white horse spoke up and addressed the original speaker. This is nothing but an ignorant peon. The contents of the load could not be anything but worthless trinkets. Push them into the gully, take the burro and mule, and run him off my land." Three of the riders turned toward the mule but Thomas quickly spoke up,

"*Oh Senor*, I have one thing in my possession that is very valuable and I beg you to let me keep it."

"Oh, he dares to speak; well let's see it then," said the white-horse rider, obviously the *jefe* of the group. Thomas unfolded the canvas cover on the burro, took out his bow with an arrow in place and held it up in the air, though not pointed toward anyone. "You dare brandish a toy weapon in front of me?" exclaimed the *jefe*.

"*Oh no, Senor*," answered Thomas, "it is genuine Comanche, I thought you might admire it."

Don Jose turned toward his foreman. "Take him out of my sight and teach him a lesson he won't forget," commanded the Don.

Thomas knew he had only a moment to change the direction of the proceedings and possibly save his life. Before he could speak, however, a lasso encircled his neck and the *vaquero* held it tight and began pulling him toward the gully. As he half led, half dragged Thomas to the bottom, the boy stumbled and fell over a bed of rocks. He rapidly rose again and was led on, but hidden in each hand there was now a round smooth rock. About one minute later there was a single rifle shot, and the riders and Don Jose sat in amazement as Thomas walked back out of the draw holding the *vaquero's* rifle by the end of the barrel and leading his horse. He presented the stock of the gun to the Don.

Thomas now spoke in perfect English. "If I can use my bow and shoot a pine cone off your foreman's head, will you let me try to prove my worth?" The *jefe*, at first, looked startled, then, roared with laughter. He knew he had chanced upon a character who was very different from what he had first appeared, perhaps someone of significance. "Where did a peon like you hear the story of William Tell, and where did you acquire your English language" He beckoned the ashen faced foreman off his horse, but rode forward and chopped off a cactus ear and impaled it with his knife.

"He is too valuable to me for you to aim at his head, but he will hold the cactus out with his hand. If you miss, this very knife will skin you alive."

Before the foreman had time to become more nervous, Thomas raised his weapon. The twang of the bow was followed by the clang of metal as both cactus and knife fell to the ground, the cactus leaf impaled by the quivering arrow. "Are you that good," asked Don Jose, "or were you just lucky?" Thomas looked around for another target and turned toward the skeleton of a dead tree, about twenty-five yards away. Two crows were perched on an outer limb watching the horsemen. The young peon aimed his arrow toward one of the birds, but Don Jose held up his hand. "Don't do that," he said, "I love crows." Both birds took wing, croaking their distain at the disturbance below.

"Hmm, I believe you are skilled," mumbled the Don, "perhaps you are worth something after all. What brings you here to this country, *pobre*?" "I have come to make my fortune. I want to be a Comanchero," answered Thomas. The large Mexican roared with laughter. "What makes you think the Comanches wouldn't eat you alive?" he said.

"I know the Comanches. I was captured, when I was a small boy, and lived with them for five years. I speak their language well."

"And what caused you to leave them?"

"I could see that the Comancheros were making all the money, and that the wild Indians were only poor peons like I am now." Once again Don Elizondo roared with laughter.

"Come, my young beggar, I may have plans for you. Hand me your genuine Comanche bow. I would, indeed, like to see it."

"I am honored, *Jefe*," said Thomas. He handed the retrieved arrow to the shaken foreman and walked over and handed Don Jose the bow.

The *vaquero* who had dragged Thomas to the gully came staggering out of the ditch, blood still dripping from his forehead, "I thought you shot him," said the Don.

"I hit him with a rock. I only discharged the gun so there would be no bullet in the chamber when I handed it to you," said Thomas with a smile.

"Juan," said Don Jose to one of the *vaqueros*, "get off your horse, and loan it to our new young friend, and lead his donkey and mule to the hacienda. I want him to ride with me so we can talk." His orders were immediately obeyed, and Thomas found himself riding side by side with the Patron. "Tell me your name," said Don Jose. "Tomás Velasquez," was the answer. "Do not start thinking, Tomás, that just because I have swallowed your tale, I cannot spit it back out. Now, don't try to tell me you are some simple, but enterprising peon. You have already demonstrated too many talents to keep yourself in disguise. Tell me who you are and why you are here."

Thomas knew he had to come up with a plausible explanation, so he created his own story. He ceased his humble mannerisms and said, "I thought, back at the road where we met, I might be dead before I was able to demonstrate any of my talents. I am a scout for the United States Army, under orders to try to become a disguised traveler with the Comanchero to evaluate the Llano Estacado as to the plausibility of establishing a safe trail from San Antonio to Santa Fe through this territory. There is great concern from the United States about the Comanchero trade with the consequent depredations along the Texas frontier being carried out by the Comanches. The government is determined to stop this trade within the next two years. I would like to discern all of the major Comanchero trails, and the main hide-outs of the Comanches before any major military movements of the Army. There is also illegal activity in our own ranks, with some opportunists taking advantage of the trade and lining their own pockets. I hope to identify them."

"It seems to me a very foolish ploy to send only one man for such an imposing mission," said Don Jose. "If I have different desires about the future course of events, all I have to do is simply let you disappear."

Thomas nodded and then smiled slightly. "I am embarrassed that my disguise was not good enough to fool you, and I know I came very close to dying, being completely unprepared for your swift command, but, that aside, my mission is not as unprotected as you might think. The army knows where I am at this time, and if I do not emerge from this hacienda they will send a whole troop to come looking for me.

"They also believe you to be extensively involved in the Comanchero trade, most of your goods unlicensed and hidden from government surveillance. There are several of the officers who have already urged that your lands and property be confiscated, and you and your men be tried and possibly hanged. What I consider more prudent heads, believe you can be of great help to us and for such help, they would enable you to keep your property and remain a respected citizen of New Mexico. The ways of this territory, and you, among all the other *hacienderos*, as being a law unto yourselves within your own property, are about to change, whether you like it or not. If you have only lived, isolated here in New Mexico, and are not familiar with the United States, you cannot imagine what force they can, and will, bring to bear upon this problem."

"When your so called Grand Army takes on the Comanches they may not have such an easy task," said Don Jose.

"It is not that the Indians are not a formidable foe," said Thomas. "It's just that the present world is already passing them by, and their population is on the decline. In the middle and late part of the last century, there were thirty thousand Comanches scattered over the territory. The government now estimates there are not more than four or five thousand.

"The army will not fight them on Comanche terms. They will simply attack their villages, especially the winter camps. They will attack the women and children and give them no respite. The Indians are already being left without enough food or sufficient supplies. There are too few of them to defend the whole of the Comancheria, and both Anglo hunters and other tribes are already invading the edges of their land. The army has orders to settle them all on the reservations, or, if they are unyielding, to exterminate them. The U. S. Army, which, as you have seen, was recently so able to totally dominate all of Mexico's military, will bring as many soldiers and as much equipment as it requires."

The riders approached the *Grande Casa*, and the headquarters station, the main house spreading like an entire pueblo. Thomas was awed by its opulence and size out in this, seemingly, isolated habitat.

"I will think on the things you have told me," said Don Jose, "meanwhile, I invite you to partake of my hospitality." He beckoned one of the house servants, telling him to put Tomás in one of the guest rooms, and to attend to his every need. "You might enjoy wandering around the compound and the corrals," said his host.

Don Jose spent a fretful night. If Tomás was simply bluffing, he would feel like a fool, but he rather thought that the young wanderer was not. He had already begun to feel increasing unease when he was in Santa Fe, and he had frequently seen Army personnel watching him, and frequenting the road in the vicinity of his *hacienda*. He had a powerful group of armed *vaqueros* who could easily intimidate the locals, but, he knew, they were no match for the United States Army.

The next morning Don Jose sent for Thomas to breakfast with him. "I will place you in a Comanchero caravan. You are to proceed into Santa Fe, and in five days from now, sit in front of the Governor's Palace. There, you will be contacted, and placed among my traders." Thomas told Don Jose that he would have to report to the army at the relocated headquarters of Fort Marcy, and tell the commander that the two of them had reached an accord, and that he would be on his way out onto the Llano Estacado.

===== *Author's estimate of approximate borders of Comancheria.*
Original underlying map Courtesy University of Texas Library,
Austin, Texas.

CHAPTER 26

Thomas retrieved his mule and pack animal and trod the rutted road on into Santa Fe. Walking into the edge of the famous town, he saw nothing but narrow streets and mud houses with tiny courtyards reminiscent of the farmer's houses along the *Camino Real*, but as he neared the center and the plaza he was intrigued with the small community, its tall trees along the tiny stream, the cathedral, the governor's palace, and the bustling market. The plaza was thronged with people, an amalgam of different races, all here to partake of a new richness of life emanating from the intermingling of varying cultures, many of which only a few had ever known before. Thomas found lodging in a modest home with a Mexican family, where he could also stow the burro and a small cart he had purchased. He found an eager market for his mule which he sold at a handsome profit.

After two days of acquainting himself with his surroundings, he made his way to the headquarters of the army. The old Fort Marcy had actually been abandoned and now the headquarters of the Military District of New Mexico was on the Paseo de Peralta, below the hill on which the fort had originally been built. He presented himself at headquarters and asked in Spanish to see the aide-de-camp of the Commander, to whom he was to deliver a letter. A rather gruff-looking, red-bearded sergeant named McRainey walked out and told Thomas he would take the letter. Thomas answered in Spanish, "I have been told to deliver this only to the Colonel or his aide and no one else, *Senor*," whereupon the sergeant kicked Thomas in the rear and said, "get out of here, you smelly peon; they don't have time to waste with the likes of you."

Thomas turned and addressed him in perfect English, "Sergeant, you have worked yourself into a bit of trouble; you have just kicked an agent of the United States Army who is trying to deliver a message from Colonel Randolph Mackenzie to your commanding officer. I think you had better take me to him." The sergeant paled, and he immediately escorted the peasant-dressed scout to the-aide-de-camp. Thomas showed the aide the letter from Colonel Mackenzie, and he was immediately ushered in to see the commander.

Colonel Gregg looked at the letter and told Thomas he had been expecting him. Thomas related the whole story about Don Jose and his own preparations to join a caravan onto the plains. "The protection of the *haciendero* will undoubtedly make you safer," the colonel said, "but there is no question that you are taking on a very dangerous mission." He called in the quartermaster and had him furnish Thomas with two of the new repeating rifles they had just received. Thomas left letters for Virginia, his Texas relatives, and Colonel Mackenzie, bade the Fort Marcy commander goodbye, and walked back to his rented quarters.

Colonel Gregg sent an army courier to deliver a letter to Don Jose. The letter thanked the empresario for his cooperation, and told him the arrangement had to be completely confidential until Thomas returned, but left no doubt that Don Jose would be held personally responsible for Thomas's safety.

Over the ensuing two days, Thomas was able to make some meager purchases to carry in his pack. He was again sitting in front of the Governor's Palace when a Pueblo Indian walked up and sat down next to him. "*Senor Velasquez?*" he asked. "*Si senor*," responded Thomas. "I have your supper," was the response. The Indian handed the young agent two tortillas and Thomas gave him a few cents. Both men then ambled off in different directions, Thomas chewing on one end of a folded tortilla. As soon as he got back to his quarters he unfolded the cakes. A note was in the second one. Thomas opened the letter and read in Spanish. "We will rendezvous at the Zapata ranch, one mile past the town of Canyoncito, tomorrow night. Bring your burro, and personal belongings."

By this time in the summer of 1873 the Comanchero trade was mostly a clandestine operation, the New Mexican traders forbidden by the military to trade with the Comanches without a special license.

Corruption was rife in the territory, however, and the trade continued through stealth, bribes and greed.

Thomas burned the letter, packed his donkey cart and left in the night. He went out of town on the Old Santa Fe Trail, heading toward Glorieta. Thomas had kept his well-worn attire and simply looked like one of the Mexican peons, trailed by a poor, tired burro.

CHAPTER 27

He met the caravan the next night. It consisted of eight ox carts, fully loaded with trading wares and ten pack mules plus a few burros. Thomas was given a corner in one of the ox carts to stow his personal wares; the donkey cart was to be his own trading vehicle. Well before dawn the caravan was underway. Personnel consisted of twelve New Mexicans and eight Indians, the natives all from the Tesuque Pueblo. One Comanche guide, named Red Hawk, accompanied the group, not only for keeping the caravan on the right trail where they could find water, but also serving to identify them and thus protect them from any wandering Comanches they might intersect. The foreman, or trail boss, was a swarthy Mexican *vaquero* whom the freighters all referred to as Chulley. He had been on many of these ventures and was quite adept at directing the men and the transportation of the wares, and was also fluent in the sign language of the plains. More importantly, he usually knew how to avoid the Americans as they tried to interrupt the trade. The language of the Comanche Chulley spoke only haltingly, sufficient for trading but not for close association.

The Comanche guide, at first, seemed quite aloof, his stern Indian features hinting of a personality, austere and commanding, but he immediately warmed up to Thomas when the young scout talked to him in his native Comanche language. Thomas could not understand any of the Tewa language the other Indians spoke between themselves, but they all knew a smattering of Spanish, sufficient to get along. No one but Thomas spoke English. This caravan was, in turn, to rendezvous with a second train, coming from the Elizondo Ranchero itself. They were to meet on the Pecos River at *Agua Negra Chiquita*, just before they started their trek toward the plains. The watering spot and the subsequent crossing of the Pecos River was the last definitely known location visited by Coronado in 1540 on his quest for the fabled city of Quivira.

The Comancheros were only a half day out of Canyoncito going through the Glorieta pass, a very narrow passage out of the Sangre de Christo Mountains, leading to the trail below, when they were confronted by a group of U.S. Army troopers consisting of a sergeant and twelve enlisted men of lesser rank. "You are under arrest and your stock and goods are hereby confiscated," said the sergeant. Thomas immediately recognized him as the same soldier who had given him the kick at Fort Marcy. A look of deep concern and indecision spread over Chulley's face. "Put your hands in the air and come out from behind those carts," the sergeant said in Spanish. Thomas walked up beside Chulley, who tightly gripped his rifle in his right hand. "These are all Americans, let me talk to the sergeant in English," he said. Chulley nodded. Thomas led his donkey forward but kept the animal between himself and the sergeant.

"Well, Sergeant," said Thomas, "you keep turning up like a bad penny. You are in the wrong place again. I know for a fact that you are not authorized to be here. Take your troops and get out of our way."

The sergeant was at first stunned and quiet. He quickly recovered his belligerent air and spoke. "I'm sorry, you young traitor, but you're the one who is in the wrong place. I seem to have caught you dealing with the enemy, and I'll take pleasure in hanging you from one of those pine trees. I know the Colonel never would have met with you if he had known what you were really about."

"I have proof that the Colonel knows who I am and what I'm doing here by what he gave me, and he will be investigating why I disappeared if anything interrupts my trip." "What did he give you?" returned the sergeant. Thomas walked over to the cart and pulled out the new repeating rifle, cocked it and held it up in the air. "One of the army's new issue rifles," said Thomas, always speaking loud enough to assure that the conversation was heard by all the troopers. McRainey looked hesitant. "Bring it to me," he said. "No!" answered Thomas, "I don't take orders from a renegade sergeant; come over here and I'll give you a better look." "You fool," he retorted, "now you've made me have to kill you. You'd be just the kind to tell the commanding officer lies about me." "It seems you had better kill all your troopers too because if any one of them decides to talk, you'll be hanged. At any rate I can save them the trouble, I'll at least have the satisfaction of taking out a renegade like you as I go," retorted Thomas.

"You really are arrogant," said the sergeant. "All I have to do is to tell the troops to shoot you, and you'll have ten bullets in you in two seconds."

"I'll get shot only if they decide to obey your command, now that they know you for the criminal you are. If you do give the order, the two seconds gives me plenty of time to put one bullet through the middle of your gut," Thomas told him.

"You think you're that able and that fast, do you?"

"Do you think the army would have brought me half way across America, then sent me alone into the Comancheria if I were simply an ordinary soldier? You give that order to shoot, or even start to ride away to get out of my sights, and you're a dead man, regardless of what happens to me."

The sergeant flushed and sat very still on his horse, a slight tremor invading his reining hand, then, he slowly turned his face toward the troops. "Boys, let's get out of here. This pack of scum is not even worth our time." Disgruntled, the troopers moved out down the path, the sergeant following, no one looking back.

Chulley walked up beside Thomas. "You are more than you first seemed to be, Tomás Velasquez. What was it you said to him, and where did you learn the language of the Americans?"

"I learned English when I lived in Paseo del Norte on the American side of the border. My English is not very good, but I made him believe that I was an expert with the rifle and extremely fast, and that, regardless of what happened to us, I would shoot him through the gut if we were attacked." The Comanchero leader laughed, "Take good care of your rifle, amigo; we may need it again." Chulley picked a horse out of the *remuda* and insisted that Tomás ride it instead of leading his donkey.

The young spy later asked Chulley if he had heard of the U.S. Army troops being involved in raids of confiscation before. "It's getting to be quite common," answered the Comanchero. "This whole society sees the huge amount of money being made through this trade, and nearly everyone around here wants to cut out his share while there is still time. There is much more to this business than you can see just from riding out on a trading mission. There are hundreds of Texans being robbed, killed and mutilated in order to obtain the livestock which the Indians use for trading; then there are greedy merchants and even army officers, raking off huge profits from furnishing the merchandise to trade for the cattle; some of the wares are even army supplies. Simply looking the other way while this illicit trade goes on is quite profitable for some of the army officers and politicians."

"Does it bother you personally to be involved in this kind of trade?" asked Thomas. "I'm no less corrupt than my fellow Comancheros," said Chulley. "Besides, everyone here detests the Texans, so who cares if they get raided and lose cattle?"

The change in transportation did enable Thomas to ride alongside of Chulley, chat with him about the trip and the land they were to cross, and in turn, with the Comanche guide, with whom he spoke in his limited Comanche language. The guide, though always assuming a superior attitude, nonetheless was intrigued by Thomas, and accepted his proffered words as making an effort to establish links of fellowship which he was willing to accept.

The caravan slowly descended out of the rocky pass, the bared stone showing different strata, where a piece of the mountain had caved off, the lines long and uniform until there was a sudden rift and the continuity of the lines was interrupted, with the layers of one side of the rift shoved upward. It was as though nature had no preconception of what the landforms should be, eliciting only a quizzical stare from the travelers, there being no geological understanding among them.

Coming down the pass out of the pine-covered Sangre de Cristo Mountains, Thomas gazed to his right to behold a huge set of ruins meandering along a narrow ridge rising from the floor of the Pecos River valley. The weathered, crumbling, rust-red, adobe walls of a long-abandoned church arose above the pueblo ruins. "What is this we are seeing?" Thomas asked Chulley. "This is what is left of the legendary *Cicuye*, the Pecos Pueblo," he answered. "It once was the dominant location, and the major trading center of this part of the country, directing the commerce of the Pueblo villages of the Rio Grande Valley with the Plains tribes to the east.

"When the Spanish came here in 1621, Fray Andres Juarez directed the building of the church. It apparently was the most imposing mission in all of New Mexico, made out of three hundred thousand adobe bricks each weighing forty pounds. It must have looked strange towering above the hovel-like pueblos around it, pueblos which had actually given it its sustenance.

"The pueblo began to lose importance under the Spaniards and eventually became a favorite raiding target of the Comanches, even though the Plains Indians needed such a trading place. It was as if they could not help killing the goose that lay the golden egg. It dwindled for hundreds of years. Even in my father's time it was still inhabited by the last stragglers. This is the place where Coronado first heard of the golden city of Quivira, and where he obtained the false guide who was to lead him there."

The caravan continued southeast between low-lying hills and across country peppered with Pinon Pines and juniper. There was no reason to be in a hurry, the oxen, with their heavily loaded *carretas*, having their own pace, a slow plodding one. Ten days after leaving Glorieta Pass, they reached *Agua Negra Chaquita* and the Blue Lake. The lake was a natural phenomenon which accumulated water in a giant sink hole, replenished from underground sources and having constant water. A small way station and community established here in 1865 had become the meeting place of many traders. The growing village adopted the name Santa Rosa.

The other caravan from the hacienda was already bivouacked around the lake when Chulley and his entourage arrived. Thomas was surprised to see Don Jose in their midst, once again riding his white horse, not hesitating to exercise his authority in all things. Thomas acted completely subservient like all the other workers.

One evening Don Jose called Chulley to his tent and told the trail boss to bring Tomás with him. "My caravan master tells me you saved our people from a dangerous confrontation with the Army," he said to Thomas.

"I think we were very lucky," commented the scout.

"You seem to have a way of being lucky!" said the Don, with a knowing smile, "Nonetheless, I am very grateful. Chulley, procure him one of the superior horses from my stock." The next morning Thomas was mounted on a truly magnificent animal with both abundant speed and stamina. Don Jose and a small party of his guards bade the caravan master goodbye, and left to return back to his ranchero.

"Does Don Jose ever travel all the way to the rendezvous with one of the caravans?" asked Thomas.

"Not any more," answered Chulley. "Don Jose is a man who always likes to be in charge, and that is never an outsider's status among the Comanches."

CHAPTER 28

After the two caravans were coupled, it was a very impressive train. Fifteen oxcarts, some pulled by as many as three yokes of oxen were now plying the trail. The pack mules were still loaded with the most valuable cargo because they were more mobile in case of danger. The *carretas* were loaded with flour, meal, blankets, baked goods, sugar, salt, trinkets, mirrors, knives, and bolts of cloth. In addition, there was an abundance of worthless chattel such as glass beads, poorly made clothes and bright ribbons. The mules were loaded with steel arrow points, guns, ammunition, coffee, sugar, and whiskey. A driver for each cart, and an additional six *vaqueros* now accompanied the train. The caravan could be heard for some distance, the grinding whine of the wooden wheels of the *carretas* turning on the dry or sometime tallowed wooden axles of the cart beds issuing an eerie sound, like the constant, high-pitched moan of a winter wind blowing against a poorly fitting window seal.

The trade group traveled south, near the east side the *Rio de Cicuye* (Pecos). Off in the distance, farther to the east, a line of blue mesas serrated the horizon, actually the bluffs of the Llano Estacado. What country was beyond them could not be imagined. Thomas knew that the caravan was already within the outer reaches of the Comancheria, so the country was likely to be devoid of any other human habitation, the land unordered and unplanned by any man-made alteration, as the roving Indians neither built nor tore down. Most people had an uneasy feeling about land devoid of human settlements, as though it might be occupied by alien life forms, perhaps those that were malevolent. Westward, to the right of the trail there was a gathering of sand dunes, seemingly plopped down as an intrusive island in this vast sea of grass, but actually formed there by the prevailing wind rising off the eroded plain extending eastward from the Pecos valley. Five days travel brought them to *Bosque Redondo*, a great bend in the Pecos River, where they were once more allowed to halt and rest both animals and men although they gave wide berth to the fort itself, in case there were new orders for suppression of the trade which the army might want to enforce.

During his study back in San Antonio, Thomas had learned of this place, the reservation where the defeated Navajo Nation had been exiled from their homeland, and held as unwilling wards of the U.S. government while their new conquerors made plans to change the very essence of these native people from pastoral nomads with a penchant for raiding to docile farmers. The Navajos had been defeated by the American army under the direction of Colonel Kit Carson in 1864 and four thousand of them herded on what the Navajos named "The Long Walk" to their new settlement on the bend of the Pecos River. Hundreds died along the way and hundreds more on the reservation. It was the failure of the farming project that induced the army to purchase Texas cattle to feed the starving Indians, giving rise to the famous early cattle drives of Charles Goodnight and his friend, Oliver Loving.

Thomas rode out among the abandoned fields and homesites. The living quarters for the Indians were less than hovels, many nothing but holes dug in the ground. Thomas could only imagine the suffering such people must have endured.

He stepped off his horse, bent down, and entered one of the spidery dugouts. In the dim light that forced its way through the cracks above, he could make out the gouged place along the side of the pit with long-dried and crumbling straw placed there to sleep upon. Several old abandoned utensils, crudely hand-crafted, mostly of bone and wood, were scattered on the floor and he even picked up a part of a hand-made doll, which some child must have cuddled in the long ago. "What an obscene testament to the ill that one people can inflict upon another," thought Thomas, though he knew from his army history, that the Navajos were far from free of complicity in the conflict between themselves and the New Mexicans and subsequently the Americans.

The trip was, by no means a great delight, the days long, tedious, and exhausting, the food, parched corn, beans, and dried meat, all meals interlaced with the dust of the trail. Thomas did study the plants, and for those he knew nothing about, he would ask the guide, who was quite knowledgeable and had an Indian name for everything. Thomas sometimes thought if the guide didn't really know a name he rapidly made one up. There was no way to translate the Comanche names into something that might be recognized by a speaker of English.

He spent much time in pondering exactly where he was in relation to the maps he had studied in San Antonio, and he spent just as much time making notes. He showed Chulley his effort at making a map of the course of the Pecos River, telling the trail boss he was making one for him, and one for Don Jose. Chulley helped him correct some of his mistakes and refine his distances.

Just before the group came to the bend of the river, Thomas spotted subtle hoof tracks cutting across the direction of their trek. He pointed them out to the Comanche, and said, "fresh pronghorn tracks." The guide dismounted, studied them a moment, and nodded. He eyed Thomas quizzically, and got back on his pony. Never before had he seen an outlander who could pick out and understand subtle tracks, much less give their age.

As they topped the next rise, Red Hawk pointed out the two does that had made the tracks. He told Thomas they were much too far away to shoot, and impossible to chase in this country. Thomas told him he wanted to try out his new rifle anyway. He set the barrel over a limb and fired. When the larger of the two antelopes fell to the ground the guide was astounded. He asked for the rifle and carefully examined it. Thereafter, the Comanche guide, himself, began to seek out Thomas as a riding companion, listening and watching attentively as Thomas worked to make him an expert marksman.

After Thomas thought he had reached the point where he knew Red Hawk well enough, he asked him if he really thought the Comanches were superior to all other humans. "Yes, it is so," was the answer, " since we are the only 'True People' other tribes haven't the ability to do the things we are able to do," his statement completely dismissive of opposition.

"What makes you believe that it is so?" Thomas asked. "It has always been so. Even, in ancient times, when our fathers came out of the country to the north, they already knew they were the 'Chosen Ones,' because it was foreordained by the Great Spirit." "How did he let it be known?" "He told our ancestors that it was so, and they have always passed the sacred knowledge down from father to son."

"Does it bother you that the Pueblo Indians, the Ute, the Sioux, the Arapaho, the Pawnees, and even the Mexicans, all think that they are the only True People, and they say that the Great Spirit or their god told them it was so?" probed Thomas.

"No! It does not bother me. Other tribes can be as foolish as they want. They only try to copy us. Hah, imagine a Ute making such a claim! I can understand that others would desire to be like the Comanches, but just because a rabbit longs to be a grey wolf, does not make him one. Whose warriors have cleared the southern plains of all other people who want to hunt the buffalo? Whose captives are made slaves for the Comanches? Our warriors have driven all others off of the hunting grounds of the Llano Estacado. If we were not the 'True People,' we would not be masters of this land, and master warriors of the prairies."

"Tell me why the Comanches are master warriors and manage to fight better than other peoples?" he continued to probe. "We train to be warriors from the day we ride our first horse when we are only toddlers, then we ride and hunt and shoot, not just from time to time, but every day. Other peoples live softer lives. They make permanent homes in one area, to farm and grow crops. We always know where they can be found and can attack them whenever we want. The Comanches, however, are never in the same place. We are always on the move; our home is the horse and the teepee, and we carry those along wherever we go, so it is much more difficult for an enemy to find us even if they are brave enough to attack. Another reason is our huge horse herds and our skill with the horse which give us long range mobility, allowing a method of war in which we can attack and surprise our enemies over a huge territory, then quickly ride away. The Great Spirit has taught us to do all these things."

"Are you concerned that the white man has better tools, better weapons, warmer houses, and even more horses than you, and that they have already driven you out of some of your hunting grounds of the hill country, and from around the rivers beneath the escarpment of the Llano Estacado, and that they have killed your buffalo until there are not enough to go around, and that all of the rifles you use, and all the ammunition you shoot, are made by the whites, and you can only trade for them. Is there any Indian who can make a rifle, or is there any Indian who can mine and smelt the iron, out of which rifles are fashioned?"

The Comanche was quiet for some time. "I will answer you, since the two of us are very close friends. I have worried some about those things, especially about the rifles," volunteered Red Hawk, "because our most hated enemies, the Anglo Texans are whites and can make rifles. They are an especially evil people. We Comanches simply want to use the land, as the Great Spirit meant for us to use it, but the Texans want to own it, and to have a legal treaty giving themselves exclusive rights to lands where they settle so that no others can hunt or ride across it."

Red Hawk lapsed back into his Comanche way of thinking, mentally ordering the universe to be what he found comfortable. "The whites may make all the rifles, but we can trade for them from the Comancheros and there is no way the whites can drive 'The People' from the land that the Great Spirit gave to them.

"What will you do if the onslaught keeps on?" Red Hawk simply consigned his confusions to the realm of the Great Mystery. "The Great Spirit will not desert his people. He will send a plague against the Whites, and he will bring back the buffalo, and we will again have all of our hunting grounds, and live like we did in the old times. I wish the same for your people of New Mexico."

"Many years ago the Comanche warriors continually raided the New Mexican people, and the Pueblo people as well, Red Hawk, and there has often been fierce war between us."

"That was before we made peace and learned to trade with one another," answered the Indian, "now we need each other, and forever more, we will be friends and have respect for the others' needs." Thomas wanted to probe more into the inconsistency of the Comanche way of thinking, but he began to recognize that the Indian had no problem with inconsistency, no practice in using an ordered method of logical progression of ideas, no need to use the contrived rationality of the white man. The native's thoughts were guided by another calling, a world governed by the expediency of the next day's meal, the next day's shelter, the next tribe with which to trade or fight, the constant struggle to wrest a livelihood from nature, and to ally himself with the eternal by worshiping the gods his fathers had known, the gods which had always worked before.

CHAPTER 29

The caravan left the *Rio Cicuye* and struck out east across undulating plains of short grass country until they came upon a series of sand hills dotted with sage brush. Fortunately, there had been recent spring rains and Red Hawk was able to guide them to small sinks in the surface of the land containing drinkable water. They trekked for days with no sign of human habitation in any direction.

Emerging from the sand hills, they finally came onto the flat plains, the Llano Estacado, and with the sudden loss of landmarks, Thomas immediately felt the same sense of desolation and dread that he had experienced when he had first come onto the Llano out of the canyons in the east. Once again he looked out upon a measureless sea of grass, stretching out beneath a never-ending sky, the expanse unfathomable, like nothing he had ever dreamed existed. There was not one tree, bush, or stone; not one landmark broke the horizon; no animals moved; no bird flew; just the flat, monotonous, and limitless prairie. It was not just the land, however; the sky seemed different; the smell was different and the wind blew across your face, unimpeded, telling you that this land was a place like no other.

The only variation in the scenery, which one could detect at all, was far out in the distance, where silvery light waves undulated in the heat, the mirages of the plains, their expanse as vast as the land. A shiver ran down his spine, engendering the feeling that he had lost his ability to cope, that he was only a pawn, an impotent hostage of this nothingness.

Thomas rode up beside the Indian guide and asked him how the new scenery made him feel. Red Hawk smiled jubilantly, "I know I am home again. It brings a peace and satisfaction over my heart like no other place. Here it is safe; the land is rich and exciting. One can find abundant game, and a warrior is free to go where ever he wants. You almost feel you can ride right up into the sky and look down with the Great Spirit." Thomas turned his horse away, riding back into the caravan to ponder the difference between himself and the guide.

He moved up to Chulley and asked him how many times he had crossed the Llano Estacado. "If you count each way as one crossing, about twenty times," answered the foreman, "but not always on this same trail."

"Are there other trails farther north?" asked Thomas.

"There are three major ones," said Chulley. "Since you like maps, I'll draw you one some evening." "So you have now become comfortable with the Llano?" asked Thomas. "Every time I come to the edge of this empty land, I proceed with anguish," said Chulley. "I believe one would have to have been born, weaned, and reared here to feel any other way. That's why the Comanches have an advantage over us on this prairie. However, we are not far from the *Agua Corriente*, a beautiful little draw, with constant fresh running water, that will at least give us a small change in scenery and make us both a little more comfortable. We can follow it eastward for many leagues before we turn south to cross the dry stream beds that will take us to *La Punta de Agua* and the *Cañon del Rescate* where we will meet the Comanches."

That evening, the Comanchero took a stick and marked a crude map on the ground. It showed the small arroyo where they were camped on *Agua Corriente* with the trail extending on down to their destination. The other trails were drawn farther north and ran alongside what Thomas thought was surely the Canadian River, one branch of the trail going south to *Tecovas*, and another one leading to what Chulley said was the greatest canyon, a *cañon grande*, where many Indians spend the winter, though he himself had never seen it. He said Mexicans called it the Palo Duro. Finally, a last trail branched away from the Canadian River, proceeding to the eastern edge of the Caprock to enter the canyon of the Quitique, the ancient homeland of a long extinct Indian tribe, its only vestige the name it bequeathed to the canyon.

"Are we on the trail where the most trade takes place?" asked Thomas.

"Oh no," said Chulley, "the trails to the north are used much more, being well marked by deep ruts, but now, they are dominated by the Comanchero, Juan Tofoya, who has the backing of the commanding general at Fort Bascom and also the rich trader-merchant Jennings at Hatch ranch. We have to stay out of their way."

"Where do they rendezvous?" asked Thomas.

"Most often they meet in the valley of the Quitique. It is a good place to gather cattle. It is also the place where the Indians prefer to bring their captives. We Comancheros call it the *Valle de las Lagrimas*, the Valley of Tears, because that is where the Comanches separate the terrified captive children from their mothers and siblings, and trade them to other tribes, or, at rare times, ransom them to the Comancheros."

Thomas tried to imprint these routes on his mind and later that night lighted his tiny lamp, and drew his recollections in his book. He calculated that he was now less than one hundred fifty miles, almost due west, of where he had first viewed the plains above Blanco Canyon, and where he had first warred with the Comanches.

As the new day dawned, the eastern sky was bright and clear, but far to the west there was a dark gathering of clouds, an embankment in the sky that seemed intent on searching out the plodding traders. By noon time the day was hot and sultry, but soon the heat was intermittently fractured by gusts of cool wind. Lightning flashed between the clouds, clouds that rolled forward as each would take its turn, momentarily outdistancing the others, then, rotate back into the common bank.

Thomas began to hear thud-like sounds across the prairie, and was looking hard to ascertain from whence the sound came, when one suddenly occurred immediately to his right. He looked down and saw an apple-sized hailstone lying in the grass. He put his arms over his head and made a dash for the carts and crawled under his own, the hail beginning to drop in profusion from the dark, mottled sky as the cloud bank rolled overhead.

The stock all turned their tails to the storm, and lowered their heads, the pelting hail flailing their bodies with blows about which they could do nothing but endure.

The men had all, at least, tried to crawl beneath a cart or wagon, some only being able to protect their heads, while their backs and legs were pelted.

The storm cleared with the suddenness of an ending symphony, the battered caravan standing in a sea of white. The animals shook themselves, and the men crawled from beneath their covers.

The train, once more, moved forward, wheels crunching over the stones of frozen water, and the men engaged in the rare experience of picking up and eating the globules of ice.

The following morning Thomas rode forward, to be back aside the Comanche. "What guides you across this place?" he asked. "I need no guidance" he answered, "this is my home and I know it like I know my own hand."

"But even though you know it, there is no feature of the land to guide you in one direction or another," interjected the scout. "You think there are no land marks, but that is because your eye is untrained. Quit looking off into the vastness of the distance and examine what is immediately around you. Sometimes a fragment shows you more than the whole."

He got off his horse and took his bow and placed it string side up, resting level on the ground. He then had Thomas lie flat on the prairie and view the distant land while looking under the string to compare the horizon to a straight line. Sure enough, compared to the straight line of the bow string, the land had slight undulation, and was not as absolutely flat as it first seemed to the unaided eye. In this manner, Red Hawk showed Thomas a slight dip in the horizon and told him that this dip was the direction in which they would travel. "I have seen this low area so often that I can recognize it without the bow," he said. In fact, I can always smell the place to turn south, from the jimson weeds that have always grown across this stretch.

He taught Thomas to look at the dust devils, with the soaring hawks circling above, to catch their updrafts, and told him the whirlwinds most often travel from the southwest toward the northeast and how to put an arrow in the ground and judge the quadrants of day by the length of its shadow as the summer sun plied its daily circuit. Finally, he showed Thomas how to recognize the subtle difference in the color of the grass as they rode farther south, and to notice different weeds which indicated lower or higher ground, or an actual variation in the grass, at times, something as subtle as the length of its awn, serving as an indistinct and irregular marker of the border of another ecology, another province. He picked some small weeds from between tufts of grass, plants that Thomas had not even noticed. "These weeds are distinct to this area," he said. "They make stickers in the fall. They do not grow farther north of this strip of land." He told Thomas he would give him other lessons at night.

Thomas reached in his pocket and pulled out a watch, showed it, then explained it to the Indian. He let Red Hawk listen to the ticking of the inner mechanism, then, hung it around his neck. The guide was delighted, and rode forward with his head high and chest out, as though he had considerably increased his dignity.

Later Chulley laughingly told Thomas there had been no need to give Red Hawk a watch. "Comanches make their own time."

The morning after, Red Hawk told Thomas to ride with him while they scouted ahead to see if any of the playa lakes had water. They came to a very shallow depression with water only six to eight inches deep, the reservoir covered by wading curlews feeding on the abundant tadpoles. As the riders approached, the birds rose in the air in huge numbers and flew off toward the east. Red Hawk said that a large flock of water birds suddenly rising into the air could be seen for a long distance by the Comanche and would always be considered, by them, as indicating humans in the vicinity, because animals of the prairie would almost never excite such a large group of birds into complete flight, and additionally the direction they flew would always lead toward another lake.

"A similar thing," he continued, "ducks are often on these playa lakes, and at night they sleep on the shore instead of the water. If, at night, you hear a flight of ducks, they have probably been disturbed by humans and you must then be alert for nearby enemies." He also told Thomas that when a group of ducks quit circling in the sky, and were seen flying in formation in a single direction, the line of flight would, also, almost always lead to other water.

The guide waded into the edge of the playa, scooped up a handful of the tadpoles and swallowed them down with relish. He brought two over to Thomas who summarily swallowed his two, trying desperately not to gag.

"Bigger water ahead," said the Comanche, and the two rode on toward the east. About four miles farther they came to a large depression in the land with abundant water filling an area almost a quarter of a mile across. Suddenly Red Hawk became very excited, and pointed out two rogue buffalo bulls. Red Hawk pulled out his bow and galloped after them at full speed, obviously eager to engage in this exciting sport. Thomas grabbed his bow as well and dashed after his companion. Red Hawk ran right past the first animal and then up beside the leader, and began to send arrows into the beast just behind the area of the last rib. Thomas was determined to emulate his guide, and with his own bow and arrows in hand, gave chase as fast as his horse would carry him after the second bull.

As Red Hawk rode almost parallel to the lead buffalo, the animal suddenly swerved, lowering its head and charging the horse just as the mount approached a low lying grove of yucca-like bear grass. The wily horse, familiar with the chase of the hunt, leaped agilely away from the bull, easily hurdling over the taller growth. When the horse's foreleg landed on the far side of the clump, however, it plunged into the opening of a badger hole which had been completely obscured by the yucca. The horse's leg snapped and both Red Hawk and his horse went flying headlong onto the prairie grass.

The bull whirled toward his tormenter and charged directly at the prostrate Indian. Thomas immediately grasped the peril of the situation. He dropped his bow, pulled his rifle and yelling and shooting, ran straight across the path of the bull. The enraged animal turned toward this new threat, and met Thomas's horse straight on. With a mighty thrust of his head and neck he lifted the screaming animal into the air, and flipped him upon his side. Thomas tried desperately to land free of the saddle before he hit the ground, but it was too late, and his leg was caught under the falling horse. He did not drop his rifle, however, and while still lying partially under the stunned mount, he kept pumping bullets into the chest of the buffalo. Finally, when the maddened bull was about four feet from Red Hawk, he dropped to his knees and gasped in vain for another breath. Even in those moments of the dire struggle, Thomas noted and marveled at how hard this creature of the wild had resisted death.

Thomas worked his leg out from under his mount which slowly rose to his feet. Red Hawk's pony could not rise. Both men began to examine themselves to ascertain what part of their own body might be broken, but though they were markedly abraded and bruised, neither seemed to have a fractured limb.

Riders from the caravan, who had heard the shots, came into sight and were soon ministering to the two scouts. The lame horse had to be shot because of its broken legs and the Comancheros began butchering both the horse and the great buffalo. One of them brought Red Hawk a large piece of raw liver from the bison, and he began to slice it and eat it raw. He held out a piece to Thomas who simply shook his head and put out his hand as if to push it away, definitely deciding his digestive system was not ready for the Indian table. "You no Comanche," laughed Red Hawk.

Though offered horses, both hunters had done enough riding for one day and together they limped back to the oncoming caravan. That night the buffalo chip fires were rich with the smell of roasting meat and the men were joyous as they feasted and listened to the scouts tell of their narrow escape. Red Hawk turned toward Thomas and said, "You and I are now brothers forever." Both men scraped the back of their abraded hands, and mingled their blood in the rite proscribed by Red Hawk.

CHAPTER 30

Nearing the vicinity of the rendezvous with the Comanches, Thomas could sense both the joyous anticipation of Red Hawk, and the mounting nervous concern of Chulley, much more somber as he approached this coming part of the venture. "There will be many head of livestock for trade," Chulley told Thomas. "Recently there have also been several captives to trade. They used to keep most of the females, needing them as mothers because the Comanche are not as efficient in raising babies as we Mexicans are, and the tribes need more people. With the buffalo more sparse, however, they don't have as many things to trade so they work hard to capture more hostages."

At evening of the next day the Comancheros saw a bloom of dust rise in the air as thirty to forty mounted warriors, yelling and whooping at the top of their lungs, came dashing over the horizon to greet, and then accompany, the caravan to the rendezvous. The braves were bedecked in a menagerie of costumes ranging from the practical, to the gaudy, to the ridiculous. "You see," laughed Chulley, "the Comanches are not just a beautiful people, they are also a decorated people." Thomas laughed. "It appears quite comical to us to view their dress, our response probably a way for us to justify looking down on the natives, until we start thinking of our own Easter Parades. The bedecked Indians and the parading Anglos and Mexicans, with their Easter finery, are not far removed from one another. The Indians, however, seem to have little concern about our evaluation of their appearance."

"The same is true about many of the things the Comanches do," said Chulley. "They care but little what we think. Our condescension when we look at their dress is likened to laughing at the dung beetle as he rolls along his prize; whether you laugh or whether you sneer, he just keeps rolling what is important to him, and you are definitely not part of his concern. Certainly, the Comanches do the same. I suspect we all do."

"We are only two camping distances away from the meeting place," Red Hawk told Thomas. Chulley later explained that a camping distance was about four leagues, and was the distance a tribe usually moved to new and clean camping grounds when there was available water, and when the tribe was under no unusual pressure. The Comancheros spent that night on the prairie, with the horses, mules, and oxen secured within the circle of *carretas* and night watchmen on patrol, the Indians remaining nearby, but they neither camped nor slept among the Comancheros, choosing their own place and mode of resting. Red Hawk was glad to leave the caravan and move out among his own people.

The following morning, Chulley, Red Hawk, and Thomas rode together at the head of the column, traveling the short distance across the remaining flat grassland to the escarpment where they could look far down on the bottom of the eroded abyss. Thomas eagerly anticipated the canyon, but to the Comancheros, the land was of no import, it was the happening itself that was their destination. An excitement possessed the two leaders as they approached. "The *Cañon del Rescate*, said Chulley" The huge rift on the face of the land seemed to be imbued with a veil of antiquity, majestic, but at the same time intimidating, almost terrifying, in its stretch into the distance. Thomas could see scattered Comanche lodges situated along the floor. They were miniscule, toy-like in appearance from this vantage point, the scope of the canyon minifying the appearance of the Indians and their meager constructions. He was awed by what a mere and insignificant claim humans make upon the whole of the landscape. "We are not nearly as important in the eyes of the Great Mystery, as we like to think we are," he said to himself. He wished his friend Dominic could be here to commune with him while eyeing this telling scene.

The caravan slowly made its way to the canyon floor, the *carretas* creaking under the extra force of the declination; a mule and rider following behind each conveyance, a lariat tied from the saddle to the back of the cart, to aid as a brake when the road was too steep. Reaching the bottom, they branched into a box canyon extending off to one side where the Comancheros routinely camped. It had a narrow opening with steep sides and back where they felt relatively safe from pilfering.

While the Pueblo Indians, New Mexican ox drivers and muleskinners remained and guarded their camp, Red Hawk took Thomas and Chulley into the Indian village to meet with the chiefs. Chulley told Thomas to be prepared for a test of his suitability as a Comanche guest, and for a feast after the council. He told him it would be mainly roast meat, but delicacies might be added that would be different from anything of which he had ever partaken, and that the Indians would expect him to eat and enjoy them all. Thomas told him about Red Hawk eating the tadpoles and the raw liver. "They'll eat anything that moves just as soon as they get it still enough," Chulley said.

The nomads knew Chulley from previous rendezvous and he was greeted warmly, as an old friend, but since Thomas was unknown to them, the Comanches were aloof toward this stranger. He was watched intently, giving him the uneasy feeling they were about to pounce like a pack of wolves. Thomas's eye was drawn to one with a particularly malicious stare, his nose long and sharp, his eyes severe. When Thomas momentarily met his glance the warrior smiled, or, perhaps, only seemed to smile. Thomas was sure this man wanted to kill him. "Dark eyes; dark soul," he thought.

The Indian's visage seemed vaguely familiar, but he was careful, at first, not to offend him by looking him straight in the face. The way in which his blade like nose melded into his forehead, stirred memories of the night the boy was caught in the wolf traps, though Thomas knew the boy was too young to be here, among this group of chiefs. The belligerent was so persistent in his stare, with its issuance of disdain, that Thomas finally raised his head, and returned the gaze, staring straight into his eyes. They were as black as char. The malice of a hungry wolf seemed to be reflected in their gaze. This time Thomas faced him with a scowl of his own, the face-off seeming to portend some unfinished matter that lingered between the two. As the Indian turned his eyes away, Thomas noticed scarring on the left side of his face, several little indentations, almost like pock marks, but the opposite cheek was clear. One of the scars sat right at the edge of his eye lid and deformed the normal closure at the corner.

The gathering of chiefs and their visitors entered a tent, the councilmen seating themselves around a central fire. A very old chief, gnomic, and white haired, began the smoke ceremony. His face was stern, but not unkind. A pipe was brought out, packed with tobacco, and lighted with a coal. With the group sitting in cloistral silence, the elder stood up before them and staggered into motion, taking the pipe and drawing in and blowing out a puff toward each of the four winds. He sat again, and in turn passed it to the other Comanches. One by one they took two puffs and handed the relic back to the elder. The old chief then handed the pipe to Chulley who likewise took two puffs and returned it back again, the rules of the pageant being strictly adhered to, as though Moses had brought them down from the mountain.

All was silent for several uncomfortable seconds. The Indians sat stiffly around the fire, their arms folded like bundles across their chests. One of the Comanches broke his posture and reached across and placed his hand on Thomas's chest, over the heart, to detect the beat, and feel if there was any scare. The heart beat was slow and true. After some unspoken, though ciphered communication between the Comanches, the old Indian smiled and passed the pipe to Thomas. Suddenly the severe countenance of all the warriors softened, and the occupants of the tepee became jovial. As they left the tent Red Hawk spoke up, "this ceremony signifies that the tribe accepts you as a brother."

When the men stepped outside the tent, one of the village dogs snarled and then barked at Thomas, another answered, then a cacophony of barking, snarling, and howling ensued. Red Hawk laughed. "The dogs will have to get used to you as well. You bring a new scent to the village, and since they have not yet learned to trust you, it makes them uneasy." The sound reminded Thomas of the melee he had encountered at Fort Sill on the reservation, during the distribution of allotments. Many people stood at a distance, surrounding the ceremonial teepee, watching the strangers.

Thomas glanced at the women and children who had gathered to look at this outlander. All eyes were fixed on him, but when he engaged them directly with his own, they immediately withdrew their stares. The sloe-eyed children appeared rather unkempt, and some were quite dirty, but still, the aura of wonder and innocence that radiated from their faces and eyes, made them attractive, under any circumstance. The appearance of the children was in contrast to the mature women, for the most part, appearing squat and dumpy in stature, with withered and wrinkled skin from their daily burdens and the elements to which they were constantly exposed, their faces appearing strikingly identical in their loss of individuality.

A few of the younger women were slightly more comely; Thomas guessing their fresh appearance was because they were not yet married. The young women eyed him intently, and he caught himself staring back, especially, at one more fetching than the rest, her head held high, demanding attention, like an Asian princess. She was clad in a fringed buckskin dress, and around her waist she was girded with a unique and beautiful belt, enlaced with porcupine quills and tendriled with dangling pieces of turquoise and elk teeth. Their eyes met for an instant, but when she realized he was looking intently at her, she quickly turned her face away, and disappeared into the crowd. Thomas glanced to his right and there was Red Hawk, smiling as he watched the young scout.

A teepee was set up in the center of the village for Thomas and Chulley. In celebration of the coming trades, games and contests were planned for the next day. Chulley said he had to go back with the Comancheros and left Thomas in the tent alone. The teepee was quite comfortable, the ground floor half covered by buffalo robes, a circle of stones was in the center for the fire. Firewood was stacked outside the flap and everyday one of the squaws would enter, prepare the wood for the night fire and bring fresh water and food.

The water was stored in a buffalo paunch, and hung from one of the lodge poles. Thomas was amazed to find wild mint leaves floating in the water. Also hanging from a pole was a buckskin bag filled with dried plums, currents and choke cherries, and another vessel filled with wild turnips, water lily roots, and wild onions. The vegetables were to be boiled in a buffalo paunch, by placing hot stones from the fire into fluid poured into the paunch. After the vegetables were cooked, the stones were removed, and the dish was ready to be eaten, paunch and all.

At night, all of the braves sat around large camp fires with laughter echoing between the hiss and pop of the burning wood. They feasted on roasted meat, which Thomas surmised, was Texas Longhorn, taken from the frontier ranches, though the taste seemed somewhat different. He turned and asked Red Hawk if this was beef. "No," the Indian told him, "we save the longhorns for trading, this is donkey meat." Thomas was handed many things for special flavors, which he summarily ingested without knowing what they were. Two women worked near by, fashioning cakes of bread, made only from water, grease, and meal, then, laid upon the coals so that when baked and taken from the fire, a portion of the ingredients which they ate consisted of ashes.

He watched with amazement as the braves wiped their greasy fingers in their hair and on their clothes and skin, a dearth of hygiene infesting the camp, though Thomas surmised that the grease had a beneficial function, to keep parasites at bay and prevent withering of the skin. Thereafter, he began to perform the same endeavors. There was much camaraderie among the Indians and between them and Thomas, as all seemed to enjoy whatever it was that Comanches relish. Thomas judged it to be mostly swapping descriptions of their earlier exploits. He chatted with them in Comanche, and everyone laughed as they corrected his novice use of their language. His acceptance into the tribe as a friend and counselor gave him a feeling of power, a power he knew he did not deserve, the fellowship tempting the natives into telling him what their nature usually forbade them to relate to an outlander.

The following day, before the trading began, came the celebration with contests and games. Thomas participated in the bow and arrow marksmanship, surprising the natives by his skill. He also entered in the horse racing but was careful not to win, in any head to head competition with a Comanche. It was also the time for exchange of gifts, a ritual and tradition which had been established by more than a hundred years of trading between the two cultures. The Mexicans gave the members of the tribe numerous brightly colored garments and other fabrics, plus knives, mirrors and beads. Lastly they had brought a hundred army caps. They were received eagerly and with much gaiety. Thomas knew these articles had to be stolen contraband with undoubted complicity by some army officer.

Red Hawk had told the tribe about his new friend risking his life to save him from the charging buffalo. "He is now my blood brother," he said to them, so the stranger was treated with great respect.

That evening, Thomas brought out his donkey and a cart, took out a large black kettle, mixed the sugar, butter oil, and water over a bed of coals, and stirred up his candy. The men scoffed at him, for doing women's work, but when he began to put small dollops of the thick, syrupy mixture on a stone plate, then, dipped his fingers into the oily butter, and began pulling the candy into long ropy shapes, the crowd gathered around. Soon everybody, even the braves, had their own dollop of taffy to pull and to taste, licking their fingers and eating portions before it was completely cured, the tribe engulfed in complete merriment.

Red Hawk walked up to Thomas and said, "In order to honor our brotherhood, I will send you a gift this night." Thomas wondered what he meant, but gave it no further thought.

CHAPTER 31

After the games and taffy, Thomas sat around the campfire talking with the braves until late into the night, finally going back to his tent where he lit a small oil lamp from his belongings and began making notes. He heard a faint stirring of his tent flap and looked up to see the young woman, with whom he had so briefly exchanged glances, crawl into the teepee and spread out a buffalo robe.

"What are you doing?" he asked her. "Red Hawk sent me here," she answered. "Are you part of his family?" he returned. "I am Running Deer, his youngest wife," she said, then gave him a shy smile.

"He sent you, his wife, here to me, a perfect stranger?" he queried. "Since you are the brother to my husband, then you are not a stranger, but a husband to me as well." She seemed perplexed by his lack of understanding. Both sat on their knees looking at one another in the dim light. Thomas was at a complete loss as to what to do, or what to say. Finally she spoke. "Perhaps you are not pleased with me." She rose and turned toward the tent flap. Thomas reached out and gently caught her by the ankle. She turned back, untied and folded her belt, knelt down on the robe, and blew out the flame of the lamp.

The next day Thomas sought out Red Hawk and told him that in the trading the Comanches must ask much more from the Comancheros than their first offer. "They make much money from what they receive from you," he said. "Money worth nothing," answered the Indian. It seemed to the young Texan that sixty percent of everything the prairie nomads traded for was of minimal value. Chulley had told him that the Comanches would trade an entire herd of cattle, which took them months to steal, for almost anything, provided it was worthless enough. The system, with its exorbitant pay off to the traders, gave the Comancheros a marked incentive for continuing the trade, even after most of it was banned by the U. S. government.

Thomas could hear the lowing, neighing, and braying of the animals that had been brought into an adjacent box canyon to be available for the trading. The two groups began bartering early in the day. The first order of business was establishing the basic unit price for a designated item, such as a rifle. Such an item might be worth three cows or one horse. Thereafter all other prices would be based on the two equivalent items, a horse for a rifle, five bolts of cloth, five sacks of flour, etc. The Indians wanted many more rifles than the Comancheros had brought, but these were no longer as readily available since the ban on these items had been issued by the government.

Thomas watched both factions in amazement. Trading the huge mass of livestock for the New Mexicans' wares required about three days, but both sides seemed relatively satisfied. The Mexican herdsmen moved out with the livestock, with ten *vaqueros*, each carrying a musket, and surrounding the herd. The trailing wagon had purposely let the canvas slip down revealing a small cannon being hauled in reserve. It was obvious the traders had prepared for any change of heart and follow-up raid by the Comanches to reclaim the stock. They wanted to make sure that the Indians were aware of it as well.

Next, the Indians brought out two captives. One girl was a very young child and one was an adolescent girl. They were dirty and unkempt, and appeared unspeakably cowed and forlorn. A young girl, between the ages of ten and twenty years was still the most valuable commodity for which the Comancheros could trade, a fact of which the Comanches were well aware. "How could such an affable and happy people, as those I saw last evening, treat other humans like this?" Thomas wondered. For the first time since coming to the villages, he was reminded of the same aroma of that awful day on the Guadalupe, and the hair on the back of his neck began to tingle. The child was quickly traded for, with the New Mexicans giving a large mirror, ammunition, a scarlet robe and some whiskey in exchange.

The Indians and Comancheros could come to no agreement on the adolescent girl, so the braves threw her back behind one of the lodges. Thomas winced at the rough treatment, and at the thought of what the future held for her. The Comanches could at once be valiant, friendly and generous, but could suddenly turn and be heartless, cruel, and menacing. Thomas decided in his own mind that the tribes were infected with some incurable distemper, a wanton disregard of other human beings not of their own ilk. A tingling surge passed through his body, stirring an urgent need for action, the incident meaning something to him, not knowing exactly what, yet realizing he hadn't time to sort it out.

"Wait!" he exclaimed. He walked back to his cart, and held up one of his gifts from the army, a new, engraved, repeating rifle, and ammunition to go with it. The braves quickly gathered around as Thomas showed them how quickly the gun could shoot. He then aimed at a gourd that had been hung from a tree limb to use as archery practice. It was almost forty yards away. Thomas hit it right in the center. He threw in his donkey and the rest of his sugar. The braves brought back the girl, and tied her wrist to Thomas's cart. "What is your name?" Thomas asked in Comanche. "Sarah," she replied. Thomas called for two horses to be brought out of the trader's remuda.

"You have bought yourself a fine wife," Red Hawk laughed. "She will get used to you, and will quickly learn to be obedient. The girl remained quite fearful, and withdrawn, and followed with her head bent toward the ground.

Chulley, Thomas and the young captive, Sarah, took a shortcut through the tents back toward their horses. To the left the walkers saw a dark figure stretched on the bare ground between two of the teepees. Walking over to see what it might be, Thomas was astounded to see a white man staked to the ground. The arms and legs were spread apart, leather thongs tied around each limb and securely staked into the earth. A final binder was stretched across the man's neck, and staked on both sides so that the victim could not raise his head.

Thomas looked into the terror filled eyes. "Help me brother," the man whispered. Thomas felt Chulley's hand on his arm pushing him forward. "Why didn't they barter him?" asked the scout. "He is for their personal use, some other night, and is not for sale," answered the trail boss. "What will happen to him?"

"You don't want to know."

Thomas probed no further, but he knew that the captive represented a future happening that no night, nor any human, had any business transacting. It was as if these people were part demon, blood lust always lurking beneath the veneer of civility, always hungering to break into the open, to reveal the base viciousness that was apparently part of their nature.

Thomas did not want to acknowledge it but his feeling of loathing toward the natives was suddenly countered by his memory of the tragic night on the Brazos. "Is this malevolence simply a constituent of society, a thing we must all endure, a thing that our natures cry out for, a ravenous desire that must be satiated by inflicting torture and spilling the blood of other humans?"

A feeling of betrayal, similar to what he had known when his Tonkawa boyhood friend was being scalped, swept over him, the feeling engendering a visceral abhorrence for what he was witnessing within this tribe, wiping away any previous doubt that he should be a spy in their midst.

CHAPTER 32

As the three continued toward the Comanchero camp, Thomas noticed a lone rider come down over the western rim of the canyon, riding as one familiar with the layout of the site. He turned off the main trail and proceeded toward the *carretas*. He wore clothes that definitely indicated that he, too, was a Mexican trader.

Later in the evening, Chulley asked Thomas to come to the back of the box canyon to meet with him. "Tomás, my plans have been altered. The messenger that just rode in, has brought me word that there is another group of Comanches coming north with more cattle, so I am turning back only as far as *Bosque Redondo*. There, a new trading caravan will be awaiting me, and I will bring it back here for further exchange. You are welcome to stay with me for the entire summer, or you may accompany these carts all the way to the hacienda of Don Jose." Thomas thanked Chulley, but said he first would like to talk with Red Hawk about staying longer among this group of Comanches.

Returning to Red Hawk, he found that his friend was already familiar with the plans for a second rendezvous. "I want to start my own business and in the future become a Comanchero *caudillo* myself," said Thomas. He offered to give Red Hawk all of the remaining goods in his *carreta* if he would guide him through the region of the Canadian River where more of the trading took place. Red Hawk readily agreed, even before he paid any attention to the contents in the cart. Thomas still had his own arms, ammunition, and all his personal things in his saddle bags and scabbards.

The guide insisted that Thomas change his clothes and wear the trappings of a Comanche, so all of Red Hawk's wives quickly changed the appearance of Thomas, who then felt somewhat exposed. He did, however, take with him enough removable clothing to keep from getting severely sunburned.

Just before the unlikely pair rode away, one of the braves walked up beside Red Hawk. "Your friend is not what he seems," he said. "I have the feeling that I know him some way. I do not believe he is a New Mexican, and I think he is a danger to the Comanches."

"He certainly looks like a Mexican and talks like a Mexican," scolded Red Hawk. "Have you ever heard him talk like a Texan?" asked the other Indian. The confrontation with the army, just out of Santa Fe, flashed across Red Hawk's mind, but he did not mention it. Finally he spoke, "Whatever he is, he is a brave man, and he risked his own life to save mine." Red Hawk turned and walked away. He said nothing more. The other warrior took his right hand and rubbed his aching left shoulder, watching the two riders disappear into the distance. "Red Hawk will unmask this imposter," he thought. "If not, it will fall upon me as a duty to do so."

Before Chulley left for the Pecos, Thomas asked him to do his best to place the captive child in the care of someone who would get her back to the hacienda without harm, and to send word to Don Jose that he, Tomás, wanted to talk to him about the young captive before he disposed of her. Most of the carts had disgorged their loads during the trading, and were empty, except for a few carts that now contained hides and a meager number of buffalo robes, plus their food and other necessities for getting home. The repayment from the Indians had almost all been in cattle, mules, horses and, to a very meager extent, by the two captives.

The trail master told the men to feed the little girl, but otherwise to leave her alone. He said she would bring more ransom if she was not so afraid and haggard. He rummaged some old blankets for her to sleep upon, and assigned her care to an older Mexican who was the cook. The child was still small enough that she was often allowed to ride in a cart. She seemed to sense the kindness of the old *caballero*, and quickly bonded with him.

Thomas took the adolescent back to the Indian village and placed her under the care of Red Hawk's wives. He asked them to see that she worked and learned the things that a Comanche wife should know, but asked them not to mistreat her. After Sarah was traded to Thomas, she began to get adequate food. Without the continual abuse, she already began to lose some of her haggard appearance.

CHAPTER 33

Thomas and Red Hawk rode out of *Cañon del Rescate* well-mounted on two horses from the Comanchero *remuda* and each led an Indian pony as well. As they topped the canyon walls they were back on the flat Llano. They rode directly north. A feeling of well-being and relief came over Thomas, and for the first time he realized how constantly the features of the topography of his homeland, the hill country, had, heretofore, enclosed him, and had weighed down upon his sub-consciousness. The expanse of this country, the ability to see out in any direction, and the time to let his mind wander, as he himself wandered across the open spaces, without pressing concerns, all combined to give him a freedom of soul he had never before felt. He had found new eyes with which to view the prairie, and he discovered they revealed a West that he had not previously recognized. Instead of the stark dread that had earlier occurred when confronting the plains, he began, like Red Hawk, to enjoy the openness. The space began to give him a feeling of rapture that engendered a kinship with the eternal.

"Tell me about Indian trade in horses and mules," said Thomas. Red Hawk had a pleasant, satisfied appearance. "Most of the animals we obtain from raids into Mexico and Texas are almost immediately taken east and traded to the Americans coming out of a region they call the Mississippi. They have a huge market for these animals, and buy as many as we can furnish. The American traders are seen less often but are better for us than you Comancheros because they have better products than we can find in New Mexico. Horses that we raise for ourselves are trained to be war ponies, bison hunters or pack animals, and we love them almost as much as we love one another, and when we raise a really superior one we will never trade it."

"Have you ever wanted to be something other than a Comanche?" asked Thomas. Red Hawk looked surprised that such a question could be asked. "As a small boy I yearned to become a Comanche warrior, and now, as a man, that is what I have become. It is the only way I want to be remembered. The Comanches were created from these plains, and they gave birth to me. I could not possibly want for anything than to be what I truly am, what the Great Spirit intended for me to be."

Thomas was amazed by the new and different subtleties of the prairie which he had not realized existed. He studied the splendid adaptations of the prevalent prairie hare, how it rested in the shade of anything as high as one's knee, digging a shallow bed in which to settle, its long ears folded across its back, even in rest, poised to bound forward into its only realm of safety, the sudden dash across the open prairie, at which this animal was the master.

They soon came to a prairie dog town. The scattered holes, with a mound around each opening, covered an area of almost a square mile. The little rodents would sit up on their hind legs when danger approached, and give a persistent warning sound that was half bark and half chirp. "They are very difficult to hunt," said Red Hawk, "because of that warning system which gets attention from every hole, and also because, when wounded, they desperately try to get into their burrows, even to die. If you can shoot one with an arrow that lodges in the body, however, they can't drag themselves back into the hole, as the protruding arrow catches on the sides of the burrow. Roast prairie dog is sweet and delicious, but it is a rare treat." Red Hawk delighted in the scene, his eyes darting across the mounds to sight the young dogs, then spontaneously searching the sky to see if circling hawks were threatening from above.

Thomas could also see the numerous little prairie owls which lived in concert with the rodents, birds which would as soon run down a hole as to fly away, behavior he had never before seen in a bird. Red Hawk told him there were black ferrets, a kind of weasel that could be seen at certain times that hunted and lived off these animals, though they are more prevalent to the north.

The travelers rode on by the outer fringes of the dog town, coming to a wide abandoned hole, probably an old fox den, out of which came a small skunk. As he viewed the riders, he turned his back and raised his tail, slightly jumping up and down on his back legs. Both men knew enough to beat a hasty retreat.

As they rode on, a fetid odor roused Thomas, and he stopped his horse, then, slowly inched forward in the direction he sensed was its origin. A high pitched buzz greeted their ears, and Red Hawk pointed out a large rattlesnake. The reptile stopped its warning and began to slither down a nearby burrow. With cat-like quickness, Red Hawk jumped off his horse, grabbed the snake by the tail and with one swift motion pulled back and flung it out on flat ground. The huge snake immediately had his rattles buzzing so fast they made a whining noise; it retracted its body into an S-shape and raised its head about eight inches off the ground, a menacing pose for any who would be an enemy. Red Hawk laughed with glee as he alternately baited the animal with the long stalk of the Bear Grass plant and instantly, after a strike, whacked the snake on the head. The confrontation lasted about ten minutes with Red Hawk obviously enjoying the death sport. Finally he whacked so hard that the reptile could only writhe, but strike no more. The Indian held it pinioned against the ground and cut off its head; then cut off its rattles and placed the latter into his medicine bag. "We will have a great feast," he said. While Thomas held the reptile by the tail, Red Hawk gutted the snake and tied it behind his saddle.

The travelers were passing through short grass country. Although it was short, it was extremely thick. Thomas looked back in the direction from which they had come. "Just like the waters of the ocean envelope the wake of a moving ship, leaving no trace of its passage, the grass closes in after us, leaving no lasting sign that we have been here." Red Hawk appeared puzzled. "Like a large canoe passing over the great waters, it leaves no trail," Thomas said. Red Hawk smiled and nodded, "Grass, when it is green and in its growth season, will wipe out the obvious trail of a whole village in four or five days." They rode by a playa lake, where they had good water, and camped for the night. "Out here on the prairie, you can lie on your back and look at the entirety of the heavens," said Thomas. "At least you don't have to worry that you might be sleeping beneath a flock of birds," commented the guide. They laughed together, and enjoyed a supper of roasted rattlesnake.

"When you come out here alone beneath this sky and the infinite stretch of the plains, do you feel intimidated by nature?" asked Thomas. "I am nature," was the answer. "Since I am already a part of this scene, I feel at home, like I belong to it and it belongs to me; we are family, and I am as one with the Great Mystery. Being alone is sought by the Indian, for it is in this manner that one gets his vision for life."

One could appreciate that the perfection of the prairies was not wasted on Red Hawk.

"Until recently the Great Southern Plains has furnished us with everything we need, grand pastures of lush grass for our horses, hunting country for the meat and hides we live upon, places to barter for the things we need from others and the Texas and Mexican borderlands where we can raid for captives and stock. The American Army is beginning to make this way of life a bit more difficult."

A stiff breeze came up during the late afternoon of the following day, and a gathering of dark clouds hurried the evening on until there was utter blackness. The starless sky tightly enclosed them. Thomas searched the darkness, longing for the North Star, but there was not a single glimmer in the heavens. "No remoteness can compare to the isolation of a dark night on the Llano. Not even the Great Mystery could find us here," chuckled Thomas. "I will show you that He is here with us, even now," said Red Hawk. He took out his piece of flint and a small rough rod of steel, held them over the makings of their dried grass and buffalo chips, and struck the fire out of the rock which the Great Mystery had put there. A spark landed in the dried grass and a blaze arose which pushed against the blackness, leaving them light to see, and heat for roasting their evening meal, though outside their immediate circle, the light of the fire, reaching out only a short distance, scarcely dispelled the dark. Instead of just pushing back gloom, the glimmer only exposed other apprehensions of the night. A circle of yellow eyes reflected the light just beyond the boundaries of the camp. Red Hawk only laughed. "Grey Wolves," he said, and flung a burning buffalo chip in their direction.

"Do they ever attack?" asked Thomas.

"Men and wolves have a storied past," answered the Indian. "We have developed a careful truce, neither side daring to probe too far."

By early morning the rain was coming down hard. Since they were out in the open, the only roof was the bank of dark clouds, so there was nothing to do but shiver and endure it. Thomas noticed that the discomfort hardly affected Red Hawk, he and his horse simply plodding on toward the north. Around noon the weather began clearing and soon they were beginning to dry out. "The weather pattern changes rapidly, out here," said Thomas.

"On the open prairie you can have cloudbursts, blue northers, hailstorms, lightning storms, and tornados," laughed the Indian. "If that's not enough to suit you, it can turn around, and scour you with sandstorms, searing hot winds, and drought, and if it's dry, you can have a prairie fire sweep across the grassland."

"What do you do if you're caught in a prairie fire?" asked Thomas. "Anything upon the prairie that cannot fly, must either, 'run, dig, or die,' and if you run, when there is wind, you'd better be as fast as an antelope. If you think you are in a sea of emptiness now, you should ride across a swath of country after a huge prairie fire."

They found fresh water in the playas, thus did not have to divert from their course to slake their thirst. It was amazing how abundantly the fauna appeared around the playa lakes, out from what Thomas thought was lifeless prairie. Frogs came out of the ground, mated, and produced the next generation of tadpoles. Salamanders would do the same, and both could be found in abundance in the shallows. Snakes slithered in and out of the water's edge, and terrapins waddled toward the dampened ground. Feeding upon this manna were thousands of curlews, and there were hundreds of yellow-legged plovers around the edge of the water, eating tiny snails that had appeared. The plover-like killdeers ran along the water's edge, bobbing and making their shrill calls to one another. When a nest was approached by a person or some animal the mother bird would feign injury, dragging her wing along the ground and running away from the nest to lure the intruding predator away from her babies. Ducks and mud hens were in the deeper water, and field mice, ground squirrels, and jack rabbits were occasionally seen hopping through the nearby grass.

Buffalo came to the lakes and the large animals waded in, the buffalo wallowing in the wet ground of the shallower ponds, coating themselves with mud for protection from insects. Following the herbivores and the rodents, there were always the predators: the Swift Fox, lynx, coyote, and the large Grey Wolves though they would very seldom approach when a human was around. Always circling above were the hawks. An occasional badger could be seen scurrying through the grass, but never far from his den. "Why don't we see prairie dogs here to drink?" asked Thomas.

"They seem to get their water from the morning dew on the grass. Some people say they dig their holes all the way down to underground springs, but I do not believe that is so. If they came here to water, far away from their holes, they would be easy prey for the hawks, wolves, and wild cats."

Though antelope were seen in great numbers across the plains, they were rarely seen at the water's edge, the animals also apparently obtaining part of their fluid from the early morning dew on the grass. Red Hawk told Thomas that they were an important source of food and hides for the Comanche, and could often be lured into shooting range by displaying some waving, colored cloth which the animals would approach, simply from curiosity. "While the buffalo migrate off the plains in winter, the antelope are always out here the year round," he said.

Away from the lakes on the flat land, especially in taller grass there were thousands of prairie chickens. Always hesitant to fly, they could hide in the grass in such a way that even seasoned hunters would not see them until startled by the sudden flush of the birds.

Thomas began to recognize that although he was continually probing Red Hawk about his surroundings and his society and the Comanche loved to talk about these subjects, in return the Comanche appeared to have absolutely no corresponding interest in the culture of the Mexicans, nor for that matter, of the Americans. "In his inner world, it is only himself he hears", thought Thomas. The natives were simply impervious to different points of view. It never even occurred to Red Hawk to make a conscious effort to expand his horizons outside the Comancheria, nor did it ever occur to the tribal elders to advise him to do so. The horizons of these natives ended at the border of the Indian territory, although that territory did include much of the Texas and Northern Mexico borderlands.

"It will be the downfall of these people," thought Thomas, "that they are oblivious to the attributes and intricacies of any other society, or any other country, even as they are being harried from every side, living only in the security of what they like to think, not what they know."

CHAPTER 34

On the fifth day out, Red Hawk said they were only about two more days of travel from the Canadian River country. Around noontime they could see a long line of figures extensively spread out across the plains, farther to the north. Thomas was at a loss to know what it was they were seeing, but Red Hawk spoke up. "It's a Comanche village on the move to a new camping site," he said, "Let's ride up close. This should be an interesting sight for you."

The two riders were spotted immediately and five warriors came riding out to see who they were. Red Hawk signed that he was Comanche, and when the five braves arrived, Red Hawk knew two of them. The five recognized at once that Thomas, even though he was dressed like one of their tribe, was not one of "The People," but since he was with Red Hawk, he was allowed a pass. The Indians were quite happy to see one another, and the two riders were invited to come along to the new camp. Red Hawk declined, however, saying he and his friend had to go on to the Canadian River. Thomas lost some of the interplay of words and gesture but he did note one pointing to a lone rider sitting off to the side of the line of the village march, as though sitting in review of the whole procedure. As the five braves rode back to the column, Red Hawk turned toward Thomas and said, "Come, we must go and greet my cousin." They turned their line of travel toward the lone sentinel.

He sat upon a black, sturdy horse. Thomas marveled at the oneness of the two, the rider, august, imposing, astride the saddle, his podium from which to direct the affairs of men, the pony beneath the stride, well sufficient unto his burden, appearing alert and eager to ply the paths of the prairies. The Indian sat erect as if posing, holding his head back and his chest forward, his eyelids at half-mast. He was not, however, overly dressed. Long braids hung down on each side to the level of his waist, his own hair interlaced with otter fur. A single eagle feather protruded backward from his hair and a silver necklace was draped around his neck He wore moccasins and a breechclout but otherwise his torso and legs were bare, his bronze skin acknowledging the power of the sun.

When Thomas got close enough to see the lone rider's face, he recognized him at once, the War Chief of the battle of Blanco Canyon. He and Red Hawk greeted one another warmly, and talked in an animated fashion with much gesture and seeming joy. The sentinel turned toward Thomas and asked, "Who is this outlander, and why are you trying to disguise him as a Comanche?" Red Hawk laughed, and said that Thomas was a Comanchero who had once saved his life, and that he was guiding the trader to the Canadian River. "Be careful whom you guide across the Comancheria," the sentinel advised, "most Mexicans and White Men have no business here."

The chief turned toward Thomas and the gazes of the two locked into a common struggle, the Comanche's eyes searching, evaluating, judging, as though they had no difficulty in penetrating to one's very soul, unmasking whatever dwelt within the mind of the one he interrogated. The stare did, indeed, seem to envelope Thomas, as though intended to cast a spell, tending to immobilize any protective mechanism that might otherwise come into play, but Thomas did not turn his eyes away in submission; his steely stare in turn interrogated the quintessence of the chief, Thomas confident in the knowledge that he belonged where he was, had hunted the sacred buffalo, smoked the peace pipe of the council, been accepted as a brother and had vanquished his foes, even the Comanches he had warred against, confident of his ability in any situation, of his equality to any warrior.

The downturned corners of the mouth of the chief relaxed as he smiled and fully opened his eyelids. "You don't look like a Comanchero to me. You look like a warrior, one we would be proud to claim as our own. My advice is for you give up your penchant for trading, and become a true Comanche, thus knowing the joy of the free and noble life." "You flatter me," said Thomas, "I will think upon what you have said." Thomas could see the faint scar on the left side of the leader's neck.

The two parties bade goodbye, and went their separate ways, the two explorers riding east to skirt the back of the procession.

"He is an impressive leader," said Thomas. "Yes," answered Red Hawk, "probably our best. He is sure of what he can do and is satisfied to let others do what they can. I have known him since boyhood when we played and rode together. I do not say this to detract from my friend, but since I knew him so well, and we grew up together I know that he is much more indecisive, and simple of nature and mind, than many people are apt to presume."

"The majority of most leader's actions, as also those of our own, are probably of such simple nature," returned Thomas.

The line of nomads straggled far back into the distance, the marchers making no effort to close ranks. The sub-chiefs rode in front, much like they were putting on a parade, sitting their horses in the way of men long accustomed to the saddle, saddles cleverly designed, light and practical, made by the villagers themselves. The warriors were in strange regalia, wearing their finery from the neck up but only breechclouts and moccasins below, because of the heat. Nearly all the warriors were carrying their lances and shields, not trusting such a sacred thing to the women. "The lance is the warrior's scepter," thought Thomas, "each man bearing his own, as a claim to his individual kingdom."

Behind the dominant males, came the wives, their burdens seeming to have no end, their tasks, more like those of a mule than a human, their faces dark and harrowed from years at hard labor, and the constant exposure to the sun and wind. Several of them had a cradleboard and papoose strapped to their backs and many had another small child riding in front of their saddles. Slightly older children walked beside their mothers. The horses they were riding were all shapes and colors, though the predominant choice tended toward paints and spotted animals. The mounts plodded onward, looking somewhat doleful, their heads slightly bowed, as ponies are prone to do when they carry a heavy load for an extended distance. From time to time, the chiefs would look back and scan the column, much like wolves do, as though to make sure each subordinate was not overstepping his or her proper place.

In addition to bearing their personal burdens and those of their infant children, the squaws were also watching and tending the pack animals, mostly mules, loaded with the meager supply of all of the Indians' worldly goods, things that were lightweight and easy to pack and move, things fitting of their nomadic society. Thomas noted that the Indians and their animals did not follow one another in a straight line, but spread out through a width of territory so that the village would not leave lasting ruts or deep trails which would endure. No travois followed directly in the path of another, an effort to avoid leaving permanent paths.

Older girls were scattered among the wives, already heavily involved in the laborious tasks of the move, trying to perfect the chores that were in store for them in their future lives. Among and behind the wives came the younger, though mobile, pre-teen children, romping and playing as they went, then the old men, and finally the old squaws. One emaciated and bowed such squaw tottered out of line, reeled back and forth and fell to one side. She struggled to get up on her knees, then, struggled even harder to rise to her feet, but finally she staggered on. There was no one to pick her up and the column left her farther behind. Thomas wondered if this was the end of her time, and she was being abandoned.

Red Hawk sensed what Thomas was thinking. "We are not a sedentary people," he said, "We are rovers. That is our nature, that is our only way of life, and when one is no longer able to rove, he or she can no longer be a part of the people. A person unable to carry his or her own load is a tremendous burden on a society such as ours. There is a history behind this woman's isolation. If this were her first occasion to need aid she would be readily helped, but everyone knows that her time has come, and she probably has no remaining family. It is the way of nature. Even wolves cull their own packs."

A heavy scattering of dogs was spread throughout the column. Some were pulling a small travois. Most were simply barking and snarling.

A group of young warriors occasionally fell out of line, and rode around the entire column, to intermittently act as a rear guard and to make sure there was no nearby danger, but after their task they rode back to their position of status. The horse herd was driven to the side of the column by the boys who were still sub-adults.

A second group of horses, consisting of shabby mustangs, was being harried apart from the main herd. "What are these animals?" asked Thomas.

"They are recently captured mustang mares, which will be used for breeding mules," he answered. "Mules from these wild mares have tremendous endurance, and make great pack animals for the nomadic Comanches."

Thomas sat his horse, holding still for some minutes, rapt by the scene, looking, not at the details, but at the whole of the happening, the whole of the image, as one looks at an entire painting without discerning the individual strokes of the artist. "What a splendid effort," he noted. "Everything moving in unison, every-able bodied person of the village participating."

"No one can do everything, but everyone can do something," laughed Red Hawk. "That is the way the Comanche people survive."

"I wonder if these tribes feel forever lost as they wander from one barren spot to another," mused Thomas. "There is no edifice, no town, no permanence to come back to after they have roamed the prairie, only a continual quest, a hunger that can never be satisfied."

Red Hawk laughed. "They are not seeking some place of satisfaction as you suggest. Wherever they go they carry their world with them, and their Comanche world has its own satisfactions apart from the place they may happen to camp. Your tribesmen try to satisfy themselves, by building permanent pueblos or towns, but when they build them, and are satisfied, then is when the towns begin to decay. I think your joy must be in the effort of building, not in the finished construction. To the Comanche, the joy is in the roving, not the location they momentarily settle upon; they will soon long for more joy and move on. The barren spots you talk about are not barren to the Indian. They find lush pasture for the horse herds, the grass beckons the buffalo and the antelope, but none of this is lasting, the horse herd, the game, the people, will all soon move on and they have the joy of renewing their surroundings and themselves."

The two mounts were suddenly harried by large horse flies, vociferous blood suckers, which drove the ponies wild by the sting of their bite. Once they had alighted and penetrated the skin to taste their victim's blood they would not be driven off, so both Red Hawk and Thomas had blood smeared hands from swatting the vile insects. "These pests sometimes follow a moving village in the summertime," said Red Hawk.

"They have now found us, so we must keep swatting and move on away so our horses will be spared."

That evening as they camped near another playa lake, Thomas walked out on the prairie to look at the western sky. The gloaming spread from the west and hallowed the horizon, the reddish glow reflecting from the clouds, casting a dim illumination most of the way around the meridian, bathing all the four winds except for a small dark swath in the midpoint of the east. He could hear the buzzing call of the nighthawks as they wheeled and dipped to glean insects from the sky for their nightly feeding. Thomas, once more, felt at peace, sensing the sublime majesty of this immense prairie, primal in its display of unsullied creation. For a long time, he only stood and gazed into the horizon.

By mid-morning of the next day they could catch the far distant glimpse of undulating land which Thomas took to be erosive channels leading to the valley of the Canadian River. Above the sky line, but still in the distance, a huge congregation of large birds was circling, and Thomas pointed out the sight to Red Hawk. "A cache of the dead or dying," said the Indian, his face wrinkling into a frown. The two riders turned their horses in the direction of the avian vortex, abnormal for its magnitude, defacing the blue of the heavens, casting a premonition of tragedy upon its surveyors. The great birds wheeled and dipped, then rose again, sailing leisurely, circling, rarely flapping a wing, but craftily soaring over the rising thermals to gather the updrafts beneath their feathered pinions and keep themselves aloft. When one would finally settle to the ground, all of the glory of its graceful flight gave way, its mighty wings "whamping" loudly to brake its speed, the dark avian creature magnified by its dark shadow, waddling and hopping into position to feast on the pulp of putrid flesh. "Some Indians think that the vultures carry the flesh of the dead up into the heavens," said Red Hawk, "but I don't think they can really fly that high."

As they drew closer, a fetid odor filled the air, and the shadows of the carrion birds repetitively crossed the line of progress of the two travelers. They rode up on a scene repugnant beyond measure. There were numerous scattered carcasses of skinned buffalo rotting in the open air. The agonal thrashing of the legs of many of the animals had scraped the ground clear of grass, and puddles of blood had collected and clotted in the flailed basins, the broiling sun drying the puddles into a pattern of cracked, dark red ceramic. Wolves were tearing at the corpses on the far side of the site, looking alien to the landscape, their normal color, that of the straw of the prairie floor, now grossly sullied by the blood smeared on their faces and fur. Buzzards were already picking at the carcasses, milling among themselves in their clerical black, always at a safe distance from the wolves. "Dominic should see this," mused Thomas, "so he could know what purgatory looks like."

Red Hawk was beside himself with anger at the wanton slaughter, this disregard for the bounty of the plains, to him, not just the slaughter of buffalo, but the wrenching out of the hearts of the "The People," the ultimate affront to the spirit of the prairie nomads, for the buffalo were not just plains creatures to be observed and occasionally hunted, but the Comanche's primary source of food, shelter, and fuel, the very sustenance of their culture.

Thomas remembered sitting in the officers' quarters at Fort Sill one night conversing with the soldiers, when one of the captains quoted General Sheridan, who said that he would like to wipe all of the buffalo from the Great Plains, because that would be one of the easiest ways to control the Indians. He wondered if the scene before them now, looked about the same, except with human carcasses, when Chivington, and at another time, Custer, decided to clear the Southern Cheyenne from the region of the Arkansas River. Lastly, he remembered when Oswego had told him that he wasn't sure he was on the right side.

The horsemen circled the sight of slaughter. They found wagon tracks leading into a rendezvous point, and then tracks more deeply rutted, as a heavier load was wheeled away. Thomas studied the site, and just from the signs left on the grass, he said, "there are three men, two horses and a team of mules pulling a heavy wagon, probably loaded with green hides. They were here within the last ten hours." Red Hawk nodded, as he had once before, when Thomas assessed the age of the antelope tracks. "You have unusual skill for a Mexican," he grinned and said. "You remind me more of a Tonkawa scout." Red Hawk waved for Thomas to follow as they loped along tracking the wagon.

The land began to get rougher as the riders approached the breaks of the Canadian River. The two horsemen came over a slight rise, and down below was a similar scene to that which they had so recently encountered. Dead buffalo were scattered about, but this time the carnage was fresh, and two skinners were in the act of removing the hides while one of the blood smeared party was toting tongues and hides to the wagon.

In contrast to the usual method of attack used by the Comanches, Red Hawk was so enraged that he let out a chilling scream and charged the bearer. The startled man dropped his load and fled toward the wagon, but Red Hawk was soon on him and ran a lance into his back. The two skinners, caught out in the open had no place to run for cover, so each crouched behind a carcass. Both had pistols and they began firing at the Indian, but he charged for the nearest one, zigzagging his approach in the same manner Thomas had seen when the soldier was killed by the war chief in the battle of Blanco Canyon. When he got close to the first skinner, Red Hawk used his rifle and shot from beneath the horse's neck, his aim deadly. He turned toward the remaining skinner, who was making a desperate run toward the wagon. The Indian pony quickly closed the distance between them, and the Comanche clubbed him in the head with his tomahawk.

. Red Hawk heard a shot ring out. Though the prairie produced no echo, the whining sound lingered in the immensity of the distance. He turned his head toward the origin of the shot. The initial hunter, that he had lanced, had not died, but had been able to crawl to the wagon. He had pulled out his Sharps Rifle which he had turned toward the Comanche. The shot was not from the big gun, however, but from Thomas's Winchester, which had dispatched the hunter who was aiming the long rifle at Red Hawk. The Comanche rode back to Thomas. "You have saved my life for a second time," he said, "it is not usual that a Comanche would, twice, owe his life to a Mexican."

To Thomas, Red Hawk seemed the perfect hero, self-reliant, fearless and competent, instinctively and skillfully eliminating enemies of his people, but steadfastly true to his tribe, family, and friends.

CHAPTER 35

Thomas was relieved and grateful that Red Hawk was still alive, though he was deeply shocked by what he had done. He had shot a white man, a man of his own ilk. He knew that if the Americans ever found out about his action he would be summarily hanged. Instead of helping to eradicate the hated enemy which so many times he had sworn to do, he had actually warred on the side of the Comanche. He was convinced he had betrayed his own people. What's more he felt he had betrayed himself and the memory of his family. He had simply been unable to sit by and watch his guide be shot by the hide packer. Red Hawk no longer embodied the connotations of what Thomas had always thought of as Comanche; rather, a friend, a confidant, a brother. The young Texan's heritage flooded him with guilt, but in the depths of his mind he felt justice required that the Indian should not be killed. He knew that the weighing and sorting of these thoughts would keep him awake late into many nights to come.

Red Hawk scalped the two skinners, and told Thomas the third one belonged to him, but Thomas declined, so the Indian rode away with three American scalps.

"How did it make you feel when you first scalped a man?" asked Thomas. "I was fourteen on the Texas frontier on my first raid, and it was the most exciting and proudest day of my life," was the answer. "Did you not feel any regret in having killed another human, or any pity for the victim?" Thomas probed. "Why do you keep asking such silly questions?" Red Hawk returned. "This was a Texan, not a human being, a despised predator of my people, living not in his own country, but upon our land." "How do you tell Comanche land from Mexican land or

Texas land?" asked Thomas. "I see you do not understand the nature of war," said the Indian.

Red Hawk said that across the river and a little farther to the northeast there was a trading company being built by white men. "These hide robbers were probably headed in that direction, so we should ride the opposite way." He also said that if the army was somewhere about, and found the death scene of the hide hunters, they might try to track the two of them so they should make sure their tracks could not be followed.

The riders backtracked to the area of the first slaughter, made several misleading forays into the surrounding prairie, finally departing from the area along a ridge of tight turf with fresh buffalo hide laced around the four feet of each horse. At the river they headed east for a mile, then rode into the water and abandoned and buried the buffalo hide horse shoes. They turned back west, and worked their way upstream in the center of the shallow, red, and opaque flowing water. About a mile from the spot where they started wading, Red Hawk spotted an area of bare hard rock, beckoned to Thomas, and they rode up out of the water.

The riders' course was west, toward an ancient and easy river crossing, called Tascosa, and Red Hawk's spirits began to lighten as they rode along. That night in camp, Red Hawk told his companion of the many canyons that cut through the eastern escarpment of the plains. "There is one that is huge," he said. "It is ten camping moves in length and so deep that no one except the Comanches and their friends can find the bottom. The white men and the army do not know of its existence, it is our invulnerable winter camp."

The two friends lay back upon the open ground and gazed into the night sky. It was a pulsing, glittering dance of lights. Again and again falling stars streaked across the sky, fleeing from the firmament into the realm of nothingness. "Have you noticed?" asked Red Hawk, "that many, many stars fall from the sky nearly every night, but there never seems to be any fewer of them." Thomas thought about trying to tell Red Hawk about meteors, but that would lead to the subject of atmosphere, and then of gravity, so he deemed the subject should be left alone. "Only the Great Mystery can tell us why," he answered.

"Haven't the Comancheros visited you in the great canyon?" asked Thomas. "They come to the edge, but we never let them in the depths, and besides one of them would never dare to reveal where it is."

"Red Hawk, your people shouldn't feel as secure as they do. If the Comancheros can find it, the army can find it. The army in New Mexico is already scouting out the Comancheros' trails." Red Hawk laughed. "You do not understand, my friend. The Palo Duro is a place like no other, a sacred place of special benevolence. It has been our secret haven for hundreds of years. The Great Spirit promised this canyon only to us. In the long ago He led our ancestors to it. He will keep this holy place safe for the Comanches through all time."

As morning broke, the two riders continued west. Looking backward over the abyss in the early morning, Thomas was blinded by the eastern sun, but by mid-morning he could enjoy looking back across the great distance they had come.

It was an indistinct image, one that lasted only for an instant, then, disappeared, but Thomas stopped his horse and grabbed Red Hawk by the arm. "I saw riders come off that far knoll," he said. Red Hawk turned and peered at the distant landmark for some time. He put his hand across his brow to block out the ambient light, thus increasing his acuity, and watched. He pointed down and to the right of the knoll. "There is red dust rising out of the bottom of the ravine," he said. "The knoll is steep, and the horses had to slide down. They are hurrying because they think we do not know of them. There must be at least four riders, from the amount of dust we see." Actually Thomas saw no dust.

"The army alone would not have been able to follow our trail. They must have a Delaware with them."

"Why a Delaware?" asked Thomas. "They are the best trackers, and the army often hires them. They hate the Comanches almost as much as do the Tonkawas. Our enemies will have horses that are much fresher than ours, Thomas, because we have now been riding for so many days. We will have to make a stand, but I know the place to do it."

They turned west again and rode about a mile before turning down an eroded gully to the river bed below. Thomas wanted to break into a run, but the Indian held him back and set a moderate pace.

"One does not want to be afoot out here leading a worn out mount."

The level of the river bottom was flat and wide, with the stream of water demanding only about a tenth of the width of the sandy bed, the stream simply meandering from side to side among the sand bars, but continuing its forward flow. Red Hawk led across the water to the opposite bank, and up a steep ravine. He no longer tried to hide his tracks as he hurried on. As the sides of the ravine got steeper the floor became wider and more flat until it came to a slight bend. Vegetation was abundant along the floor but the rift formed into a box canyon with high steep walls on all sides except for the inlet. Next to one wall, Thomas noted knappings of flint and chert, relics of a distant past.

There was no obvious way out of the box canyon except the inlet from whence they had come. Red Hawk tied the horses where they could be seen from the bend and beckoned Thomas to bring his rifle and follow. The two walked behind a rim of red juniper and in one corner Red Hawk pointed upward. Thomas stared at the sheer wall and, at first, saw nothing. Red Hawk pointed to a subtle scalloped indentation in the red sandstone, and Thomas realized there was a series of indentations that had apparently been chiseled up the precarious side of the bastion. The steps were almost invisible in the shadows of the canyon and he would never have found them if they had not been pointed out by his guide. He could see that the ladder had long been abandoned because the cups were filled with debris, but he guessed it must have originally been carved by ancient tribesmen whose bones had long since turned to dust, probably designed for the same purpose for which it was now being used.

Red Hawk took a juniper branch to wipe away their tracks that led up to the ladder, then clinging with his fingers, leaning flat against the stone, began toeing his way to the top. After eyeing the technique of the climb, Thomas, likewise, strapped his rifle across his back and started the fearsome ascent. Twenty minutes later they were both on top, standing on a flat bench of ground, the tabular summit on a level with the adjacent plains, and like the adjacent plains of the Canadian River country, dotted with clumps of juniper. From the sheer rear wall in the back, the butte extended along both sides of the box canyon, before erosion angled it downward to descend all the way to the canyon floor where the ravine began, but still well above the level of the river.

Red Hawk pointed the way around one side to Thomas and he

took the other. There was no hesitation in his directions, proceeding as though incapable of miscalculation; no "perhaps" residing in his thinking. Thomas saw that the Comanche had assigned him the easiest and most protected side, with better concealment because the scrubby bushes were more thickly placed, but this was not the time to argue, so Thomas began working his way down the ridge as Red Hawk did the same on the more exposed opposite edge. Both found a good spot where they were well camouflaged and sat down to wait. Thomas knew he would soon have to decide whether or not to fire on the U.S. Army. He feared he could not do that, even in order to save his own life. The quandary, however, was that he also knew that he could not give himself up by surrendering to the Americans and, thus, betray Red Hawk.

CHAPTER 36

The army patrol and their tracker approached the mouth of the ravine very warily. As Red Hawk had surmised, they were being led by a Delaware scout. He was frowning as he slowly followed the four sets of horse tracks from the river bed into the floor of the ravine. Thomas eyed him intently; he was savage, but fascinating, like a wolf trailing its prey, his approach ominous, but magnificent in its display of primitive prowess. The scout and all the soldiers were obviously at full alert, their rifles cocked and pointing forward.

When the Delaware came to the bend of the canyon and saw the four tied horses, he immediately backed from the line of sight, and again looked above to scan the rims on each side. He dismounted and walked to each bank to make sure there were no tracks leading back out, motioned for the Lieutenant, and they began a discussion while the other four stood guard, their rifles remaining cocked and held in position ready to fire. The scout and the officer eased forward toward the bend of the canyon and when the horses again came into sight, they shot all four, then, retreated back again to the mouth of the ravine. All of the six trackers dismounted, and one trooper was assigned to sit on his horse and hold the other five mounts at a position just outside the entrance into the gulch.

The lieutenant assigned one older sergeant to go up the left ridge where Red Hawk was hidden and the Delaware scout took the right ridge which was Thomas's side. Thomas breathed a sigh of relief, for he had no compunction against firing on a Delaware. The remaining three soldiers carefully worked their way back to the bend, disappearing beyond the curve of the high canyon wall, apparently intent on flushing out the fugitives while their two compatriots looked down from above.

The sergeant, picking his way up the ridge, came to an area about fifteen feet in length which was devoid of cover. He crouched with his rifle in his right hand, then, sprang for the next clump of juniper. Simultaneously, a shot rang out. The sergeant slapped his hand across his chest as he tumbled backward and rolled to the edge where he fell headlong into the ravine, the only noise, a sickening thud of irrefutable finality. Every sound was abruptly stilled and utter silence encased the canyon.

Thomas kept trying to see even the faintest movement or different color among the junipers of his ridge, but he could only stare into the shrubbery at nothing, no hint of the presence of the Delaware. Gradually an unrecognized scent drifted on the air, and Thomas knew the stalker had to be very close. He stilled his own breath so there would be no break in the effort of his own listening. Faintly, he detected the sound of the Delaware's breath break into the quietness. A rock landed just at the heels of one of the horses being held by the soldier on the canyon floor, and the animal shied forward. The horse guard reached to quell the excited animal and in an instant, Red Hawk, who had someway worked around behind the horses, leaped up behind the guard and cut his throat. Thomas sickened as he saw blood spurt forward and discolor the sand.

A second shot rang out and Red Hawk was knocked from the back of the army steed where he lay imperiled among the horse's legs, but the offending barrel of the rifle had been exposed, and Thomas put three bullets into the juniper where the Delaware had to be crouching.

There was a muffled groan, and then labored breathing, but Thomas could see nothing but juniper. He heard a rock land in the dirt behind his back, but he did not look or move. He recognized the sound as a ruse thrown by his enemy, and braced himself for an assault. He listened. The foe drew in a deep breath, as though to rinse his mouth with air. Suddenly, the Delaware came out of the brush with the charge of a wounded boar, flinging himself at the shrubs which concealed Thomas. Though the Indian scout was experienced and agile, he was also wounded, overestimating his own remaining ability, and underestimating that of his foe. Thomas met him in the air with a rifle butt to his jaw. The Delaware crumpled, then, pitched forward into the ravine, his surprised scream puncturing the silence, and echoing from the canyon walls. Thomas took no chance and shot him twice where he lay. The Lieutenant and his two troopers appeared at the edge of the bend, but Thomas put a bullet into the wall just above their heads, and scree showered down on them, causing the soldiers to quickly withdraw from the line of sight.

Thomas hurried to his friend who was now sitting upon the ground among the horses' legs. He still held his rifle in his right hand but his left arm and side were covered with blood. Slowly Thomas pulled the arm away from Red Hawk's body, and a pulsatile jet of red shot forth. Thomas worked his thumb up into his friend's axilla, felt the bruit of the open artery, and pushed down. The bleeding ceased. The wound was along the inner side of his upper arm and did not involve the chest, but Thomas could tell the bone was broken. Though Thomas was pressing down directly over the fracture, the Comanche made no sound. With Thomas's thumb staunching the hemorrhage and his other hand on the rifle they sat where they were for twenty minutes, waiting for the blood of the open vessel to clot. Thomas slowly eased the pressure of his thumb away, and this time there was no active flow of blood.

He ripped the sleeve off the dead trooper's shirt and wadded it to make a tamponade, taking the rest of the shirt and making a sling for the arm, and binding it to the chest wall. Red Hawk said he could still sit a horse. Thomas picked out the best two mounts to ride and two more to lead behind them, then shot the remaining unlucky two. He helped Red Hawk onto his horse, again shot his rifle toward the neck of the ravine, and headed to the river, hoping that fear of being sighted and shot still held the three remaining soldiers at bay in the head of the canyon.

The two horsemen rode down to the river, letting all the animals drink, and the scout filled the army canteens. Thomas turned the mounts to the south and the two riders and four horses came out of the breaks, then turned back east toward the site of the second buffalo slaughter. The trek was the most difficult that Thomas had ever taken. He tied his horse side by side with that of his friend so that he could hold Red Hawk in the saddle. They rode on through the night, using the river breaks on their left as their guide. After twenty-four more hours they rode back into the presence of the herd of dead and partially denuded buffalo. It had now been almost three days since they had left this spot. The team of mules, now crazed with thirst, were still securely tied to the wagon.

Thomas threw the raw and bloody buffalo hides out of the wagon, leaving only three at the bottom of the bed for Red Hawk to lie on. There was a small amount of corn and some rations in the front that had not been disturbed except by the flies. Thomas took all the animals to the river to drink and then brought them back to the wagon. He fed the mules and the one horse he might have to ride all of the remaining corn. The best two horses were tied to the back of the wagon; the other two were shot. Even though the mules appeared in terrible shape, Thomas put them in the traces and turned the wagon south to try to retrace his trail back to *Cañon del Rescate*.

The wagon went only five hours the first evening. They had come to one of the playa lakes where Thomas was determined to take full advantage of the water and the summer grass while it was available. Red Hawk was in terrible pain but he still had a faint pulse in the wrist and his arm was not febrile. He recognized the playa where they camped the first night, and instructed Thomas extensively on what to look for on the way back. Both scouts thought they would not be followed since only three of the original pursuers remained, and all three were afoot with no tracker.

The next morning, the mules were remarkably revived. Thomas found it hard to believe how tough and resilient they were. He killed a jack rabbit with his rifle and roasted it and fed Red Hawk as much as he was able to eat. On they went, mile after weary mile, Thomas's long training as a scout serving to keep him on the proper route. He had his pocket compass and Red Hawk was able to repeatedly recognize their locations, though the various landmarks that Red Hawk recognized all looked the same to Thomas. As Thomas had previously learned, he always drew a line from the back of the wagon toward the North Star as they camped at night so if weather prevented seeing the sun as it arose they would always start toward the south.

On the fifth day Red Hawk's arm was swollen and red and his pain was much more severe. Thomas was willing to stop and let him rest, but Red Hawk insisted they keep going, because he felt his only chance was to get back to the medicine man of his tribe. Thomas acquiesced to the desire: if your blood was Comanche, and your thinking and acting had followed that vein all of your life, it followed that there was no alternative in the mind of the wounded warrior.

"If I do not live, Thomas, please take my body back to The People, that I may have a proper burial, so that I can go to the realm of the Great Spirit. I know you will do that even though you are not a Comanche."

"I will never abandon you in life or death," said Thomas. "I may not be Comanche, but I am your blood brother." Red Hawk grasped Thomas by the arm, gave him a slight smile, and then lapsed into a coma. Thomas detected a putrid odor on the Indian. He searched for the origin of the smell. It was not the arm. Eventually he traced it to Red Hawk's medicine bag. There, tightly stuffed into the pouch were the three scalps taken from the skinners. They were so important to Red Hawk that he had carried them all this way, even through the climb, and the encounter at the box canyon of the ravine. Thomas tied them beneath the wagon, to distance the odor.

For the last four days of the trip, Red Hawk appeared to improve, and though the jolting wagon was very painful to him, he seemed to enjoy talking and eating around the evening campfire. Red Hawk asked Thomas if he felt he had learned enough to go out on his own as a Comanchero. "No," said Thomas, "after seeing the hunters and the army on the plains, I don't believe that type trade can survive. That means the Comanche cannot continue in the old ways." Red Hawk smiled. "You are talking about what may happen tomorrow; we will not worry about that tonight. There will be plenty of time to consider this problem after we see the next morning's sunrise."

The days were long, dry and tedious. No feature appeared upon the prairie to mark one's progress, making the grassland imponderable and threatening.

One night, Thomas asked Red Hawk if he had ever been on the reservation at Fort Sill. "I have ridden there to look, and to see some of the Indian people who have yielded to the way of the Whites, but I would never choose to live there, or to take orders from them, even if I were starving. For me and my family, we want to live, not just survive. We choose to exist as we always have, on the free buffalo plains."

"Does that mean you will continue to raid on the Texas frontier, and trade with whoever you can still find?" Thomas asked.

"That is the way of our lives. Why would we want to change? If we did not go on raids, our young warriors could not gain honor and learn to be worthy and brave. They would be only slaves, and warriors no more, and the Great Spirit would no longer be proud of 'The People.' I have decided that it is time to gather many other braves, joining all of the tribes together, and drive the Americans and the Texans totally from our land, and all the way back to the great waters. Your people of Mexico should join us."

"What makes you think you can drive them away?" asked Thomas.

"Because in spite of everything you have told me, I think there are more of us than there are of them. In all these years of fighting the army, I have never seen more Blue Coats than Comanches. Also, we are better warriors," he said.

"I agree that you are the greatest warriors, Red Hawk, but you are mistaken if you think there are more of you, than there are of the Americans. They have a huge land and it is thickly peopled, all the way from the frontier to the shores of the great waters. We Mexicans thought we could defeat the Americans when they decided to take our land, but they have several armies a hundred times larger than anything you have seen on the Llano. They have huge war canoes that can carry whole armies and have cannons many times as large as the one you saw in the back of the Comanchero wagon. Be careful you don't hold to your opinions simply because that is what you want to believe."

"It's what the Great Spirit wants us to believe and to know," returned Red Hawk sternly. Thomas turned from the subject, realizing there was no use to continue, the shroud of native conceit never waning enough to allow the plain facts to shine through.

It was late evening when the explorers rolled into sight of *Cañon del Rescate* and the Comanche village of Red Hawk. The young boys ran and laughed and all the village people gathered round. Much concern was expressed about Red Hawk's wound, though they seemed to recognize it as a great badge of honor. There was also rejoicing over the three scalps that Red Hawk had brought home, and everyone wanted to hear the story of their battle. Red Hawk was not shy about telling of his great victory over the hated buffalo hunters, but he did give Thomas credit for shooting the wounded one. He became very serious as he told them of the escape from the army patrol, and he praised Thomas for killing the Delaware scout, and for again saving his life and bringing him home.

That night there was a scalp dance generating much excitement and the appearance of much joy throughout the villages camped in the canyon. At least two hundred souls answered the call for the dance, including many people from the neighboring camps, for scalps were more and more difficult to come by, and this celebration of a victory over the hated hide hunters should be a prestigious occasion. Red Hawk was exhausted and was in considerable pain, but he and Thomas sat together and watched the rite. The dance was a frenzied thing, surreal and bizarre, as if it were from some nether part of the world, orgiastic, primal, and devoid of order, the discordant rhythms sweeping the Indians deep into the night, chanting until they were hoarse, beseeching the Great Mystery to affirm the supremacy of "The People," the truth of "The Old Ways."

The teepee where Thomas had slept before was still in the same place. Red Hawk's wives had brought the captive girl and put her in his tent. The rags that she had previously worn had been replaced by Comanche clothing and the unspeakable grime, which had encased her, had been washed away.

Chulley had returned with his new load of goods, and most of the trading had already been done. He told Thomas they would leave in two days. Thomas greeted most of the Indians that he had met during the previous trading that were still in the area, though some of the villages had already left, and there were new ones to take their place. Only once did Thomas see Running Deer. They made eye contact long enough for each one to smile, then she looked down and walked away. Thomas and Chulley sat with the braves around the fire and ate roast meat. They listened to Red Hawk recount his battle story, and heard Thomas confirm the details and say he had never seen such a warrior before. Red Hawk exulted in his new-found prestige.

When Thomas went back to his tent he saw the captive girl sitting on the robes. She quickly removed herself and sat on the ground. Not able to conceal her fear, she ventured to communicate. "Am I to be your wife?" she asked in her limited Comanche. Thomas motioned her back on the robes, came close enough for her to hear a whisper, and spoke in

English. "You have suffered enough. You are free, and I will try to see that you get back to your people, but we must say nothing of this, and never speak in English again until we are in Santa Fe." He could hear her softly crying during the night, but he knew she was shedding tears of profound relief, at last hoping that her long and terror-filled ordeal might come to an end.

Red Hawk went through all of the ministrations of the tribe's medicine men, the incantations, the sprinkling of herbs, the sweat lodge, the crow's wing placed above his doorway, and the continual dancing around his teepee, but his arm began to swell and the skin grew dusky.

Before going their separate ways, Thomas and Red Hawk sat together in his tent, each reluctant to be the first to say good bye. Finally Thomas spoke. "You have been a great teacher for me. I have learned to love the buffalo plains, and have learned what fighting skill, endurance, and courage are. You will always be a part of my life and the brother that I have always wanted. The deep regard I have for you is beyond human words."

Red Hawk took his friend by the arm. "I would not be among the living, here today, if you had not come into my life, though I know that my time is now short. I accept my fate and it is well with me. The people will not see me beseech the spirits for one more day or one more hour. I have already received the many blessings of the Great Mystery. I have stood on the top of the mountain after my fast, and received my medicine, which has guided my life, the soaring majesty of the Red-Tailed Hawk, who screamed his oneness with me. I have ridden into battle as a Comanche warrior should. I have sat in my lodge with my little ones and my squaws around me, all happy and content together. I have seen my sons grow into strong young men and I know they will forever honor me.

"You have given me many things to think upon and as I consider all you have said to me, it often makes me disagree with myself. I have thought often on what you told me about no Indian being able to make a rifle. Though it makes my heart ache to say these words, that means that in some ways we are not equal to the Mexicans or the Whites. My Comanche brothers do not realize this, and if anything happens to me there will be no one but you to make them understand. I know that as a brother to the Comanches you will accept this task."

"I promise you I will do my best to see that the Comanches remain an esteemed tribe, respected by friend and foe alike, honored by all who love the freedom of the open land," Thomas said to him. He could see the febrile flush of Red Hawk's face and a slight dullness in his eyes. He knew he would never see this warrior again.

CHAPTER 37

The exit from *Cañon del Rescate* was the same as before. The drovers had gone ahead with the herd, and the carts with their meager supply of remaining goods tailed behind. Sarah was assigned to help the cook and she had to walk. Thomas almost never even made eye contact with her, but he noticed that most nights she slept as close to him as she could manage.

It was hard for Thomas to adjust to the plodding pace of the caravan after having had free rein over the plains with Red Hawk, but Thomas busied himself with his own thoughts and again rode with Chulley, learning about his boyhood in a Mexican village. Chulley had decided that Thomas was certainly no trader from New Mexico, but he had the capacity to let other people's mysteries alone, and accept them for the persons they wanted to be.

On the trip back to Santa Fe, with the slow pace and sufficient time to talk, Thomas began to get beyond the everyday vernacular, so that he and Chulley could actually discuss things in depth. The caravan leader was an able student of the native pueblo people, and to a lesser extent, of the Comanches of the plains.

He was familiar with the oral traditions of the Comanches, telling of their ancestors coming on foot out of the north, around the first of the eighteenth century, a poverty-stricken people, grubbing out their existence from roots, rabbits, and reptiles, eating carrion if necessary, only rarely securing an abundant meal of fresh meat with an accidental encounter or exceptionally fortunate hunt, certainly used to hunger during the late winter months.

Out of this unpromising material was fashioned through the next few years, from 1706 to 1750, a new society. With the help of their cousins, the Utes, they acquired the horse and the skills of raising and using them. Within the next forty years they became as one with these animals. They mastered the hunt of the buffalo and the trait of the hit-and-run tactics of war, becoming a society which dominated the plains, creating, what many people thought, the outstanding riders of the world, their presence striking fear into the hearts of all who challenged their hegemony.

The Comanches knew who they were and where they were from, not in a geographical or accurate historical sense, but in the sense of continuity and intimate closeness to the land, its grass, its space. The prairie had become their home, their haven, the land of their growing up and of their dying down, of their highest elation and, at times, of their profound despair, a place, a climate, a lifestyle, all of which had allowed them to develop and endure on these flats for ten generations – their culture, in turn, still influenced and partially directed by their past, their ancestors, the embodiment of inherited feelings, habits, and mores stretching back another fifty lifetimes, the past and present now melding to allow this creation, these "Lords of the Plains."

"How effective have they been?" continued Chulley. "For two hundred years they have utterly halted the spread of Mexican culture. Instead of this area all being Northern Mexico, it is the Southwest of the United States, and even the great country of America cannot yet control it, because a small group of nomads won't let them."

Thomas began to confide in the trail boss, telling him about the Canadian River experience, and also, of the gifts he received from Red Hawk. "With the Comanche, the act of giving is a display of the greatness of the giver," said Chulley. "Without doubt, Red Hawk garnered a wealth of prestige by his actions."

"I want to talk to you, Tomás, about what we are really doing here, and because you are young, and have not yet set your final course in life, about your part in it. We are participating in the fringes of war, yes, somewhat removed from the battle site but war nonetheless. We are in a war being waged between the Plains Indians and the Whites, and right now we are profiting from the spoils of this conflict, but you and I both know that the ultimate struggle is not far away; this type of life will come to an end, and, in ending, there will be much human tragedy.

"I can see that you are involved in ways that do not just relate to the Comanchero trade, though of course your exact allegiances are not known to me. In the short time I have been acquainted with you, I am aware of your involvement in at least four confrontations, putting yourself at extreme hazard, and I can see that you are very skilled in the arts of battle, but outcomes of these clashes are a result of both skill and chance, and you may be overdue for the imposition of chance upon your fortune, for chance sometimes allows the skilled to be foiled, and the fool to succeed.

"You revel in the thrill of the battle, in no small part because of the danger involved, but I do not believe you yet understand how precious is life, and how absolute is death. While you are still young, I want you to quit this profession of war and enjoy a family of your own, and the love of a wife and children, as well as the joy of creating a home and a treasure you can hand down to your own offspring."

The words were sobering to the scout. He had no idea that the rough, and somewhat crude, New Mexican had such feelings, or that he had been so insightful. Thomas felt that Chulley was, in many ways, an extension of Oswego, the accumulation of many years of experience, and from that experience, acquiring wisdom, an understanding, that training and effort could not furnish apart from many years of ripening. Thomas mused upon how difficult it was to learn from someone else, simply from what they said, rather than going through the trials yourself. Most of our knowledge is, in reality, hand-me-down lore, and those of us who cannot recognize it are both vain and ungrateful. Even the most experienced and tried of us only add an infinitesimal bit to the pool of culture in which we swim. No wonder the primitives worship their ancestors.

CHAPTER 38

On the sixth night, they were again back in the sand hills and though caution was still present, it was more lax than on the open plains. The carts and wagons were circled with most men sleeping beside or under them. Thomas made his bed beside one of the dunes, while the captive girl slept more in the open. Thomas was sound asleep when he was abruptly awakened by a scream from Sarah. He looked up and even through the darkness he could see a figure on all fours, crawling toward him. The stalker stood up, and raced toward his intended victim. A shot rang out and the dark figure stumbled and dropped his tomahawk, but just as quickly rose again and continued. Reaching out with his hand, the intruder touched the startled Thomas on the shoulder, then whirled and fled into the dimness of the night.

A second shot rang out just as he topped the dune and the raider sprawled into the sand. Thomas looked back and saw Chulley standing with his rifle. The two walked together and stood over the Indian. One of the *vaqueros* came behind with a torch. The bullet had entered the left side of the back and passed through bone of the pelvic crest. It appeared not to have entered the abdominal cavity, but the bone was badly shattered, and the overlying soft tissues swollen with blood. Thomas recognized the Comanche by his long angular nose, pointed chin and the pitted scarring on the left side of his face. On seeing that he was Comanche, Chulley chose not to kill him. A bandage was placed over the wound and the Indian was bound and staked to the ground in Comanche fashion.

There was no more sleep for the rest of the night. At dawn, Chulley and Thomas took their rifles, and followed the tracks into the dunes where they found one high enough to conceal a horse. A pinto pony was still there, tethered to a bush at the foot of the dune, the tracks coming in from the east. "You must have quite a history with these Comanches," said Chulley. "I think I know why it occurred," said Thomas. "I called him a coward once, and he counted coup by touching me on the shoulder to prove to me and also to himself, that it was not so." Walking back to the convoy, Thomas traipsed over the dunes and retrieved the discarded tomahawk.

When the two came back into camp Thomas saw the girl sitting alone and far apart from the rest of the camp. He walked over to her and asked in English, "How was it that you happened to detect him?" "I smelled him," she said. "The smell awoke me. I know exactly who it was."

"You mean just from the smell you awoke and could actually tell who the person was?" asked Thomas.

"I have been waked in the night by that smell before," she said. "I know it only too well, and never in my life will I forget it."

"Who is this man?" asked Thomas. "He is the sub-chief they call Stone Face," answered Sarah, "because he is so solemn and unyielding. He is considered a fine warrior, even though he has a deformed shoulder because of an old bullet wound, which he received in earlier years of raiding, but he always thinks his voice is the only correct one, and he is never at ease, his every moment crowded with some kind of endeavor. They say he is still obsessed with the thought of revenge for his shoulder wound, and he seems to be deeply ashamed of the wounds on his face. I know that he can be a very cruel man."

Thomas remembered his own feeling of familiarity with him the night of the council, even if that familiarity seemed also to be enmity. He recalled that the struggle to remember had been enhanced by a smell.

"His face has a sharp nose, does it not?"

"Like an axe," she answered. Thomas reached out and gently squeezed the girl's shoulder in a gesture of thanks.

Early the next morning Chulley called for Thomas, and the two discussed what to do with the prisoner. The boss of the trade mission felt he should not execute a Comanche with whom they did business, but he could not permit one to attack his caravan. "He was not attacking you," said Thomas, "he was solely after me. He thinks I am an enemy of the Comanche People. Let me take him back to *Rescate*." "Will you be safe?" asked the trail boss. "I will be safe," answered the scout.

Stone Face was securely bound and placed back on his horse, and tied to the saddle. The two riders headed east with Thomas leading the Indian's pinto. As soon as they were well out of sight of the caravan, Thomas took out his hunting knife. The Indian looked at the knife, but in spite of what it suggested to him, his affect was stoic and he sat still and unflinching upon his mount. Thomas reached out and cut the thongs that bound Stone Face's hands to his saddle. He tied the pinto's reins together and threw them over the pony's neck to the Indian, then reaching back into his saddle bag to retrieve the tomahawk, he handed it to Stone Face. The two travelers continued to the east, both men astounded by what had just been done, though the release did not ease the tension between them. Thomas wondered if he had made a mistake, the prisoner's eyes looking across at him with the feral stare of a prairie hawk.

They camped together the four nights on the trail, the travel of the days slower because of the Comanche's wound. Though obviously in great pain, Stone Face did not complain or moan, only stoically rode on. Thomas said nothing to the Indian, and, in turn, nothing was said to him, the alienation between the two much too great to allow companionship or fellowship. Only the concept, be it right or wrong, that an act of mercy, and an acceptance of this act, should take place for the greater good, for the redemption of their two peoples, for obedience to the will of the Great Mystery, drove the journey on.

The trek took on a life of its own, a happening, not of themselves, but spontaneous, without reason or obvious justification. Thomas provided the food and water, the Comanche simply taking and consuming it, without comment or any show of gratitude. At the start of any ride, Thomas had to boost the Indian upon his mount. At night, the deep sleep of total exhaustion would come upon the wounded Comanche as Thomas sat watching him. The Indian lay prostrate, totally vulnerable; the archfiend, the one he had so long sought, forever hoping to tear out the raider's heart with his own hands. Thomas stared at the eight pitted scars on the side of his face, wondering what they could represent. He reached beneath his shirt, and unfolded his packet, taking out the shred of purple cloth that had once been tied around his halter rope, and retied it around the Indian pony's bridle. He felt a sense of relief come over him; it was now permissible to resume the enmity.

The tribesmen spotted the two riders when they both appeared at the rim of the canyon. Once again, young people surrounded the warrior and the scout, the two riding into the center of the village, causing major chiefs to suddenly appear as the two arrived. Thomas spoke to the crowd, "Your warrior is badly hurt. He was shot while attacking one whom he considered an enemy of your people. I saw him, without fear, count coup on his enemy. He is one of the bravest of men." The Comanche sat on his horse, speechless, astounded, for the first time looking at the scout with eyes that were not threatening.

The Indians helped Stone Face off his horse, again causing much pain. He stood and looked Thomas in the eyes, then made the sign for peace, but the arduous trip, the pain, and the loss of blood had taken its toll, and the warrior fainted, dropping unconscious to the ground. In the crowd that picked him up, there was a young brave, his features mimicking those of the wounded warrior. Thomas knew it was the same young Indian whose terror-stricken face he had seen some years before. He was just now coming into adulthood and was a fine looking specimen. Their eyes met only for a moment, but a moment that affirmed mutual recognition.

Suddenly the crowd of people in front of Thomas parted, allowing the passage of an ancient, tottering, but regal figure, the old chief of the night of the council fire, his unexpected presence causing a poignant hush to come over the crowd. His eyes were now clear, his stare deep and unblinking, penetrating into the innermost depth of Thomas's being. He realized that the old one understood. The toothless smile came again, the same smile as of the night of the council. An unsteady hand reached in his shirt, removing a long leather pouch which he handed to the young scout. Within the packet was the peace pipe of that memorable night. The old man nodded and turned away.

The scout remounted his horse and searched the crowd for Red Hawk. At the outer edge of the village he saw a young woman in mourning, walking with head bowed, her clothes torn, her hair chopped off, and cuts across her face, neck, and arms: Red Hawk was no longer alive. Thomas turned his horse to the west and rode back out of the canyon.

CHAPTER 39

The headquarters loomed large on the horizon as the trading caravan approached home base. The cattle herd had arrived two days ahead of the wagons. Don Jose and his entourage rode out to meet them, and he seemed in quite a good mood. The herd of cattle was in better shape than usual, and there were more animals than he expected. Though the *carretas* were almost barren, he was not surprised, since he knew that the buffalo herds were being decimated by the American hide hunters. He looked at the captive and offered, "I know how to get a handsome price for this one."

"The girl is mine," said Thomas, "I traded for her with my own rifle and she would still be back in the Comanche camp if I had not intervened."

"You make a mistake, upstart!" said Don Jose, "all of the merchandise from this Comanchero venture belongs first to the maestro, and he distributes out rewards to the workers as he sees fit."

"Then I pray you see fit to distribute her to me," said the young scout. Don Jose let out one of his loud and prolonged laughs. "I hope this is not what you recognize as the riches for which you became a Comanchero." He laughed again. "Your boon is granted, take her and go, and, in the future, when you decide you want to work for a *grande hacienda*, bring your new wife and come back to me."

"I have one suggestion to make to you, Don Jose, if I may be so bold."

"Yes," he answered.

"Sell the child who came with the first caravan to me. I will take her back to the army in Santa Fe. It will make them think that you have been

Americanized and the act will pay big dividends for you in the future."

The commandant let out a low chuckle, "And what price are you willing to give?"

"Whatever you require," was the answer.

There was a prolonged pause. "Tomás, you would spend your last dollar like it was a leaf, and you owned the forest." He then turned to his men and ordered, "Put her in a cart and let him take her." Turning back to Thomas he said, "Now, get out of my sight before you try my patience more than I can tolerate."

Thomas bade good bye to the Don, and then rode over to Chulley. "You and I must meet again some day; there are still many things we have not discussed, and many maps we have not yet drawn." He got his rifle and his small packet of belongings, and, with the two girls, rode north toward Santa Fe.

He had no difficulty in obtaining an audience with Colonel J. L. Gregg, commanding officer of the Military District of New Mexico. He had not realized how hungry he was for the sound of agile Anglo voices and in the ensuing conversation he sat there and listened with great satisfaction. He turned over the care of the American captives to the Army officers who promised to find them a way home. He also related to the commander his experience with Sergeant McRainey at the onset of the excursion onto the plains. Thomas was not surprised to learn that he had been arrested for pirating of trade caravans, and was now in a federal prison. The commander knew that the army was planning a campaign on the Llano the coming fall, and knowing that Thomas's information might be vital, he bade the scout God's speed, again furnished him with supplies, and sent him on his way.

Thomas hired one of the Tesuque mule skinners, who had been with him in the Comanchero caravan, to take him to follow the trail of the stolen cattle toward northern New Mexico and Colorado. They traveled over the high road to the ancient pueblo of Taos. The year had advanced into the fall months and the mountains were radiant with their cloak of gold from the turning of the aspen leaves. Thomas had seen pretty autumn colors in the hill country of Texas, but this display of the aspens, with the golden cloak of the peaks had turned the country to glory, a gift of the Great Spirit, magnificent beyond description. He took a long time to stamp this vision deep into his memory, for he doubted he would ever see such grandeur again.

Thomas's guide took him into the village of Taos where he felt he was a pilgrim, visiting the shrine of the Kit Carson legacy, certainly an idol of his boyhood, and a scout he had tried to emulate. They visited the Taos Pueblo, an ancient edifice, renowned as the longest continually occupied structure in North America. "It must be viewed with reverence," thought Thomas, "because it has endured." He marveled at its symmetry and beauty emanating from such simple basic design. Since it was raised from adobe, the elements of the earth, it produced no clash with the nature of the valley which it occupied.

Although colder weather was approaching, the two explorers continued north. They came into the valley of the Cimarron, then onto the flat grasslands and low hills of the northeast part of the territory, now sparsely populated with Texas cattle. They continued north, through the foothills of the Rocky Mountains and through Trinchera Pass onto the vast pasturelands of Eastern Colorado. The great Rocky Mountains loomed to the west, many of which were snow-capped, something Thomas had never seen before, but to the northeast the flat grasslands rolled forever into the distance, much like those of Texas. Thomas recognized when he saw this unpopulated plain that the only way to stop the raiding in Texas was to control the Comanches. The market for cattle would go on forever.

By the time Thomas and his guide returned to Santa Fe, winter had arrived, and the city was covered with snow. Confined to the city due to the winter weather, he returned to army headquarters and was allowed an office in which he was able to edit his notes of the experience of trading with the Indians and of the territory over which he had traveled. Colonel Gregg quizzed him at length about his findings and especially about the cattle which were being herded north to the open plains.

CHAPTER 40

One day, Thomas was summoned to the colonel's office and invited to dinner in the commander's home. "I would like you to join us tonight, Thomas. We are having an interesting group of people and I think they would like to hear about your experiences with the Comanches. I believe they are people you would enjoy knowing."

He went by a store to purchase some passable clothes for such an occasion and appeared at the appointed time at the colonel's house. There were three other army officers, and their wives, two couples that were local merchants, and the Reverend Bishop Lamy, the Bishop of the Vicariate of New Mexico. The colonel and his wife were surprised by the ease with which Thomas mixed with the guests, expecting him to be rather crude, having served in the wilds as an army scout and spy, but the social exchanges among the men and women, made him feel quite at home, reminding him of formal gatherings so often attended at his grandparents' house outside of San Antonio.

"Thomas has just returned from a mission among the Comanches out on the Llano Estacado," said the Colonel.

The members of the Santa Fe gentry were enthralled by listening to Thomas talk about the details of his experience with the Comanches and overwhelmed him with questions about the wild tribes. "Are those Indians becoming any more amenable to a civilized way of life?" he was asked.

"In no manner," Thomas answered. "The only way they will give up their nomadic existence and their depredations is from being subjugated by force of arms."

"Similar to what we did to the Navajo?" questioned one of the merchants. "I would think it could be no less ruthless, if they are to be brought under control," returned the young scout. "Their wild way of life and their penchant for war is now so ingrained into their society that I believe it will require utter defeat to turn them toward any other way of living."

"Do you think for us to perpetrate such a defeat on these natives is a moral thing to do?" asked the Bishop. "That's not a question I can answer," returned Thomas. "There are three societies involved here, the Comanche, the Mexican and the Texas Protestant. The so-called morals of all parties involved are so very different. If it's the Texas frontier people you ask, they probably think it quite moral to exterminate them, for they don't think the Comanches deserve any moral consideration. If it's the Indian morals, it means stay off the Llano Estacado and, otherwise, leave things as they are. If it's the morals of the church, I'll have to defer to you. At any rate I don't believe it will be settled according to anyone's moral precepts; it will be settled by raw power, and the whites have the upper hand because of their superior equipment and numbers."

"How were you able to go among them?" another of the merchants asked. Thomas unabashedly told them the truth. "I took on the guise of a Comanchero and traveled on a trading mission so that I could spy on the Comanches, in essence, deceiving them and betraying the cordiality of both peoples."

Later in the night, conversation turned toward Bishop Lamy, the group wanting to know how Christianity was faring among the pueblo natives of New Mexico. "It requires much patience to convince them of anything new," said the Bishop. "They readily submit to being baptized, but there seems to be no way to actually convert them completely, the Indians persistently hold on to their old ways, ways, of course, that we consider heathen in nature."

"Does the church have a problem with the Indians maintaining their own culture?" Thomas asked. "Not as long as they do not sin against their neighbors or the Holy Father, claiming other gods, or blaspheming the scriptures or the Lord."

"Are the Indians of Acoma any different from other pueblo Indians?" asked Thomas.

"It's funny that you should ask that question," said the Bishop. "The Acoma Pueblo has a history of rebelling against new ways as far back as the end of the sixteenth century. The Mission San Esteban Rey, which was founded in 1641, and which was one of the few churches not destroyed in the native rebellion, has always maintained a bit of the native religion mixed into their church. As a matter of fact, as soon as the weather allows I am traveling to Albuquerque to meet with a young and very able priest who is transferring from Ysleta, in the hope of better serving those people." "From Ysleta!" Thomas exclaimed. "Is his name Dominic Castaneda?" The Bishop was completely taken by surprise. "How in the world do you know him?"

"We traveled together from San Antonio to Paseo del Norte. As a layman, I judge him an able and true servant of God, and I count him as one of my closest friends on this earth."

"I understand that you, too, are about to travel south. Why not travel with me and we shall see Dominic together," said Bishop Lamy. One week later, under a bright clear winter sky, they were on the way toward Albuquerque. The bishop was accompanied by his assistant, Monsignor Fernandez, a man less complex than the Bishop, but no less compelling. Thomas loved the wit of both men, and it was good to be back in the company of the learned.

The two men of the cloth were also grateful for their new companion. Although it was obvious that Thomas's inner direction was very different from their own, it was refreshing to discuss other views. They probed Thomas for information about the Plains Indians, and listened intently as he related the many stories of his experiences. Thomas told the Bishop about his coming upon the Indian villages in the *Cañon del Rescate*, and how minute and insignificant they seemed when viewed against the vastness of the landscape. "How can we believe that God holds that the lives or actions of such negligible creatures as we all seem to be are significant?"

"You are right in realizing that what we, as humans, consider significant, may or may   not be significant in the mind of God, but He does allow a great equalizer for the unimportant. You as a man are only an infinitely small part of the plan of God, but so integrated into his nature, that even the shadow you cast upon the ground is a determining factor. Block one ray of sunlight from a single blade of grass and you have altered its growth. No matter how infinitesimal the change, all things are connected and this one alteration cascades down through all of creation for all of eternity. Who knows? The change caused by your shadow may be more important to the course of the universe than all of the actions of the College of Cardinals in Rome."

The ride south beside the Rio Grande was quite rewarding. The few draws that crossed their path were filled with snow drifts, cloaked in the pure white array of the season, and in the quietness they would ride upon Pronghorns nuzzling the ground for food. The animals raised their heads and stared at the passing strangers, then flicked their short tails, and disappeared over the next rise, vanishing as quickly as they had appeared.

When the three travelers passed into the edge of Albuquerque, the Bishop turned to Thomas. "I shall remember you in my prayers, my son."

"When I think on the many things you have told me," answered the young Texan, "my heart will always feel that I have been blessed by an insight that only few in this world can deliver." The prelate turned toward his aide, "What more could one ever ask?"

The Bishop rode up to the cathedral in Albuquerque exactly at his appointed time. "Punctuality is an acknowledgement that you are laboring for God and have no time to waste," he said. As they walked down the center aisle of the church, Thomas lingered behind. Dominic, who was also a punctual servant, arose from his bench and went forward to meet the Bishop. He bowed his head and took the offered hand and the three stood talking for a long time. "I have brought you a splendid surprise," said Bishop Lamy. He turned back toward Thomas, and beckoned him to come forward. Dominic was completely stunned. He ran forward and embraced his friend. "You could have brought nothing which could give me greater joy, Reverend Bishop."

Following the conference between clerics, the young priest was assigned to return to Acoma, hopefully with new insights into his duty to his new parish. Thomas asked Dominic to show him the ancient citadel, and both friends seemed to be delighted.

CHAPTER 41

"Why are you not still in Ysleta?" Thomas asked him, as they rode west from the meeting. "A strange set of circumstances," Dominic replied. "I was contacted by the office of the Bishop with whom we have just been talking, requesting that I consider moving to the church in Acoma because they were operating with a congregation who clings to their own beliefs, and the Bishop, oddly enough, had reason to think I could bring them into the fold. I replied that my church on the Rio Grande, was doing well, and since I had so shortly just arrived, I was loath to leave. One month later I was notified that the previous priest from Ysleta had recovered from a severe illness, and wanted to return to his parish. Simultaneously I was appointed to the Mission San Esteban del Rey and told I would have everything explained to my satisfaction as soon as I met with the Bishop."

"Well, is everything explained?"

"I'm more confused than ever," said Dominic. I was told that the Indians are rebelling against the authority of the church, and that I am to set it right." "Right for whom?" asked Thomas. "That's just what surprises me," he answered, "the Bishop distinctly told me he wanted it made right for the Indian, not just for himself, or the professed church."

"I don't know about your Pueblo Indians, Dominic, but all the Indians with whom I have ever dealt have their own ideas about life and its meaning and have never readily fit into the trappings of the European societies. If the Acoma people have not adapted to the Spanish ethic since Coronado was there in 1540, they are not suddenly going to change during your lifetime. My only suggestion would be to respect and love the people for their own sakes, and they will respond to you on that basis, but to change their basic beliefs has to be a matter of their own choosing alone."

Late on the second day out of Albuquerque, Dominic pointed out to Thomas the distant mesa on which the Acoma pueblo was built. The adjacent landform was different from any Thomas had heretofore seen. Giants of the earth guarded the approach to the Sky City, in the form of huge sandstone boulders, grouped in numbers, ranging from two to twelve, the groupings isolated and widely separated across the plain, their vertical visages reaching upward to challenge the sky. Thomas and Dominic rode on between these giants until the Acoma mesa appeared near, solitary and solid, a seemingly impregnable fortress, rising vertically 347 feet above the flat land below. In 1540 Coronado had called it the strongest defensive position of the world. Thomas knew from history, however, that its unassailable appearance was illusory, for the bastion had been breached and conquered by the Spanish, not once, but repeatedly, its people enslaved and its warriors, having one foot chopped off to issue a harsh and bitter reminder that the Spanish were supreme.

Overlooking the precipitous cliffs on one corner of the mesa was the Mission San Esteban del Rey, dwarfing the other structures of the pueblo, its bell towers reaching upward, proclaiming the glory of God, its mighty timber beams manually transported across a hundred miles of scorching desert, borne by the conquered Indians under the urge of the Holy Word and of the lash. Thomas looked at the steep cliffs at the foot of the church over which the monks had been tossed in the Pueblo Rebellion of 1680, martyring them in the Spanish mind, ridding an oppressive and parasitic pestilence in the mind of the Indian.

They rode to the foot of the mesa, to begin the ascent to the top, up a narrow path, enclosed by unscalable, sloping walls of solid rock, the narrow floor worn into steps by centuries of passing feet. Walking up the trail ahead of them was a group of young water girls, large pottery jugs balanced on their heads, as they trudged on their daily route from the rock cistern that served as the well. The young women had dark bangs guarding their foreheads and longer hair woven into a large knot in the back. Their boot-like moccasins extended up to the knees and long loose cloaks were draped over their shoulders. A miniscule burro with a young Acoma boy leading him forward followed right behind Dominic and Thomas, the donkey dwarfed by its burden of sticks, dried tree and cactus roots, and stubby brush trunks, none of which were heavy and solid, but a good supply of quick burning fuel for the cook fires.

Reaching their destination, Thomas looked out on the pueblo, stark, but with an appealing symmetry, somewhat akin to the natural beauty of a mud-wasp's nest. "We are standing on blood-soaked ground, holy to the ancestors, are we not?" asked Thomas. "Indeed we are," answered the priest. "I do not believe we will ever be able to atone for the historical injustice we have done to these people. '*Gente sin razon*' (people without reason), the early Spanish had called them, deeming them wild and uneducated, and thus clay for the Spaniards to mold. Their resistance to being shaped by foreign civilizations, however, has been formidable. Even to this day, after hundreds of years of proselytizing they give only token allegiance to our Lord. They still bury feather offerings next to the pueblo in order to win favor of the cloud-gods. It is as though they have no receptors within themselves that will allow the message of the gospels to alight." "Maybe the receptors are located in the foot," proffered his guest. "I see you have not lost your penchant for blunt assessments," returned Dominic.

"So what is your hope and your purpose?" asked Thomas.

"Much of what I want to communicate to them does not lend itself to the forms or words which the church puts at my disposal. My hope is to acquire for myself some of that 'Indianness' which we have forced them to overtly abandon, but which lives on in the secret chambers of their souls. If I can grasp enough of those concepts, then maybe I can share a vision which God may have given them, one that may be worthy of adoration as much or more than some of our own holy traditions; then our church will no longer be driven by the fear of evil, but attracted by the expectation of good."

"Dominic, I can't believe I am hearing those words from your mouth. What has happened to your previous beliefs? Your Bishop and his church will never allow, much less condone, such a view from one of their own."

"I am sure I seem different from what I previously professed, yes, but I don't think it is so far from what I have always truly believed.

The mind needs to be able to work without imposed trappings, and I think my experiences with you loosened some of my fetters. Our God is not an exclusive God, but an inclusive one, and I believe the insightful Bishop is saying as much to me.

"And tell me what has become of your life's quest?" said Dominic.

"Most often, I don't know what my life's quest is," answered Thomas. "I think I have never really known. I do know that I have become a killer of men, and the task that I took on for the army was to live a lie, and I have not even been able to be true to the lie, much less to myself."

Thomas told the young priest of his experiences as a spy, of his acceptance as a brother by the Comanches, and of the buffalo hunters, and the army patrol with its Delaware scout. "I originally committed myself to revenge for the killing of my mother and sister, but now I have become what I never intended, a mercenary, fighting or even killing for whatever authority is directing me at the time. Chulley tells me that I revel in the war action, but I know that I end up doing things that I don't think of as acts that I desire to do."

"That's what a warrior does; he gives obedience to authority, authority whose aims may or may not coincide with his own goals. The life of a warrior has been your chosen profession for as long as I have known you," returned the priest. Thomas turned his head and for a long time stood looking off into the distance.

"I must go now," said the scout. He saddled his horse, tied on his saddle bags, embraced his friend and rode off of the mesa. He looked back toward the Indians living in this isolated land. "I could learn much here," he thought.

CHAPTER 42

Eager to get back to Mackenzie, and his friend, Oswego, and knowing that there was more water than was usually found on the plains, Thomas sought out men who were in the Santa Fe-Albuquerque area wanting to go back to the Texas frontier. He found them in a group of cowboys who had initially accompanied John Hittson, one of the cattle kings of Texas – a man of action, who had brought up a heavily armed group of eighty cowboys in order to scour the New Mexico ranches looking for stolen Texas cattle obtained from the Comanchero trade. Hittson's group would help themselves to the territory, and when cattle with Texas brands were found, unless the owner could produce a valid bill of sale, they were confiscated by force of arms. The group had been quite successful, though often operating outside the law, but now with much of the work done, many were ready to return to their homes.

The thirteen Texans, Thomas, and two Mexican traders rode from Santa Fe in the late spring, first traveling to the Pecos River and then turning south on the Goodnight-Loving trail, departing from the Pecos River at Horse Head Crossing to proceed through Castle Gap, and from there to the headwaters of the middle fork of the Concho River. Strong memories lingered with Thomas as he rode into the gap.

The cleft through the mountains gradually narrowed down until the party reached an area where it was only a few yards wide. After emerging through the narrows, Thomas looked upward to scan the top rim of the pass. Standing upon the ledge, hundreds of feet above was a single sentinel, a band around his forehead and a rifle in his hands. Thomas knew that he was Apache and that there were undoubtedly others beyond the bluff. The scout grasped his own rifle and held it high in the air, in salute to the warrior who summarily returned the gesture, neither wanting engagement, each acknowledging the prowess of their enemy.

Thomas and his party were not fearful of an attack. They were all well-armed and seasoned fighters, but the Texas cowboys and their three cohorts were much more anxious to get home than to seek confrontation with the natives and they rode on. Five days later they entered Fort Concho.

The Fourth Army was still south, stationed at Fort Clark, after their abrupt war with the Kickapoo Indians, who had been raiding and destroying South Texas ranches, but Mackenzie and his men were soon ordered back to Fort Concho with plans to organize a force to return to the plains for action against the Comanche and Kiowa tribes.

As soon as the Fourth Army arrived, Thomas went directly to the office of Colonel Mackenzie to report. The Colonel was very glad to see him, although Thomas thought that he was somewhat surprised that the scouting mission had been successful, and he had returned. Thomas relayed to Mackenzie the four main rendezvous camps and their general whereabouts. He said he could lead him directly to *Cañon del Rescate*, or to Tascosa. He discussed the trafficking of illicit goods through Fort Bascom on the Canadian River and the complicity of some unscrupulous army personnel in the trade. Finally, he told the Colonel that one of the canyons, less used for trading, was the favorite winter campgrounds for the Comanche. This information was of particular interest to the commander. The colonel told Thomas that he and his staff would debrief him in every detail later in the week.

"Colonel Mackenzie," added Thomas, "I may not be a scout you will want to keep any longer. I spent a lot of time in Comanche villages this summer, and to be truthful, I found the inhabitants a very different race from what I thought they would be, in many ways, a noble people, and in spite of what happened to my own family, I can see the beauty as well as the blemish of these Indians. I have mixed feelings about whether or not they should be eradicated." The colonel pushed back his chair and beckoned for Thomas to sit back down. "You are a long way from the young boy that first came to me, swearing that you would make any sacrifice to achieve vengeance upon these hated people. After living among the Indians for this length of time, do you think you have, as they say, 'gone native'?" asked the colonel.

"No sir, it's because I have been close enough to look into the faces and the souls of the enemy, and the attributes they display, seem, in many ways, superior to my own," said Thomas.

"After the experiences you have had, Thomas, I want you all the more because you do have such feelings. I have no burning desire to kill Indians and would prefer that my soldiers did not either. I feel those people have as much right to live upon this earth as I do, but I also know that these two cultures will never exist side by side without wreaking immense carnage upon one another. The Texans are aggressive, volatile, and violent. They covet land more than life, and their credo is, 'just as it was meant to be, a Texas without Indians.' The Comanches on the other hand, consider themselves as the only true human beings. They have a violent society that has evolved to be incredibly cruel toward anyone they consider a foe, and the very essence of their value system is based on raids and war and inflicting devastation upon their enemies. A raid to the Indians is a noble cause; to the Texans it is a vicious depredation. Both sides are generously supplied with duplicity and moral blindness.

I don't pretend to know which system is more just. I seek no vengeance, and I hold no hatreds. I do believe, however, that the white world is in its ascendancy, and will wipe the Indians from the face of the earth if the natives are not rendered helpless to practice their desired way of life. For this reason, I am willing to destroy their wild society, and drive them, to a man, woman, or child off the plains and on to the reservation. It is a poor choice but, I believe, the only one that is available."

He dismissed Thomas and asked him to return to the Tonkawa scouts.

Thomas realized that his own ambivalence about the coming conflict had simply been brushed aside by the colonel, as though it were of no importance. He walked back to the scouts as Mackenzie had directed, unable to grapple with his own misgivings, yielding to the inexorable rush to war, a decision made in the chambers of Washington, by people who had not the slightest idea of what was involved.

Thomas asked the troopers if any of the Tonkawa were around and was pointed toward a small campsite down toward the river. At the camp he was told that Oswego had gone all the way to the water, and Thomas walked off to find him. He spotted Oswego walking up the bank, dripping wet. He stopped where he was, without invading his friend's space, and watched him carefully as he walked up to his clothes. The light beaming down showed many grey hairs which were mixed with the black. His back was bowed slightly forward, and the many scars across his body glittered in the sunlight. The giant pectoral muscles, that Thomas had always known, now looked a bit lax and hollow, and the skin on his arms and body was more withered and wrinkled than he remembered. Thomas had never even considered frailties involving Oswego, and had never given one thought to his aging. A lump came in his throat, and Thomas turned away as a tear welled over his eyelid.

Oswego quickly donned his clothes and walked out of the thicket. He saw Thomas looking upstream as though he were searching the water. He called his name. Thomas turned toward his mentor, and muttered the Tonkawa word for father. They clasped right arms and stood looking deeply into one another's eyes. "Come," said Oswego, "I must hear all about your travels."

They sat apart on the edge of the campground and Thomas relayed the story of almost the entire episode, from the trip with the Franciscan priest, to the encounter with the Apaches, to his disguise in El Paso, the trip up the Rio Grande, his near death experience on the hacienda of Don Jose, the journey with the Comancheros to the Comanche camp, on to the Canadian River and their encounter with the buffalo hunters, the trading, and the return to Santa Fe with the captives. He achingly told him of his and Red Hawk's confronting the patrol and of his shooting of the Delaware scout. He also told him about his conversation with Colonel Mackenzie. He did not tell him that he had also killed an American buffalo hunter, nor did he tell of his entanglement with Stone Face. While he talked, Oswego sat rapt as he listened to every detail.

"I know you have conflicting thoughts about what you have done on the Canadian River with the hunters and the army," said Oswego. "Let me tell you that I believe there is no right or wrong answer when you are in such a dilemma. All one can do is to be as sure as he can, that his choice is not serving an unworthy cause, and that it is not simply self-serving. It is not that I don't value loyalty, but blind loyalty in the face of circumstances that cry out the injustice of your original cause, is no loyalty at all, only blind worship of the creed of a demagogue. War puts us in strange moral conflicts, but there is no one but the person involved who can determine what is just and what is not. If we truly seek justice we must not allow second thoughts about difficult decisions, which we encounter in a crisis, to ruin our lives nor function as a stain upon our honor."

As the two walked back among the Tonkawa scouts, Oswego told Thomas of their action against the Kickapoo Indians, and the army raid into northern Mexico, in the interval of time while he was away.

He also told him what he knew about plans for the coming campaign against the Kiowa and Comanche. There had been an uprising of Indians on the reservation, apparently in response to a medicine man who had organized the warriors under the influence of the drug, peyote, and they had attacked a group of buffalo hunters in the north portion of the Llano Estacado in a united effort by the tribes to drive the white man, once and for all, from their sacred hunting grounds. The attack had failed, and the discouraged Indians had broken into small marauding bands and gone on a wild spree of raids and killings along the Texas frontier. In response, the army had been ordered to initiate a massive campaign to annihilate any tribes that did not immediately go onto the reservation and submit to all government regulations. Mackenzie's army was one of five groups moving out into Indian Territory to converge on the headwater region of the Red River.

The troops, consisting of both cavalry and infantry, under the command of Colonel Mackenzie moved out from Fort Concho August 23, 1874, designated as the Southern Prong. Thomas, Oswego, and the remaining scouts were already out ahead of the troops. They traveled northwest, up the North Fork of the Concho River and then turned due north across the Colorado, and finally to a spot just beyond the Fresh Water Fork of the Brazos River, onto a small defensible mesa named Soldier's Mound, where they established their supply camp, constructing breastworks sufficient to defend it. The army halted at this spot for twelve days, to further drill and train the troops in the discipline required for confronting the warring Comanches. They also used this time to let those units catch up, which were on the way to join the force.

Abundant game was still in the area, and both Oswego and Thomas enjoyed hunting to furnish the troopers with fresh meat from both buffalo and antelope herds. Thomas had seen many buffalo before, but he had never seen such a massive herd as was now moving across the landscape. It stretched across the valley to the distant mesa, like some giant had scattered the beasts, as though seeding the prairie with living flesh. The breeze gently blew the bovine smell of the herd across their nostrils, a detail that would not ever be forgotten.

The two scouts found a spot where they could ride out close enough to the herd to watch them in every particular, carefully making sure that the two of them kept down wind and very quiet, because buffalo have relatively poor eyesight, but extremely acute senses of smell and hearing. The scene was magnificent, a pristine glimpse back to an earlier age, the entire herd slowly grazing across the grassland, all moving in the same direction, seemingly in unison. Each of the massive bulls had his harem of cows, surrounding him, while the younger bulls were pushed to the outer fringes of the pods. There was a constant recurrence of, low, bellowing sounds, almost growls, emanating from the dominant bulls, warning the younger and lesser males not to get too close – nature's way of selecting the strongest genetics for the herd.

CHAPTER 43

On September 20, the army again moved out, going fifteen miles up the valley and on toward the Staked Plains. Meanwhile the scouts fanned in every direction, and began probing the territory for Indian signs. The first hostile encounter was when a scout, alone on the left flank, was attacked by a group of twenty Comanches. He rode his horse hard to the northeast to rendezvous with his fellow scouts where the increased fire power caused the Indians to break off their attack. Indian tactics were organized to grasp the initiative any time odds were greatly in their favor, but they believed that only fools would engage in a pitched battle.

The scouts came in and reported the twenty Comanches to the army, and the cavalry immediately moved out to trail the war party toward the headwaters of the Wichita and from there on to the headwaters of the Pease River in the Valley of the Quit-a-Que. The Tonkawa scouts could trail the Comanches on the run while regular members of the army could see almost no sign at all. Thomas recognized the valley into which they rode from the previous description given him by the New Mexicans. "*Los Canoñes del Valle de las Lagrimas*," he said, "The Valley of Tears."

Far out in the northwestern sky, clouds began to gather and then appeared to tumble over one another as though they were fleeing to escape the flaying lightning bolts that continually seemed to drive them on. In the distance the army men could see the rain, its inexorable sweep over the bare and unimpeded plains, aimed directly toward them. The storm hit the troops like a slap in the face, for which they were unprepared and unprotected. Everyone and everything was almost instantly drenched, the swirling wind gusts pummeling them from every direction. The sodden smell of wet horses mixed with that of wet leather foretold of a long and miserable night.

The initial rainstorm passed right over them and continued toward the southeast, but immediately in its wake, dark blue clouds again began to congregate, out of which bone-chilling winds swept down to envelop the column in one of the "blue northers," for which the plains are well known. As exposed as they were, there was no respite for troops or beasts, and all had to endure the same numbing chill through the rest of the day and night. All the troops ached and were bone-tired the next morning. Several of the horses could not move on because they were completely spent. The depleted mounts were shot to keep them from falling into the hands of the Indians.

The following day the company was determined to get all men and equipment out of the breaks and on to the plains. The scouts were out as usual, though Thomas stayed with the main body in order to help the movement of the wagons out of the canyons and onto the flat land above. Several ridges were too steep for the mules so teams had to be unhitched and wagons drawn up by ropes, the expended effort by both man and beast extreme and exhausting. When the entire southern column had reached the top, the scouts once again directed them north.

As the army lumbered forward, the scouts kept probing outward, episodically coming in with reports of more and more Indians hovering around their outskirts. At one point, with Oswego on the outer edge of the scout group and Thomas the next rider in, three Comanches appeared and started circling Oswego, riding closer and closer as they circled, and when within range, began firing. Oswego recognized the enemy rifles as muzzle loaders and when all three had fired, Oswego with his Winchester repeating rifle charged them. The three fled over a small rise, with Oswego in hot pursuit, but just as he came to the top of the rise, a planned ambush was apparent, with numerous other Indians hidden in the grass who started shooting. Oswego stopped his horse, raised his rifle in the air, shook it at the Comanches, and slowly trotted off as though he were impervious to Comanche bullets, a show of Indian bravado, often exhibited in skirmishes among the natives.

That night the army bedded down in a group of small ravines at the head of Tule Canyon. Every precaution was taken, with the horses very securely staked and hobbled and an outside line of pickets on constant guard. Troopers slept with their boots on, and in a circle around the horse herd. After helping secure the herd, Thomas and Oswego rode off into the evening heading west, to reconnoiter the territory of the left flank before the column moved farther north.

The two riders went on for almost half a mile and stopped to look back from whence they came. At the escarpment edge, the horizon was broken with dark swatches of small juniper and mesquite trees silhouetted against the eastern sky, a faint orange tinge caused by the gloaming pouring forth from the West. The quietness of the plains was engulfing and both riders moved on with no exchange of words. Once the moon came up, its slanting rays allowed only a faint view of their surroundings.

Almost three hours into the night, Thomas held up his hand to signal a stop. He held a cupped hand to his ear and strained his attention, trying to discern the bare break upon the silence he sensed. It was more of a suggestion than a sound, and Oswego could not sense it in any way. The Tonkawa dismounted, cleared the grass from a small piece of earth and placed his ear flat against the ground. He then motioned for Thomas to take his place. Thomas could now hear from the ground the rhythmic beat of hundreds of horse's hooves drumming across the prairie. Oswego smiled to himself. He knew ten years ago, he would have heard the disturbance before Thomas did. "The carrying of the ensign is, indeed, passing to the next generation," he thought to himself.

"A Comanche raid on our troops to try again for the horse herd," said Oswego. "This time they won't budge Mackenzie," opined Thomas. The two scouts rode on for two more hours and then bedded down by a playa lake in the bottom of a small basin.

Before there was any light of day, both scouts were again in the saddle. They watched the tawny dawn push the horizon into view and then clear the overlying sky of the last vestige of stars still lingering in the West. Thomas rode up to the edge of the basin, looked across the flat land, and waved for Oswego. Curling into the sky about a mile to the northwest was a single plume of smoke, buoyantly rising from the plain, only to pale into the ever reaching firmament. The two scouts watched for a minute before Oswego spoke. "It probably is a small group of travelers, but not Indians. They would never have a fire with the army about."

"The campers must not be afraid of Indians. They may be traders, and actually want the Comanches to find them," said Thomas. "This small amount of smoke cannot be seen from very far away," said Oswego, "I think we have time to take a look even though it could be a signal to some of their compatriots. You approach from the sun so they will not see you at first. I will approach from the west so they will see me, and I will try to divert their attention. We can meet back at the lake if necessary."

The two scouts rode out to begin their maneuver. When Thomas got within less than a quarter mile, he could clearly see the *carreta* which was hitched to two small mules. He could also see a single man turned toward Oswego holding his rifle. "*Senor,*" called Thomas as he approached from the rear. He held up his own rifle, then put it back in its scabbard, and signed for the man to do the same. At first the stranger looked around as though searching for a place to flee, but seeing the two riders coming steadily on, he put his rifle in the cart and stood out into the open.

Thomas rode up and said hello in English. The Comanchero shook his head and said, "*no hablo Ingles.*"

"Senor Jose Tafoya," said Thomas, "*no me recuerdo?*" Thomas saw him blanch, even beneath his dark, swarthy skin. "Where are you going?" asked Thomas in Spanish. "I am only wandering the llano, hoping to come across some tribe with which to trade." he answered. "Why don't you just go to the Comanche villages," said Thomas. "*No se adonde esta,*" he pleaded. "So you don't know where they are, eh?" said Thomas. "Then you must come with us and we will find them together." There was desperation in the trader's face. He knew he was now a prisoner in a land where prisoners were only pawns, to be used or traded for someone else's purpose.

The scouts took his rifle and led Tafoya and his *carreta* back to the lake where they had camped, placed him on one of his mules from the team, and turned the other loose by the lake. The three men then rode to the northeast to find Mackenzie. "Had you known him in New Mexico?" questioned Oswego.

"No, I guessed who he was by the description that some of the other traders in my own group gave of him."

"He likes to be a loner, I suppose."

"I think not, but sometimes he ventures out away from the main caravan to set up the location for the coming rendezvous, always carrying small quantities of goods that are especially chosen to entice the Comanches to want to be present for the main attraction at some future time. There must be a caravan somewhere behind him, probably bringing winter supplies." Six hours later, the prisoner and two scouts rode in sight of the army column.

The colonel was told what the scouts had brought in. He walked up to the Comanchero, asked Thomas to translate, and told the prisoner that he wanted him to take the army scouts to the Comanche encampment. Once again Tofoya answered that he did not know the whereabouts of any such place. The colonel turned to Thomas and asked if there was any chance the trader was telling the truth. "None whatsoever," said Thomas, "he knows every inch of this country." The Colonel turned to the troopers and ordered the Mexican trader tied by the ankles, hitched to a wagon tongue, and lifted into the air upside down. Tell him he has ten minutes to change his mind or he will be brought back down, tied by the neck, and hoisted up again. Tafoya pled and moaned but only claimed ignorance so he was lowered, a noose placed around his neck, and the soldiers went forward to string him up. He immediately reconsidered and agreed to guide the army to the winter hide-out.

Oswego bound Tafoya's two hands together, placed him on a horse, securely tied his wrists to the saddle horn, and placed a noose around his neck, which he made snug and then secured it so the noose would not slip to be either tighter or looser, tying the free end of the rope to his own saddle. The two scouts, the prisoner, and one extremely able army sergeant, rode out of camp on fresh mounts. The prisoner began to complain bitterly about the chafing effect of the rope around his neck, but Oswego gave the rope a hefty jerk and shook his head. The complaining abruptly stopped. Meanwhile, the army prepared to move five miles farther north, and camp for the night. The prisoner was warned that if he led them into a trap, they would execute him on the spot.

Tafoya had led the scouts due north for about twelve miles when he motioned for them to dismount. It was night and though there was some moonlight all that the group could see was flat prairie. Oswego held on to the end of the rope around the Comanchero's neck as they crawled forward. Just as Thomas decided to halt the crawl because he judged it to be some kind of ruse, they came abruptly to the edge of an enormous chasm which, heretofore, the army had known nothing about. The immensity of the canyon was stunning, even in the moonlight. It looked to Thomas that it must drain the plains all the way to the Atlantic Ocean. Dotted below, on the floor of the canyon, was an assemblage of hundreds of camp fires, still faintly glowing from the evening before, and stretching out for at least three miles up the stream. No wonder the Comanches were hard to find. Whole hosts of them could disappear from the plains and reach a safe haven as quickly as a prairie dog darts into its hole. "The Palo Duro," Thomas murmured to himself.

Thomas and Oswego decided to scour the canyon edge to see if there were sentries. Handing the end of the rope to the sergeant, Thomas told the soldier in Spanish so Tafoya could understand, and then in English, to kill Tafoya if he made a sound or a suspicious move, being sure that both understood the command. "I warn you this man is a wily, able, plainsman, and by no means the subservient peon he makes out to be," he told the sergeant. The two scouts left in opposite directions. Tafoya smiled and rose to his feet, but the old sergeant jerked the neck rope and flung him back on the ground. He put his pistol barrel in the startled trader's mouth and cocked the gun. There was no more trouble. Both scouts were back in thirty minutes with no evidence of any Comanche picket on the canyon rim.

Oswego and the sergeant took Tafoya and rode back to fetch Mackenzie and the army, leaving Thomas on the rim to keep surveillance on the happenings below. They had to take his horse with them, so there would be no silhouette for the Indians to spot if it became daylight before the troops arrived. The two scouts agreed to use the call of a Red-Tailed Hawk as their signal to each other when Oswego returned since they were afraid that daylight would break before the troops could be in place. Thomas would answer only once if there was danger, but twice if all was clear. As he saw the party ride off to the south and disappear from the moonlight, he had never felt so alone. He knew he was at the brink, not only of this geological wonder, but of a great human conflagration which might well be the defining point of the future of the Southwest.

Looking to his right, along the canyon wall, he sighted an ancient juniper, a silent sentinel, gnarled and twisted, extending from between the rocks of the rim among which it was rooted, one of the two great branches leaning back over the plateau toward the plains and the other out over the sheer precipice to look down on the chasm below, its aged trunk embossed by the swells and shrinks of good and bad years, its great arms twisted, dead spikes of long ago fractured branches attesting to the strength of the storms it had endured. The obvious history of the living thing and the perception of its enduring presence made Thomas reflect on how unimportant to the inexorable flow of nature were these struggles between men.

He quickly abandoned his ponderings and turned to his work, seeking a way down into the canyon. Hoping for a trail with some degree of concealment, he followed the rim rock to the southeast, finally coming upon a hoof-worn declivity that went through a break in the rim, from whence it snaked back and forth down the sharp side of the canyon wall. Thomas judged it to be an old buffalo path, but could see that it was also being used by horses of the Indians. Noting the landmarks along the canyon that would allow him to quickly return to this trail, Thomas went back to the previous lookout.

Dawn broke out of the east and began to send shafts of light down into the canyon, at first producing a soft pink glow hovering over the floor, but with increasing emergence of the sun, swiftly evolving into a pungent orange, the glow extending along the length of the rift and reflecting off the scalloped walls of the far side of the gulch. The rays of sunlight colliding with the bare surface of the red sandstone mirrored upward from the rock to produce an emanation which seemed to belch fire into the yawing sky.

Although Thomas was not trained to think in terms of geological time frames, or to recognize the portraits of age-worn eroded walls, he knew there was a timeless history being displayed, that the Great Plains escarpment had allowed the creation of this canyon by the effect of hundreds of thousands of years of running water issuing from the Llano Estacado, breaking through the rim rock and eroding the underlying land into these canyon forms. In past eons it must have been a mighty stream.

The reddish haze of early morning was ephemeral, for very quickly it was replaced by the clear yellow light of day which pushed the fire away, and spread out to delineate the landscape. With the more vertical rays of light Thomas could see into the bottom and he gasped at the vastness of the crevice. He groped for a vocabulary to express what he was seeing, but his senses had never confronted such a spectacle before, and he had no reference for comparison, nor any way to comprehend the enormity before him. His mind drifted back to the time he sat above the Marathon Plain looking down on the desert with Dobie, and he was suddenly overwhelmed with reverence for the essence that had allowed this canyon's creation.

In the distance he heard the cry of the Red-Tailed Hawk, turned and pulled out his reed whistle, and gave two answering cries. Oswego was soon by his side, and Mackenzie and his officers silently walked up behind. They had marched fifteen miles through the night to arrive here at dawn. Thomas immediately led them to the trail he had discovered. Mackenzie turned to him, "It looks like you've found for us the low road to hell." He ordered the party of scouts to descend, clear out any sentinels, and hold the base below.

Palo Duro Canyon

CHAPTER 44

Thomas led the scouts through the break in the rim rock and off the cliff, first dismounting to lead his horse, then tentatively sliding and stumbling down the path to reach the canyon floor. The entire command now dismounted, and began the arduous task of following the scouts. One by one, they crept and slid down the same path into what many feared might be a descent into a land of no return. No sentries had been found on the floor but a few of the Indians farther up the canyon had apparently seen Mackenzie's forces, though they didn't seem to recognize what they were seeing. They did begin manipulating the horses toward safer grounds. Among the nearer teepees, one could see a stirring of the natives, but no alarm rang out. As soon as the troops reached the bottom they restored their ranks, readied their arms, and charged up the canyon toward the horse herd and the string of villages, the cavalry men hurling their mounts into the charge, the onslaught rolling forward, sudden and indiscriminate in its destruction.

The Indians had been completely surprised, not so much because of the failure of the sentries, as by their inability to believe that this sanctuary could ever be breached. Heretofore, the Palo Duro Canyon had always been invincible, and they could not conceive of themselves being vulnerable with an enemy in their midst. The natives were in complete disarray as the troops charged through the camps, shooting, trampling and knocking down lodges. Braves found it impossible to fight because they were completely engulfed in their scrambling women and children. Squaws grabbed their offspring and their most valuable equipment, and dashed for the crevices on the side of the canyon, then began scaling up to the top. Thomas looked up at the fleeing women as a cradle board, holding a papoose, came loose from a mother's back and cascaded down the sheer canyon wall. A resounding wail arose from the side of the cliff, a wail rising distinctly above the clamor of battle below. It seemed to embody the ultimate of human despair and shocked the dashing troops into silence as they gave ear to the mother's cry for her lost child, but the squaws below her only prodded her onward in their desperate scramble to escape. The few braves that were armed were able to effect slight delaying action, but the Indians were so hard pressed that they abandoned all organized defense, dropped most of their belongings and fled, clawing their way up to the canyon rim, and disappearing onto the plains.

The galloping troops passed hundreds of abandoned lodges. The valley floor was strewn with Indian goods, and many of the pack animals which had broken from their tethers were running loose, also trampling goods, lodges and people underfoot. A few of the mules were bound so tightly all they could do was pull back, kick, and bray.

"A Troop," which had been the first contingent to gallop forward in the charge, soon came riding back down the canyon with nearly the entire Indian horse herd in tow. Surprisingly, very few dead Indians were seen, but the rout had been so spectacular that at least ninety-five percent of everything in the way of possessions owned by the natives had been abandoned. In addition to the dwellings there were huge stores of food, hundreds of buffalo robes and blankets, cooking utensils, bows, lances, shields, and hide tanning equipment. Goods that had been accumulated over decades, all lay scattered across the valley floor. Whole crates of unused carbines and huge stores of ammunition were found. Worst of all for the Comanches, nearly the entire horse herd had been captured, and most of the braves, whose very limbs and feet had practically been supplanted by horse flesh, were now afoot to face the inexhaustible plains.

Even as he galloped up the stream, and through the tented villages, Thomas thought how unnatural a thing was war. Here a whole nation of people were routed, desperately fleeing for their lives, discarding everything they had acquired over many generations, tearing themselves away from the very fabric of their culture, and forcing themselves into a future of utter deprivation. And whom were they fleeing from? For the most part, from a group of rather kind though durable men, who loved home, parents, wives, and children, who simply wanted to be happy, and to have their own chance to work the land and engage in commerce, so as to earn their share of nature's bounty. Once the mantle of war was put on, however, they became hardened, fearsome, and cruel, discarding every reverence for life and moral precept they had spent an entire lifetime acquiring, to wreak havoc and death, to seek revenge, and to stamp mastery over another people. Societies had failed both the Whites and the Indians.

Mackenzie ordered everything gathered into piles and burned. Tents, lodge poles, robes, and blankets; all went up in black smoke. The entire larder of stored food for the winter went the same route. While gathering things for the flames, Thomas picked up a broken peace pipe from a spot where it had been trampled into the sand. He stood there thinking how ironic the situation, then pitched the emblem of accord into the consuming fire.

As the young scout walked up the canyon to the next village surveying the debris and crushed tepees, his searching eyes caught sight of a buckskin clad leg protruding out from under a fallen tent. He pulled back the flaps of hide, and there, lying face down, was a lifeless squaw holding a dead child beneath one arm. He gently turned them on their backs. A chill ran over his skin, as he recognized the somewhat contorted and scarred features of Running Deer. He murmured her name, though he knew there would be no reply. Around her neck she wore the watch that Thomas had given to Red Hawk. He wrinkled his brow for a warrior's valued possessions are buried with him. For some reason, Red Hawk had given his young wife the watch before he died.

In the cradle board was a small baby, a daughter, he thought. Thomas unlaced the cradle board and lifted out the child. She looked as though she were only in a pleasant sleep, though in looking closer he could see and then feel tears that still remained wet on her cheeks. The back of the hair was gathered into a tiny braid and at the end was a small, frayed piece of cloth tied into a bow. It was the rare color of royal purple.

Thomas looked under the tent and pulled out a soft buffalo robe. He took the robe and laid it beside the creek on a bed of soft leaves, then went back and carried both bodies and laid them side by side. He cut off a small lock of hair, both from the baby and the mother, undid the purple bow from the braid, and tied the two together. For a long time Thomas simply sat there with bowed head. Eventually a trooper walked by. "Hey," he said, "we can't leave that robe here. It's got to be burned. "You leave that alone," snarled Thomas. His glare appeared so vicious that the trooper beat a hasty retreat back to his company. He told of the incident to his captain while Mackenzie happened to be sitting on his horse right beside the other officer. Both Mackenzie and the captain rode down toward the creek and looked at the scene for about a minute. Mackenzie turned to the captain and said, "Would you please see to it that they are not bothered?" He turned his horse and rode away.

The captain rode back down the canyon, where he crossed paths with Oswego. "We need you to go back to the bend of the stream and bring Thomas with us," he said. Wondering what had happened, the Tonkawa scout rode his horse toward the bend, dismounted and walked down to the stream. He glanced at the head-bowed Thomas and the two still figures and stood in silence. Then, as he had done many years before, beside the Guadalupe River, he once more gently placed his hand on the young man's shoulder. "The time for war has passed for you and me," said Oswego. "Let us go home." Thomas slowly rose, turned away from the mother and daughter, walked over to his horse, mounted and turned down the canyon. Oswego stood looking at several large boulders at the edge of the chasm. He picked up his rifle and continued his survey for some minutes. Although he had a slight unease, he mounted and started in the direction following Thomas. Periodically, he kept looking back at the boulders until he came to the bend in the canyon, and lost sight of the area of concern.

CHAPTER 45

The two scouts followed the command and the horse herd up the trail and out of the Palo Duro. The next day, the entire herd of captured horses was driven down into Tule Canyon and up a barranca into a dead end trap. Mackenzie knew he could not get such a herd back to the frontier without the Indians stampeding and recapturing a major portion of them. He had been through that problem before and had learned his lesson. He turned to a young officer and said, "Lieutenant, take a detail of twenty men with rifles and plenty of ammunition and slaughter this entire herd. The young officer turned white and then muttered, "Sir, could you spare me that job? I love horses so."

"That's exactly why I want you," said Mackenzie, "I will not have it said in the annals of military history, that we executed this war with any relish, but rather that we carried out the duty that was required of us with a protest in our hearts as to the nature of what had to be done." As the shooting proceeded, Thomas heard sounds from the crazed animals that he had never heard before. It was almost as if they were screaming. "This is always the way of war;" said Mackenzie, "the innocent pay the price while the warriors spar with one another and claim glory for themselves."

The troopers looked back over the rim of the Palo Duro, and watched the black smoke curdle into the sky, only a few of them recognizing what had just happened. Most thought it was only another, though arduous, skirmish where nearly all of the Indians had, once more, slipped away without any decisive battle having occurred.

The principal Comanche Chief of the encampment, O-Ha-Ma-Tai, standing on the opposite canyon rim, however, knew what it meant. The storehouse of the Comanche nation was gone. It was too late in the year to procure and shape enough lodge poles or to kill game and tan enough hides to cover the teepees, or even to clothe their own bodies. It meant hungry bellies, and shivering huddles of people, facing this coming winter on a barren, unforgiving plain. It meant the destiny of Comanche babies, old men, and old squaws, was abandonment, hunger, and cold, raw death. It meant deep sorrow and wailing as the tribe yearned for the days as they used to be. It meant loss of the social order, with members of the tribe disregarding the needs of others, shrinking more and more into themselves, with a selfish grasping only for their own survival. The arsenal was gone, the food stores were gone, and most of the utensils were lost forever. It meant the Comanches no longer had a safe haven where they could escape the constant pursuit of the hated enemy, and with the loss of arms and the horse herd, it meant the dash and fire of the most formidable light cavalry the world had ever known, would be no more.

Mackenzie, and his group of officers, knew what it meant. Although they had fought more than a hundred engagements, never having slaughtered enough of the foe to substantially reduce their numbers, with the army never having won a decisive face-to-face battle, they had now won the war. Although there were a few scattered tribes who were not in the canyon that day, and there would still be sporadic confrontations, the arsenal, the horse herd, and the stored supplies of the Comanche nation were gone. The Indians who wanted to remain alive now had no choice but to surrender to the White Man and proceed to their designated reservations, and a new and alien way of life.

Oswego and Thomas knew what it meant. The deep enmity acquired in their younger days, and the grueling life style they had endured to satiate the hungers of their deep animosity brought them nothing of the triumphant feeling that they dreamed they would experience in victory. Each of them had a deep sadness, not relating to himself personally, but arising from the immense tragedy being acted out on the canyon floor, a tragedy which pervaded through the souls of all who could understand the consequences of that day's conflict.

Thomas thought that the Texas frontier would now be safe, but he knew that in this entire campaign he had personally sacrificed his claim as a moral and respectable human. In order to help attain this goal, he had left his ordered life, had put aside the love of neighbors, family, and sweetheart, had deserted his education, and had become feral and ruthless. He had lied, scalped, killed, spied, and betrayed. Most of the noble characteristics of life, which he had always ascribed to himself, now seemed more prevalent and inherent among his enemies than they were within his own being.

After the death of his mother and sister, he had called his enemy cowardly. He no longer harbored any such thoughts. Only thirty thousand Comanches, at the height of their population, had ruled a land as big as the state of Texas. They had, until now, successfully defended it against all intruders: Indians, Spaniards, Mexicans, Texans, Confederates, and Americans. They had been a far more formidable enemy to the Texas nation than Mexico ever pretended to be. For almost two centuries, they had been an absolute barrier to the incessant, probing, coveting, and land-craving advance of the Whites. The complete downfall of the Comanches, in some large part, had to be their failure to adapt, brought about by one of those recurrent human frailties: believing, even to the bitter end, that they were the chosen ones, superior to all other beings. "Perhaps, in the distant future, it is destined to be the downfall of our country as well," thought Thomas.

After leaving Tule Canyon, the command again moved out onto the plains, heading cross country, toward the escarpment of Blanco Canyon and beyond to the Clear Fork of the Brazos River, and their base of supplies. This night would be their last night on the storied and infamous Llano Estacado. All precautions were again taken, with the livestock herded to the middle of the camp and sentries posted in a complete circle about the bivouac.

Mackenzie and his corps of officers rode out to the edge of the encampment to watch, for one last time, the dazzling colors of the unique sunset on the Texas plains. Far out on the horizon, as though emerging out of the setting sun, they saw a lone rider approaching. A sentry went forth to challenge him, but the Colonel signaled for the men to let him come on in. It was a lone Comanche, wearing all he had left of his ceremonial regalia. He carried his lance and shield, his head held high. A countenance that was both haughty and condescending enveloped his person. "Arrogant to the last," said one of the aides. "That arrogance is the ichor that runs through their veins, which enabled them to become Lords of the Plains," said Mackenzie. He told one of the officers to go get Thomas, so they would have an able translator.

As Thomas rode into the circle, both he and the Comanche seemed to recognize one another. The Indian rode up beside Thomas. He reached beneath his shirt, pulled out a buckskin pouch and handed it to the scout. Thomas unfolded the skin. It contained the weathered scalp of a young girl, a small swatch of royal purple cloth, and a small belt plaited with eight strands of leather with large beads tied to the frayed strands of each end. Suddenly he realized what the scar marks of the Indian's face represented. Thomas felt a surge of blood rise to his neck and face as he sat looking at the belt, the urge to strike engulfing his being. How could one forgive the unforgivable? The Comanche sat looking straight into Thomas's eyes, his own eyes never blinking and his countenance never wavering. Finally, the young Texan's flush began to wane. He held the packet to his breast, then reached in his pocket and took out a tiny bit of hair, a small purple ribbon of cloth tied around the tresses, and laid the locks within the packet. He slipped the package beneath his own shirt, and made the sign for "Peace." The Indian nodded, and without changing his countenance, turned his horse, and rode west, back toward the dying sunset.

Mackenzie, who had watched the drama, reached up and took off his hat. "They will leave no lasting mark upon this land. The grass will cover every trace of them in a few years, but those of us who were fated to have seen and met them know that the souls of these people will always roam free across this prairie, hunting the phantom buffalo."

EPILOGUE

After returning to base camp, the scouts were released, and Thomas and Oswego rode, together, back to the Texas frontier. As they rode by the old camp near the San Saba, Oswego stopped once more near the ant bed and walked over to the large hollow tree, pulled out the long rested shotgun and placed it in Thomas's saddle scabbard. "We need to put away the tools of war," he said. At the Llano River they parted, Oswego turning east toward his people and Thomas continuing south toward his own. Thomas reached out and took Oswego by the arm. It was a time when words were of no use at all, when they would only invade the camaraderie and the love between them, so neither spoke. Finally, Oswego placed his hand on Thomas's shoulder, as he had done only twice before. The silence was fitting, marking their final farewell. The two diverged, and soon, could no longer be seen by one another.

Oswego was not allowed to reap any of the benefits of a peaceful frontier for which he had given so much. He returned to his own people, and there, he was revered as a great chief. The Tonkawa were not wiped out by the Comanche; they were destroyed by their allies, the Texans. They were banned from Texas soil, again forced to move from their homeland, to a more distant reservation, because they were Indian, and all Indians were the same, no matter what their history or allegiance. They interfered with the white people's high estate, impeding progress and enlightenment. The Tonkawa and a few Lipan Apaches were amalgamated into one group, and in a few years lost their identity, disappearing forever as a tribe.

Thomas continued south toward home. In the early dawn he came to the little mesa overlooking the homestead beside the Guadalupe. From the top of the trail he could see dried corn stalks still standing in neat rows where they had grown in the summer, but there was something different about the scene, the house, the corral, the bend of the river. They all seemed smaller than before, more ordinary. He wanted to feel intimate, that he belonged to what he saw below, to know that it was his, that there was no other place like this one, but as he looked down, what he saw was only another structure, a house, not his house, a farm, not his farm. When he rode up to the gate the latch was rusty. No tracks passed through the gap. He opened the gate and rode through, continuing up the trail to the giant oak tree where his parents and sister were buried. He got off his horse and with his hunting knife and bare hands, dug a deep hole beside his sister's grave, and placed the scalp and the remnant of purple cloth in the common plot. He walked around to the other side of the tree and buried the two tresses in their own unmarked grave.

Thomas unsaddled his horse, turned him into the corral, strode up to the house, and opened the door. There was a stale, musty smell in the room. He took his sleeve, wiped the dust off the fireplace mantel, and laid the plaited belt back in its place. He stood remembering how the smells used to be – the crisp smokiness of the fresh fire, the aroma of baking bread, the sweetness of freshly washed linens. He felt very alone. He turned back toward the open door, walked through to the porch, stepped down onto the faded path and started walking up the riverside trail toward Virginia's old home. Across the stream a Great Blue Heron arose from the river shallows and flew off to the east, squawking in angry protest at Thomas, who had disturbed its early morning repast.